Buying the *Ranch*
BOOK II *Escaping Reality*

AN ADVENTURE STORY

WRITTEN AND ILLUSTRATED BY

VIRTUE HATHAWAY

LA HACIENDA PUBLICATIONS
JALISCO, MEXICO

Buying the Ranch
BOOK II Escaping Reality

PUBLISHED BY

LA HACIENDA PUBLICATIONS
APDO. POST. 20, MASCOTA, 46900
JALISCO, MEXICO

ISBN 978-0692940693

I dedicate this work to those beloved individuals who once having entered my life, changed it irrevocably; Penelope, Peter and Charlie.

They, like the little girl who had a little curl right in the middle of her forehead; when they are good, they are very, very good, but when they are bad, they are horrid.

Virtue Hathaway

A man without a woman
Is like a ship without a sail
A boat without a rudder
Or a kite without a tail
A man without a woman
Is like a wreck upon the sand
There's only one Thing worse
In the universe
And that's a woman
Without a man

Very old Folk Song

ACKNOWLEDGMENTS

I would very much like to thank those people around me who have made this book possible. My children, Penelope, Peter and Charlie for their love and support, the very talented Graphic Designer, Paul McBroome who has overcome serious health issues to put my work together and the family who helps me survive my own health situation in order to write: Herminia, Rosie and Susanno Pena Rosas.

CONTENTS

PREFACE

The use of the expression, "Buying the Ranch" which I use in the title of my book seems to need an explanation. Part of the story of Joanna Botticelli is set in California where the colloquial meaning of "buying the ranch" means someone has died! Where I come from in the Midwest the equivalent meaning is "kicking the bucket". John Doe has died, he has "kicked the bucket" in Illinois and in California he has "bought the ranch".

The expression is used in two ways in my books, as a metaphor for the problems and obstruction that the heroine faces in her struggle to realize her finest instincts with death as the ultimate payment for violating the patriarchal rule. In our society, it rarely comes to that, suffice to withhold economic and social advances to ambitious women. And there is domestic violence against women. Misogyny kills the soul in its own way through drug addiction, alcoholism and suicide. However, certain aspects of the Islamic religion do condone the actual killing of women for violating its laws against certain female behavior.

The second use of the expression is exactly what it says, buying agricultural land for the purpose of cultivation and the maintenance of delightful domestic animals such as cows, pigs, horses, burros, chickens, dogs and cats.

I hope this will explain the titles of the books in the series.

Thank you for your interest,

Virtue Hathaway

CHAPTER I

Christmas in Tucson

It is still dark in the early morning as I tie my shoe laces frantically, almost dressed for the Christmas Eve flight to my families' home in Tucson. The doorbell rings and I see by the light of the street lamp it is Vincent standing outside. The air is so cold his breath is condensing into a ghostly mist around his mouth. I open the door for him.

"Hi honey. Huh, so you're actually going to fly to Arizona in that flimsy Super Cub with Kelly, who can't fly worth shit....I sure hope you make it to 1963." He speaks angrily and doesn't even kiss me as he thrusts a heavy, oblong cardboard carton in my direction. "Merry Christmas," he growls, crossing his arms, waiting for me to open his gift.

There is a tiny figure of Santa Claus glued to one end of the carton that says "To Joanna, with love forever, from Vincent, Merry Christmas and Happy New Year". I use a small paring knife to pry open the box and pull out a pair of long, black, shiny Head skis with my name, 'Joanna Botticelli' printed on them.

"Vincent, how sweet of you, I can't believe you would do this for me...I...I have nothing for you, except the portrait I am painting of your daughter and...and, I'm afraid it's not finished." A part of me is feeling very guilty, unfaithful, ungrateful, you name it. *Why has he done this I wonder?*

He slumps down on my sofa, takes out a cigarette, lights it and sits back to contemplate me. I still have things to pack up but I dare not offend him. I rush to bring him coffee and hope he is appeased. He looks rumpled and unhappy. He has a rough stubble of beard on his chin and he doesn't smell good. I love him, and another part of me glories in his misery, his thwarted love and the deterioration of his marriage. I know I should be sad for him but I am not, I can never pity him somehow. He is beyond such a trifling emotion.

"So what's Kelly gonna do at your folk's house, ask for your hand in marriage or something?" The smoke curls around his large noble head like a crown and I know he is mine forever.

"No, of course not, he's not even divorced yet and besides, we haven't talked about getting married, you know I am not ready to get married...we're just going for a holiday. I haven't seen my family for over a year and it will be nice to go home again, briefly, before all the old problems surface. Thom doesn't really have anywhere else to go, now don't you think that's sad for a wealthy, famous doctor, not to have a place to go for Christmas? He's been nice to me, he has helped me a lot."

"Too nice." he says acidly as he sips the coffee.

The phone rings and I know it is Thom, anxious, ready to leave.

"I'll be right there Thom," I speak quietly into the receiver, "just let me finish some coffee with Vincent, I'll be outside the door by the time you have the car ready."

I replace the receiver and rush to finish packing, put some make-up on quickly, pull on a jacket and grab my suitcase.

"Here, I'll help you with that." Vincent says as he takes the suitcase from me, the cigarette dangles from the corner of his mouth. "What about your new skis, you're just gonna leave them in the middle of the floor?"

"Uh, no...let's hide them behind the sofa and when I come back from Tucson, we'll go skiing, okay?"

I carefully lock my door and we go out into the cold, dark foggy morning. Thom is wiping the windshield of the Thunderbird and barely acknowledges Vincent. The cigarette still dangling, Vincent helps load the suitcases into the trunk.

Feeling extremely uncomfortable, I move to get into the car, Vincent jumps ahead of me and opens the door. He stares at me coldly as he shuts it. A quick glance to his face reveals a tear coursing down his cheek. It is unbelievable. I am shocked. Could he be jealous? Could what started out as an amiable passing back and forth of a new girl on the scene grown into love? True love?

No, I think cynically, as Thom and I speed down Highway One in virtual silence. He, locked in his own thoughts while I struggle with the turmoil of mine. Nothing has been resolved between Vincent and I. He continues living with his wife and coming around for me when he feels like it or has time. His display this morning seems to confirm that he just wants what he can't have, like Thom told me, and if he can have it, he won't want it. Why is that I wonder, a person forever pushing away contentment and fulfillment for some unfathomable illusion. A passion that flares hot and intense and then slowly cools down into a numbing, domestic routine punctuated by tiny insults to relieve the monotony. The danger inherent in this deadly, emotional game between men and women is that if one feels forced to act as if one doesn't give a damn about the other person, eventually one simply *doesn't give a damn.*

It is still dark when we pull into the parking area in front of the Half Moon Bay Airport coffee shop. There is one light on inside and Jake is bent over the counter reading a newspaper, drinking coffee. He barely raises his head as we enter. He is so imperial in his rudeness.

"What stinks?" He asks brusquely with a slight sneer.

"Oh, uh, crabs, I bought some Dungeness crabs to take to Joanna's folks for Christmas eve, I sure hope they don't get bad." Thom mumbles. He seems intimidated by Jake.

"Throw some more ice over them things." Jake orders, nodding his head in the direction of the freezer.

"Got the Cub ready to fly?" asks Thom, in a jovial tone of voice.

"Oh yeah, it's outside...say, you ain't gonna leave that black jalopy parked there while yer gone now, are ya? Those things are sure easy to steal ya know...whyncha park it in the hangar?"

"Oh sure, Jake, good idea, thanks." says Thom as he fills out his flight plan.

Thom almost trips in his eagerness to take advantage of the proffered parking privileges and scurries to drive his beloved black T-Bird into the sanctuary of the hangar.

The first glimmer of dawn begins to light up the eastern sky as we load the Cub and prepare to take off. I squeeze into the back seat and spread the air chart across my lap, folded so as to follow our flight path. I am very excited. Thoughts of my irresolvable love affair begin to fade away. Thom turns and smiles back at me when he finishes the check list. He puts his hand on mine briefly and we share the camaraderie of immanent adventure.

"We'll land in Palm Springs to refuel and you can fly from there, how's that sound? Get some good cross country experience," he shouts back at me as he maneuvers for take-off. Jake is standing off to the side of the runway, barely visible in the pale light of dawn, a bemused expression on his face. I wave at him and surprisingly he waves back.

The motor accelerates, Thom releases the brakes, the small aircraft leaps forward and in a few moments we are airborne. Thom seems to be more confident of his flying, for one thing he didn't drink too much the night before, and sensibly we both went to bed early.

He heads inland in a south-southeasterly direction and we watch the sunrise over the snow-covered Sierra Nevada mountains from the air. The vision is incredibly beautiful from this altitude. The mountain snow painted in shades of pink, orange and yellow. The farm lands of central California unfold beneath us, below is the controversial canal that takes the water from the wet north to the dry south. As the morning progresses I see a thick, dark gray-yellow mass off to the right, hovering on the horizon in the clear air toward the southwest. "Los Angeles," Thom informs me, "Smoggy as hell, don't ya love that we live in San Francisco?" I nod in agreement, studying the distant polluted air mass with distaste. An ignorant population, Thom would say, who in their mad scramble for material gain, have fouled their own nest.

Thom lands in Palm Springs, tops off the gas tanks and buys a bag of candy bars and salted peanuts in cellophane bags. I slip into the pilot's seat. My heart pounds as I strap myself in, tune the radio frequency to the airport tower and wait for take-off instructions while Thom coaches me from behind. The voice on the radio tells me which runway to take off from, the heading and exactly when. I set the altimeter for air pressure and altitude, receive the wind velocity and direction and poise the tiny craft for take-off. I can scarcely breathe as I move the throttle forward, frantically pressing the rudder pedals, struggling to keep it going straight down the runway, (I imagine the traffic controller judging my take-off after hearing my female voice.) gradually pull back on the stick and we are flying! Once achieving our assigned flight altitude and setting the correct heading for Tucson, there is not too much to do. It is hard to hold a conversation over the noise of the engine so I just settle back and enjoy it all. We fly over the Sierras which are not too high at this end, then the Mojave desert stretches out before us. A few craggy mountains break up the bleak expanse but that is all. The hours pass and I begin to feel drowsy and hungry. I didn't think to pack a lunch, Thom had not mentioned it. Food seems to bore him so I content myself with a sickly sweet chocolate, coconut and peanut concoction.

"Hey, pilots don't fall asleep there girl, wake up, you're losing altitude!" Thom is shaking me.

"Sorry, we should have had breakfast."

"If you eat, that means you have to go to the bathroom, what goes in must come out and how do you go to the bathroom in this plane I ask you?" Thom thrusts forth a handful of little pills, another candy bar and a bag of peanuts.

"But Thom..I don't",...

"Take two, they'll wake you up at least until we get to Tucson, you've got to land this thing, we can't change places in the air and I can't see worth a damn from back here."

I can't get the pills down my dry throat. *We didn't even bring water along, how could we be so short sighted*, I wonder. Then, I did leave the flight plans up to Thom. *Perhaps I should have taken more responsibility for the trip, but I trusted him,* I answer back to my inner voice.

The plane seems to fly itself except for a gentle rise and fall due to the desert up and down drafts. I begin to drift off into my dream world. There we are, Vincent and I, among the colorfully dressed, beautiful people skiing on the cold, steep, snow covered slopes of Squaw Valley. We look so attractive that people wave to us and smile, desiring to know who we are. I want to try my new skis but they feel stuck in the snow and won't move. The desire to dash down the slopes together is overwhelming, Vincent and Joanna Cooper, the fascinating new couple around town. But something is holding me back, the skis feel nailed to the snowy mountain. I lean forward, angry, gravity decrees that my new skis with my name on them take me swooshing down the mountain to the sprawling ski lodge far below. But they don't budge. I cry out to Vincent to do something but he and the whole vision fade into hopelessness and the future becomes dark and difficult. I am left with a bitter foreboding that a life of material ease and pleasure will never be mine, I know this as well as I know my legs and arms, feet and hands, fingers and toes. Vincent was not sent to me to give me credit cards, luxurious ski vacations, fine clothes from Magnin's, an elegant car, a lovely home in Marin with a swimming pool or diamonds, pearls, gold and silver to adorn my body. My portrait will never appear in the society section of the Chronicle and my beautiful, hypothetical, yet unconceived daughter will never become a San Francisco debutante. None of that will ever happen. Vincent was sent to me...for what? He has already married his trophy wife and is still chasing women. I know I am not trophy wife material so what comes next?

My dark mulling thoughts are interrupted by Thom leaning over my shoulder and shouting into my ear, "What we are doing is illegal you know."

I hear the pleasure in his voice and I respond, "Why?"

"You are not supposed to be flying without an instructor on board."

"Oh, so why did you tell me to fly?" I shout back to him.

"Oh, what the hell, like I said, it's good experience for you for your solo cross country."

"And what if I crash land it in Tucson."

"So what, life is short...a hell of a way to go." He leans back in the seat, his cynical half smile twisting his mouth, he is not bored.

Suddenly I am wide awake, my dark thoughts relegated to a murky corner of my consciousness. We are passing the Gila Bend omni station and Tucson is only 45 minutes away. Mentally I go through the steps of landing. The Super Cub is different from the Cessna 140, more primitive and less responsive to the pressure of your hands and feet. Thom leans over me and tunes in the Tucson radio frequency, I put on the head phones and listen to the tower giving landing and take off instructions, weather, wind and flight conditions. It is hazy and the sun is low behind us on the western horizon.

I wish for a cup of hot coffee, possibly with some sugar in it. Then, with Thom's urging, I give the number of our plane and our position to the air traffic controller and wait for instructions. The controller acknowledges the Cub which thrills me, since this is the first time I have flown away from the Half Moon Bay vicinity, away from my nest as the pilots say. The instructions sound garbled so I ask him to say it all slowly and he does! I wonder if he is shooing all the other planes away since a woman pilot is coming in to land. No matter, I descend to the correct altitude and compass heading and keep going, my heart pounding in my chest. Everything is forgotten in this intense concentration on getting back to earth. In the distance I can see the landing lights at Tucson International. Thom indicates the landing field for general aviation and I carefully aim us toward our destination. It is almost dark when I make my straight-in approach, the controller coaching me in, I pull full flaps as we are high, the stall warning goes off so I push the nose down slightly and we begin to sink, a slight thrust forward on the throttle so we don't drop too abruptly, fumbling for the flaps. We are hovering over the concrete as I pull the stick all the way back. The plane settles to the ground then bounces back into the air and we are flying again.

"Push it into the ground and keep it there, remember give more right rudder to compensate for the reverse thrust of the propeller." Thom screams in my ear as I frantically push the stick forward. We hit the pavement again with a heavy thud and I can feel it wanting to bounce but put all my strength into holding it down. It feels as though the prop is going to scrape the concrete and we are going to flip over, but miraculously, we don't. It stays on the ground this time. I struggle mightily with it to keep it going straight. I pull it off onto the taxi strip and we both breathe a great sigh of relief.

"You need to work on your landings miss, Merry Christmas." says the air traffic controller over the radio as he continues to give me taxi instructions. Was there also a sigh of relief in his voice or did I imagine it I wonder as I taxi the plane to the tie-down area.

"Don't say anything to anyone, pretend I am your instructor." says Thom as we push the plane to tie-down position. I feel as though I am going to faint which seems to happen frequently when I am with Thom Kelly.

"Joanna!"

I turn to see my mother and younger half brother walking briskly toward us. She looks beautiful and I feel happy to see them again.

"Mom, how have you been?" We embrace, and kiss each other on the cheek. She smells like expensive perfume combined with the slight whiff of pot roast. I embrace Paul, a gangly seventeen year old with pimples, he is sweet and brotherly in his response.

After introducing Thom, Paul helps get the luggage down along with the leaking box of crabs while we secure the aircraft. Then we walk to the general aviation office to close our flight plan.

We can't stop talking. I am so eager to tell them I flew the plane myself all the way from Palm Springs and that I landed it. Badly, but I did it.. I have to wait until we are away from the airport officials. But it is all right, no one questions us and we are soon speeding away into the night in my step-father's luxurious Chrysler sedan.

My mother shakes her head disapprovingly, "I can't believe you flew that plane yourself from Palm Springs, weren't you afraid?"

"Mother, if we don't do the big things we want to do but are afraid to do, we will never live our lives. Did you see me land it?" I am exhilarated, unconquerable...in command of myself and all I survey.

She frowns at me, "No, I didn't see you land."

All that she wants for me is to be a nice, middle-class housewife like herself, safely married with a couple of kids, dedicated to taking care of a husband, cleaning house and cooking. Any move I take away from her vision of my future upsets her. Flying around the country in a private plane, with older professional men is not her idea of a proper life for her daughter.

The lights are blazing as we swing into the driveway of the huge, sprawling, ranch house in the foothills surrounding Tucson. My step-father's large frame fills the open front door as he awaits to greet us.

"Thom Kelly, I'd like you to meet my, uh, step-father...Bill Robertson. Where's Jimmy?" I ask as I push past him into the spacious living room.

"Oh he'll be along, how about a drink..." I see that Bill has one sitting on the cocktail table that he is probably nursing along, waiting for the strange guests from San Francisco. He seems older, but I know he is just as mean as ever. He considers me wild and rebellious, in need of masculine control. My defenses begin to fortify at the sight of him, the criticism will begin soon, it is a sport for him. I can see a smile of pleasant anticipation cross his mouth and I feel like prey that he has cornered.

"Great, I'll show Thom to the guest room, okay?"

Thom collapses on the large bed in the guest bedroom while I draw the drapes on the picture windows framing the view of the city stretching out to the distant mountains. In a moment he is sound asleep. I am amazed that he can fall asleep so fast in a strange place. I close the door softly and go to my old bedroom, all pink, red and black. My thoughtful little brother has my suitcase sitting on a chair waiting for my attention. After organizing my clothes, showering in the tiled bathroom, I put on a red silk chiffon, ankle length dress, trimmed with a mink collar, that I had found in a Pacific Heights thrift shop for five dollars. The cast-off of an anonymous society matron. I will make my obscure statement against consumerism to my affluent family. The dress is beautiful however, in a traditional, romantic way, so the message will probably be lost.

I am dying for a cigarette and some food. Fresh powder, rouge and lipstick make me look less exhausted than I feel. The effect of Tom's energy pills has worn off. Starving, I head straight to the kitchen where I know there is ample food.

"Well," exclaims my mother by way of greeting as I enter the beautifully laid out tile, chrome and stainless steel kitchen. "You certainly look nice, too nice to be doing any cooking around here. But you are way too thin, that's not good for you. What do I do with these crabs?"

She wears a white ruffly apron over a floor length dress in a red and green Christmas holly pattern that she has sewn herself. A thick gold chain is entwined around her neck and her ears glow with large diamond earrings. She is energetically mashing up cream cheese and sour cream, adding chopped nuts, onion and garlic to make her yearly Christmas Eve cheese ball to go with the highballs, as they call the evening drinks. I scoop some of it up on a cracker. It is delicious, the first real food I have eaten today. Her hands work quickly and efficiently, they show the signs of a life of hard work striving for prosperity. The tendons and veins stand out under the tension of manipulating the kitchen utensils, her nails short and broken.. Her left hand displays a new, sparkling diamond and wedding band on her ring finger. I wonder where she keeps the simple rings my father had given her when they were engaged and then married.

My mother refuses to have a maid or any kind of a servant, and does all the housework, cooking, baking cleaning, sewing of the clothes, drapes, covers for the chairs, washing, ironing, gardening, shopping and entertaining.....alone. Housework is her employment, her justification for living in the upper middle-class and a maid would simply be doing *her* work. It is work that would have to be paid for. Then what would she do, what would that mean in the whole scheme of their values? My mother prefers not to think about it.

"I certainly hope you and Dr. Kelly are not on intimate terms, physical that is, you know what I mean, your bedroom and his are right next to each other...it is better to avoid intimacy before marriage," she says sternly, handing me another cracker loaded with cheese ball stuff. "Your marriage will be better because of it, believe me, why Bill never even kissed me until after we were engaged you know."

I am curious about the conversations that have led up to this little counsel, she has dispatched her duty and now we can continue with the festivities. However, the most shocking aspect of her comments is that apparently they think I am going to marry this well-off, successful, (though much older) physician! They don't want to understand that I consider the institution of marriage as voracious, a vacuum, sucking unsuspecting, freedom loving, happy-go-lucky individuals into its cavernous maw in order to sustain it's desperate need to prevail as an institution. I am just having fun these days.

I don't answer her. She looks up at me, waiting for a response, her blond hair is pulled back behind her head in chignon, with some fluffy curls on top, falling onto her forehead in a coquettish manner. She is still quite beautiful. It looks like she is coloring her hair, but she will deny that.

She continues, "It will be something for us to have a doctor in the family, even though he doesn't practice natural medicine, we can always change him, after all, he is my age." She titters on, delighted that my worrisome condition as a single, divorced woman, nearing her thirties will soon be cured by the doctor.

"I don't know if we are getting married or not, mom, you shouldn't plan these things before you are aware of the situation, you know what I mean?"

"Don't speak to me like that young lady..." she says annoyed with my infernal attitude, handing me the cheese ball and plate of crackers to take to the living room. "There is no reason for you *not* to get married, all that education and talent, for what good is it if not to make some man a good wife." Her words follow me into the living room, bringing the old depression down onto my soul.

The living room as well as most of the house is decorated in shades of cerulean blue to flatter my mother's blond hair and blue eyes. Scattered amongst the new furniture were pieces I recognize from our old house in Chicago.

My step-father is preparing manhattans at the bar, a sweetish concoction of southern comfort whiskey and vermouth over ice with a maraschino cherry.

"Where's your boyfriend?" Bill says to me.

"I'll go wake him up, he's pretty worn out from the trip."

"Too much for the old fellow, huh?" he says, chuckling.

Thom is snoring loudly. I turn on the dresser light and study him. I shouldn't do that. His mouth is open and white spittle has gathered at one corner and is sliding down his cheek.

"Thom, wake up!" I say softly, close to his ear. "Wake up." I say with more emphasis, and tug at his shoulder under the covers. He ignores me and rolls over to continue sleeping. Those pills I think.

I grab him and pull him into an upright position. "Thom, please wake up, it's Christmas Eve and everybody is waiting for you."

"Huh, what...lemme sleep."

"No, you can't, take some wake-up pills, please, they all want to talk to you, they have heard so much about you from me, please...."

With a tremendous force of will, he rises to a sitting position, his eyes half closed. I pull his legs around so they hang over the edge of the bed and grab him before he falls back into the comfort of the blankets. I rummage through his medical bag as he directs me to a syringe and a small bottle of fluid.

"Gimme that." He orders groggily and takes the hypodermic needle, sticks it into the small glass bottle, sucks it all up into the needle, and plunges it into his thigh. I almost faint.

"Uh, yeah, that'll do the trick." he smiles at me sleepily. I rush for a glass of water from the carafe in the bathroom, drink it down myself and then refill it for him..

In a few minutes he comes to life, smiles coyly, and goes into the bathroom to begin dressing for the evening.

In the living room, Bill serves up the "manhattans" to all of us gathered there. My mother walks around holding the plate of crackers and cheese, her dress brushing the carpet, she is smiling happily...these are her moments to shine out of all the long, boring, lonely days she spends in her gilded cage.

The men are discussing the war in Vietnam of which I am only peripherally aware, being far more involved in my own mental crisis and love affairs to care. Paul is nearing draft age and worried about it. The phonograph is playing 'Silent Night' and I sip my drink slowly, wanting a cigarette badly. Smoking is strictly prohibited.

Thom tells his hero World War II story; "Yeah, war is hell all right, I was a medical officer working out of Baltimore, trying to put those poor guys from the European front back together again. We lost the best and the brightest of our manhood in that one, I tell ya."

Paul is sitting on the footstool, listening to Thom intently, mentally envisioning the scene of the bloodied, horribly wounded and dying men. It makes him very nervous.

His longish, dark brown hair is swept back across his head, his features sharp and angular. I think he is handsome. He looks like a photo of my mother's father who was dark. Of all of us, he received the sweetest disposition, generally mild of temperament, he was not subject to the dark moods and barely controlled rage of his older brother, James. I think much of that had to do with the unhealthy domination of my step-father who favored Paul while my mother took the side of James and thus they maintained an eternal, roiling, destructive stew of dysfunctional family confrontation.

"I have to report to the induction center next month." says Paul, clasping and unclasping his hands, his forearms resting on his thighs.

"The Roman empire fell because of a series of scattered, small wars that eventually drained Rome of its strength and resources." says Thom in his professor's ponderous voice. "They also lost their best and brightest and ultimately were ruled by the effete. Guys like Nero, you know, the emperor who fiddled, while Rome burned." Thom shifts gears playing to his audience. Bill looks impressed as Thom continues. "I believe our nation should carefully think through all the ramifications and pitfalls of entering into the political problems of other countries."

"Why I'd go over there and fight in a minute if I were younger," states Bill, standing up abruptly, his chin thrust foreword and his fists clenched.. "We gotta teach those commies to stay in their place goddammit, all this protest nonsense should be stopped, and I mean *right now!* If we don't go in there to save those poor, backward, ignorant people, Russia is going to take over, enslave the country and if one country falls to them, the rest are going to follow, like dominos. It's not a war, we are going in there to *save* those poor people from slavery, to give them *freedom!*"

We all turn to look at him, surprised at Bill's outburst, his face reddened, he looks as though he were about to lead the troops into action. He was exempted from the second World War because of an asthma condition, and then having married my widowed mother, was further relieved of military obligations by her pregnancy.

My mother flutters about, slightly embarrassed, not really aware of what is being discussed, her mind on what to do with the crabs and what she is going to serve next as though that will solve everything.

Thom clears his throat, carefully contemplating his next words, "Of course, at this point we aren't sure about the extent of Soviet ambition in Southeast Asia...."

"Well, I'm sure, they goddamn want to take over the whole world, and we'll be next, right here in Tucson." Bill stares steadily at Thom, who looks intimidated having unwittingly unleashed this torrent of patriotic fervor; "Instead of a nice, well paying private medical practice you'll be working for the state for minimum wage, no fancy airplanes, no young women (he snickers in my direction), no big homes or cars, how'd you like that?"

He takes a hearty swig of his manhattan. Thom lights a cigarette and doesn't respond. My step-father can be unnerving at times and resolute in his conservative convictions. My brother continues to nervously clasp and unclasp his hands. I look at him closely, and do not think he is so eager as his father to enter the Asian war.

"Uhm, Bill darling, please make us a fire in the fireplace and Joanna, light the tree lights and let's not get into any political discussions, tonight we celebrate the birth of the prince of peace," declares my mother, ignoring Thom's smoking and determined to dissipate the dark clouds of war.

"I sure don't want to go over there." says Paul, quietly. The thought of having to leave his comfortable life to fight a nasty war in some remote country he never heard of before horrifies him. Never had it occurred to him that such a thing would come to pass, but the papers were sent; *you must register for the draft.*

Thom studies him a moment and says, "Uh, do you have any kind of medical disability?"

Bill has left the room to refill the pitcher of manhattans.

"Yeah," replies Paul, his voice lowered, "as a matter of fact, I have a touch, if that's possible, of what they call traumatic epilepsy from a head injury during a football game last year. Don't say anything in front of my father, he loves football more than anything and really encouraged me to go all out for it. He hates to be reminded of my injury, doesn't want to think that maybe I can never play ball again." He glances furtively toward the kitchen

"Well, there should be no problem, visit your sister in San Francisco in January and come to my office. I can fill out all the forms for your medical exemption, I do it all the time. Stupid wars, I often think mothers and doctors should rise up against the defense department once and for all, they undo everything worthwhile we work for." He lights another cigarette and hands it toward me as my step-father returns with refills. I shake my head and look alarmed. Thom smiles devilishly and inhales my intended coffin nail happily.

"How's this? A *doctor* smoking?" says Bill, wrinkling up his nose.

Thom chuckles slyly, turning his head and dropping the hand holding the smoking cigarette between his thighs, like a naughty boy caught in the act. "Unfortunately, I am addicted to nicotine, among other things, if you prefer, I'll go outside and smoke."

"No, no, perfectly all right if a guest in our household has the unfortunate habit," says Bill. "I used to smoke too, but then I got smart and decided I wanted to live for a while, got these two boys and I hope to see them become men someday!"

I sense we are on our way to getting tipsy this Christmas Eve. I can see Thom suffering with the sweet drinks and I wonder if there is any vodka close by, probably, but it is all too complicated at the moment.

The evening continues as we all play out our little games of revealing and concealing, as so many other families are doing at the same time across our nation and the world. It is as though we are in a juggling act, balancing conflicting ideas and temperaments in order to keep them all up in the air in some kind of harmony. If one of us becomes angry, it will be the spark to ignite a family war in spite of the fact that we are rarely all together. My step-father unfortunately thrives on provoking family conflicts, it is the elixir of his life and he is totally oblivious to the psychological damage this nasty little habit of his incurs. He always wins.

"Say, do you by any chance have some beer, I feel my blood sugar about to hit the ceiling." says Thom, setting his drink aside, untouched.

Glad to be out of the house I make my way to the outdoor patio and pool area to the utility room refrigerator where Bill keeps his beer. Steam is rising from the heated pool. The air is cold and crisp. The reports says there is snow on the White Mountains which means skiing. I think of my new skis and my love, so far away and wonder what will become of us all.

I change the records to Pavarotti singing the traditional Christmas carols, pour Tom's beer, bring more snacks, pickled herring, cheeses, cut up vegetables, olives and crackers. My step-father is discussing the stock market with Thom and Paul. We appear to be on our way to a Merry Christmas. The tension hovers in the corners, ghost like, while my mother and I struggle to find a common ground on which to tread forth into the evening.

My mother is anxiously awaiting the arrival of her oldest and most favored son, James, who is always late.

"Can I help with anything mom?" I ask as she chops up a large head of cauliflower at the huge cutting board built into the island in the center of the large kitchen, along wtih a double stainless steel sink and six restaurant size electric cooking burners. An enormous exhaust hood with a fan churns out all of the unwanted cooking odors into crisp night air outside.

"Well, yes, I guess so, better put an apron on and let's get the supper going. I wonder where on earth James could be." she frets.

Tonight she will serve a traditional Italian Christmas supper called 'Bunya Cauda'. My father, when he was alive loved this food and it became a tradition on Christmas Eve. Bill has tolerated it. This meal is built around a chafing dish of simmering olive oil, with lots and lots of garlic and anchovies. Surrounding the chafing dish are plates heaped with thin strips of beef filet, bowls of sliced Italian bread and sour dough bread, several kinds of cheeses, long green garden onions with shiny white bulbs, large fresh mushrooms thinly sliced, artfully sliced sweet red bell peppers, radishes cut to look like flowers, celery strips, green and black olives, spicy hot yellow peppers, romaine lettuce, cauliflower and cabbage. We don't eat this in the dining room because of the carpeting but here in the large breakfast room where the mess can be washed up off the tiled floor in the morning. The purpose is to bring the family back together in peace, love and goodwill.

I arrange a hand embroidered tablecloth from Mexico across the large oval table, carefully place the silver chafing dish at the center and light the candle underneath. The aroma of olive oil, garlic and anchovies begins to rise into the air. Matching napkins, spotless and carefully ironed are stacked next to the gleaming silver ware. Then the crystal wine goblets are circled around the table and finally, incongruously, a two gallon jug of cheap table wine from Armandetti Vineyards somewhere in greater California. My step-father is not a wine drinker like the rest of us, loving his whiskey above all. In fact, he objects to everything Italian but makes a concession to his wife this one night of the year. Finally, I stack the bibs, large, home sewn affairs that tie around the chin, protecting the diners' holiday clothing from the travesties that await. I carefully arrange the dungeness crabs from San Francisco, breaking them into pieces and piling them into a large bowl. A whiff of the sea here in the middle of the desert.

I imagine that Thom has finished his beer and check out the liquor cabinet for vodka. I spy a dusty bottle of some good stuff and prepare a drink for him, wanting Thom to enjoy his time here.

Quietly I enter the living room. Now they are talking about labor unions, organizing and corruption and Thom barely looks up from his conversation as I hand him his drink which means he must be enjoying himself. Great.

As my mother and I make the last minute preparations in the kitchen, she remarks, all too casually, "Well, you better think about getting married pretty soon or you are going to be too old to have children, women should have their children in their twenties or early thirties or not at all. A life without children can be very lonely and sad you know, growing old by yourself, I hope you know what you are doing."

"I hope so too, mom."

It would be useless to try to explain to her how I feel about marriage and family. How I hate the way she and her husband spend their time together bickering about trivia, about who is right, if she says something is white, he will say it's black, no matter if in reality it is white. How he picks on her and denigrates her at times and how she takes it. How he tried to do that to me, strip me of my self respect and esteem, forcing me to leave them to maintain a few shreds of self esteem and sanity, and how I hate that she never defended me against him. How she must ask him for money for everything they need. How together they despise working women who strive to achieve independence in their lives. Women who don't want to be unpaid housekeepers and then when they reach their fifties, be dumped for a younger woman. Wives living out their best years in servitude. I don't think she wants to think about that even though my brother Paul has hinted that Bill has a girlfriend in Yuma who is probably half the man's age. So where is this all going to lead, and yet my mother is determined that I repeat it all. If Bill ever asks her for a divorce, she will be lost, she knows nothing of the law, of finance, of earning money except as a housekeeper and she is entering her middle 50's. I really don't want to think about it.

I strike a match to light the two huge silver candelabras on the table while my mother announces in the living room, "manga", in Italian, even though she is forbidden to speak Italian, the manhattans must have gotten to her. The garlic fumes have permeated the whole house, overwhelming the pine scent of the tree. But the booze flushed group is unaware and file into the kitchen laughing and joking. Thom, however, is clutching his vodka like his life support system, nervously out of his element. But he will do all right, I know him, maybe I will bring him another shot of amphetamines after we eat to keep him going at least until my other brother shows up. I can almost see his nose turn up at the sight of the cheap, Italian jug wine.

I grab the offensive jug and begin filling the crystal goblets almost to the brim, we may all fall on the floor before the evening ends. Once safely in the crystal, the wine looks fine and I set the offending jug under the kitchen counter.

"Merry Christmas!" announces our host, Bill, his thinning gray hair somewhat in disarray. We all lift our glasses and drink.

"Say, that's not all that bad," says Thom frowning, taking another sip.

"That's all we can buy, dad won't spend more than $4.50 a jug." laughs Paul, finishing off his glass and holding out for another.

We plunge into this spontaneously creative feast laughingly tying each others bibs around our necks. Each diner takes a long silver fork with a bone handle and combines the elements spread before us, spearing the filet and an onion or a pepper then plunging it into the simmering communal pot, perhaps taking a piece of mozzarella for the bread and putting the hot meat and vegetable over it so it melts. My lipstick smears onto my bread but it doesn't matter, I eat it all, the bib absorbing the drips and drink half of my goblet of wine. Faces become greasy, shining by the candlelight, the forks plunge rapidly in and out of the steaming chafing dish. One must take care not to get stabbed in the hand. I feel like we have reverted to the cave, the tribe huddled around the fire, tearing chunks of meat from a still warm carcass and throwing them over the flaming coals, satisfying our primitive hunger.

The doorbell rings. There is an imperceptible halt in our eating orgy and at my mother's bidding, I clean my hands and rush to the door, knowing who will be there.

"Ho, ho, ho," exclaims James, the older of my two half-brothers. "I hope you haven't eaten yet, I am starving...oh, I smell wop food, let me in, by the hairs of my chinny-chin-chin!"

He grabs me and kisses me on the mouth, this outrageous other brother who is over 6 feet tall, with a shock of wild, reddish blond hair. He brushes by me and drops a load of gifts under the tree.

I interrupt Thom in his struggle to spear an elusive anchovy with his fork and introduce him to James. James is very drunk and smirks as he shakes hands with Thom. I can almost read his thoughts; *I have myself a sugar-daddy, a rich, old man who will take care of me*. I imagine he approves, or does he?

"Bunya Cauda hey, dago food, let's all get nice and greasy." he laughs and takes a plate while our mother happily ties a bib around his neck so he may safely join our pagan feast.

Conversation is suspended while we move back and forth around the table, spearing here, picking there, piling it all up and savoring the wild combinations of foods. We bump into each other, wine and food pieces fall on to the once immaculate floor which become slippery and dangerous. No one cares. The big simmering caldron of olive oil is now filled with pieces of meat and vegetables and begins to resemble a stew, the flavors intensify and I eat without regard to my figure, gorging happily, secure for the moment in the barbarous fold of family custom.

My visions overtake me and the reality recedes before my images of our ancestors many thousands of years earlier, eating freshly killed game in their caves over the large communal fires. The light from the flames flickers over their primitive, ancient faces, casting shadows on the rough stone cave walls. I hear the cries of the children as they reach for the choicest, meatiest bones and fill themselves hungrily. I feel the dirt and stone floor under my bare feet and the walls of the cave glow with paintings of antelope, bison and pheasants, both the companions and sustenance of our ancient relatives as they roamed the young earth. I hear the dogs snarling over the leavings we fling their way.

"What's with you, day dreaming again?" James nudges me reluctantly into the present. I almost expect to see a skinny dog tearing at a bone under the table.

"I was just imagining... oh never mind, you would think I am crazy."

"My dear eccentric sister, I *know* you are a little off." He pours more wine into my glass, "but that's why we love you."

He was my first passion. I was barely eight years old when my mother brought him home from the hospital and I loved him immediately. He was like a real live doll and I could hardly keep my hands off of him. As he grew, my girlfriend and I would play with him endlessly, combing his curly red hair, dressing him up in outlandish clothing and taking him wherever we would go in the neighborhood like a pet. We cried when my step-father insisted his hair be cut because everyone thought he was a girl. After the hair cut, he wasn't the same child in our eyes and we began to lose interest in him. A miniature Samson, shorn of his allure.

I help my mother clean up after the dinner, sipping more wine, feeling drunk and tired after the long day. She turns on the dishwasher for the first load and we join the men in the living room where they are discussing money.

"Money is the most important thing in the world and ya never wanna make a move in this life without thinking if it's going to bring in the bucks!" declares my step-father.

"Then when the hell are you folks gonna splurge and get some decent wine in this house, I'm sick of this cheap stuff. Here, unwrap this." declares James, thrusting a package from under the tree toward our mother.

She carefully takes the paper off, she will save it for next year, then works off the ribbon with her bony fingers, the diamond flashing by the light of the Christmas tree. She lifts the lid and peers inside. "Look, how nice." she exclaims, three bottles of red wine." There is the faintest hint of disappointment in her voice, she has always been bad at covering up her feelings.

"From France mother, that bottle that you are looking at is from one of the finest vineyards in France. Twenty-five dollars a bottle, only the best from now on, for dinner tomorrow, there's another box under the tree." He smiles smugly.

"Why thank you, but so much money for such a little bottle, why the Armandetti only costs five dollars for a whole gallon and everyone likes it." My mother smiles her weak, submissive smile and carefully replaces the bottle in the box and returns it to the tree, waiting for her husband to chime in.

"Throwing your money away," growls Bill, disgusted, never missing an opportunity to critisize James. The sick, vindictive smile dominates his puffy face and I remember why I had left home as soon as was possible.

James looks over at me and changes the subject. "So, you really did go through with the divorce, huh? So whattarya gonna do now?"

I have become the focus of family misbehavior, the black ewe. "Uhh, what do you mean, I will do what I have been doing, painting...you mean what am I going to do without a man, or what?"

Bill picks up on this. "Yeah, threw away your meal ticket and you aren't such a young chick any more."

He humiliates me the way he talks and it gets worse when he drinks. I loathe the man and look over to Thom for support. Thom has his old cynical smile plastered on his face and I know that he is amused by all of this.

I continue in the absolutely futile attempt to explain myself. "I am painting full time, I've had a show in San Francisco ar the Aldrich Gallery which is one of the best in town, and I invited all of you, but of course, you could care less about my achievments, also, for your information I am doing medical illustrations for Doctor Kelly and for some other lawyers around town."

Bill tosses down the rest of his drink and looks at me angrily, as though I have violated some unspoken cardinal rule. "You can't depend on that you know."

"Why not?"

"You should go back to teaching school, like when you were married...be a school teacher."

"I didn't like teaching all that much, and besides, the schools are cutting out all the cultural programs like Art and

Music, and then they put the new teachers in the worst schools to be policemen. And hardly anyone cares about teaching well any more, all they care about is their next pay check."

Bill is now furious, he hates when I make judgements, he has always seemed to take it as a personal insult when I expound on my personal opinions or experiences.

"So what's wrong with that, paychecks are what everyone cares about, who the hell do you think you are not to care about paychecks, if you don't care about your paycheck more than anything else, you are a complete fool!" he fumes, his teeth clenched. If I were 11 years old and no one was around he would take the belt off from his pants in one sweeping movement and lay it into me for my insolence.

Silence hangs heavy in the room after his angry tirade. I feel like throwing my wine glass at him, my hatred is almost overwhelming and I want to leave immediately and put endless space between me and this odious man. I fight back the familiar tears of anger as he continues, pleased with himself.

"You're no artist, you just go around saying you are an artist," he sneers, fixing himself another drink at the liquor cabinet, my mother has left the living room.

"I have had a show." I reply weakly, knowing it will make no difference in his opinion of me. His patriarchal stone walling has haunted me all of my life. There was the time I told them I wanted to go to college and he declared firmly that "women should never, never be educated. Ruins em." I went to college anyway, mainly working my way through, to his sullen disapproval. At times I fear I will never overcome his incessant attempts to destroy any brilliance in my destiny.

I silently gather up some dirty dishes and glasses and retreat to the kitchen. James follows me.

"Why aren't you more supportive, you don't respect him, even if he is your real father." I hiss angrily. "I would like to leave right now if it wasn't for mom, the guy always ruins everything. He embarrasses me in front of Thom, and Thom is so wonderful, so helpful to me. You know, people need that, moral support from their family and here all it is is fight fight, critisize, denigrate and fight some more."

"You look like you're gonna cry." He says. "I know how you feel, I hate him too but what can I do, I work for the guy.... much as you hate the fact, he's got the dough around here."

"So he's you're meal ticket, everyone needs someone to pay their way and we all must grovel before the master."

"Kiss ass is what you mean, Joanna. Now just forget about it, you're mad cuz you can't beat me up anymore, I'm bigger than you."

He nudges me in the hip and I spill water from the ice tray onto the floor.

"Now look what you made me do!"

"Clean up for chris sake, or don't you clean house anymore either?"

"No, I have a cleaning lady once a week." I lie as I swish an old towel over the mess, my red silk chiffon dress trailing through the puddle.

"You are going to be spoiled."

"For what?" I ask hotly, pulling myself up to my full height.

"Well, for marriage I guess."

"It's not having the cleaning lady that spoils me for marriage, besides, look who's talking, you are only twenty-one and on your second divorce, no one harangues you, maybe you are spoiled for marriage."

"The difference is I have a job that makes money and you don't." His teeth are bared in a triumphant smile.

"I do make money, doing something I like very much, painting and drawing."

"That's not real work."

"I can't believe you, why isn't that work just like any other kind of work that one does and is paid for?"

"It just isn't that's all."

I am more furious than ever and have only been back home a few hours and tomorrow remains yawning ominously into the future. But I can't resist the bait and I foolishly retort.

"What is wrong with someone earning a living doing something they like and giving pleasure to people? You hate the tool and die factory but you do it because your father gave you and Paul half the business and it makes you a lot of money, besides all the property it sits on close to downtown Tucson. No one gives me anything except a lotta shit but I've accepted that, you all want me to suffer, that's it. The sobbing virgin, the mater dolorosa, the martyred woman who always fails in what she does, poor, without funds, a failure. That way you will all be happy feeling sorry for me, getting punished for stepping out of line. What you all really fear more than anything is the possibility that I may succeed in what I do in my life. And I will succeed I assure you, once I get my priorities straight that is."

The condescending, patriarchal chuckle closes that part of the conversation but the attack continues.

"You should have stayed married to Stanley, you could have adopted kids you know, lotsa people do."

"I want my own children, I want a belly that grows bigger everyday and to feel life inside of me, kicking and squirming around. It's a woman's birthright, and I have to do that before I get too old, not like men who can have kids in their 70's. I crave morning sickness, labor pains and a tiny baby sucking away at my breasts."

"Your teats, not mine." James says, retreating from the subject while I wallow in images of my fulfilled womb.

"Like an earth mother, all powerful, with sweet milk flowing from my engorged breasts like a pagan goddess." I continue, seeing myself almost but not quite, on a throne like a painting, like a Botticelli mother and child painting, with cherubs flying overhead, I struggle to retain the vision but his next comment smashes it.

"You'll never make Playboy centerfold with that attitude."

"Oh you and your damned Playboy mentality, that's what's causing you a lot of your problems with women you know, along with mother's constant belittling of your last wife Sally. I don't blame her for leaving you the way mother talked about her and you didn't defend *her*." I grab the bottle of Southern Comfort from the kitchen counter and take a swig to calm my anger, he takes the bottle from me and does the same.

"You're just jealous because I make so much money, yeah yeah I know Bill handed it all to Paul and me, but still, we have to work and you don't want to put in the kind of effort needed to be successful. America is for the strivers and you just walk around with your head in the clouds, dreaming of some Utopian existence that can never be." He slams the almost empty whiskey bottle down on the counter for emphasis, and brushes his red blond hair back from his forehead.

"I guess our disagreement is lodged in the fact that I grew up with El Greco and Renoir and the likes of them and you grew up on Hugh Hefner and the stock market and never the twain shall meet."

"Actually, ya know what I really think, and here's where dad and I come together, I think Art is un-American. I mean an artist, or writer, or film maker, for that matter can make what they believe or think look real, or appear real. That is subversive, un-American, they can influence people in whatever way they want to through their paintings, films and books. They can be anything, communists even!"

"You and your communists. Karl Marx's, "Das Capital", was not allowed to be read in my college, nor "Mein Kampf", not even in the political science classes where that stuff should be read as much in the original as possible.. I mean that's stupid, a student should at least get to read what those fellows had to say, whether you agree or not."

"It's people like you who can be brainwashed, I'm going to get you some books so you can read the truth about your hippies, draft dodgers, druggies, all those weirdos from San Francisco…anyway, so you gonna marry this doctor?"

"No, I don't think so, he's really too old for me, besides I am more seriously involved with a lawyer there."

"And how old is he?"

"You don't really want to know that do you?"

"Yeah."

"Fifty-one."

"Good lord, just three years younger than our mother, he's gonna be an old man when you are still relatively young."

"So what, age doesn't matter if you are happy with someone, and really, I can't picture Vincent, that's his name, Vincent Cooper, I can't picture him older than he is right now."

"Good God, are you dumb…I bet you'd love a cigarette right now, wouldn't cha?"

"You still have a Chicago accent, I managed to ditch mine somewhere after the divorce and no one can tell where I'm from unless I tell them."

"I learned a lot in Chicago, more than you in that old Art Institute you hung out in, I learned not to let anyone take advantage of me." James takes out a pack of Luckies and waves them in front of my face, tantalizingly.

"I'll learn that when it's time, but doesn't it seem unpleasant to you to have to live your life suspecting that everyone is trying to screw you over…where can we go for a smoke?" I am craving a cigarette.

"Hold your horses, they'll be going to bed soon, but I think that's better than going through life getting screwed up and over just because you don't want life to be unpleasant, well life is goddamned unpleasant at times. Your problem is you give people qualities they don't have because you want them to be that way and then you get disappointed and upset about them not being what you want and cut them off…you keep doing that Joanna. Look, don't cry about it, have a drink."

He hands me a glass of whiskey and takes his in his long fingers, we clink glasses.

"Here's to dog eat dog, kill or be killed, money, sex, Merry Christmas!" He laughs like Lucifer himself.

"Now, now you two, alway arguing, stop that, " says our mother entering the kitchen with a load of dirty plates balanced on a tray, she is somewhere between the hostess and the maid right now. We squeeze by her to the living room.

Thom looks very tired and drunk, the combination of pills and booze is doing him in. He is slumped down in the blue over-stuffed chair, his eyes half closed.

James doesn't sit down, but pulls on his coat from the hall closet. "Well folks, gotta go, party's winding down it looks like, have to hit the town tonight, looking for Miss Right, there may just be some luscious babe out there dying for Mr. Right, me of course, ha, ha, ha." He stretches his lanky frame and shakes back his shock of red blond hair, like the golden crest of a fighting cock. "Nice ta meetcha Doctor Kelly, see ya tomorrow for dinner."

He breezes out the door as Thom collapses back into the chair, passed out or asleep I am not sure,

Bill is laughing at my consternation. "The poor old fellow can't handle it can he now..I'll help you get him to bed."

As we tuck Thom under the covers I think that probably Bill is younger than Thom, he looks younger, Thom won't say his age for some reason. Then I think about Bill's mistress in Yuma, probably around my age. I hate thinking about all this.

As I drift off to sleep it occurs to me that just this morning we were in San Francisco and I was saying good-by to the love of my life, it seems like light years ago.

I awaken sometime after 6:00 A.M. to what sounds like a thrashing machine in the kitchen. Just one more day to get through without an ugly family battle, I sure hope we can make it. Thom plans to fly back the next day to San Francisco. Feeling a bit hung over and tired but unable to sleep, my nerves screamingly on end, I put on a robe, after a stop in the bathroom, head toward the kitchen. Guilt wells up inside of me at the thought of my poor mother having had to do all the clean-up herself. *But then again, she likes that*, I think to myself.

"What's going on mom?" I say loudly, noticing the source of the thrashing machine noise. A three legged flour mill is grinding away on the counter top while my mother, in her pajamas and house coat is peeling the skins off of blanched almonds.

"Oh good morning, isn't it kind of early for you to get up?"

"I can't sleep, what's this thing?"

"Oh, that's my flour mill, it's grinding the unsprayed, organic whole grain wheat from the Mormon Temple to make whole wheat waffles for breakfast, everyone loves them."

The machine screams and whines, chaff and flour splay out from it's electrically driven stone grinders. One can feel the energy going into this metamophosis of grain to flour. It fascinates me, this is the one aspect of my mother's character that I find interesting, her dedication to organic food preparation and her rejection of doctors. That is what redeems her for me, seeds of rebellion still stir within her.

"Can I help with anything mom?"

"Well I supppose so, finish these almonds while I get the coffee going, then we'll make the fruit salad and open a can of real maple syrup, it's so good you know, right from the North Woods."

My mother's philosphy of life is very simple, we are put on this earth for the express purpose of working. It is the answer to everything, love, health, wealth and happiness. You just have to keep your nose to the grindstone, work your ass off and the world will be yours. Could this be true I wonder as I squeeze the skins off the hot, slippery, white almonds. It certainly eliminates a lot of hard thinking along the way. What if you hate to work, I mean utterly hate to work? And what about the kind of work one does? She has never gone into detail with her philosophy and I have never prodded her too much because it makes her angry. Although I agree with her there is something despotic about it all.

We begin the preparation of the turkey, giblet gravy, chestnut stuffing, candied sweet potatoes, cranberry relish, pumpkin pies with whipped cream, salads, French cut green beans with slivered almonds and butter, homemade dinner rolls then the formal setting of the huge dining room table with the polished silverware, linen tablecloth, napkins, ornate china dining plates, a floral center piece and the silver candelabra, glistening with eight tall tapering blue candles. The preparations will take us all day and finally the table will look like a page out of Good Housekeeping magazine.

"I sure hope Doctor Kelly is one of the good doctors," my mother says as she hands me the pot of cooked liver, heart and neck to chop.

"Yeah mom, I think he's pretty good at what he does, bone surgery."

"As long as he doesn't prescribe drugs, you know, just a drug doctor, they give you anything to make money and then we have to suffer the side effects, I hope you don't take drugs."

"Well no, or maybe once in a while, for cramps sometimes." I chop away at the grey, greasy meat on the cutting board, hoping my mother does not chance upon the small satchel filled with Thom's pills. I dump the chopped mess into a big stainless steel pot and start on the mushrooms.

"Well, don't take anything, all those little pills have side effects, they destroy your organs. I don't trust doctors in general, maybe once in a while you find an ethical one, but very seldom. All our friends are sick or dying and they all take drugs."

I have been raised with this belief, the suspicion of the medical profession, that somehow they were on the side of some amorphous enemy out there, an enemy motivated by greed and love of money rather than the creation of a healthy populace. She believes the health of the family begins in the kitchen and is an aficionado of organic, unsprayed , unprocessed fruit and vegetables, meat raised without hormones or chemicals, before any of these concepts became fashionable. I wonder how she reconciles all of this with the money god her husband worships, that anything goes as long as it makes a profit. I glance up at her in profile and think that inside that head of hers she must have to block out a lot of straight thinking in order to live her contradictory life. I wonder if this might eventually damage her brain function in general after so many years, and perhaps lead to a sort of atrophy of the brain. After all, they say that what you don't use, you lose. And then she is thrilled about the idea of me marrying a rich doctor, a pill pusher and consumer par excellence. We don't discuss it but I suspect she rationalizes the prospect by thinking she will change her husband. I hate to admit it, but I am beginning to think we can't change anyone over 12 years old.

I put "Oh Little Town of Bethlehem" on the phonograph while the rest of the family awakens, dresses and congregates in the living room to open gifts. Thom wobbles in, looking pale and wan, his hand trembles as he lights his first cigarette of the morning then collapses back onto the sofa. He will need several more pills to get him through this day.

James comes in, very hungover from his Christmas Eve night on the town.

"Hi", he says to us as he slumps his long frame down onto the ultramarine colored lounge chair. "Would you be so kind as to fix me a 'Bloody Mary' for my hangover? I think I met Miss Right last night, hey that rhymes, anyway, there we were at the "Last Chance Bar" when this gorgeous blond walks up to me and at that minute I fall in love. So I say to her, 'what is a nice girl like you doing in a place like this?' She laughs and I know that she is smitten too, so I have a date with her tonight. We couldn't stop talking...she's Norwegian, Italian with a little Navajo Indian thrown in from a great, great, grandmother somewhere. She is beautiful!" He leans back, closing his eyes in pleasant reverie while I make Bloody Mary's for him and Thom. He can wash down his amphetamines with it.

They down the strong drinks quickly and I prepare refills. The only way to cope with all of this.

Bill enters the living room, looking like a true patrician in a finely tailored red plaid sport's jacket, a white shirt, a red bow tie and black pants. "Well, well, well, what have we here..buck up boys, this is Christmas morning and we have to open our gifts!"

Paul bursts in wearing a bright red Santa Claus suit our mother made for him, with a white cotton beard and a pillow stuffed under the front of the jacket to make him look fat.

"Ho, ho, ho!" Paul chants as he reaches under the tree to begin delivering the gifts. "What have we here, says 'to James from Santa'." He hands my gift to James. It is a brightly colored, ceramic piggy bank. A communal chuckle ripples through the living room.

"Why thank you sister Joanna," he says as he turns the pig around admiring it, "A perfect gift for a budding capitalist I would say."

"You better just start saving before you start spending." declares my step-father.

"That is the reverse of true capitalism." retorts James, "one spends before one gains, preferably other people's money of course. Now Santa, how about the long, red and green papered box over there next to the manger scene...yeah, right there next to baby Jesus, that's to Joanna from me."

I open the box and there lies a 15 inch long doll. But it is not an ordinary doll, it is a male doll, dressed in a business suit and tie, hair greying at the temples, carrying in his hand a brief case that says, 'Chairman of the Board'.

I hold the doll up for all to see. They laugh again awaiting James' interpretation of the gift.

"Well, you know you need a man so now when some one says that to you, you can tell them you've got a man, a business man, maybe chairman of the board even."

"Oh," I smile in wry amusement.

Thom has given me a long, white silk scarf to wear flying, while I give him an IOU for a painting of him I have in progress, operating on Gladys von Rhor's hip.

There follows the usual array of ties, socks, gloves, watches, pen sets, earrings and perfume.

Then, breakfast of whole wheat waffles and bacon is served.

Afterward, my mother and I return to our kitchen labors while Bill and Paul take Thom on a tour of the grounds behind the house, the stable housing Bill's jumping horses, the mock football field with the dangling stuffed dummy for Paul to practise on, the fruit orchard and then the pool where despite the chill morning, they sit down in the lounge chairs.

Meanwhile in the kitchen, my mother continues to expound on her wealth of acquired knowledge while we pound, chop, wash, mix, boil and dry pots, pans, and bowls. She pours two glasses of wine to fuel our efforts. The wine hits my stomach with a welcome splash.

"I just hope you aren't taking birth control pills, causes cancer you know. I don't take estrogen even, that's the first thing they try to push down your throat when you go through menopause, and another thing, you will get older like me someday and don't let them take out your ovaries, your uterus or anything, you need all of that until the day you die no matter what lies the doctors tell you. It's like a man getting castrated at 50, what man would allow that, but those poor stupid women do whatever the doctors say. They can always find a reason, but you lose your force without your reproductive organs." My mother has a very low opinion of female intelligence as well as our medical practicers.

"Mom, I agree with you, I mean you are so radical, even if you hate the word. I am thinking I would like to have a baby, have children some day. I can't even conceive of never conceiving. And, well, as much as I care for and respect Doctor Kelly, I could never marry him. I think you could understand that, I don't know what I am going to do, I am in love with a man in San Francisco, but uh, he is married."

"A married man?" she howls at me, her face contorted in the old familiar anger and I curse myself for having mentioned it. I should have remembered never to share an inappropriate thought with her. She would really cringe if she knew how every month I visualize my voluptuous, eager egg traveling happily down my fallopian tubes anxious to meet the spermatozoa of her life only to be flushed down the toilet, lost for eternity.

"Don't ever get involved with a married man, or get pregnant, or Bill and I and the rest of your family won't have anything more to do with you young lady, there is no future there whatsoever. You have to find someone to marry and soon so you will be taken care of, do you understand that?" She pounds the chef's knife on the cutting board of the food preparation island for emphasis, her face knotted in anger and something else, fear maybe.

I say nothing as I tear up leaves of romaine lettuce for the Caesar's salad, nothing to be gained. Though she can be quite wise about health and medical problems, anything that suggests deviation from a women's carefully proscribed role and position in life, was greeted with outrage. If only she knew, I think, peeling the garlic and praying for strength to get through the day.

She hands me a tray of toasted bread cubes and I pour melted butter and garlic over it all, then open up another can of anchovies, without which Italian cuisine does not exist.

"Go set the table and make sure there are no spots on the silver ware or the crystal wine glasses, sometimes the dishwasher doesn't get everything perfectly clean and Bill doesn't like that, you have to check everything, then cut some roses from the garden if there are any for the centerpiece. She continues giving me my orders for preparing the ritual dinner where all of her children, for better or for worse, will be present. A truly happy event for my mother.

The house is filled with the aromatic scents of cooking, the savory and sage of the turkey roasting in the oven, the gravy simmering on the stove with it's special herbs, the aging of last night's left overs from the Bunya Cauda which will reappear at today's dinner table as a vegetable sauce. Waste not, want not.

By two in the afternoon it is all beginning to come together and we dress in our finest for the occasion. We seat ourselves at the glowing dining room table and my mother says grace. She thanks God for the food we are about to eat, for the family gathered here, she prays for our health, well being and prosperity for the coming year, 1963.

The turkey is placed next to Bill for him to carve on a table with the heated plates stacked neatly to one side of it for him to serve. My mother places heaping plates of Caesar's salad in front of each of us while I pour the Armandetti wine into the crystal goblets. Then she passes around a basket of hot fresh dinner rolls with sesame seeds, right from the oven. The butter goes around the table and I lavish great hunks on the hot rolls and pop the hot, melted butter and bread roll into my mouth. This is not a time to worry about fat, it is so good.

"Now I see why you are such a good cook," Thom says to me and to those gathered, "Really Mrs. Robertson, your daughter amazes me when my friends and I are fortunate enough to have her come to my place and fix dinner for us. This is wonderful, and then besides that, that Joanna is such a talented artist, why we never cease to marvel at her abilities."

This last is greeted with silence, Thom looks about the table for a response of some sort and receiving none, reaches for his wine.

"How can you people drink this stuff, wait," says James, rushing to the living room for the French wine.

"Well, I hate to say this, but that guy is turning into a snob, that's what happens when ya spoil the boys, never had to work like a dog like I did as a kid, don't know how hard money is to come by, don't appreciate nuthin!" pronounces Bill, his face dour, the words coming out like a snarl, casting a dark portent over the family and guest assembled for Christmas dinner.

"Now, don't get angry at the boy Bill, he's just trying to contribute to the dinner, please let's be calm and co-operative," says my mother as she removes the salad plates. Then in front of each person we place the large dinner plates filled to overflowing with turkey, dressing, green beans with slivered almonds lightly fried in butter, glazed and baked sweet potatoes, mashed potatoes, cranberry relish like at Thanksgiving and finally passing the gravy bowl so that everyone can ladle the rich, mushroom filled thick giblet gravy over it. I put Glenn Miller's 'In the Mood" on the phonograph in hopes of dissipating the family demons.

James ostentatiously uncorks the French wine, filling a large crystal goblet with the deep red Cabernet, holds it up to the light from the chandelier, swirls it around while seemingly admiring the color, then sniffs it. We are mesmerized by the performance as he finally takes a gulp, then holds the beverage in his mouth as if to savor every nuance and finally, to everyone's relief, he swallows it.

"Now *this* is real wine." he pronounces as he places clean goblets next to the Armandetti and fills everyones wine glass whether they like it or not.

"Yes, it is very good," says my mother seated at the foot of the table, smiling benignly.

"You'll go broke drinking wine that expensive," comments Bill, with an edge to his words, as though he might just relish the idea of this arrogant son going broke.

Thom lays down his fork and says conversationally, "We have very excellent wine produced in the vineyards of Northern California, why in San Francisco you can buy Chardonnay, Zinfandel and Cabernet as good in my book, as this French wine."

"San Francisco produces a lotta kooks, commies, hippies and draft dodgers in *my* book, never been there and never wanna go, can't see how Joanna here can stand the place."

My step-father's little speech causes an awkward silence, he is angling for a really good dinner table squabble which he loves since he always wins. It makes him feel powerful, in control and breaks up the tedium of his normal work days. And of course it only works with the family because if he treated his workers at his tool and die plant in this manner, provoking and insulting them, they would all quit. As a matter of fact, he is considered a model of the fair, square, small business owner and has a trophy awarded to him from the Better Business Bureau of Tucson, testifying to that truth.

I begin to dream of how it would have been like in my family if my father hadn't been killed in the war. My distant recollections of him are bathed in an aura of sweetness and golden, celestial light. He would be a patriarch in the regal, ancient sense of the word. He would understand my desire to develop as an artist, he would have loved San Francisco and attended my shows, he would have encouraged me and been proud of me. Perhaps he would not be so wealthy as my step-father but he would have struggled to keep the family unified rather than divided, he would be a wise man and would see the destructiveness of pitting us all against each other, of denigrating us and of belittling and bickering constantly with my poor mother who was always on the defensive. The toll that must take on her I think. I can see him there at the head of the table, hosting the family Christmas dinner as Bill shrivels into nothing. But there would be more people at the enormous table, there would be aunts and uncles and cousins, all of those family members from my mother's side who had been alienated by Bill, there would be much laughter and friendly joking as we reveled in the joy of all coming back together again for the holidays.

The vision crystallizes further and I see my real father standing up and tapping his wine glass for attention. He has become a great land owner in northern California, his extensive peach and grape orchards are renowned for their quality. He is a handsome man with a small mustache that adds to his dignity. His hair is graying and he has a slight paunch and is not nearly as big or as menacing as Bill. He looks like a saint from a Caravaggio painting only with a haircut.

He speaks in a deep. pleasant, resonant voice. "Let us give thanks for this opportunity for us all to come together, that you Joanna can be with us once again and we hope that your experiences in San Francisco are adding to your womanly wisdom. Ahh, San Francisco, that most beautiful city, how glad I am you live there so we can visit you often. And of course, you must all know how successful my beautiful daughter is as an artist, why she even wanted to give me some of her paintings but I insisted on buying them in order to help her economically in these early days of her struggle to establish herself. Mother and I could not be prouder of her achievements and on top of all that she flew here to be with us by herself, well, Doctor Kelly advised from the back seat of the plane but imagine, a chip off the old block of Amelia Earhart herself. An heroic, admirable young woman."

"And then of course my two wonderful sons, different in their abilities., but each a prince in his own way. James, an astute and imaginative businessman, while Paul could charm the pants off you, he's great with people, I want you both to know, that if you can overcome your natural, innate sibling rivalry, together, you can conquer the world and live life as it should be lived, in happy, joyous cooperation, mutual trust and harmony. Now my dear family, friends and beloved children let us drink to that with this excellent French wine that my son James has been so generous to give to us for this occasion."

We all drink it down but of course it is not as good as the wine we make here at the family vineyards.

Then my mother stands to speak as the staff of servants clears the table. "Thank you all for coming such long distances to be with us here in the Sonoma Valley. It has been so long since I have seen all my brothers, sisters, cousins aunts and uncles that you will excuse the tears I shed. But all this is possible, this grand dinner, in this magnificent house, and this grand reunion because my Universal Organic Food and Beverage company has enjoyed it's most successful year ever and I am making plans with the help of James here to set up a series of franchise stores all over the world. Thanks mainly to my wonderful, beloved husband Giovvanni, who encouraged me to get out of the house, stop being a frumpy housewife complaining about everything, always asking him for money, and to use my innate talents and abilities, we are able to live like a Queen and a King here in our castle in the coastal range mountains, close to the Russian River. I could never have done all of this without him and his loving support."

"And one more thing," she continues to announce, "I plan to buy several thousand acres of ranch land close by here where we are going to specialize in organic farming, and I want my most beloved daughter Joanna to oversee the production. Of course, I will be giving it to her in her name and I know that she is organized enough to continue painting while she runs the ranch. She is a daughter after my own heart, talented, lovely and ambitious and I would hate to see her throw that all away by getting married."

My mother is beautiful, smiling and radiant, her grayish blond hair floating around her perfect face like a halo. She is a fulfilled woman, a mother and a wife, but also a fabulously wealthy and famous entrepreneur in the health food business. I begin to clap for them but sadly, they fade away and Bill is there in Giovanni's place continuing his harangue.

"Why are you clapping?" says Bill indignantly, as though I am making fun of him, "Joanna, you can't even get a job there in Frisco, how long has it been since you've been employed I ask you?"

Now it's my turn to run the gauntlet of familiar derision, my turn to have my ego and self- esteem poked, prodded and eroded so that there will not be any hope of me ever being successful in what I do, of ever being or even thinking that I am as good as they are.

Again I stupidly rise to the bait, striving to placate him, "But Bill, I told you I do work, I'm self-employed, like you, I illustrate, I paint...I am an artist."

He throws his head back in a great gesture of guffawing laughter, "You try to say you're self-employed *like me?*" More outraged amusement. "That's no work, you just don't want to go out there and get a real job...you're lazy that's your problem, lazy do you hear me." He is shouting by now and his face is red with fury.

"Now Bill, that's enough." says my mother quietly, the wine is getting to all of us.

"I don't see you working all that hard down at the plant Dad, I mean you made it during the war and right after, it's harder now to make your first million." says James, his face flushed.

"Don't you talk to me like that, you ungrateful brat." Bill is on his feet and begins pounding the table, the plates and glasses bounce and waver. I gasp, anticipating the next move and without being aware of it everyone else is on their feet as Bill starts screaming at his oldest son..he runs and grabs James by the tie and begins choking and shaking the younger man. James' hand reaches for the empty wine bottle, grabs it and manages to clobber his father on the head. Bill staggers backward while my mother and Paul grab at the two of them trying to pull them apart. The wine glasses spill and the table cloth is yanked to one side in the fray, spilling plates of uneaten food onto the carpeting. Thom moves off to a safe corner, lights a cigarette and watches the family drama play out in quiet amusement. My mother and I pull James toward the door, his face is flushed, he wields the winebottle like a weapon, swinging it overhead as Bill grabs another bottle and moves toward us despite Paul's restraints. We manage to get James out the front door. I slam the door with my mother and Bill inside. James is shaking with fury.

"Let me at him, the fucking bastard, I'll kill him, he can't do anything except make money, I hate him. I'm going back in there and get him once and for all." He takes his key chain with the front door key on it, as he inserts into the lock, I grab it and throw it into the cactus plants. Screaming with anger, he pushes the doorbell and some idiot inside pushes the door open. I quickly slam the door again and plead with him to get into his Porsche and *leave*. His face is crimson and his chest is heaving with primal fury.

I try to think of a book or a movie I have seen to get me through this moment. Perhaps an old war movie where a woman is restraining a family member from going to a sure death in a futile effort to destroy the enemy. She talks to him, that's right, talk....

"James, I know how you feel, he has treated you badly all your life, he is a selfish, self-righteous asshole but he is your father and he is getting older, it is better if you just leave and go back to your apartment and cool off and let him cool off. He loves to fight, you know that, he does this every time we all get together, he just goes around the table picking on everyone until someone gets pissed and answers him back, he is in his glory and look at you, if you were any older, you'd be having a heart attack. He is hard to take but you just have to take it and get through the day, He is *ignorant*."

I carefully pick his keys off the needles of the Sahuara cactus and open the car door for him. He hesitates, "I'd love to go in there and..and.." he clenches his fists.

"Nothing would come of it James, he's old, and we are all a little drunk, it's too bad we can't drink wine together and enjoy each other's company, but we can't and that is the sad, sad truth of our family."

He plunks down on the front seat of his sport's car, still breathing heavily.

"Please, just go home to your apartment, order Christmas dinner out, call your new girlfriend, try to rise above this." I plead.

His mouth still clenched, he swings one leg in and then, the other. I slowly close the car door and hand him the keys through the window.

Without speaking a word, he shoves the gear in reverse and punishingly, guns the motor, laying a strip of rubber on the driveway, he thankfully screeches away.

The dining room is a mess. Paul and my mother are trying to repair what is left of the Christmas dinner. She is crying. Bill has vanished and Thom is smoking and sipping wine in the living room, staring off into space.

"I was afraid of this." I say as I sit down next to him with my wine.

"Typical family get together" he comments, offering me a cigarette which I refuse, "same thing used to happen when my mother tried to get us all together, those Irish tempers. Everyone fighting and arguing, slamming doors, leaving before dinner, same family shit. I used to punch hell out of my brother John, maybe that's why he's such a wimp. It didn't matter what, start the drinking at the baptisms, funerals, weddings, birthday parties, holidays..it got so we even looked forward to it, kind of a family catharsis, even my mother and sister would have a go at it sometimes, rolling around on the carpet, tearing each others hair out."

"Personally I hate it," I say, "it would be nice if we could have interesting dinner table conversations like we do at your place without fearing that someone's teeth are going to fly across the table."

"Speaking of teeth, I've got a bad toothache... when we get back I have to see the dentist." He takes a pill out of his pocket and washes it down with the wine. "You have great teeth haven't you," he says, "makes me jealous, what does Vincent think about those beautiful choppers of yours?"

"Why, I have no idea, I never thought about it and he never said anything about my teeth." *Other parts of me* I think, *but not teeth*.

"He's not jealous?"

"Why should he be jealous?

"He doesn't have a tooth in his head you know."

"He does so, I've seen them…."

"Plates, every last one of them is false." says Thom with a smile of satisfaction at the possibility of eroding my infatuation with Vincent.

I am shocked at the thought that Vincent is toothless, it had never occurred to me, only old people lose their teeth, not Vincent, my virile hero, the love of my life, it can't be true and I promptly put the thought out of my mind.

I bring Thom more of the good French wine then continue helping my mother with the mess. It takes us hours and we don't talk too much about what has happened. Some catharsis I think as I load the dishwasher for the second time. These family fights are never about anything critical, a difference of opinion politically or morally, criticism of a girlfriend or one of us, or how money should be invested in the business. Once my brothers had a brutal battle over who would sit at the head of the table when Bill was away. But then, perhaps that's what all fights are about, seemingly innocuous differences or greed or the ego-maniacal desire to dominate. I am feeling the same thing that I did when I divorced, life is not meant to be lived like this, miserable, without soul, tear drenched amid all the material riches. Death is preferable to this style of ongoing quiet desperation

We salvage what is possible of the meal and my mother, Thom, Paul and I eat our Christmas dinner silently in the kitchen. It is delicious. Then Thom and I go outside on the patio and I take the moment to light up with him. The smoke fills my nicotine deprived body with a wonderful relaxing peace. We contemplate the colors of the desert sunset in shades of red, pink, yellow, purple, lavender and a pale green-blue. It is like an untended palette, the turpentine spilling over paints so they merge freely and spontaneously. I look over at Thom and he looks relaxed, maybe the battle did act as some kind of catharsis. He catches me studying his face.

"I'd sure like to take you out tonight Doll, get away from the family but I'm kinda tired...you understand, we should get an early start tomorrow morning, we'll have head winds."

"I sure am sorry about what happened today, Thom, it is really humiliating, I probably should see a psychiatrist, it takes so much mental energy and discipline to overcome what they do to me so I can live a decent life. It isn't right."

"No it's not, but it happens all the time and we just have to accept it and do the best we can. The sad thing is that you never really overcome that kind of psychic destruction. Love and creative work are the only things that help and you can see how hard those things are to come by these days."

He smiles at me, we clink our glasses together in a gesture of hope for the future.

The next day Thom and I fly back to San Francisco in the Super Cub.

CHAPTER II

Winds of Change

Vincent arrives late to his office after a meeting with the marriage counselor that Phyllis had insisted upon. He hated the meeting and the counselor. She treated him a like a wayward child, him, Vincent Franklyn Cooper the third, at 14 years of age, youngest pilot to ever solo from Mills Field, World War II hero, best lawyer in California. The nerve of that bitch, admonishing him to stay home nights, quit chasing after women. The truth is that he is feeling obsessed with the young artist on Upper Terrace, thinks about her all the time, he hopes he isn't in love because that means you lose control. He is suffering over it, thinking of her with Thom. As he thumbs through his messages he thinks about calling her, they must be back from Tucson by now.

The counselor, or psychologist, whatever Phyllis called her had the nerve to tell him to give her more money to run the household, then to present him with a bill for fifty dollars an hour for her services. And here he is battling bankruptcy. He had felt like punching the woman in the mouth, but he prided himself on his gallantry with women, but this one hardly qualified as a woman in his estimation. Why the bitch would shit in her pants in a high-speed stall. For a moment the pleasant fantasy of the bulbous-eyed, hyper-thyroid counselor, with bleached blond hair, gains his attention. The woman a vision of petrified protoplasm, strapped into the cockpit of an AT-6 while the earth spins in circles beneath her, above her, around her..the horizon lost. That would fix that aggressive know-it-all of a female he thinks. Ten years ago wild horses wouldn't drag him to a shrink and now it has come to this. He makes up his mind in this moment not to go back, *let Phylllis pay the woman out of her house money. Her idea wasn't it?*

He calls.

"Hi honey, how was the trip to Tucson? How did Thom handle the Cub, no downwind landings?"

Cradling the paint smeared receiver between my chin and shoulder I set down my paint brushes. "No, he did fine, actually, I flew part of the time and even landed in Tucson, can you imagine that?"

"Yeah, you're good, you have an instinct for flying, you'll be a fine pilot one day, how are your folks?"

"The same, had to go through a family row, but that's normal. It did Thom good to get away, he seems calmer for the time being."

"Because I'm not around, but once he sees me he'll revert back to his angry self...speaking of coming around, can I stop by for coffee later on in the afternoon?"

"Sure." I answer, my heart pounding. He still affects me like that, even after the time that has passed.

"See you in a bit."

As I shower I wonder if I am being a fool, is he just using me I wonder. Well, I can just use him too, if he doesn't love me at least we have great sex together, and besides, I still don't know what I really want. My mother's marriage has ruined me for the institution. Probably, a good marriage is the best way to live out one's life, but it's all so difficult....

He stands in my doorway, disheveled and unhappy looking, Icarus in the process of taking his fatal fall, his wings drooping and beginning to melt away.

I barely have the water boiling for coffee when he has me down on the bed beginning his urgent, almost desperate love making.

In the middle of the act he stops suddenly. "Did you screw Kelley in Tucson?"

"No, my mother wouldn't let me, not that I would anyway."

"Good for her."

By the time we are finished and enjoying the ubiquitous cigarette, the water has boiled away and the teapot is burning.

"You didn't really want coffee now anyway, did you?" I ask him as I put on a Japanese patterned robe that Thom had given me. To make me look like a geisha he had said. Women who combined their beauty, sexuality and intelligence to please men.

"Better to bring me a drink. Got any Tangueray gin around here?" He lays naked on my bed. He must like it here I think, a refuge of sorts. "Over the rocks with a twist of lemon rind, please dear, you know how I like it. I need to rest a while, I feel like I am in a cave here, away from my problems."

"What problems could you have?" I ask, bringing him his drink.

"Oh, honey, if you only knew, let's get away from here while we can, just the two of us, away from the office, Kelly and all the rest."

He sips the gin and sets it down on the floor next to the bed, then lights two cigarettes for us, inhales deeply and blows smoke rings into the air, seeming to fall into a reverie. I sit quietly next to him on the bed, smoking and thinking about escape. The routine of my life, the struggle to paint everyday and the tense hoping of a sale in order to pay my expenses. I live cheaply but there is only so cheap one can live and the money from the paintings seems to fly out of my hands. It would be so pleasant to run away to a beautiful tropical place where one could almost live off the land, some place untouched by civilization, with Vincent. The thought is half formed in my mind, where he could pay for everything and I would just dedicate my economically liberated talent to my work. But then my old muse pops into my thoughts, laughing at me, that Vincent taking care of me is a hopeless fantasy, along with the house with a swimming pool, the I. Magnin credit cards and all the rest of it. So, let's just run off together I reply to my inner voice. That's okay, Inner Voice answers, *just don't expect too much from him.*

He grinds out his cigarette in the ashtray on the floor and sits up. "I know just where we will go, to Puerto de las Peñas right after I finish this case for Lloyd's, you'll love it. Just beautiful, right on a big bay on the west coast of Mexico pretty far south, a tropical paradise."

"When will you be finished?" I ask, eagerly.

"April or May, you'll love it there, perfect for an artist, I'll find you an apartment, I know lots of people who live there."

"Really now, is it wild and primitive, like the South Sea Islands? Will we go around in sarongs?"

"Like Fleishaker Zoo without cages and a warm climate, actually no, it's like Hawaii, same latitude, high mountains that go right into the sea, volcanic mountains with crazy rock formations and clear, clean water. Great fishing and all sorts of sea animals, the whales migrate from off the shores of Alaska to spend the winters there. Smart of them. And you can practically live off the land, mango groves, avocadoes grow wild, coconuts drop at your feet or sometimes on your head, just wait honey, you will love it."

"I can hardly imagine it, the only time I was in the tropics was when I was thirteen years old we drove from Chicago to Mexico City and then on to Acapulco. But it was a city, even then, with hotels and apartment buildings. I wanted to go into the jungle but my parents were not interested." I say, as the phone rings at my feet.

I lean over and pick up the receiver and hear Winston Hoffman's pleasant voice on the other end of the line. He wants to come over and see me, he will bring champagne and we will work on the bathroom mural, he can't forget me he says.

"Um, I really have to work, Winston, I'm sorry." I hedge.

"You can't work all the time, it's bad for an artist, you need some recreation. I'd like to take you to a bar in the Mission where they play Mexican guitar music, we can drink wine, I want to talk to you, badly." He insists.

"Well, alright." I agree half heartedly wondering what he wants of me as I hang up the phone.

"Who is Winston?"

"Winston Hoffman, the artist, you've met him at Thom's, they get along great together, he invited me to go to the Mission District and listen to guitar music, I may as well go since you will leave me shortly to go with your wife."

"He just wants to get into your pants."

"Oh, Vincent, why do you think every man is just out to screw me?" I say, irritated with him, the lovely dream of Puerto de las Peñas evaporating before his irrational jealousy. How can he be possesive of me when he continues being married and living with his wife I ask myself. As long as he does that, I am perfectly free to go around with whoever I feel like and do whatever I want. Right? *Right.*

"Honey, you are either very dumb or very naive or both, then what the hell do you think this Winston wants out of you, artistic inspiration?"

"Maybe, or possibly he is looking for a wife, he is in his thirties, thirty-seven I think, and he probably wants to have a family, sex is part of it but it isn't all of it...besides I have no plans to go to bed with him, he is just a nice guy, fun to talk to, I am learning a lot about old fashioned classical painting too and it's better than staring at my four walls all night long."

I stand up abruptly and am conscious of a warm wetness running out of me, down my inner thighs. At least at this point in my life I may be an old maid but I am not a sexually frustrated old maid.

Vincent won't leave it and continues, "I don't want you to go out with him, I want you to stay home here and stare at your four walls all night, or paint or read a book I want you to wait for me to come to you, I don't want you to go near other men."

"How can you ask such a thing from me, you are married, you have girlfriends from time to time, Thom has told me. I've seen you with them and even entertained them for you. How can I sit here and just wait for you? I love you Vincent but I would go mad doing that, sitting by the phone waiting for it to ring, hour after hour, day after day, hating you for all the lonely hours you have failed to fill for me. I would not love you then. Better I go my own way and love you for who you are..."

"And who am I?"

"You don't know at this late date?" I laugh at him.

"So, what you are trying to say to me is that you are running around with other guys, lolling around with Kelly upstairs, because I know he can't do much more with you than loll around and all of this because you love me, is that correct?" He lights another cigarette, he is the interrogator, the trial attorney accumulating evidence against me from my testimony, trying to make it all very clear. He smiles coldly, with only half his mouth, his teeth looking strangely unaligned, his blue eyes narrow and penetrating, wondering who I am trying to kid.

But I am serious about this, having given the situation a great deal of thought and now I have momentum. "Yes, I love you because I am free of you, if I were a possession of yours, deprived of my own free will and suffering from whatever, your unfaithfulness, venereal disease, neglect, any kind of abuse, I could no longer love you. I would utterly hate you, the way slaves hate their masters."

"I'll be damned, you know you probably missed your calling little girl, you shoulda been a lawyer, like my mama always told me, I could find an excuse for anything."

I make more drinks, the day is over as far as my painting goes.

Vincent is trying to figure out how to handle me, ultimately, he knows as a lawyer, that the truth is hard to beat, you can run little circles around it, bend it this way or that way, but when someone is flat out truthful, one is in trouble. Clever the way she handles the fact of her dating other men he thinks, maybe she isn't going to sleep with the guy, maybe she is telling the truth. Maybe he has met his match at long last, maybe that's why he wants her so badly, she is like him, his mirror image.

I study his teeth, as surreptitiously as possible, unable to accept his toothlessness.

We part, with an ambiguous embrace.

My evening out with Winston Hoffman is predictable. He claims to have fallen in love with me, that artists should marry artists. And as I suspected, he is at the age where he very much wants to settle down and have a wife and children.

We sit comfortably at a table in a dimly lit Mission street Mexican restaurant while a slender man with a black mustache and longish hair sings mournful Spanish melodies while strumming an acoustic guitar seated on a small stage beneath a bluish spotlight. The place is filled with what appears to be Mexican migrant workers. No one is speaking any English, not even the waiter. Winston orders by pointing to Bohemia beer and guacamole with tostadas on the menu. He smiles amiably and we are soon sipping the cold beer and dipping into the thick, spicy avocado guacamole.

"I like the atmosphere here, the music is incredible and, (ha, ha.) it's cheap."

"I would imagine there are a lot of people in San Francisco who would be terrified to walk into this place." I say, resisting the desire to drink the whole glass of beer all at once, it is so good.

"Yeah, probably, but I have worked a lot with the Mexicans, on construction jobs mostly when I really needed money and most of them are kind, generous, sweet people. They send a large part of their paycheck back to the old country to help the family, things like that you know. Hey, let me get more beer here, this first round went down fast, didn't it."

"I am going to be perfectly frank with you Joanna," says Winston, "artists, male artists anyway, usually marry someone who will take care of them, you know take care of the nitty-gritty of life like grocery shopping, cooking, washing the clothes, that sort of thing so the guy is free to concentrate on his work. They almost never marry beautiful, exotic women who may be artists in their own right, the guy doesn't want the competition and god forbid the horrible thought that she may be more successful than he is. It's kind of dumb, but that's how it is so usually their kids aren't too talented, it's been watered down by the housewife syndrome. Call it egotism, or the need to focus, whatever, but that's how it is."

"Winston, I'll be perfectly frank with you too, I don't want to marry, not now, not ever." I light my own cigarette since Winston doesn't smoke.

"You mean you *never* want to marry, *never* settle down have a home, children, husband the whole ball of wax, the American dream." He appears incredulous.

"The American Nightmare, is a better word for it, why is everyone always getting divorced if marriage is such bliss? I would like a house of my own and I would like children and lots of money to raise them properly, maybe have a maid to take care of everything while I concentrate on developing my talent for what that is worth. That is my American Dream. Traditional marriage is so stifling with the woman expected to be the housekeeper, the mother, the sexual receptacle and certainly not to concentrate on her career and reap the rewards the way men do. I mean, it would drive me crazy. I *hate* washing dishes."

"Actually I do too, but *someone* has to do them. And it just seems to work out better if women are taking care of children at home that they may as well do the cooking and cleaning up while they are at it...then talented women should never have children is the way I see it. It's just that simple, you will never reproduce as long as you think the way you do." Winston drains his glass and orders more.

I feel like something stronger but am reluctant to order a tequila, I am still drinking what the man orders.

"So you think I will die a barren woman?" I ask, somewhat mischievously since I know that will not happen.

"Definitely." he almost shouts, he even seems angry. "If you married me you could still paint, I would let you, while the children are sleeping. We would have beautiful, talented children between us, can't you just imagine us combining genetically?"

I can hardly keep from laughing out loud at him. "But children don't sleep all that much Winston, where one could really concentrate on drawing, painting or illustrating. I mean I am just thinking back to when my brothers were small, it seems they were awake all day long, even into the night and always needing something or other."

Winston heaves a long, heavy sigh, stretches his long arms out to the side and clenches his fists in a minor artistic temper tantrum. The lone guitarist has been replaced by a small mariachi band and the music bounces along happily in a polka rhythm. I notice people singing along in Spanish and drinking tequila with lemon and salt. I dip a tostada into the greenish mass, squeeze lemon and some salt and bit of chili over it and pop it into my mouth. Winston watches me eat silently, he is scowling and I feel his disapproval. It is a familiar feeling, I felt it constantly as a child, then often while married, recently from Thom, this afternoon from Vincent and now from this man. Who needs it I think as I wash the guacamole down with the last of my beer and smile sweetly at Winston.

He turns from me and motions for the waiter to bring the bill. He pays and we leave, still with the dark silence between us.

Paul, my younger brother comes to visit me in February and to see Thom for his medical military deferment. I arrange the living room sofa for him to sleep on while he is with me.

After the routine examination in the office on Sutter street, Thom invites Paul and I up to his flat for dinner. Thom has Nancy his secretary fixing the dinner. I have been displaced. I put music on the phonograph and help Nancy with the meal preparation while Thom and Paul have a drink in the living room.

"Did Thom tell you?" Nancy asks me as I wash tomatoes for the salad.

"Tell me what?"

"I am getting a divorce from my husband, remember he left me, well he came back and threw me out of the apartment, imagine that. Thom is letting me stay here until I can find a more permanent place to live."

"That's too bad, what happened between you and him?" I am slicing onions and tears are welling in my eyes. Nancy appears happy rather than upset about her marital problems.

"He was a brute, violent, he beat me up for no reason," she lifts her skirt to show me the ugly bruises on her thighs and calves. "He knocked me down and kicked me to get me out. Sometimes he used to give me a black eye, remember when I would wear dark glasses at the office, well, that is the reason."

"How horrible for you, what did you do to make him so mad?" I ask, wiping my eyes in a napkin and smearing the mascara all over.

"Nothing actually, in fact I was a very good wife, *I think*, I gave him my paycheck twice a month, I did all the cooking and cleaning for him, then suddenly, without any warning, not even a little fight or disagreement, he would fly into these awful rages and attack me for no reason whatsoever. Thom thinks he is probably a psychotic, you know, crazy, these people that do these awful things and consider themselves guiltless."

"Life really is not fair Nancy, you are such a good person, I notice you working overtime often for Thom, always smiling and pleasant, you never seem to lose your temper, Thom says you have the patience of a saint."

She laughs merrily, joyous over her release from her persecutor. We serve the dinner of fresh broiled red snapper, peas, potatoes with butter and parsley and a large salad with fresh, hot sour dough bread, topped off with a bottle of my favorite Chardonnay. Then, comes Nancy's favorite, Napa Valley Zinfandel. The winds of change are in the air.

"Great view," comments my brother as we sit down at the elegant table. The night is cold and clear after a week of rain and snow up in the mountains. The lights of Market street sparkle like a long golden necklace then end in the blackness of the Bay, above which glitters the urban sprawl of the East Bay.

"To peace." announces Paul, raising his glass and we drink. Thom chuckles, reminding us that the war in Southeast Asia is escalating.

"You are in excellent physical shape Paul, I would suggest however you choose another sport for diversion rather than football. Golf or tennis are much less brutal," remarks Thom in a fatherly way.

"Unfortunately that is not going to be easy since I have a football scholarship to Purdue University." His face is serious, he might escape the war but now this is before him.

"I suggest you have a serious talk with your dad, he seems to care a great deal for you and ask him to scrape up the tuition money for your university studies, he seems rather well off and that's a whole lot better than sustaining a lifetime injury for that silly game." Thom finishes his Zinfandel and Nancy pours him the Chardonnay in a clean wine glass.

Paul laughs nervously as he butters his bread. "You see, my father is exceedingly proud of the fact that I won this scholarship, he is not going to be happy about paying for my education even if he can afford to. He thinks football makes men out of boys."

Thom starts coughing and choking on a piece of lettuce in his throat at this statement. Nancy jumps up and lifts up his arms while I pound him on the back and it comes up.

"Sorry about that," he manages to say as he sips the Chardonnay. "It's just that garbage about football making men out of boys that got me, I'm surprised your father thinks at that level."

"I can't imagine you being surprised after the exhibition you witnessed at Christmas," I say, in my most sardonic manner. Paul is his father's favorite and doesn't want me to bring the matter up.

"Hurummph!" exhorts Thom, finally getting back his breath and his composure, eager to go on with the conversation. "The only thing that makes men out of boys is your cock and balls young man, and don't forget that. We are either born men or born women, some of us are born something in between but we won't talk about that now, but his thing of having to go through football hell, or war hell, or knocking women around hell, or businessman hell to be a man is total shit, pardon my French, but that's the God's truth." He leans across the table, his face a glowing red with a joyous smile on his face staring straight into the soul of my younger half-brother who is backing up into his chair in an effort to escape Thom's ferocious pronouncement of the truth. I feel a great warmth pass over me, these are the moments that I love Thom the most, and the moments I will miss most about him.

Thom is laughing, "Sorry to frighten you, look, your epilepsy can be controlled easily with a light program of drugs, you are very young and youth heals a lot faster than us old farts, I suggest you will probably grow out of it. But stay away from those team sports, don't get involved in fraternity hazing since that's another dumb way of making you kids victims of the ass-holes and a lot of times kids can get injured. Just a way of enforcing the old boy hierarchy, just see it for what it is and stay away from it. The best thing is that you won't be sent off to war now after my examination and the appropriate papers that I will send off right away to your draft board. Say, Nancy, don't forget to do that first thing tomorrow." He downs his glass of wine which Nancy immediately refills.

I suddenly see them as a couple! Thom and Nancy. Of course, I should have seen it before. He will want to marry her, and she will want to marry him and be the third wife of a wealthy, famous, successful San Francisco Orthopedic Surgeon. Dr. Thomas Kelly. She is my age, perhaps a few years older, and has worked for Thom since she was fifteen years old. Practically a lifetime. They must know each other well, more so than he and I for we haven't really passed the stage of putting on our best selves for each other. We haven't examined each other's warts up close. It dawns on me that I have missed my chance with Thom, for better or for worse, the moment has passed into eternity. And now Nancy, having faced up to the brutality of her husband, rejecting it, has the whole world before her, no wonder she seems to glow with happiness. She now has the only man she probably has ever loved in her life. How wonderful I think, but something about the scene passing before me gnaws at my sense of reality, something is wrong somehow.

I play Montovani on the phonograph. His heavenly sounds are soothing for the flux in our present lives. Thom opens more wine after dinner and we sit by the cozy fire for a while. I forgo the wine since tomorrow I have a flying lesson and I plan to take Paul up with me.

I yawn ostentatiously while they talk medicine and aviation. Finally, I can't bear it anymore and stand up. Nancy will have to tackle the kitchen on her own.

"Thom and Nancy, thanks so much for a great dinner and great conversation as usual, I am so happy no one got into a fight, ha, ha, ha...we have to go down to my lovely little cave under the house and sleep. I have a flying lesson tomorrow and Paul wants to see what flying is all about...Goodnight."

"Oh don't leave so quick, what are you going to do, solo cross-country?" ask Nancy, who is learning fast.

"Probably just do touch and go's until Jake thinks I can handle cross country alone, but you know I can do it Thom, I flew cross-country and landed in Tucson. I don't want to be tired and hungover, Jake picks it up and gets mad at me about it."

Nancy jumps up and reaches into her handbag on the sidetable next to the pouf. "Here, please Joanna, take these, they are great, you won't feel a thing tomorrow." She grabs my hand and turns up my palm, shaking many little white pills into my hand. "We take these all the time, keeps us going with a smile, right Thom?"

"Really, thanks so much Nancy, but...."

"Oh come on, you've got some crazy notion about medicine, remember, the knowledge of medicine and the ability to cure what ails us is what separates us from animals. You get your crazy notions from your *mother.* " says Thom, standing up and staring at the pile of pills in my hand, challenging me, insisting. As though to reject the pills is to reject him. I feel I must take them or else he will be profoundly insulted and after *all he has done for us.*

I clutch at the pills while he continues his harangue. This is when I hate him. The drugs feel gritty and alien in my sweaty palm. I envision myself throwing them into the garbage the minute we get down to my apartment.

"Goodnight, and thanks ever so much." I say backing away. We make our escape down the back stairwell, past the new tenant's flat where all my memories of Vincent are still living. As soon as we enter my dark, dampish cave of an apartment, I throw the pills away.

"What do you think I should do?" asks Paul as we make up the sofa bed for him to sleep in. "About the football I mean, Dad will have a fit if I give up my scholarship. And to tell the truth, I'm sick of it, I'd just like to study at the University and maybe get smarter than I am at the moment."

"Sounds like a good idea, if you go to the state school it won't cost so much, and really you don't want to end up a life time zombi because of that stupid game. Maybe just get started at it, then drop it and let Bill pay for it." I fold the sheet back over the blankets and tuck him in like a baby.

"That's devious you know."

"Women like me have to think devious, or else we would never survive in this life. Now let's get some sleep and I'll take you for a spin in the Cessna tomorrow."

A smiling, charming Vincent meets us at the Half Moon Bay airport coffee shop at ten in the morning. The three of us stride out to the Cessna 140 waiting for us in front. I check the oil, drain the gas tanks of any water condensation, wiggle the ailerons and the rudder and look at the tires.

"You act like you know what you're doing." says Paul, with an amused smile on his face.

"She's a damn good pilot now, don't underestimate your sister, son." adds Vincent on my behalf.

"Well, back at home they talk as if she is crazy and can't do anything right." laughs Paul as I strap myself into the pilot's seat.

"Well, next time they say anything like that, you defend me, tell them that they are flat out *wrong!*" I say as Vincent gives the prop a few turns then steps back and smiles at me. I sense his pride in what I can do and I know that that is the most important thing to love in a man. He wants me to be good, to be successful in my endeavors, he helps and encourages me. I am so overwhelmed by him I wonder how long it will last. I keep thinking he is too good to be true.

I turn on the ignition, shout "Clear!" then push the starter button and the plane roars to life. I taxi to the beginning of the runway and go through the check list, glance over toward the two most important men in my life, they wave and I wave back. Happier than I have ever been in my lifetime, I push in the throttle and start rolling down the runway until that blessed moment of release from the earth and I am in the air. A breathless moment that never ceases to exhilarate me.

After two touch and go's I taxi back to Vincent and Paul. Vincent yanks open the door and practically pushes Paul into the co-pilot's seat, then slams it again.

"Oh my god, you are really going to take me up in this rattle trap thing?" my brother gasps.

"Yeah, so you can tell our mother and your father that you flew with me and see what they say."

We fly the traffic pattern twice. It is a beautiful day, and I am happy that I am able to do this. I make a perfect landing then taxi back to the coffee shop where Vincent fills in my pilot's log book.

We go to Dan's for a couple of martinis and an Italian lunch.

"So, brother dear, what do you think of my flying, tell the truth now, were you scared?"

"Uh, uh, no, I trust you even if they don't, after all you used to take care of me and I don't think you ever dropped me on my head when I was a baby, did you?" he says laughing, feeling very relieved that he doesn't ever have to go to war.

"Of course not, I adored you, changed your diapers, fed you, dressed you, you and James where my little darlings."

"So you do have a maternal instinct after all Joanna." says Vincent, leaning over, lifting up my hair and kissing me on the back of my neck.

"Oh, that tickles, yes of course I have a maternal instinct, Thom says my womb gives me pain every month to punish me for not having babies."

"Well now, we have to see about fixing that little problem."

"Somehow, I can't see you as a mother Joanna, not with your painting and your flying and your, well, your men friends." Paul says as he finishes his martini. We order Lasagna and a bottle of Pinot Noir from Sonoma.

"No more so-called 'men friends' for you Joanna, and you know what I mean." says Vincent with a twinkle in his eye, totally confident that I am his. No matter that he still lives with his wife. Sometimes I think I can't handle all of this and really would like to run away from having to make such important life decisions. *Just do nothing and see what happens I think, but that is not so smart, replies my inner voice.*

That evening, Vincent and I drive Paul to the airport in the big, white Buick for his flight back to Tucson. As I kiss him good-by I feel that great change is in the air and that sadly, I may not see him again for a long time.

CHAPTER III

Wedding in Marin

Perry Atkinson and Barbara are getting married in their home in Ross, Marin County. Vincent and I are invited to the wedding as a couple! Thom is also invited but declines to go, for some reason he is sulking as of late, things do not seem to be going his way and he has the habit of withdrawing from social life.

Vincent and I arrive in style for the event, in his yellow Austin Healey sports car with the top down of course. All eyes are on us as we walk up the flagstone walk and I imagine that it is us getting married and living happily ever after.

The house is a large, spacious ranch style with shingled outside walls, a big swimming pool, huge old redwood trees, extensive gardens and an outdoor fireplace and grill with big wooden picnic tables set all around.

There is Jake and Annie, Hamm Sado and Doctor Burkhart, besides all the men from the San Francisco Sheriff's Air Squadron, their wives and families as well as Atkinson's fellow lawyers and acquaintances..

The ceremony is performed in the huge living room by a judge who is a friend of both Perry and Barbara, while a string quintet plays soft background music as the couple exchange their vows and legally become man and wife before our eyes. Afterward we all file out onto the patio and garden to the strains of the wedding march and there huge tables are laden with the best delicatessen and gourmet food available, served by caterers dressed in black and white attire.

The men represent a cross section of the top echelon of San Francisco and Northern California politics, business, banking, law and medicine. The whole place radiates masculine power. The best domestic Champagne flows freely and I feel wonderfully alive and happy. I have even splurged my hard-earned painting and illustrating money to purchase a lovely silk, garden print Galanos dress for the occasion and am not unaware of the sly glances I am getting from the men.

The day seems special, blessed somehow with portents of human love and happiness. I feel a bond between Vincent and I as we mingle and talk to the guests, drinking ice cold champagne and nibbling on tiny little open face sandwiches of cheeses, anchovies, herbs, cold meats and pickled fish all cunningly decorated with red pimentos, parsley and pieces of olives. A photographer follows Vincent and I around taking our pictures, we must radiate some euphoria called, for want of a better term, love. We both seem to be floating through the day on our hyper-actuated senses. I love to touch him, his hand on mine sends steaming signals to the nether-parts of my body, we can hardly stay away from one another.

It is a joyous gathering of people. A live, 5 piece band plays music from the 50's in the corner of the very spacious living room.

"Can you do the two-step?" asks Vincent whirling me around him, bumping into the other dancers. "Beg yer pardon Mam." he says as we break into a waltz.

"Hey you do that pretty good. I bet you could do the polka too." he says as we continue flying around the room, the photographer following us with his camera like we were celebrities. The king and queen, we must radiate love and the bliss of being together.

We waltz through the open French style doors and continue dancing on the flagstone patio amid the blooming roses, jasmine and columbine. He is the most marvelous man on earth for me in these moments, his beautiful, perfect teeth are his own, firmly rooted in the bones of his jaws, despite what Thom says, I decide that this must be true. His body is lean and hard, I feel the muscles of his arm through the light blue suit jacket, I adore the wine colored bow tie he is wearing. Our fingers intertwine and at times I feel we are the only two people in existence. Could all this rampant erotic energy be coming from the new marital status of Perry and Barbara Atkinson, have they bathed us in it so that we too will join them sometime soon as husband and wife?

No, says my inner voice, that will never be, you are destined to work out your own life by yourself, and it will not be easy. I brush the inner voice away as the music stops and we all wait expectantly.

Barbara, tall and statuesque in her ivory wedding gown is standing on one of the picnic tables tapping a fork against a glass to capture our attention.

"Having fun you all?"

"Yeahhh." The crowd replies in boozy unison.

"It's time for me to throw my wedding bouquet to see who will be next to tie the knot, okay ladies, arrange yourselves and here it goes!" Me, the secretaries, daughters, and divorcees all form an eager phalanx, our arms outstretched.

Barbara turns her back on us and flings the flowers high into the air and they land right into the hands of Perry's top secretary, a stout, middle-aged woman, her face very red from the excitement and the champagne, she waves the bouquet wildly above her head, screaming with pleasure that it might just be possible that her many lonely years as a spinster may be ending. Despite knowing it will never happen the crowd cheers her on anyway.

Perry steps up onto the table with his new bride who lifts up the satin skirt of her dress to expose her well tanned, long legs with a white garter trimmed with lace and tiny roses right below her knee. The men roar lasciviously as Perry seductivly slips the garter off her leg.

Vincent joins the groups of unmarried young men, students and apprentices at the law offices, waiting to try their luck in catching the garter and perhaps be the next to take a wife. Vincent is the oldest among them, and everyone knows for a fact he is still married.

Perry turns his back and flings the delicate garter high into the air behind him and it lands right into the waiting hands of Vincent who let's out a whoop of pleasure.

"Boy oh boy, what luck now, how do ya like that...hey honey, what d'ya think? I just might be next in line for the halter." He laughs in my direction as he pulls the garter up over his arm and his suit jacket and displays it for the eager photographer.

The flash keeps going off, recording each scene for posterity, the moment frozen for eternity as we, the subjects keep going on, living our lives for better or for worse, getting older, sicker and eventually dying. The pictures will live on beyond the grave. But I don't think about this, I am too happy and it feels as though it will go on forever. The crowd breaks up and heads for the bar for an afternoon and evening of serious drinking. There are colored lights strung across the pool and patio. The music has moved outdoors and Vincent and I dance to the romantic songs of the past, the two-step, waltz and polka. He won't jitterbug with me however, claiming that that is not dancing, "Just a lot of jumping up and down and around."

Perry and Barbara whirl by, Barbara points at us and says, "You two are next."

"Say honey," he whispers into my ear, "It's getting dark and it's a long way home, what say we leave? Sunday night traffic on 101 and all."

We say goodnight to everyone, wish Perry and Barbara a long, happy life together, then zoom off into the night in the yellow Austin-Healey.

The Golden Gate Bridge glows with it's double string of amber lights and the red tail lights of the traffic crawling its way back into the City. We inch along the bridge, smoking cigarettes and talking idly while he fondles my thigh, foreplay while driving. After the bridge, Vincent turns off onto a side road, we pass through the Presidio and end up in front of the old abandoned Presidio Fort Point, underneath the bridge. The traffic now roars and flows above us while we find a parking space among a few other cars parked there in the total darkness.

The incoming tide crashes against the sea wall, the spray from the waves washing over the rocks, inundating the area with salt water. We get out of the little sports car and walk as far as we can to where the old Fort building ends and look with awe at the base of bridge suspension tower. The buoys clang mournfully and the fog horns groan their two-note refrain into the night. A ship is entering the bay, it's lights glimmering over the dark black waters as it sails slowly and majestically in with the tide.

"Excuse me while I pee." Vincent says laughingly as he urinates into the wild water beneath us. I too need to relieve myself but am unable to do more than a prudent puddle on the ground, my anatomy prohibiting me from making such a grand gesture as mingling my water with that of the Pacific Ocean.

"Handy gadget to take along on a picnic." he says merrily, zipping himself up.

Returning to the Austin-Healey, he pulls up the top, fastens it down and we wiggle inside. Our lovemaking, which has been pent-up since early afternoon, begins immediately. In an erotic frenzy, he lifts up the silk, Galanos garden print dress and spreads my legs as much as possible between the gear shift, hand brake, steering wheel and dash board. Hungry for him I acquiese in a daze of lust. I wear no underpants, just a garter belt with nylon stockings that hooked on to it with little button like affairs. It was a style that prepared us for sex at any time, practically anywhere and one could stay fully and properly dressed during the whole event. I am pinned against the door and window handles which gouge painfully into my back but I feel nothing as he nestles down on me and his tongue begins it's artful probing and licking, driving me to the brink of orgasm. Suddenly there is a flashlight shining in through the driver's window, focusing on our love making. A cop on the beat! Vincent slowly, painfully pulls himself out from under my garden silk dress to face the grinning face at the car window while I swing my legs around and sit primly in the bucket seat and stare straight ahead at the ship in the distance now turning toward Oakland.

Vincent rolls down the window and the policeman illuminates our faces for a moment then shuts off the flashlight.

"Just a little serious necking here, nothing to get upset about sir." says Vincent politely as he opens his wallet and takes out a card of some sort and shows it to the cop. The officer flicks on the light again and studies the small document. I have visions of him taking us to jail, spending the night there and our faces in the newspapers the next day. I have this inherent fear of the law, perhaps because I know so little about it

The waves crashing below add to our little drama. I sit still, wanting the cop to leave so we can keep doing what we were doing. How can this eternal act between men and women be against the law I wonder, *whomever are we hurting out there by giving each other pleasure?*

"Okay," the cop says finally, returning the card to Vincent who slips it back into his wallet. "So you're with the Sheriff's department, you're in like Flynn, ha, ha..sorry I bothered you there, just be careful now and I'll see to it that no one comes around."

Vincent rolls the window back up and says, "Don't be upset honey, he won't bother us, in fact we'll have protection, nice fellow. Here, have some champagne, I took a bottle along for this occasion, I want to finish what we started."

He reaches behind him into the back seat and pulls out a bottle of Dom Perignon, not too cold but no matter. He uncorks it with a chaste little pop and we drink from the bottle. It is so good, the champagne sliding down my throat while his fingers continue to probe me down there, satisfied that I am thoroughly craving him he dives once more under my skirts until he finishes me off as I give myself over to him and his power to take me out of myself, I scream and moan uncontrollably.

"Gee honey, I think they heard that all the way up on Telegraph Hill." he whispers into my ear as he slides into my still pulsating body to take his pleasure from me. He finishes with equal fervor to mine and I feel myself convulsing inside along with him, we are in total harmony, playing each other's bodies in an erotic symphony. Now I finally know what sexual love is all about I think, in its higher forms, it is art, as the two of us join, it is oneness with sea, the sky, the bridge, the glimmering city and ultimately the universe.

After an indeterminate length of time we sit up and tug our clothing back into place although nothing was removed. We pass the bottle back and forth and he lights us both cigarettes. We smoke and watch the water dreamily, enjoying the sweet physical calm of ebbing sexual desire. We are utterly satiated.

We drive to Upper Terrace and as he swings around to park I notice the light is on in Thom's place. It is not late, only around 11:00.

"Stay with me." I plead at my door, not wanting to let go of him, wanting more, now and tomorrow morning and perhaps forever.

He holds me at arms length. "I can't tell you how much I want to sleep here with you tonight little girl, my sweet young artist, I love you so much, I think of you constantly and that is the truth, this has never happened to me before and I am afraid of it. But listen to me, you have to understand, I am going to divorce Phyllis and I think she is having me followed just to get something against me in case I follow through on the divorce. Already she has me seeing a marriage counselor who is costing me, not her, a small fortune. And besides, I have this problem down at the office, but you don't want to hear about that."

"Oh." I respond, not knowing what to say since none of this makes sense to me at all, it is as though he were talking about space aliens and it makes me feel that I never want to know or experience that place called, 'contested divorce proceedings'.

We kiss goodnight and he tucks the bottle of champagne under my arm. I lock the door behind me, and hear the sad sound of the Austin-Healey driving off down the hill.

I ready myself for bed, pour what is left of the champagne into one of Vincent's wine goblets that has found its way into my apartment and drink it all. Very tired, I slip beneath the covers of my warm, cozy bed and am about to drift off to sleep when the phone rings.

"Hi there Doll, how was the wedding?" says Thom, with a forced amiablity. I know him so well that I can sense how he feels.

"Oh fine, wonderful, people were asking for you, why you didn't show up. How are you?"

'Okay I suppose, kinda tired and not in the mood for a party, all those people to talk to, you know I get that way sometimes. Say, whyncha come up here for a night cap and tell me all about it." It sounds like an order.

"I uh, I'd love to but to tell the truth I'm awfully tired Thom, and a little drunk. I have to finish a project tomorrow for Perry Atkinson's office and I have my period." This last is a lie.

"Aw, come on, I have something that will fix that right away, that poor unfulfilled womb of yours. Nancy was here earlier but had to leave, I'm feeling depressed for some reason, lonely maybe and I'd love to have your company for a while, I think this is going to be an insomnia night."

I sigh heavily, why do I have to go through this I ask my inner voice. That's the way it is, get used to it because you'll have this all your life, like it or not, inner voice answers. *No, it's not*, I talk back to Inner Voice.

"Thom, I would love to come up and have a drink with you but I am totally, completely exhausted, half asleep even as I talk to you."

"Well, if that's how it's going to be, that's how it's going to be. Oh, and by the way, you won't forget you owe last month's rent to me." he says testily, bad at covering up his annoyance..

"I know that, I'll pay you Tuesday, I promise. They'll pay me half for the preliminary drawings I have to show them on Monday."

He hangs up the phone abruptly, without further comment. I sense trouble ahead, serious trouble endangering my fragile existence here. I love my little apartment but slowly and surely new terms are being laid down for my continued occupancy. Why should he be angry I think as I turn off the light. He has Nancy now, I am no longer the love of his life and he knows I'll pay him. I am too tired to think more about this and drift into sleep, the better to face tomorrow.

CHAPTER IV

Escape To The Tropics

"Oh, I'll just stay a month or so, till my money runs out. I would like to paint the Mexican children there, enjoy a change of scene, climate, be adventurous for a change. You know Nancy, I have never done anything like this. Gone off on my own I mean." I say as I pack up the carton containing my art materials.

Nancy is down in my apartment moving her things in, preparing to occupy it while I am off to Puerto de las Peñas in Mexico to begin living out my dreams.

"This will be wonderful experience for you, you are so talented Joanna, why you could sell your paintings there and stay even longer." She shakes her head happily as she puts her clothing on hangers and slips them into my closet, then starts in on the kitchen. My things are pushed to one side as she carefully washes the shelves of of accumulated dust, then cuts flowered, plastic shelf paper from the super market, to size and carefully pastes it onto each shelf before she places her dishes in the cabinets.

Our understanding is that she will sublet the place from me until I return from Mexico at which I time I will move back in.

"Oh, and here is my portable Singer sewing machine that has clothed me through my social life since I was seventeen years old. If you like, you may use it, I know how careful and conscientious you are Nancy, and of course, my furniture, what there is of it is at your disposal."

"How kind of you Joanna, oh, did Thom mention to you that he would like his skeleton back?"

"No, but of course, I'll just leave it here for the moment and when he needs it you can take it back to him. Of course, the place won't be the same without these old bones, I will miss him, or her."

Nancy laughs politely at my idiosyncrasy and continues her moving in process.

Vincent is going to fly me to Puerto de las Peñas in a rented Cessna 185. His Staggerwing is in the hangar waiting for parts. Our plan is that he will stay with me there for a few days, getting me settled in, relaxing a little with his friends and then return to San Francisco. It will be during this interim, that we will both think hard about our relationship, if I am committed enough to marriage for him to continue with his divorce. He has made it clear, he needs a wife, period. I am feeling the weight of adult responsibility on my still youthful shoulders while at the same time I am wildly excited about going back to Mexico after so many years and being free of commitments to anyone or anything. At twenty-eight years of age, I have probably lived a third of my life and have only the vaguest notion what I want to do with the rest of it.

The night before we are to leave, Vincent stays in the apartment with me. Everything is packed and ready to go. Clothes and personal items, some books, my paints, easel and a roll of canvas. My rent is paid up. Thom is barely speaking to me. I do not say good-by to him.

It is still dark in the morning as Vincent and I start loading the Buick with my things. The streetlights are still on. I put on some jeans, a Mexican embroidered blouse which I think is appropriate and pair of guaraches. I take a sweater along as it can get chilly up there in the air. A knot of excitement grips my stomach and chest, I can hardly believe we are actually leaving. I have my Mexican visa which is valid for six months, my birth certificate and as much money as I was able to scrape together. As Vincent turns the car around to go down the hill I glance back at the building and it seems that I see Thom glaring down upon us, two burning eyes filled with impotent anger. I feel a portent of something, both good and bad and my inner voice tells me I am going to have to be strong. I do not argue with inner voice.

Vincent and I hardly speak as we speed along Highway 1. Dawn is slowly breaking over the Eastern skies above the coastal range. The Pacific surges and ebbs next to us along the rocky cliffs. Soon we will be where the sea is warm, where the water does not chill one to the marrow of one's bones.

The coffee shop at Half Moon Bay airport is well lit. Jake is expecting us. There is some fog but it appears to be lifting, the sun will burn it off they say. It is early June and that is when the fog is the thickest.

"Hi Annie, you're sure up early today. How about some bacon and eggs to hold us until we get to Guaymas?"

Vincent is jovial, his face relaxed and happy, he looks so handsome at this moment, anticipating an adventure. He is dressed casually; a white shirt and khaki pants some dark aviators glasses that contrast with his thick, silvery hair. If possible, I am even more excited to think we will be in Mexico this afternoon. on a sandy beach, carefree for the moment, no Thom, no Phyllis, no bankruptcy proceedings, only sensual pleasure, exotic sights, food and music and who could imagine whatever mystical delights may await us, *or me.*

Jake comes in and grunts a greeting in my direction as we eat our breakfast at the counter. Then Vincent goes over to the office part and begins filling out our flight plan.

"You lucky dog!" comments Jake, lighting a cigarette.

Vincent chuckles and sighs happily, "You only live once you know."

The Cessna 185 is ready for flight, parked outside the coffee shop. After paying the fuel bill we begin to load it, filling the whole luggage compartment and backseat area mostly with my stuff. It looks as though I was going to stay permanently. Vincent has given me a small, portable radio to take along and I carefully place it in the box with my art materials. We make a last stop in the bathrooms since there is nothing available during flight for our elimination needs except Vincent's famous pickle jar. We board the plane, lock the doors and wave good-by.

"Good-by and good luck you two, bring me back a coconut." shouts Annie, smiling and waving, her face red in the cool morning breeze off the ocean.

Jake gives the propeller a couple of turns then steps back out of the way. Vincent shouts "clear", and starts the engine. It catches immediately, a sign that the plane is in first class condition mechanically.

He taxies to the beginning of the runway and goes through the safety checklist. It is now daylight and the fog has lifted enough for us to take off. We start down the runway, picking up speed until that magic moment when we are airborne, leaving our earthly concerns below us somewhere, to deal with at some vague, future time. Nothing exists now except Vincent and I and the plane, we are one cosmic entity. I trust him implicitly.

I am the navigator sitting in the co-pilot's seat. Vincent has given me the job of calculating our air speed, maintaining our heading, confirming our position with the air chart before me and identifying the land marks over which we pass. The forced concentration brings on a wave of air sickness. I struggle against it, realize I am losing the struggle and fold up the air chart, swallowing mightily. The thought of splattering this morning's breakfast all over the instrument panel is not attractive nor is it compatible with being a cosmic entity.

"Hey, what's wrong, you look a little green, don't look at the air chart," shouts Vincent over the roar of the engine, "look straight ahead out the window, try not to barf, don't even think about it. Okay?"

"Okay."

We enter a turbulent air space over the Santa Lucia mountains, we are overflying Big Sur. I force my stomach into reluctant tranquillity, breathing deeply and slowly, not wanting to miss the spectacular panorama unfolding below us. Vincent is flying low, around 2,500 feet so we can appreciate the force of the sea against the dramatic, tree covered cliffs. The water is a gorgeous blue-green, I try to think of what color I would use to paint it if I ever did seascapes. Cobalt blue and viridian green I decide and the whitest white I could find to define the cresting waves.

"Pretty isn't it?" says Vincent looking over at me and smiling, enjoying the intensity of my aesthetic experience. We are beginning to communicate without words, knowing without speaking what the other is feeling, our selves having merged.

"We'll be landing in Mexicali to go through Mexican customs, probably get there a little later this afternoon. I hope they let all this stuff into the country."

In the back seat he has a box of fishing gear, a small motor for a dug out canoe he calls a 'panga', a small diesel generator, toys for the children of a friend from San Francisco named Roland Adams and his Mexican wife, Hermalinda. The names are strange to me but will soon become well known.

We change course inland after Morro Bay, leaving the coast behind us. He shows me where the omni stations are that give us our directional headings. I am learning cross country navigation. I feel totally comfortable and secure with him, I trust him completely, something I have never felt before with any man, this has to be love, the love of my life.

The snow capped Sierra Nevada mountain range towers off to our left, the coastal ranges to our right as we fly down the central valley of California and soon are over the Mojave desert.

I glance over at my love and am startled to notice he is sleeping!

"Vincent, wake up, we are losing altitude.." I shake him awake.

"Oh sorry, Honey, could you fly this thing for a while, I really am tired, I just need a few minutes and I'll be fine. We'll be skirting the Eastern edge of the Los Angeles basin, keep an eye out for other aircraft, stay at this heading of 155 degrees and don't crash, Jake will be furious to lose customers."

I take the controls as he slumps back in his seat, falling asleep almost immediately.

Nervously I scan the instrument panel, this plane is more complex than either the Super Cub or the 140. There are adjustments to be made for fuel mixture, for propeller pitch, the controls are electric and then there is the radio navigation system and on top of all of this it is a large aircraft, much larger than I am accustomed to.

Vincent is snoring loudly as I scan the skies for other planes, check my compass heading and shift my attention back and forth between the altimeter and air speed. My air sickness has vanished with my responsibility. Furtively, I take this opportunity to glance over at my love's teeth. They look slightly ajar as his mouth is half open in deep slumber. Yes, I will have to accept the fact that he is much older than I am, and it is very likely that he wears false teeth. Well, so what, I think to myself, *no one is perfect*, I'll be old someday with my teeth falling out of my head. I am in love with Vincent the man and that is that and I must overlook and accept the natural failings that human beings are subject to with the passing of the years. Then I congratulate myself on my noble sentiments, not really feeling or accepting that I shall ever become an old woman.

I notice that I have strayed from my compass heading by 5 degrees, correct for that and look down at the distant earth.

There is a jet liner climbing in our direction in the distance toward the southwest. That smoggy yellowish area must be Los Angeles. The flight south is becoming familiar. The jet is turning toward the north now, probably heading for San Francisco I imagine.

The radio starts up and through the static I think they are asking us to make contact with the tower in Los Angeles. They must have us on radar. Not feeling competent to deal with them I wake Vincent up. He snorts and looks around for a moment, as if he doesn't quite know where he is, then smiles at me and takes the radio. He gives LAX our call letters, altitude, air speed and heading. They tell us to climb 5500 feet and to stay out of the way of commercial air traffic.

He pulls back slightly on the stick and we begin to climb.

"An hour and a half more and we will be at the border, you aren't bored are you honey?"

"No, on the contrary, I am loving every minute of this."

"Have to pee?"

"A little, but I can wait."

"We've got some headwinds, slowing us down a bit, probably get to Mexicali about 1:00 PM. Let's make love to pass the time, you ever made love at 6,000 feet in the sky?"

I giggle at that and ask girlishly, "How can we do that?"

"Easy, here.." he unzips his pants and puts my hand on his half hard penis, it is very silky under my touch and begins to enlarge.

"Slip one leg out of your jeans, come on, no one is looking."

"Not even God?" I say, remembering my Sunday school lessons that God is everywhere watching us, knowing when we sin, the all powerful, inescapable, punishing father.

I do as I am told, then he pulls my head down on him and I hear him moaning in ecsatsy while his hand slips down between my legs and begin fondling my creamy, throbbing flesh.

The plane feels as though it is bobbing around, I pull away from him and see that we are losing altitude, in fact we are almost in a dive position and he doesn't care.

"Vincent, look we are losing altitude...." I shout anxiously.

"Don't stop, I'll take care of it." He murmurs, pulling back on the control with one hand and pushing my face back down onto him. He ejaculates into my mouth, and the plane continues to bounce around.

"Oh my lord, wasn't that great, now look, you straddle me, yeah, like that, good lord, you are ready aren't you honey, that's it, sit on my cock and you do the work while I keep us straight and level."

I forget about God watching me as I move up and down on him, performing the ancient ritual between men and women, pressing at times against the control, we fly erratically until I climax, screaming into the side of his hot, pulsating neck. Never before have I been so liberated from learned sexual repression, this man has truly uncastrated my libido.

He smiles happily, loving my lusty outcries, feeling what I feel. "Isn't that wonderful honey, what our bodies can do, how they can take us to another place of pure wonder, now why is that bad, why isn't it part of our religion, like the images on the ancient temples in India where sex was worshipped by the people as divine?"

I look at him curiously, wondering what he is talking about, dabbing between my legs with a kleenex to dry myself up a bit, feeling totally alive.

"What do you mean, the worship of sex?" I ask, pulling my jeans back into place.

"Exactly that, I saw the temples during the war when I was in India, there are these large relief carvings in stone of men and women in different sexual positions, even homosexual positions. A woman sucking on a man's penis then a fellow behind her screwing her from behind, it is really something that you could hardly believe if you didn't see it for real."

"And their God approved of all of that?"

"It is God's gift to humanity according to their religion, the gift of life."

"Wow, just think of that, a religion that worships sex and the body."

"I want to make love to you at high altitude in Mexico, there is something about the lower air pressure at high altitudes that makes sex more intense, didja feel that, a celestial orgasm I call it."

"What do you think God thinks of us now?" I ask impishly, lighting two cigarettes for us.

"I think He would approve, at least that old Indian God would, and I think perhaps we should educate the Christian God about the beauty of sexual intercourse, don't you think so?"

We smoke silently, thinking our separate thoughts but feeling strangely at peace with one another, feeling the rightness of what we are doing, the utter honesty of our acts.

I drift into reverie, imagining Vincent and I as ancient god and goddess, sitting on the throne of pagan India. Incense rises around us, mingling with the scent of the many flowers growing in the gardens, while beautiful women dressed in colorful silk saris play string instruments as others fan away the flies. The babble of our children rises pleasantly from the courtyard, like the sound of a stream flowing over rocks.

A temple guard announces that a messenger has arrived at the gate of the temple. Our servants lead him to us and he explains that he has been converted to the new religion and has been sent to educate us all, that we must renounce paganism for the new ways. He assures us that the entire eastern world is renouncing the old ways for the new ways. There have been many such rumors for a long time but no one believes them. No one can imagine a religion that negates our natural selves and our love and worship of earthly beauty. Who would ever espouse such a religion?

"Vincent, my beloved," I say to my consort, "don't you think that fellow that is announcing the new divine order is very ugly. I mean, we and all of our people are so beautiful with our honey colored skins, silky dark shiny hair and light eyes, while this man is hideous, deformed with unwashed hair and beard, dressed in sackcloth, why his ungodly odor is noxious even from a distance of many meters. He looks unhealthy, I wonder what they eat?"

"Ahh, most precious light of my life, they say that all of the new believers are the unwanted and the unloved, for that reason they are initiating the concept of fleshly sin so that we may be controlled by them. They say they eat strange food that is not natural, that it is contrived food rather than that which we eat from our extensive, organic vegetable gardens, this makes them unhealthy, depressed and ugly. They say they use something called money to fulfill their needs rather than exchanging worthy products produced by their own efforts, and this makes them all thieves at heart."

Vincent shifts uncomfortably on his throne in his golden silk robes. Rubies, diamonds and emeralds gleam in the golden crown on his princely head. He strokes the thin mustache that curls enticingly around his mouth and his brow is knotted in an unaccustomed frown.

I reply nervously, gracefully dismissing the messenger with a wave of my hand. "Tonight the moon is full my darling and I will go to the holy shrine of the Buddha and wait for a message from our gods, to find out how we may prevent the corrupting of our beliefs by those who hate their own flesh with all of the wonders of the body that we are born with and the earth we live in."

That night the Goddess of the full moon comes to me. Her words are not pleasant to hear. The light of the moon becomes more intense as I invoke her spirit until the giant stone carved Buddha and I are encircled by her silvery light and she speaks.

"My blessed child, I must tell you that your beliefs are doomed to destruction from the outside forces who will make you feel unworthy, evil and separate from the earth and your own natures. The human spirit will become suspect, forced to live apart from your bodies, humanity will be lonely, alien and suffer great sadness. Joy will be lost to you. Greed and destruction will become an integral part of the new religion and you will be powerless to stop it. First, humanity will separated from the earth and her creatures, then men and women will be separated from each other, hating one another, then, parents and children will be divided by competing and loathing, until finally, the human organism will be separated from it's own spirit and begin to mindlessly pursue self-destruction."

I feel myself weeping at her words as she continues.

"You who believe and have faith in the old ways will survive, but in secret, for 2,000 years and then you will return, slowly, little by little, with great difficulty and sacrifice, but eventually you and all wom-men, including the men in 'wom-men', will come into your own, you will come back to love, cherish, maintain and possess the earth with all it's plants, it's animals, the air around it, it's seas, rivers and lakes. You will cease destroying the gifts of your earth and the treasures of your humanity. I am speaking the words of the great spirit, return and tell my words to your lover Vincent and your people, prepare yourself for the dark times but know that as long as you respect the true gods of nature, love the spirits of the earth and yourselves, you will eventually triumph."

Tears stream down my face, smearing the kole around my large Indian eyes as I sadly return to the temple court where supper is being laid down on the tables alongside the lavish, hand embroidered cushions. The musicians are playing evening music while the large tigers trained to guard the temple, prowl around the periphery of our dining hall waiting for scraps.

"My heavenly darling, you look strange, please seat your self next to me while I fondle your most supremely beautiful body, here eat a date that has been marinated in mare's milk brandy."

"No, my most divine love of the universe, Vincent, I can't eat anything, please pass me your silver chalice of mango wine and I shall take a big sip before I relate to you the terrible prophecy of the Moon Goddess."

I hear the roar of the Cessna engine as I reach for the chalice and never get a chance to taste the ancient, mango wine.

"Hey, Joanna, what are you talking about, what moon goddess for chris' sake, what are you mumbling about?"

I am abruptly in the moment, "The altitude has gotten to me I think, never mind, I was just thinking about the Indian religion and also, how sexual you are. I imagined us as, well, like we were in high school together and making out in the backseat of 50's Chevie in the back row of a drive-in theater."

"Thanks honey, nice to hear it, you got a great imagination. How about some music while you fix your face, your mascara is smudged." He finds a music station on the radio, they are playing a Frank Sinatra love ballad.

"Uh, how did you like it, the sex I mean." he asks, turning to me, his face slightly beaded with perspiration, the cabin is hot even though the vents are open. The odor of his masculinity emanating from him, embracing me, making me feel womanly.

"Yes, I like it Vincent, very much, I have never known a man like you, you are everything for me."

He smiles, "You ain't supposed to say those things, you're supposed to play hard to get you know."

"Oh, but it doesn't come naturally to me, pretending I feel one way, when in truth I feel the opposite."

"Yeah, you could go nuts making a practice of that sort of thing, I like you cuz you're pretty straightforward there, girl. In fact, I would say I can read you like a book."

"Yes." I murmur, still not totally accustomed to *his* frankness.

"I want to do everything for you and to you, sex is wonderful, our bodies are wonderful. For me there is nothing like making love to a beautiful woman, I forget everything, all the problems of the office, the divorces, everything, it's almost like...like a drug for me."

He continues, "When I was a little boy," he continues, "we were prohibited from touching ourselves, down there. My mother was a great woman, but she was from the old school, cunts and pricks were dirty, sex was bad, you know all of that. When I was around 3 or 4 years old I would play with myself in the bathtub, like children do you know, and of course, I'd get this baby sized erection. My mother would be furious and threaten to get her sewing scissors and cut the thing off if I kept it up. I was terrified she was going to do that but I couldn't make that erection go away no matter what."

I gasp at the thought, thinking how much so many women would have missed.

He lights a cigarette and stares dreamily into the skies, transported to the past. "She thought she was teaching me the correct behavior, and God rest her soul, that she was simply doing her motherly duty by me and my sister. In every way she was a wonderful mother, loving, fun, hard working, they don't make 'em like her anymore totally dedicated to family and home."

"Yeah, my mother is like that too..but she was really kind of frustrated, she did it all just like "Good Housekeeping" but she was furious the whole time and not loving at all, chasing me around the dining room table with a riding crop because she didn't have any other way of venting her anger. You suffered the part about sex is bad but I was the family whipping boy, or girl, the scapegoat, I think that's worse. "

"Really, how do you deal with it?"

"Well, I got away at the first opportunity and mostly stay in touch by letters and an occasional phone call. The Christmas visit was more of the same, two days is the most I can stand to be with them. Mainly I have had to make myself over in my own image, no other way because to accept their negative view of me, I mean, that would ultimately mean suicide."

It is his turn to gasp and turn to me with a mixture of what? Surprise, shock, maybe all of it mixed together, but I also see compassion there in his ruddy face. He hands me his damp handkerchief to wipe the sweat from my face.

We fly in silence, he makes a radio check then goes on.

"My father's father was a Baptist minister, real strict, from Kansas. I think my father ran away from home, and settled in San Francisco in the early 20's. He came to make his fortune and he did, for a while anyway. He bought property on Bryant street and built an industrial laundry. He did all washing for the big hotels, the Fairmont, the Mark, all of the big ones, imagine, he washed all the bedding, towels, tablecloths and uniforms. I can remember those huge vats of fabrics boiling and churning, then passing through huge wringers to the mangles where they ironed linen as big a a football field. Not quite, but to a kid it looks like that. My mother was a 'Kelly Girl." You don't know what that is but they were like stewardesses on planes but they served the trains. They were real strict with those girls, no hanky-panky and they took good care of them. The girls had to be smart and good looking, hard working and, virgins, hopefully. A good way for a girl to see the wild west without too many problems with men and most of them married well.

It was almost like a convent on wheels, preparing them for a proper marriage but with a man of course, not with a religious spirit." He looks over at me and smiles as I imagine his mother, beautiful and blond, chaste, serving these tough, handsome guys on the trains, adventurous men wheeling and dealing with the new found wealth of California. What fun that must have been, everything possible, wide open to whoever was spirited enough to go for it.

"My dad fell in love with her and they got married, like most everyone and he bought a huge family house on Buena Vista Avenue where my sister and I were born, I told you how we were born in the kitchen didn't I? We grew up there, I went to Dudley Stone school and then my father bought a car, a Packard touring car that we could all drive around in. That car was his pride and joy, he loved it more than he loved us my mother used to say."

"Then came the crash of '29, which began the Depression in the 30's, but you were too young to remember weren't you?"

"I remember something but I thought it was fun, everyone had to stay with us because they no where else to go, my cousins, my grandmothers, my aunts, people were alway coming and going, I liked it a lot, a lot better than afterwards when everyone scattered and we hardly came together as a family anymore."

"You are strange, happier in the bad times than in the good times...I'm gonna have to watch out for you. Anyway, to go on with my family history, dad lost everything, the hotels went bankrupt and with no more commercial laundry to do, the place closed down and he put the building up for sale. I think they sold it for less than it cost to buy the property. He sold his Packard. Real sad. So he gets sick and the last thing I remember was him in San Francisco General with tubes coming out of him. He didn't have money for a good hospital. I'd go visit him and once there was this woman with him, crying, I never knew her but my mother told me she was his lover, or his mistress, or maybe she said his whore. She left right away when she saw me."

"Then one day when I went to see him, the nurses and the doctors were having fits, he had pulled all of his tubes and whatever out of himself and was swearing at all of them, telling them to leave him alone, to let him die in peace. And a little bit after that he did die. And you know what, that woman came to the funeral, can you imagine? My mother told my sister and I not to speak to her but she seemed to know some of his friends and to tell the truth, we could hardly keep from looking at her."

"What did she look like?"

"She was kind of dark looking, maybe some Mexican blood in her, she had this veil over her face, it was hard to tell, we never saw her or heard from her, ever."

"And why did your father pull all those tubes out of him like that."

"Lost everything, car, business, couldn't pay his employees, couldn't put food on the table, it was too much for him, for his pride, he preferred to buy the ranch."

"Why do you say, 'buy the ranch'?"

"Kick the bucket, you know, *die*."

A strange expression I think, one would think that buying a ranch, or a farm would be a positive event, a chance to enhance life, cultivating the earth, breeding animals but here in California it means death.

We slide into our private reveries mesmerized by the sky, the clouds drifting by us and the landscape unfolding below. I ponder how life can deal with people, how terribly vulnerable we are to forces beyond our control.

Finally, Vincent breaks the silence. "Half an hour more to the border." he announces, patting my thigh and tuning in the radio. A man's voice surfaces, speaking in Spanish.

"Mexicali, you speak any Spanish?" he smiles at me.

"Yes, a little, I brought my Spanish grammar book from high school with me, you want me to talk you into Mexicali in Spanish Vincent?"

"Lord no, just kidding, we better stay in English, that's official air talk language or else they revert to Spanish and ya don't know what in the hell they are telling you to do."

"Oh."

We begin losing altitude in anticipation of our Mexican touch down.

I scan the land below as we drop. Dry. Desert with jumbles of buildings and towns. It doesn't look so great but it's a foreign land, promising change, challenge and possibly adventure. It is thrilling. I listen to the garbled English giving Vincent landing instructions, he lines up with the runway, we touch down and taxi over to a building with a large sign in Spanish that says, ADUANA.

"These are the customs inspectors honey, just smile and be nice and hope they don't find the rifle under the seat."

He opens the doors of the plane and a blast of hot, dry air engulfs us. The building is shabby, the wind is blowing gum wrappers, leaves and dust around the cracked pavement.

Four uniformed men are walking toward us, they make me feel threatened and serve to cool my excitment at landing in Mexico. They are wearing greenish gray uniforms and billed caps, none of them too clean. Vincent almost leaps forward to greet them with a humble smile of appeasement, acknowledging their superior power over him at this moment. They are laughing heartily among themselves at some private amusement and I feel we may be the source of some denigrating joke we are unaware of. The Captain motions us to follow him to the office while the others stay behind, touching and fondling the Cessna 180, walking around the plane, peering inside and tugging at the propeller.

In the office, Vincent fills out several forms stating the purpose of our trip, our destination and what we have with us. He notes his pilot's license registration, number of our aircraft, closes the flight plan and opens another to Guaymas, Sonora.

"Vincent, where is the bathroom?" I ask in a whisper.

"Dónde están los baños para damas?" inquires Vincent, proud of his Spanish.

"Por allá." motions the Captain without looking up from his paperwork.

'Allá' is a rambling concrete, box-like structure painted an utterly garish shade of chipped, ultramarine blue that must be the main terminal for Mexicali Airport. I make my way through the swirling, dusty winds and manage to shove open the main entrance door. The building is poorly maintained, suffering a border-town malaise..the floors and windows badly need cleaning, the supporting concrete pillars are straight out of bureaucratic hideous. Form follows function as I was taught in my art classes, but these can barely even function. They are unpainted and chunks of concrete have fallen off the corners, exposing the iron reinforcing bars. The floor tiles do not properly meet the bases of the columns and garbage has collected in the cracks.

I feel let down as I push open the door to the ladies room only to be accosted almost to unconsciousness by the order of ripening feces and fermenting urine. I back off to regain my senses, take a deep breath and plunge forward to relieve my aching bladder. There are no doors on the two toilets available, there is no paper and no running water. The toilets are filled with who knows how many days of excrement to which I can only add as there is no choice. I leave as quickly as possible, convinced I have seen the worst women's restroom in the world. I have not envisioned this aspect of my dream country, south-of-the-border.

Vincent and the Captain are back at the plane. I see Vincent giving the Captain some money. Palm trees bending in the wind are planted around the buildings in a half-hearted effort to beautify the place. They should have hired an architect from the school of Porfirio Diáz and made a proper airport in the beginning, I think. The small planes parked here and there, bounce slightly in the hot wind.

"Well, glad that's over honey, I'm going to the men's room, you stay here and take care of the plane, I'll be right back." says Vincent.

Three of the military looking fellows are still here, lolling around the plane. One approaches me. He sports a heavy dark mustache, spikes of straight, jet-black hair poke out from under his military style cap. He is short, just my height and brown skinned with an overweight belly that hangs over the belt of his trousers. He is smiling broadly, revealing large teeth, some with flashing gold and silver fillings. I am fascinated by his strangeness. He apparently misunderstands my artistic curiousity.

"Pritty laady, wot es jur naime pleez?" he asks, his smile growing even wider.

"My name is Joanna." I respond politely as I was taught to do. The other two officials are watching this little drama with undisguised pleasure.

"Ahh, Juana, Juana es jur naime." he says.

"Yes, I mean si."

They all laugh when I say 'si' which is very puzzling to me, why is that funny I wonder.

"My naime es Evodio, an I am mucho pleeze to meet wit ju my laady."

He hold his hand out to shake hands, I extend my hand cautiously, he takes it and won't let go.

Still smiling he says "I wan keez ju, I laik jur preety blu iezz."

I panic slightly, thinking perhaps I should not be so nice and polite, then forcefully yank my hand away from this rude man, wishing Vincent would hurry back.

I move away to the other side of the plane, still feeling responsible for guarding our means of transportation. The Mexicans are speaking rapidly in Spanish and I wish very much to know what they are saying.

Finally Vincent returns with the Captain, somehow, they are talking and laughing, Vincent having charmed his way through the bureaucracy.

As we settle into the plane and prepare for take-off, Vincent turns to me and asks, "What was that all about, was that spic trying to get cozy with you? They love gringas you know. They think they're easy to make out with."

"What's a gringa?"

"A girl from the U.S., a guy is a gring-o. masculine and feminine, you know how all the Spanish nouns have their own gender, basic high-school Spanish."

Evodio gives the propeller a few turns, still with his broad smile while his compadres look on, They appear to live in a world of perpetual amusement.

"Clear", shouts Vincent, he starts the motor and we are off and airborne once again. It feels good to be putting distance between us and the border.

"Next stop Guaymas honey, hungry?" he asks, handing me a candy bar he must have bought in the airport.

"Uh huh," I murmur, taking the wrapped up Mars bar. I eat the sickly sweet, slightly stale chocolate and nut concoction, then wipe my fingers in my handkerchief.

"We'll stay overnight there and get an early start for Puerto de las Peñas tomorrow morning." he says as he adjusts the prop, fuel mixture and stabilizer for cruise altitude. "Below us is the Sea of Cortez, or the Gulf of Lower California as we call it.

Those immigration inspectors at the airport, they tried to get too friendly with you while I was gone, didn't they? They think all Amercian women are easy lays."

"Well yes, sort of, I was just trying to be nice, polite I mean seeing as how we are visitors in their country, something like that, but the guy grabbed my hand and wouldn't let go, and then he said...." I didn't finish. the sentence.

"You can't be too friendly you know, a woman that is, they get the wrong idea right away, here, a respectable woman doesn't even look at a strange man let alone speak to him."

"Really, then won't they think we are 'ugly Americans' being rude to them in their own country?"

"No, the funny thing is the more aloof and unfriendly you are, the more they respect you, don't forget that, this is an authoritarian country and meaner you are the more the authority you have, or so it seems."

He hands over his pack of unfiltered camels, for me to light one for each of us. We are beginning to communicate without speaking, each others needs and feelings shared without words.

The cabin fills with smoke and I push open the outside vent all the way to let in the thin, high alitude air. I wonder how I am going to deal with this place, it will be different from Mexico City I know where the people were almost like those in San Francisco, just speaking Spanish. The great cultural gap looms ahead as I contemplate the months before me of painting, drawing, photographing. absorbing the life of this strange country.

Vincent likes to tell me things. "The Mexicans have a Madonna/Whore image of women, either you are one or the other, a saint or a devil, nothing in between."

"No kidding, isn't that unrealistic? I mean no one is either totally good or totally bad the way I have been educated to think, we are combinations of qualities and then people change...like Thom changed from being my saint to being my monster."

He looks over and laughs at me, as though I am hopelessly naive. "Well honey, you'll see what I mean when we get there, you've always been with someone taking care of you, shielding you, parents, school, husband but now you are a divorced women in the world, you have to be careful of how you handle yourself. Thom was your protection for a while, like a father wasn't he but he wanted his pound of flesh out of you and you pulled away from him and lost that. I'll be with you for a while but then I have to leave Mexico, unless you change your mind and want to come back with me to San Francisco?" He exhales big smoke rings into the air, they hit the windshield and disperse.

I stay silent, not knowing what to say, thinking how depressing all of this is and we haven't even gotten to the tropical paradise yet and are talking about going back. And the pitfalls. Always these warnings, this burden of female virtue we are forced to lug around with us all the time, the predators out there, all around, waiting their chance to snatch it away in some unguarded moment. It takes the fun out of everything. I feel it settling in around me. I wonder if he thinks I will take up with one of these predators, I have no intention of doing anything of the kind, but then I don't really know what lies ahead.

I stare down on the blue waters of the Sea of Cortez. The beaches are great sandy, empty expanses melting into deserts punctuated by startling rock formations and mountains in colors of gray, beige, peach and lavender. It is wildly beautiful, with not a sign of human habitation, glaringly inhospitable terrain.

I feel tired and doze off, unsettled by Vincent's little lecture.

I dream of Mexican cowboys, dashing fellows, adorned in silver with huge sombreros mounted on great beautiful horses, stallions I would wager. They thunder by me as I stand on a dusty road somewhere, each man more handsome than the next, they smile their flashing, devilish grins, showing off perfect rows of strong white teeth. The horses tails are raised like flags of joy and fly high in the wind behind them as they gallop past me and toward me, pounding the road, I feel their stirrups graze my arms. Inadvertently I reach out to the last rider as I see him approaching, a dark skinned, lean man with a black mustache and dark brown eyes. I gaze at him in longing and he understands my look, leans over, puts one strong arm around my waist and in a moment I am tucked neatly on the saddle while he rides the straining flanks of the silver and gray spotted stallion. The horse is galloping so fast I feel we are almost flying, flying....

"Hey there," Vincent nudges me slightly to rouse me, "What the hell you dreaming about, you're jumping around like a cat on a hot tin roof?" He doesn't wait for me to answer. "Joanna, you fly this crate for a while, I need a little nap myself, you okay?"

"Oh yeah, I'm fine, where are we?" I look down and see that we are over land now, no water anywhere.

"A little west of Hermosillo, you slept a while you know. Less than an hour and we'll be landing in Guaymas...all right, it's your chance to practice being Amelia Earheart, wake me up if the engine quits...."

He is snoring almost immediately. I take a heading of 145 degrees and maintain an altitude of 4,500 feet.

I think about my dream. These fantasy situations had the power to take me over completely and become as real or more real than what was supposed to be reality. I wonder if I am crazy but dismiss the thought, though doubts linger. If I am mad, I must cherish and protect that madness as instinctively I sense it as a great source of energy. As a child, I was so unhappy I would conjure up romantic stories at night as I lay in bed waiting for sleep. The stories would continue into my sleep and the next night I would pick up where the one the night before left off. They would be fantastic adventures of which I was the brave, beautiful heroine and the boys, they were boys then, would be idealized versions of the latest school heart throb, they would be my companions whether we were flying airplanes in the war, saving our nation from the enemies or riding the range in the wild west rescuing our herds from the rustlers. It was the only way I was able to cope with the mundane, dinginess of my life.

Vincent snores on. I wonder what the radio frequency of the tower in Guaymas is and fantasize about landing there, but then, think the better of it and rouse my sleeping lover.

"Ummph, rumph." he sputters, "where are we?"

"Close to Guaymas I think, you better call the tower there and check the heading."

He talks in English over the radio, giving our position. The radio crackles with static and I can barely make out the landing instructions in the broken English of the controller. I can't understand a thing he is saying and wonder how Vincent can proceed with such confidence on the basis of those garbled words.

"Roger, over and out." Vincent turns off the radio and we begin our descent into Guaymas.

He makes his usual perfect landing and we taxi to the aviation gas pumps where he tops off the tanks, then to the airport tie-down. After unloading and locking the Cessna we check into the office to close the flight plan for the day. The atmosphere has gone through a sea change. We are still on the Sea of Cortez but the breeze is languid, laden with salt, warm and calming. The airport is small but nicely designed and well maintained. Still, the women's toilets leave a lot to be desired but at least there is running water. However, the booths are so small that my head hits the door in the process of peeing and I find I must leave it half open in order to achieve the proper position. Either the women are half my size here or someone doesn't know how to measure, I think as I wash my hands and face in the cool tap water of the sink. A definite case of form *not* following function.

The palm trees are tall and robust, with an abundance of coconuts bursting forth under the swaying fronds. Some have ripened and have fallen to the ground and just lay there. I imagine how costly these tropical products are in the north and pick one up to take with me. Vincent laughs. My depression lifts and I begin to anticipate the rest of the afternoon and evening here in this lovely tropical village.

A rattle-trap cab takes us to a simple, sea-side motel where we check in.

"Let's go swimming." I say, rummaging through the mountain of clothing I have packed for my stay in Puerto de las Peñas for a bikini. "I love to swim in the sea."

Vincent is stretched out on one of the twin beds, in his lazy lion attitude. By now I know what he wants, a drink and sex in that order.

"Let's order a drink honey, aren't you thirsty?" There are no telephones, so one of us has to go order the drinks, and it will be me. I slip into my bikini in the bathroom, then dig around for a beach robe to wear to the bar. But look, he is asleep. I will take my swim and then get the drinks I think happily, grabbing a towel and walking swiftly down toward the sea. My love is exhausted while I am seething with energy. The stony beach hurts my bare feet but I don't care as I gingerly pick my way into the gentle surf. A tenderfoot I think, an urban cowgirl as painfully I get to where I can let myself unto the water and relieve my delicate feet. I paddle my way out through the shallow waves and marvel at the tepid water, such a difference from the bone chilling waters off the coast of northern California. I roll over on my back and study my surroundings. Birds careen overhead, screeching at each other. Their species is unknown to me. Coconut palms line the shore, interrupted here and there by a palm thatched shanty. Children frolic on the beach while fishermen work on their small boats and canoes, mending their nets. The tensions of the flight dissipate, the sun lowers on the horizon and the gathering clouds promise a great sunset. The place feels rural and untouched. I continue to loll on my back, treading water occasionally, doing the side stroke, then a few back strokes. Then, after maybe an hour, Vincent appears on the beach, shouting and motioning for me to come back to shore. Almost reluctantly, I swim back to my love, who is now rested and eager to get on with things.

I crawl through the beach surf on my hands, reluctant to subject my feet to the stones only at the last moment. He waits with my towel and brusquely begins drying me off, scrubbing me down to my ankles. He kisses me at the nape of my neck, we are almost alone on the beach.

"Aren't you going to swim, the water is incredible, it is so warm, like a bath tub."

"No honey, put on your little beach robe that you sewed up for this trip and let's head for the bar, you look beautiful...you never brought me my drink you know."

"You fell asleep you know." I say smiling as we walk along a dirt path, my feet still bare. *I'm going to have to buy some sandals* I think as he opens the door to the motel bar and restuarant.

There is a big stuffed blue Marlin hanging on the wall above a myriad of liquor bottles. A colorful juke box is playing "Rancho Grande" while a few Mexican fishermen drink Dos Equis beer at the bar. They turn to look at us curiously as we slip into place on the bar stools.

"Dos margaritas." orders Vincent from the amiable bartender. Everyone seems so laid back here, what a startling change from the city, no wonder Vincent loves to vacation in Mexico.

The drinks come, along with a small clay bowl of peanuts. The clear liqour is frosting the champagne goblets while a thin line of coarse salt rims the glass edges. Drops of moisture form on the glasses from the humidity.

"What is this?" I ask.

"Margaritas, tequila with lime juice, ya gotta learn to drink Tequila if you are gonna live in Mexico my love, salud." We clink our glasses together and then sip the cold and firey drink, that is salty and lemony and a tiny bit sweet. It is delicious.

"This beats the vodka martinis from Upper Terrace." I say with pleasure, loving this man who takes such delight in introducing me to these sensual experiences. The drinks go down incredibly fast and he is ordering more. The peanuts are good, a little on the damp side but they help keep drunkeness away from our empty stomachs. The words on the slightly chipped, clay peanut bowl fascinate me, "Motel La Playa', Bienvenidos, Guaymas". I decide I will take it with me for a souvenir, everything feels free here. Like all we have to do is ask, or reach out and whatever we desire will be ours.

"Happy?" Vincent asks, lighting cigarettes for us.

"Uh huh, very..you look very good yourself, very handsome after your rest Vincent."

He reaches over and takes my hand in his. "You make me very happy, but that makes me afraid, do you love me, I mean really love me?"

"Yes, very much." I respond, meaning it. I want to say something about the problem that he is married but he beats me to it.

"I am going to get divorced you know, and you must understand that I am divorcing Phyllis in order to marry you. I am much older than you, when you are my age I will be 74 years old, whaddya think about that? Are you going to still love me when I am an old fuddy-duddy?"

"That won't matter to me," I say blithely, "for me we will always be the way we are right at this moment, you a handsome, successful, incredibly charming San Francisco lawyer and I will always be a young, beautiful artist, forever and ever."

Vincent lifts his noble head back and roars with laughter, then crosses his arms and looks at me with his inquisitive stare usually reserved for a court of law. "That's exactly what worries me about you honey, you are not practical, you are not realistic...you haven't had too much experience with life, the first hard times hit, you are going to come apart."

"Hah!" I snort after a large gulp of this ambrosia called 'Margarita', "you aren't the first person to say that to me, and sometimes I think I may be hearing the same thing all of my life. But to say I haven't had to face hard times, well, maybe not horribly hard times but I know how to work, and I'm not afraid of work."

"I worked like a dog when I first married," I continue, "I did it all, my senior year in college, cleaned, cooked, washed and an after school job.. and you know what?"

"What?"

"I got the best grades in all my four years of study that year and graduated in the upper quarter of my class." I finish off the drink and set it down, happy with myself.

"Hmm, maybe you are one of those types that need adversity. But I want you to know something, I need a wife, I mean I *need* to be married, I don't function well alone and I want you to promise me you will be faithful to me while you are down there painting away. I will go ahead with divorce proceedings against Phyllis, I'll think of some reason, always could. And then, I'll come down here for you and we will be married and live happily ever after...I'll give you all the children you want or can handle. How does that sound?"

He motions for two more drinks. We are on our way to becoming bombed.

"Sounds wonderful Vincent, I do love you, but how can you ask me to be faithful when you are still married, isn't that what is called the old double standard?"

"I just have to ask you that's all, so you know and trust that I am telling you the truth about divorcing."

"Maybe I should wait until you are actually divorced before I promise you anything, right?"

He shifts uncomfortably on the bar stool and looks off into space, somewhere in the direction of the hundreds of liquor bottles then looks at me quizzically, analyzing, the sense of sexual exchange vanquished for the time being as I become a person in his eyes rather than an object. I sense the change and feel slightly disturbed by it. It implies responsibility which I don't want.

"I have a lot of problems in the office, I think Thom mentioned that to you, I'm not all that well off financially." He puffs smoke rings into the air as the juke box blares out a Mexican corrida. The men next to us become louder and more boisterous, while we gringos from the the states become more introspective and paranoid.

"Money doesn't concern me."

He laughs again and shakes his head as the waiter sets down two more frosty goblets of the wonderful new drink.

"Salud!" he says and we clink our glasses while the Mexicans stare at us in wild amusement before laughing and guffawing even more than ever. I know they are laughing at us.

"Ignore them." orders Vincent.

I search for my train of thought and then grasp it. "I think what I want is to have my own work, to be successful at it and not to have to depend on a man to live. I mean, how would you like to have to ask someone for money to live on and maybe they give it to you or they don't. But if the man and the woman are equal partners they can just live to give each other pleasure, to make each other's lives happier, more fulfilling perhaps rather than this bickering modern form of marriage I have seen around me all my life."

I think of more things to say in condemnation of modern marriage but decide to hold my tongue since it all seems to be hitting too close to home and I do love this man. "I like the way you and I are together, pure pleasure and escape, I'd like to live like that forever with you and forget about marriage." Amen.

He turns toward me, a half smile playing about his mouth, a strand of gray-blond hair falling over his forehead. He is relaxed and looks youngish, virile, handsome. "You know Joanna, you don't really sound too upset that I am married, you almost sound like you prefer it that way, like having your cake and eating it too."

"Like you said, I haven't had too much experience in the world and I want children some day, probably some day soon the way the years are going by. If there are children there is responsibility and a mother should know something about how the world works, politics and all. I mean, I hardly pay attention to who is president, the Vietnam war is something I barely pay attention to."

"John F. Kennedy is president, he's a Democrat."

"See, that's what I mean, I don't know what I am, Democrat or the other thing, Republican or Communist maybe. Like my step-father says, all of San Francisco are Communists. Now what really is a Communist? We never read the Communist Manifesto in Political Science. How can you be against something or for something if you don't even know what it is?"

"A man has always told you who you are and what to think."

"Exactly."

Vincent considers his own inner conflict, how he always falls for attractive, smart independent women but then they make him nervous, they don't always do what he wants them to do… He feels more secure, more comfortable with a woman he can control, like Phyllis who is happy to be his chattel but who bores him with her whining illnesses and dependence on him. He is tired of thinking about it, of talking about marriage versus freedom, fucking is really all that matters to him at the moment, to get his fill, satiate himself with this young woman blabbing away next to him.

He snuffs out his cigarette. The music is beginning to grate on his nerves, he can't understand a word of it.

"Hungry?"

"I am starving. We haven't eaten anything since those eggs this morning in Half Moon Bay, seems like years ago."

"I did buy you a candy bar in Mexicali."

He pays the bill and we walk along the beach holding hands, like high school sweethearts, to a small restaurant with a thatched roof. The sun has set and the air is warm and sultry. We are both somewhat drunk and perspiring profusely. I am still barefoot, with my dampish bikini under the floral print silk beach robe tied around my waist. My skin is pale, as though permanently drained of color by the San Francisco fog. I long to lay on the beach in the sun. Soon, I think.

There is an old man on the beach with an array of items to sell. Among the jewelery, blankets and hats are sandals. Oh I think, just what I need. Vincent buys me a pair of handmade Mexican sandals. "You will love these," he says, "they will form right to your feet."

The floor of the restaurant is hard swept dirt. There is a small kitchen toward the back where a plump, smiling dark skinned woman is drying dishes behind a brightly painted pink concrete counter. Her dark shiny straight hair is pulled back from her face and contained in a bun behind her head. There are five wooden tables with four chairs each placed around the room. The tables are covered with flowered oil clothes and plastic roses of shades of red and yellow in recycled sauce bottles. There is no glass on the windows which are simply openings between the upright supports of the palapa. Wooden shutters are locked above the opening on hinges. The sound of the surf is not far off and we dreamily pull out two rataan chairs and arrange ourselves at the table closest to the beach.

"You know honey, we are still on gringo time, we are late for lunch and early for supper." says my lover lighting our cigarettes. We inhale luxuriously, the problems of the world far, far away.

The woman approaches us, smiling as though her mouth would split, revealing several missing teeth and several rimmed in silver.

"Buenos tardes," she says, laying a hand written menu in front of us, "quieres tomar algo?"

"What did she say?" I ask, wanting to understand this language, to pass this barrier.

"She asked if we wanted anything to drink, beer, right? Maybe some fish, ceviche on a tostada...is that okay with you my love?" He reaches over and places his hand on mine, he has changed imperceptibly having crossed the border, as though the border were not just geographic/political but mental/spiritual. He has been released from whatever grips him in San Francisco to become more himself.

Vincent gives our order in what I think must be fluent Spanish and we sip our beer quietly, his hand caressing mine.

"Wouldn't it be fun to stay here another day and go fishing?" I say..

"Well, yeah sure, but wait until you see where we are landing tomorrow, why this place is the dumps compared to there, honey I swear, tomorrow I am taking you to paradise."

I giggle happily. I can hardly wait. I am in his hands and he is going to reveal more of life to me than I had ever known existed.

After another round of beer, the meal begins to arrive at our table. A steaming basket of fresh yellow hand made corn tortillas, tostadas with ceviche, enchiladas with yellow, hot running cheese and a green sauce spilled over them, a side dish of red snapper we didn't even order, a dish of sliced cheese that is home made, a plate of sliced tomatoes, avocadoes, cucumbers, onions and another plate heaped with refried beans. There are several small clay dishes of sauces. Our hostess informs us which is 'picoso', hot to the taste. She comes back with more beer and a plate of sliced limes and salt. There is enough to feed the masses and here we are with our bird-like appetites, not wanting to get fat or gaseous in the night, torn between the food and our sense of romantic aesthetics.

"You think this will hold you honey? Here let me show you how to make a fish taco." He breaks off several pieces of the soft steaming white fish and places them on an equally hot tortilla, then a spooning of hot sauce, a few beans, two slices of avocado and finely chopped onion, a sprinkle of salt and a squeeze of lemon then rolling the tortilla up into a lumpy tube, he smilingly presents me with this most basic of Mexican culinary concoctions, a taco.

I bite into it. Stuff squirts out and he shows me how to raise the far end of it so as to trap the contents inside. It is so good, it tastes like food for warriors, the combination of ingredients will impart to me a superhuman strength to endure whatever vissicitudes life may present.

"Good huh?" Vincent asks after making one for himself and expertly lifting the drooping, dripping end of the taco with his little finger.

"I'll let you in on the secret," he says. "The fish was just caught while we were getting drunk at the bar, the avodadoes, lemons and onions grow in the family orchard, the tortillas are made from their own corn harvest, the chilis, onions and tomatoes for the sauces grow in their vegetable gardens and the cheese is made in the family kitchen from the milk from their dairy cows. They probably just buy the salt from somewhere up the coast, the rest is profit to keep the family going."

"Wow," I mumble between mouthfuls, "that's great, reminds me of the old farm in Makanda when I was a child, they lived like that."

We eat all of it and I am stuffed. Unaccustomed to eating very much for fear of getting fat, but the food is irrestible and the consequences will just have to be endured.

Afterward we walk along the shore, it is dark now and shallow waves glisten with phosphorescent algae. I let my sandles get wet in warm water. We are holding hands, it is very romantic. I see us as though we were in a movie, when suddenly, Vincent farts long and loud.

He jumps in mock surprise, "What was that?" he exclaims, laughing, looking behind him, "must be some animal back there behind us making all that noise."

I am very embarrassed. This is the first time we have confronted our bodily functions but it had to happen.

"Oh Vincent," was all I could think of to say.

"Better out than in, you don't want to be marooned in this wild country by yourself with your pilot dead of a burst gut, now would you?"

I laugh and we have passed a plateau.

"Are you happy little girl?" he asks as we near the end of the beach, a rock formation looms ahead in the dark, the lights of the town glow softly behind us.

"Yes." I murmur, meaning it.

"Come here to me, I want to make love to you here on the beach."

"What if someone comes by?"

"No one will come by, come here."

He pulls me close to him and we sink down into the warm sand, his hands begin to fondle me and our blood rises…he doesn't bother to remove my bikini but roughly pulls it aside and enters me. I feel the sand going in along with him but it is not unpleasant. The tide is coming in and laps at our feet and we pursue our mutual satisfaction. Vaguely I see the shadows of persons passing by but nothing can stop us, not even their giggling. Finally he pulls away from me, our passion spent… he closes his eyes and sleeps. I sit up, alert, aware that we were seen and wondering what will happen. Maybe this is illegal I think…we could be arrested. How humiliating, for him more than for me.

I run into the waves and submerge myself in the water, it is cleansing. I swim out a ways and paddle about for a while, wanting to make these moments last, prolonging them.

Vincent is sitting up when I return to the beach.

"Hey, you could get eaten by a shark, aren't you scared of the water at night?"

"No."

The next morning after a quick breakfast, we take off on the last leg of our trip to Puerto de las Penas. The sun is just rising over the Sierra Madre Occidental, the high mountain range that marches across the west coast of Mexico. It is actually the continuation of the rocky mountains of the United States.. The terrain beneath us becomes greener and more lush as we enter the tropics. As the hours pass, Vincent becomes more excited until he grabs my hand.

"There it is!" he shouts over the roar of the engine.

"Look, that's the Bahia de Banderas and there is Punta de Mita. Roland is expecting us, I am going to buzz his beach restaurant to let him know we are finally here…he will come get us at the airport. Isn't that a pretty sight now?"

The huge bay spreads out before us as we drop lower and lower until we are over the beach. Lucious, green jungle mountains tumble steeply right into the sea. Below us are fishermen and children running around, pointing at this low flying plane in excitement.

It is all jungle except for the village of white washed adobe houses with tile roofs creeping up into the hills from the blue green sea. Thick jungle presses in on every side. A silvery river angles its way down from the high mountains cutting through the middle of the village.

"That my dear is Puerto de las Penas and its all ours for the next three days!"

He flies low along the beach hanging his arm out the window as we roar pass what looks like big thatched palm roof huts, people jumping and running along trying to tell us something. We are skimming along the waves, Vincent keeps shouting but how could anyone hear him? He pulls the Cessna up into a steep climbing turn and then dives back down over the waves to make another pass. I realize we are living dangerously at this moment and loving it.

He is hanging his arm out the window of the Cessna shouting out to the people on the beach, gaping at us in amazement, sure that we are going to crash at any moment. Then he makes another steep climbing turn, flies down over the thatched roofs. He looks over at me laughing, "I sure hope the wings don't come off this thing!"

I giggle inanely. I am smudging the window glass with my nose, in an effort to see everything at once. The thought of a month in this gorgeous place fills me with rapture. No money worries, no Thom watching over every move I make. The promise in real life of all my fantasies. The promise of books I have read, D. H. Lawrence, Hemingway, Isak Dinesen, Beryl Markham and others, of every photographic exotica displayed in fashion magazines advertising their beautiful, rough outdoor clothing, of every adventurous woman's dream of the wilderness and primitive sensations, all awaiting me in this magical place we are flying over. I feel my other self that watches me, dancing about with pleasure and we are brought together for once, for the moment at least.

"They just built a new runway, paved with an airport… before it was just a dirt strip where cows grazed." Vincent informs me as we head north of town to land. Below is the airport, and landing field, a very small building sits to one side of the taxi area. It all looks miniature. Vincent makes contact with the terminal below us, lines up the Cessna and makes a perfect landing. We taxi over to the fuel pumps which sit on big metal drums of aviation fuel and disembark from the plane. The hot humid air envelopes us as we stretch our legs. A small, smiling Mexican man amiably begins to fill the fuel tanks of the plane.

"The rainy season begins in June, where we are now, ya got to be careful when you fly. See those clouds forming out there over those high mountains?" Following Vincent's instructions I look out into the distance and see the whitish fluffy clouds, with gray shadows hovering over the mountains. He continues, "they can wreak total havoc on a small plane caught in their storms. The rains bring riches to this area but you have to respect the damage they can cause."

It is relatively early, around 2:00 in the afternoon. We are now in the tropics, having crossed the Tropic of Cancer around Mazatlan. Vincent takes the bill for the aviation fuel which he will pay in the airport office when he closes his flight plan.

We taxi to the area for private planes, there is no hangar, and there an employee of the airport helps Vincent tie the plane down securely. There are other small planes there, Vincent explains to me that the identifying numbers on the planes that have an N in front of them, are from the United States. Fellow countrymen seeking respite from the pressures of the North. There is a a large, twin engine Cessna parked off to one side with a soldier guarding it. It has the Mexican emblem on the tail, an eagle with spread wings holding a snake in it beak. The Mexican man who is helping us tells us that the plane belongs to the Governor of Sinaloa. Curious, I think.

Vincent locks the plane after all of our belongings are removed to the office. There are some people at the edges of the tarmac looking at us curiously. There are no fences. I feel elite. We are part of the aristocracy of the privately airborne. I like it.

The airport office is a rustic, humble affair. On one side is the office where Vincent is closing his flight plan and on the other side is a bar where a few men are congregated, enjoying an afternoon tequila.

I sit on a wooden bench waiting for my love to finish his business. A tall, handsome man walks in. He has white blond hair and blue eyes. He is wearing a khaki shirt open almost to his belt, some khaki shorts and Mexican sandals. His face is flushed and he is smiling. He is not Mexican. He looks over at me and must think the same thing. This must be Roland Adams I think, Vincent's great friend down here.

"Well hi there pretty miss, you must be Vincent's new love of his life, the artist he talks so much about." I stand to greet him and he engulfs me in his arms and kisses me on the mouth! He smells like booze, but I will get used to that.

I think I must be blushing but I can't tell. I fumble for words, "Well, yes, we are together as much as possible, you must be Roland."

"Welcome to Mexico, you will love it. Come on, Let's have a drink while Vincent finishes up with the aviation bureaucrats." He waves to Vincent at the office desk, Vincent waves back as Roland propels me to the bar.

"And our luggage?" I ask, worried about possible theft.

"Martine will watch it." He indicates a dark, serious looking, young Mexican boy who had followed him into the airport.

We slide onto the bar stools. "Hola Miguel," he says to the man behind the bar.

"Que tal Roland," the man responds as he shines a glass. They appear to be friends.

"What'll you have?" He asks me, smiling broadly. They all seem so happy here.

"Oh, beer I think, its too early for a drink."

He throws his head back and laughs heartily as though I had made a big joke.. "Sweetheart, here it's never too early for a drink, Here we have raicilla in the morning with our coffee." He stares into my eyes, resting himself with both his arms on the bar.

"But you can have a beer if that's what you want."

"I'll have a beer too and a raicilla, so the little lady here can try it and see what it's all about." says Roland, leaning in toward me.

The two men make small talk in Spanish. Roland amazes me with his fluency, somehow it is incongruous with his white, anglo-saxon coloring.

The drinks are set before us. "Here, take a sip of the raicilla, it's mountain brew, firewater, made from the lechugilla cactus. It's supposed to be psychedelic, great stuff."

It tastes like nothing I have ever tasted before, truly it is like fire, fire from the sun. I set the little glass down on the bar and take a deep breath.

"Honey, what are you drinking?" Vincent is behind me, his arms around me. "You guys trying to get my girl drunk here?"

"Vincent, how the hell are ya?" The two men embrace, Mexican style, both very happy to see each other again. Old friends.

"Jeezus Christ, ya look great Vincent, how was the trip down here? Come on have a drink here with Miquel before we hit the road. Unwind from all the Frisco business."

He sits down next to me so that I am between the two men. I feel protected. From what I don't know. The beer is wonderful and before I finish it a second bottle appears before me, waiting with beads of moisture running down its sides. "Bohemia" it says. Gee, I think to myself, that's where my grandmother is from, amazing right here in Mexico. I don't mention that fact to Vincent and Roland who are busy catching up on gossip from Vincent's last trip here. Before I have a chance, Roland fills my glass with the second bottle of beer. A large clay dish of peanuts is placed before us. I feel as though I am floating. I ask for the Ladies room.

Miguel motions over to the desk to his wife. "Blanca, Miguel's wife will take you to the bathroom." says Roland. "This is Blanca and this is..uh.."

"Joanna, Joanna Botticelli…like the artist." I say, trying to be helpful

"Right, Joanna the artist, Blanca speaks a little English, don't you Blanca?"

"*Poquito*," says Blanca, much amused by the situation. She is a nice looking woman, in her late thirties I would guess. "We go to badroom," she continues. I follow her to a bathroom door that is marked "Hembras" which is right next to a bathroom door marked "Machos". She enters first, grabs a towel and wipes the mirror and the sink, then peeks into the toilet stall and flushes the toilet. Thankfully.

"Que bueno, hay aqua…wadder," she explains. "Ju wan sumzing, ju tell me, okay?" She smiles kindly and leaves.

I relieve myself gratefully, wash my hands and repair my hair and face. My reflection in the mirror reaasures me that I am young, healthy and pretty. All of which I feel I will need very much on this adventure.

Outside the airport office sits a rickety Ford pick-up. It has been painted blue, with a brush, the brush strokes are clearly visible. Vincent and Roland are casually leaning against the vehicle, smoking, waiting for me.

"All set?" says Vincent as he helps me into the cab. Roland is trying to dust off the inside of the truck which is in the last stages of deterioration. Wires going to nowhere, they hang from the dash which is pocked with gaping holes from better days of an ashtray, a radio, heater, gas and oil gauge, and cigarette lighter. Below, one can see through the remnants of the floor to the road underneath. A lovely Mexican serape is thrown over the torn upholstery to hide the ravages of time. There are no windows besides the cracked windshield. The passenger door can only be opened from the outside.

Roland grabs some wires from underneath the dash and the motor reluctantly starts. I am sandwiched in between them, he looks at me and grins sheepishly. "You see, here we oppose planned obsolescence. It gets worse my dear, I hope you are not one of those rich girls from Pacific Heights who expect everything to be new and hunky dory."

I laugh at that. "No, I am not Roland but tell me why you are not sweating while Vincent and I are dripping?"

"Oh, you will get used to that after a while, at first everyone from el Norte sweats buckets. Say, how long are you going to be with us?" The truck lurches into a pot hole, disconcerting me. I wonder how the thing can stay together.

"Uh, oh, probably about a month. I would like to organize a studio for painting and do some work while I am here, I hope to pick up a little Spanish so I can communicate with the people. It all looks so fascinating. How long have you lived here.?"

"Many years, I came here right after the war, met Hermalinda my wife and never left."

I imagine I will know that full story soon.

Martine, Roland's helper rides in the back of the truck, he never seems to smile which seems unusual here. We pass groves and groves of coconut palm trees. Here and there an adobe hacienda with earth colored tile roofs. Occasionally we pass some burros, their owners walking behind them. They are loaded with sacks of beans, corn or wood for cooking.

We pass an old taxi that looks like the cars my boyfriends drove in high school. There are old Chevies, Fords and Pontiacs, patched together with wire and tape and somehow managing to run.

Abruptly the blacktop turns to cobblestone and we are entering the Village. The homes appear very old and are painted in soft shades of brick red, pale cerulean blue, dark forest green, lilac, yellow ochre and cream. Behind the homes are spacious patios and orchards that extend way beyond the façade. There are cooking smells in the air, toasted chiles, tortillas and beans being prepared for the lunch and supper. There are many children, laughing and playing, carrying mechate bags full of fruit and vegetables from the market, or in their uniforms returning from school, eating mangos or pineapples on sticks.

"Say Roland, how is the Oceano Hotel these days? We could stay there, right on the water, it's nice," says Vincent, as he wipes his forehead with an already very damp handkerchief.

"Vincent Cooper, don't you even say such a thing, that is an insult and you know it! Hermalinda has the guest bedroom all decked out…by the way, we have a new little girl, we call her Tami. She's almost two now, cute as a bugs ear."

"You're not too busy, I mean, we won't be imposing on you and Hermalinda?"

Vincent can be so humble at times, I find that is part of his charm.

Roland smirks. He doesn't even bother to reply so that arranges everything.

We pass the downtown plaza and the gardens filled with roses, daisies, bouganvillias, copa de oro and jasmine. The kiosko in the center of the plaza is constructed of hand wrought iron and painted white. Some children are playing there. The fragrance of the flowers, combined with the salt air is intoxicating. Women in colorful dresses carrying baskets of fruit and vegetables pass back and forth. A few men wearing white shirts and pants and the traditional wide brimmed straw hats are standing around talking or sitting on the benches smoking. The bell tolls the hour in the church directly behind the plaza on the hill. The houses of adobe, painted in their bright pastel colors march up the hill behind the church. Apart from our truck motor, a few gulls calling from the shore and the bees buzzing around the flowers, the place is quiet and serene. The palms sway in the hot afternoon breeze off the sea. I feel we are in another world, a smiling, kind, innocent world that is in danger of extinction: a totally generous world where want is unknown, where one can gather ones sustenance from the earth. A veritable Eden, but like Eden someday we will all be thrown out by god, the money god, and the place will be sold to the highest bidder.

"You are going to love Hermalinda," says Vincent as we roll over the bridge that spans the river. Women are washing their clothes there on the shore of the river, their children splashing about happily in the clean, clear water.

"I'm looking forward to meeting her." I respond, politely, not having any idea of what to expect of this unknown woman.

"She's a *great* woman," expounds Vincent in his lawyers voice.

Hmm, I think, perhaps he over-expounds the virtues of Hermalinda.

We continue bumping along the uneven cobblestone streets heading toward the beach…finally pulling up to the palapa covered bar and restaurant that we had so recently hailed from the airplane.

"We'll have a few drinks and lunch here at Roland's restaurant and then head back to their house, only a block away and rest up," explains Vincent in his tour guide voice.

The restaurant is named appropriately, "La Ramada" and is furnished with plain, square wooden tables and leather covered chairs in the equipale style; so comfortable for sitting around and drinking all afternoon. A small group of musicians are playing ranchero music off to one side. Petrified tree trunks with vines curling around them provide the supports for the enormous canopy vaulting above us of dried palm leaves. The surf is lapping up at the clean, sandy beach only a few meters away. I feel like I am in a dream.

Vincent and Roland are talking about their mutual friends from San Francisco. Roland is from a socialite family and became an instant black sheep by dropping out in Mexico and marrying an Indian woman. They discuss illnesses, deaths, divorces, alcoholism, desertions, bankruptcies and women. Beer arrives for Vincent and I in brown bottles dripping with moisture. Roland drinks straight tequila in the little glass, with lemon and salt, he chases it with beer. Then a plate of cucumbers arrives, sliced in long strips, covered with lemon juice, salt and chile. After that a dish called *quacamole,* mashed up avocado with lemon, cilantro, onion and salt which is served on tostadas, toasted tortillas. It is all very delicious. I am soon feeling drunkish from the very strong Bohemia beer. The main course is fresh caught red snapper along with beans, rice and other condiments. I try to master the art of the taco as Vincent had instructed me in Guaymas, whereby one lifts up the far end of the rolled up tortilla with ones little finger so that the contents of the taco do not spill out all over the table, clothes, ones hand and down ones arm.

There are other Americans eating and drinking. The musicians, called *mariachis* begin to circulate among the tables, strumming their instruments, demonstrating their talents in the hope of engaging clients for their music. Soon, of course they begin playing around a table of boisterous American men. They play the Mexican country music, the corridos that tell of lost ranches, loyal horses that have died for their owners, of beautiful women that betray their men, of getting drunk, of fortunes made and lost, of being poor and suffering, of loneliness and murder. The instruments look home made. A large bass fiddle, two acoustic guitars, a trumpet and a vocalist who also plays a guitar. At times they all sing in a chorus. It is beautiful music.

A plump, older man with a cheerful face, named appropriately, Smiley Jones, sits down with us. He is Roland's business partner. A retired lumber worker from Northern California, he financed the bar and restaurant on the beach. He now spends his days sitting here in the beach restaurant, drinking his time away. A rather timid man, with deep blue eyes behind his thick glasses, he steals what drops of happiness that he can out of the dryness of his waning years. He is accompanied by a pretty young Mexican girl.

"Hi there" he says helping the girl into an equipale. He does not introduce her. Her eyes are downcast and she is silent. "I have some accounting for you Roland, ya want it now or later?" He sets a portfolio down on the table and orders a beer for himself and the girl.

"Later is fine, I'm not in the mood for business just now Smiley, I want you to meet a new visiter from San Francisco. A good friend of Vincent's, an artist no less. She is going to be staying with us for a month or so, right Joanna?"

"Yes," I say. I don't know what else to say. I smile my most ingratiating smile.

Vincent picks up the conversation, "Yeah Smiley, you know, you kind of have to look out for my girl here, keep those fellows with the bad intentions away from her. I need to get back to San Fran and keep to the old grindstone. Joanna doesn't speak too much Spanish, actually none, so you have to show her the ropes. She is going to paint beautiful pictures of the people of Puerto de las Peñas."

"I'll drink to that!" says Roland and we clink our glasses together and drink it down while the *mariachis* play "*San Francisco, Open your Golden gate*" and the sun drops a little lower into the sea.

Afterward we drive in Roland's rickety pick-up to his house. Hermalinda his wife, is a dark, heavy set Indian woman…her black hair hangs in a braid down her back to her waist. Her eyes are dark and almond shaped. She looks as though she had just stepped out of a Gauguin painting from Polynesia. I find her fascinating.

She greets me cooly as Roland and Vincent unload our things and set us up in the bedroom. She offers her hand to shake which I do. She turns back to her cooking. Two little boys are romping around the simple adobe house, they are around 6 and 3 years old. A little girl hangs on her mother's skirts, and she seems to be about a year and a half. They all have honey colored skin, blue eyes and light colored hair. They are beautiful.

"How's the boat coming along Roland?" asks Vincent as he stands before the hull of a fishing boat in progress. The boat is propped up on wooden horses in the patio. "I brought you a motor for the boat."

"Oh great, thanks, I noticed that motor there with the generator, thanks a million Vincent," says Roland, knocking his fist on the side of the hull. "I just haven't had too much time to work on it."

Later, in the guest bedroom of the house, Vincent tells me, "Roland is really lazy, he has been working on the boat for more than five years now. He was always a rich kid and never learned how to work. He's getting worse here, drinks all the time, a lot of guys go to hell in the tropics."

"Oh," I say, unable to comment on the phenomenon of not learning to work. Coming from the working class I have little experience of not working and drinking all day and every day. The concept goes against everything I was ever taught.

"Let's sleep honey, I'm pooped, how about you?" He is stretched out on the bed on top of a gaily flowered bedspread. His eyelids droop and he seems to fall asleep before my eyes.

I undress as he snores. The bathroom is outside, across the patio. I throw on my silk beach robe and venture forth. I seem to see Hermalinda there behind the concrete wash sink through the fronds of the vegetation but she disappears. In the bathroom everything is exposed, there is nothing around the shower so I just turn it on and take a quick shower in the cool water. No gas heaters here.

Thunder begins to growl in the mountains behind the village and the sky is darkening. Returning to the bedroom the cool drops begin to fall on my shoulders, they feel refreshing.

Vincent is stretched out naked on the bed, still snoring luxuriously. I arrange the mosquito netting carefully around the bed then climb in beside him, closing the netting behind me. He is damp with perspiration. The thunder grows louder and closer, then the torrent begins. The skies are unleashed of water and it falls down in a seemingly solid mass, like water being poured down on us from a giant bucket. I crawl out of the netting and go to the door to watch this phenomenon of which I have only read about. The *monsoon.* It is still fairly light and I can see the patio begin to flood but it all seems expected. The little rivers collect and run into little brick and concrete gullies below the pillars supporting the patio roof then down through grates into a drain system. The water is pouring off the roof. There is a kind of rosy glow in the atmosphere and I feel like stepping out into it but am afraid the Hermalinda is somewhere watching me and that would not be too dignified.

Suddenly, feeling chilled, I go back and crawl into bed with Vincent. I draw the sheet over us and absorb his animal heat. It feels very good and I am soon asleep.

We sleep the sleep of the exhausted and do not waken until late the next morning.

I hear the chatter of small children outside the door. They are playing with the toys that Vincent has brought them. Little cars, a wind up airplane, a rubber ball and some blocks. They call him "Tio Vinco."

Roland opens the door and looks in on us. "Hey you two, you going to sleep all day or what?" He boldly pulls back the netting. Vincent murmurs something about another half hour of sleep but Roland will have none of it.

"Get dressed and let's have some breakfast…or lunch."

"Lunch?" mumbles Vincent.

""Yeah, it's almost noon. You need some coffee with a little tequila to get going again."

Good lord, I think to myself, *I will certainly become an alcoholic if this keeps up.*

Heremalinda is busy in the kitchen, she is managing to smile and seems nicer than she was the night before. "Café?" she asks as we sit down at the wooden table, covered with a flower patterned oil cloth. A flyspecked light bulb hangs from the ceiling by a frayed cord over the table. In the corner is a small stove with a counter next to it where she works. There is no water in the kitchen, one must go out to the patio with a bucket to collect water from a spigot over a rustic, concrete sink. That is where she washes the dishes.

The little girl hides shyly behind Hermalinda's skirt, following her mother around the kitchen and peeking out at us from time to time.

"You, you," Hermalinda struggles with the pronunciation and it comes out sounding like "chew". "You stay in Puerto de las Peñas y Vincent goes back to Saint Francis city?" she asks me as she sets a pitcher of hot water on the table in front of us and pushes the sugar and a jar of Nescafe within our reach. Vincent begins stirring the powdery coffee into a large clay mug filled with the steaming water.

"Yes, I mean si…I am an artist and I plan to spend a month or two here, painting. Then I will go back to San Francisco, I think." I fix myself a mug of coffee.

"Oh," Hermalinda acknowledges, unimpressed. Her weight makes her appear to be older than she is. She may be pregnant. She is younger than I am. She has three children and I have what; my youth, my figure, a modicum of talent that has not truly been tested and I am becoming more and more undomesticated. Then there is Vincent, I can have him if I decide I want him and that's about it.

Vincent says no to a shot of tequila in the coffee. "Say Rolando," he says, did you come up with an apartment for Joanna? Someplace cheap where she can stay for the time being?"

"Yeah, as a matter of fact, Smiley Jones made a deal with the owner of the hotel Marsol, right down the beach from the La Ramada. It's not too luxurious but adequate. It has a kitchen, a bathroom, bedroom and a little terrace that looks out onto the street and the beach of Los Muertos."

Vincent laughs, "Honey, you are going to be staying on the beach of the dead, now what do you think about that?"

"I don't know what to think really, why do they call it that?"

Roland pours half a mug of tequila into his coffee and looks at me with a smile as he relates the story of Los Muertos. "It seems around a hundred years ago, a ship wrecked in the Bay and the bodies of the sailors washed up on the shore there. The natives were terrified at the sight and the beach became know as the beach of the dead, Los Muertos. Now the tourist department wants to change the name to Playa del Sol, Beach of the Sun, but everyone still calls it Los Muertos."

"That Bay can be dangerous, looks calm, but…" Vincent looks at me fondly, his expression, protective.

I sip the hot coffee. Hermalinda returns with a basket of sweet rolls with a sticky frosting. She sits down with us and begins spreading butter on one of the sweet rolls which are warm. She finishes one and starts eating another one.

"Hey" says Roland, "you're gonna get fatter on those rolls."

"No importa," she answers him with a toss of her head, "you are going to get borracho, drunk, on that tequila".

"How dýa like that Vincent, she doesn't care if she gets fat, doesn't give a damn."

I, who do give a damn, refrain from the rolls, thinking of tacos on the beach. Maybe some eggs ranch style.

After coffee, I put on my bikini, my beach robe, new sandals and grab a beach towel. I look forward to seeing my new apartment by the beach. Vincent and I walk hand in hand along with Roland, the short distance to the beach. There are great gaps in the sidewalk so we end up walking on the cobblestone street. The houses are walled in with great bouganvillia flowers overflowing from their sheltered gardens inside, trailing down onto the ground around our feet. Tall palm trees sway in the morning breeze, the air is crystal clear, warm and humid from the rain.

"We'll have breakfast at the "Ramada" says Roland, his face beginning to flush from the liquor.

"Pretty here, isn't it?" remarks Vincent as we sit down at the rustic tables. The walk has made me hungry.

"Really beautiful Vincent, thank you so much for bringing me here," I respond sincerely.

The waves lapping at the shore just meters away are small and delicate, nothing like the roaring surf of Northern California. They make a soft, rhythmic sighing sound, like background music in an expensive bar in San Francisco. Fishermen are mending their nets or bringing in the catch for the day, or setting forth in their hand made canoes, called pangas. There is so much sea life that there is no time when not to go fishing. No one is swimming, there are hardly any tourists about. It is getting warmer and we begin to perspire. The jungle begins just down the beach and the mountains reaching up from the sea shore are covered with lush, tropical vegetation. There is no hint of the corrosive development that would someday compromise the beauty of this spot of earth.

Smiley Jones is seated at a table across from us. Vincent motions for him to come over and sit with us. He slides into an equipale and sets his beer down in front of him.

"Buenos dias to you lovely people," he says, smiling.

We both answer, laughing, in broken Spanish. I will have to study this language in order to communicate in this nice place, I think to myself.

"You look really pretty miss, I forget your name, I'm sorry." Smiley is so humble and self effacing, one would forgive him anything.

"Joanna, Joanna Botticelli, Botticelli, like the Italian artist, remember?"

"Never heard of the guy, but that don't mean nothin, I never made it out of high school. I have a place for you, just half a block up the beach. But shucks Vincent, you ain't gonna let this pretty lady down her by herself now are ya?" Still smiling he sips his beer.

Vincent hands me the menu to study. "I gotta get back to the office, I've been gone now three days. I told my partner Walters I'd be gone five days, two to fly back. Hell, I should leave here tomorrow. I have to leave you and Roland in charge here."

He is leaving me *alone*. I am torn between missing him and the thrill of unknown freedom. Not any kind of freedom but *exotic* freedom. The thought of living in an apartment on the beach is almost unbearably exciting.

I stand up. "Order me some Mexican style eggs, I want to see what the water is like." I sense their eyes on my body as I remove my beach robe exposing me and my new bikini. I turn swiftly and run down to the sea. I dive into those gentle waves, they caress me. The water is as warm as a bath. The salt flavors my mouth and I swim. The water is clear, tiny fish dash about my feet. I float on my back and study the sky, deep, deep blue. There are pelicans flying overhead and skimming over the waves, fishermen in boats, putter by. Toward the south there are three enormous rock formations poking up from the sea. I will learn later they are called, "Los Arcos", the arches. They are cave-like and boats can go through them. Toward the East, the mountains soar, marching higher and higher, each receding range a paler shade of blue. I think about painting the mountains, then wonder what lies behind them. Where do they go? I feel relaxed, free from anxiety, as though I am in the process of discovering a secret that I need for the peace of my soul. It is heavenly. I dive under the waves like a fish or a dolphin, a part of the sea for a moment. The water is like a drug; relaxing, calming. Time floats. I receive a premonition of destiny, of passing a stage in my life. I absorb the healing power of the ocean's waters in order to prepare myself to face whatever is looming on my personal horizon.

Vincent is on the beach, motioning me to come in for breakfast.

He hands me a towel. We rejoin Smiley and Roland at the table. I am dripping water, I push my salt laden hair away from my face. I catch Vincent looking at me with what; admiration, love, lust? He catches me looking at him and abruptly erects his emotional shield when he feels vulnerable. He too is on unfamiliar ground.

The table is laden with sauces of various degree of spiciness, plates of eggs over tortillas, smothered in bright red sauce, heaps of refried beans, beer bottles glistening in the heat, avocados sliced, salted and drenched in lemon, baskets of steaming hot, handmade corn tortillas.

Unceremoniously, I gobble it all up, it is all *so good*.

"Let's go see your new home," declares Vincent when we finish eating. I pull my beach robe around me, slip my sandy feet into sandals, gather up my bag, and the four of us begin the walk up the beach.

We pass a grove of coconut palms, then a small hotel called the Tropicana. Soon we are in front of the Hotel Marsol, a rather dilapidated second class place badly in need of repair. Entering the dingy reception hall, Smiley asks for the key to the apartment. We file back outside and stand before a termite ridden, wooden door that fronts on the sidewalk. There is a hole in the sidewalk that Smiley must straddle in order to place the key in the key hole. He struggles with the key, a large elongated cast iron object which finally gives in to him. The door swings open to a flight of stairs. We quietly mount the steps and are in the bedroom. The apartment is basic. Basically ugly. There are twin beds with some faded ruffled bedspreads and mosquito netting hanging over them, an old wooden wardrobe, walls that are peeling pink paint. There is a terrace which is a saving grace to be sure. The bathroom is tiny, behind the stairs. The shower outlet is a large, rusty thing with clogged holes. There is an interesting viridian green mold growing between the tiles. I will soon see that there is no hot water for bathing. The toilet is old and cracked and lacks a toilet seat. The closet is a concrete wing next to the bathroom and features a faded cotton sheet strung onto a pitted old water pipe that serves as a clothing rack. The ceiling is stained from water probably, numerous insects have left their marks around the room, spider webs adorn the corners of the ceiling. Then I see the French doors, there are two sets and each opens out onto a balcony over looking the Ocean. Like something out of Romeo and Juliet. There are faded curtains gracing the French doors, the panes of glass badly need washing, the salt air gives no mercy but how amazingly lovely framing a view of paradise. Certainly not a candidate for *Architectural Digest* but I can imagine going to sleep to the sound of the waves washing the sandy shore.

Smiley laughs apologetically, his glasses bob up and down over his watery blue eyes. "Needs some work," he says, "The owner says he is going to fix the water heater, get a new toilet seat and pàint the place right away."

"Yeah, right," says Roland, with a smirk on his face, "remember this is Mexico."

"The kitchen is right through here," continues Smiley leading us out through another door onto a second floor balcony that looks over a small, untended garden below on the first floor. We follow the balcony around to a large room that serves as a kitchen. There is a concrete sink that doubles for washing clothes with a spigot for water similar to what Hermalinda has. The floor is dark red tile which has seen better days, a small refrigerator and a two burner stove connected to a gas cylinder complete a functioning kitchen. One fly specked light bulb hangs from the ceiling over a wooden table and some chairs. The other half of the room is empty except for some boxes. A studio I think, a studio in the kitchen, art and home economics combined. Woman's art, you do it wherever and however.

Vincent grimaces, "This ain't exactly Telegraph Hill. How much are they going to rob us for the month?"

"The owner wants a lot of money for this dump," says Smiley, smiling, "he wants $70 dollars a month, too much, but they ain't too many apartments available and it is on the beach ya know."

"It's okay Smiley, I can handle it, artists are adaptable, you have to be to survive." I say as I see Vincent take out his wallet and hand Smiley $70, dollars for my first month's rent. I have some money but not a whole lot. I feel gratitude toward my lover.

"Right on the beach," continues Smiley, stuffing the money into his pants pocket, "you hardly spend time here you know, you could have breakfast here and lunch at the La Ramada."

"It's kind of dim for painting," I comment, thinking of installing a light fixture of the same style of those so redundant here. So I will be able to see to work.

Roland covers his mouth and chuckles, "you won't be doing much painting here dear girl, too much social life, lots of artists come here to paint and end up…"

"Drinking their time away on the beach, right Roland?" says Vincent. "But my girl here is serious, had a show at a big important gallery in San Francisco…she's here to work!"

"Oh," says Smiley in a tone of polite disbelief, his bloodshot, watery blue eyes narrowing in an effort to size me up.

I look up at the high ceiling, "maybe we could string an electrical wire up there and put in another light, there are no windows in this room, only the door."

Why is it I never have everything I need at the same time to work I think. In San Francisco I had light but very little space, here I have space and hardly any light. Oh well, as my dear mother used to say, where there is a will there is a way.

"Sure honey, but let's try to make it better," says Vincent as we walk out. "We'll go to town this afternoon and get some electrical wire and a socket to hook up a light for you, maybe a can of paint for that kitchen, It's kind of depressing."

"Well, I'll be on my way, I hope you enjoy the place and if I can help in any way, you can find me everyday at the La Ramada," says Smiley as he hands me the heavy key.

We return to Roland's house and borrow the pick up to transfer everything to my new apartment on the beach.

We carry the boxes and suitcases up the narrow stairs. I have brought a few sheets and towels. Vincent sets up my easel in the kitchen while I sort out my paints, brushes and canvases. The paints make me feel at home with their familiar technical names; alizarin crimson, zinc white and my favorite yellow ochre to name a few of my friends. I have a small notebook where I note the supplies I will need. Turpentine, how do you say that in Spanish I wonder. I am encountering my first quandary in this very foreign place. To solve the problem, Vincent produces a Spanish/English dictionary from his suitcase. "Agua raz," he pronounces and I kiss him thankfully on the cheek, noting it down.

"I hope you are going to leave me that dictionary Vincent."

"Of course, I brought it for you, you just have to study it, and here in the back are useful phrases…"

I am going to miss him I think.

We take cold showers in the trickling water with a tiny left over piece of soap. He pushes the beds together and we lie down in a close embrace. The sex is as much to calm me as to satisfy our ongoing desire for each other. We sleep for a while. I feel warm and secure in his arms afterward and silently question my desire for freedom and adventure.

We shower again but the water runs out half way through the process.

He laughs as he dresses, "Not like the states, where everything works. You hungry honey, you have to eat more, you are too thin."

"I guess so, I like being skinny, it seems like we just ate breakfast."

"Yeah, well, there is a saying, the closer to the bone, the sweeter the flesh, or something like that. Say, I'm going to buy you one of those lacy Mexican dresses with the flowers, so you look like a Madonna, the ones they have in the churches, and only I will know what a sexy number you are in bed..what do you think?"

I am putting lipstick on in the cracked mirror of the bathroom and don't really know what to think. I decide to laugh at his Madonna/whore fantasy and go on to look for something appropriate to wear. My clothes don't suit the climate here and a new dress would be just fine. I take a colorful flowered sheath I had made ages ago and slip that over my bra and panties. I pull on my sandals and then comb my hair which is rather long now. Maybe I will have to cut it short I think.

"Vincent, this place is great for all the problems, Hermalinda isn't too friendly is she?" I ask as I watch him button up a white men's shirt with lace trim, he looks wonderful in it.

"Mexican women are jealous, especially of blond, blue eyed gringas. I know you aren't blond but to them you are. Anything lighter than black hair is considered blond."

"I like your lace shirt."

"I don't look like a fag now do I?"

"You could never look like a fag Vincent, no matter what you wore. Were you saying that American women aren't jealous?" I am thinking of his wife and her fits of illness and rage at Vincent's philandering.

"Yeah, I guess they are too. What about you, are you the jealous type?"

"No, not so much…I always figure if a man wants another woman, that is his choice and not much that I can do about it. Just accept it."

"Thom says that homely women hate men, do you think that is true?" he says as he lights two cigarettes for us.

"I have no idea, but with all the props, diets, fashion, make-up, no one has to be ugly these days. And say, what about men…do homely men hate women as well?" I open the French door to the terrace to let in the sea breeze and take away some of the cigarette smoke.

"Could be Joanna, a guy that gets rejected by women could get kind of mean about it."

He is sitting on one of the twin beds, without sheets, patiently waiting for me to finish primping. The ashes from his cigarette are falling on the floor.

"Mexican women, not all of them but many of them tend to get fat after they get married," he continues, "they figure they have their man sewed up and they don't have to worry anymore. The church forbids divorce so that helps."

I stuff my hairbrush into my purse and tug on his arm. He stands up and we embrace, I can feel his erection against my dress. We laugh at his boundless virility.

"Let's go shopping!" I announce and we are off.

After a few beers and snacks at the La Ramada we borrow Roland's pick-up and go to town to further outfit my new home.

The commercial section of Puerto de las Peñas is simple. Small stores fronting on the sidewalk with apartments above for living quarters. The hardware store, or 'ferreteria' as it is called in Spanish is a rustic place, small, dim and dusty. It offers rough looking items like machetes, shovels, sickles and saws, harnesses for horses and mules, heavy road maintenance things like pick axes, sledge hammers, plows and rakes meant to be used with oxen for planting and much more.

The proprietor is a middle aged, dark skinned man with a mustache and a weathered face. We seem to amuse him.

"Que desean Ustedes?" he asks.

" Vincent, what did he say?" I ask anxiously.

"I think he is asking us what we want to buy here," replies Vincent thumbing through his dictionary.

"Foco," he says, pointing to the ubiquitous light bulb hanging from a wire hooked into the wooden beams that support the high ceiling.

"Uh huh," says the man and disappears into the back of the store. He emerges with a 20 watt light bulb.

"Ah, si, but more watts and electric cord!" Vincent is almost shouting as though the sheer volume of his voice and repetition of the words would force the man to understand English.

I take the dictionary and rapidly begin searching; cord, alambre, electricidad…that seems understandable. I point the words out to the owner. He breaks into a broad smile and disappears into the labyrinth of shelves. He returns with a piece of electrical cord, a 40 watt light bulb. We are all perspiring from this ordeal which has only just begun.

"More cord, more!" shouts Vincent.

"Mas alambre?" shouts the man in reply.

"Si," I interject, "*mas* mean more I think," I whisper to Vincent. An audience has gathered around us, several children on their way home from school. Several young men lean against the entrance to the hardware store enjoying the unexpected bit of entertainment. A young woman resembling the store owner has joined him in this sale of electrical goods and all of its cultural ramifications.

"Cuanto?" shouts the man, not in an angry way, more as though he were mimicking Vincent, he is still smiling.

"That means how much," I say.

"I know, I know, but we didn't measure how much we need to go from the existing light fixture to the new one you want to install."

"I don't know, several yards I think, maybe 4 yards."

"Here they measure in meters, not yards, let's say five meters, it's better to have more than less. Then we have to say socket."

"I need a stronger light bulb, like 75 or a 100 watts, tell him that."

Vincent ends up going into the back shelves with the young woman who is apparently the daughter of the shop owner. I wait patiently, considering the difficulty of a simple transaction, regretting that I didn't study Spanish harder in school.

I smile at the children, pretty youngsters with classic Mexican faces, large brown eyes, smooth dark skin and black hair. They turn away from me, embarrassed for a moment then continue to stare. I look back at them quickly and they begin to giggle. I hear the word 'gringa', I suppose I must get used to that name.

Vincent comes back with the young woman who is carrying the merchandise.

"Vincent, I need turpentine."

"Look that up in the dictionary," he orders.

"Here, it says 'aguarras', I excitedly point it out to the shopkeeper and his daughter, eager to terminate this ordeal.

"Ahh, aguaras…si…si, donde esta su bote?"

"He is asking us where is our bote," explains Vincent, "look it up, it must be under 'b' or 'v'. He takes out his handkerchief and wipes his forehead and behind his neck while I frantically flip the pages.

"Here it says 'bote', -jump, thrust, rebound. Now that doesn't make sense." I sigh heavily, frustrated that I cannot make my order understood by this kindly shopowner who obviously wants to sell us our lighting needs.

A tall, handsome man steps forward, smiling profusely in a very friendly manner. "May I be of some servicio to ju nize peoples?" He asks in heavily accented English. His black hair is swept back and he sports a medium size mustache. He has twinkling light colored eyes that look perpetually amused. He wears a beige colored khaki shirt, open at the throat, light blue cotton trousers and Mexican huarache sandals. He has an aura of charm and sophistication that immediately suffuses the humble hardware store. He is very attractive.

I do not know what to say, he seems to be addressing me, his eyes bore into me, insolently.

Vincent leaps to the opportunity. "Oh, great, some one who speaks English. Could you please tell this man we need turpentine, maybe a quart or more. Aguaraz I think it's called. It's for her painting," he nods in my direction.

Still smiling, the tall Mexican man speaks in rapid Spanish to the shopkeeper who answers equally fast and at length. The poor man must be as frustrated as we are.

"He has the aguaraz, he sells eet from a tambo, or drum I think ju say. You need some kind of bote, bottle…they say 'bote' here, to put eet in." I show him my dictionary open to the word 'bote'.

"Thees don halp you Meez, thees dictionario ees for España. Here een Mexico, we speak differently."

Vincent and I confer. We have nothing to put the turpentine in.

The Mexican man sees our plight and explains to the shopkeeper who once again disappears into the back of store, emerging with a brandy bottle filled with I what I hope is turpentine. This all seems so complicated.

The Mexican man looks happy, he introduces himself. "I am Ingeniero, Antonio del Valle, a sus ordenes." He extends his hand to Vincent.

Vincent responds, introducing himself as "Licenciado Vincent Cooper from San Francisco, very happy to meet you.."

"And this lovely lady who has the problems shopping without knowing Spanish is Joanna Botticelli, an artist."

Antonio takes my hand and gently shakes it, almost bringing it to his lips to kiss. I am astounded. I manage, "Pleased to meet you."

"Gracias, muchas gracias," effuses Vincent with sincere gratitude as the shopkeeper tallies our bill and hands it to him.

"No hay de que," responds Antonio. "If ju need any halp here you can find me at zee Las Olas on zee beach. I am the Secretario de Tourism here. I be very happy to serve ju."

He hands Vincent his card, we all shake hands again and he is gone.

He slips the card into his shirt pocket.

"Wasn't that nice of him," I murmur as we gather the light bulb, electrical wire, the tape, the socket and turpentine together in an old sack the storekeeper has loaned to us.

"Very nice," answers Vincent, "I wonder if he is the guy who…oh never mind, I'll tell you later. This system here is really different, when you go shopping you have to bring all your own bags, jars, cans, bottles..someday they will catch up to us in the states and have plastic bags jars and bottles for all that available, you know, they'll have *progress.*"

We go out into the hot sultry afternoon, the ocean glistens only a block away, beckoning me to its warm, invigorating waters.

"Vincent, let's go to the market, I want food in that rusty old refrigerator."

We go to the market on the river, next to the bridge. I am feeling domestic, not even aware that I have forgotten my apartment in San Francisco, Thom and my life there and have completely centered myself, my life here in this wild, beautiful, difficult place.

The stalls are filled with tropical fruits and even some not so tropical fruits like orange, grapefruit and lemons. There are glistening avocados, voluptuous papayas and mangos, tomatoes and bananas…onions and dirt encrusted potatoes that turn out to be as sweet as sugar when cooked.

There are colorful hemp bags in varied sizes hanging on the sides of the stalls. Vincent takes a large size one in bright colors of red, blue and yellow.   We take our purchases to the scale which works with a series of weights loaded on the other end of the fruit. Then it is all dropped carefully together into our hemp bag.

"Eggs, look it up," I whisper to Vincent, not knowing why I am whispering. He flips through the pages, leaning the dictionary on a stack of oranges.

"Huevos," he says.

"Cuantos?" says the proprietor.

I hold up six fingers, already beginning to understand what he is saying.

He puts the eggs into a paper bag and into the large hemp bag.. I worry about them.

"Okay honey, what else to keep body and soul together?"

"Some bread, some butter and cheese should keep me, I can buy fish from the fishermen on the beach, really fresh."

We buy a chunk of butter from a larger chunk The woman has to lend us a jar to put it in and we are made to promise to return the jar to her. The plastic age has not arrived yet.

We buy rolls and tortillas, more than we can ever consume.

We buy beer in loose bottles, warm.

Vincent looks at me with a half smile, "You are going to have fun here, I rather envy you, but I will come back here as soon as I can to take care of you…I will miss you."

Back in the apartment I begin by scrubbing the dirt, grime and mold from the refrigerator. Vincent plugs it in and thankfully, the motor kicks in. We immediately put the beer in to chill and I continue to wash the fruit under the spigot while Vincent begins measuring for the new light fixture.

Two of the eggs have broken and made a bit of a mess on the new hemp bag but no matter. I transfer the butter to a bowl I find on the shelf and wash the jar to return to the kind woman who sold me the butter.

Vincent installs the light fixture while I hand him the tools to do the job. I place my easel close to the wooden table that holds my paints and brushes. The turpentine rests in the brandy jar and I think maybe I should label it so no one mistakes it for booze.

"Voila!" exclaims Vincent as he switches on the light. The bulb sways slightly in the afternoon breeze, it will work fine.

With the groceries all tended to and my light bulb installed, we open two beers, return to the bedroom and walk out onto the terrace to watch the activity on the beach. There is a fragile looking wooden dock stretching out into the surf and up and down the beach fishermen are tending to their nets and their boats. Children and a few adults splash around in the gentle surf.

"Don't you feel just great here," says Vincent handing me a lit cigarette. I mean free, we can do anything we want to, we are in love and we have each other. Finish that beer and let's make love, I want to fill myself with you before I have to leave.."

Afterward, we take Roland's truck back to him and walk to town. Vincent wants me to meet the "local gentry"at the Oceano hotel bar. He wants them to "look after me" when he leaves.

I wonder at this necessity everyone has for seeing that I am looked after, as though there lurks some great invisible danger of which I am unaware. What exactly this danger is teases my curiousity. I subliminally anticipate shaking off my bodyguards some time in the future to know for myself what it is that I must be afraid of.

The clouds are beginning to form for the afternoon rain by the time we get to the Oceano. A sultry breeze off the ocean wafts through the open windows that surround the bar room. A few men are seated at the bar and a group of tourists occupy several tables.

After Vincent orders our Margaritas he sits back relaxing and casually slips the business card of the man we had met earlier in the hardware store from his shirt. "Antonio del Valle" he reads aloud, "Ingeniero Civil…yes, I think he's the fellow, I will ask Roland when I see him."

"What fellow?" I ask.

"Well, I suppose you should know about the political pitfalls here. He's the fellow that Roland is suing for his part of the Las Olas restaurant that is just across from the La Ramada. Roland and Smiley Jones were partners with him in the creation of the original restaurant and bar. Then, according to Roland, this Del Valle fellow, or maybe it was his cousin I forget his name, robbed Smiley and Roland of their share, something about not being able to own land next to the beach if you are gringos. This was back in the 50's. I understand he paid them something but not nearly what their shares were worth so Roland and Smiley made their own restaurant, the La Ramada right across the street from the other one. There were death threats involved between them so now they are mortal enemies."

"Gee," is all I can think of to say at this turn of events, life is becoming more complex here than I had anticipated. "We should walk along the beach tomorrow and really take notice of the two restaurants."

Vincent is taking notice of the Margaritas being set down before us along with the ubiquitous clay dish of peanuts. He raises his glass to me "Here's to your health honey and may you make lots of great paintings so you can support me someday!" I laugh at how preposterous that seems and we down our drinks.

Roland strolls into the bar, grinning, greeting some of the men there then sits down with us and orders a 7-up and Tequila.

"So, what have you two lovely people been up to today, I heard by the grapevine that you met the cousin of my number one enemy in town, Antonio del Valle, is that right?"

"Godammit Roland, how does news travel around this place without telephones?" Vincent takes out his pack of Camels unfiltered and lights one for him and one for me.

"We call it the telephone of the talking mouths, gossip in other words. The bad guy, the cousin of del Valle is called Sergio Montes Cruz, he's the one who screwed Smiley and me on the property. I guess Antonio is alright, he's not such a greedy bastard like Sergio."

The waiter brings our drinks. Vincent leans forward, concerned about the conflict. "This Antonio fellow was really helpful, a gentleman it seems, hard to imagine him as a crook. But tell me, does this news get around so fast, it's incredible."

"Word of mouth, It's the way everyone knows the latest news. Like here in the Oceano for instance. You can do all kinds of business, rent a house, buy property, find a woman, locate a relative right here in the hotel, it is the heart of Puerto de las Peñas." Roland pops a peanut into his mouth and follows it with his drink.

Suddenly, lightening starkly illuminates the room closely followed by a nerve shattering bolt of thunder that has people cowering in their equipales. It has turned dark and menacing outside as the late afternoon storm prepares its onslaught.

Roland continues, thoroughly accustomed to the drama of the monsoon. "Whaddya think of Hermalinda?" he asks me while reaching for another peanut.

"Great girl," Vincent answers for me.

"Yes, she seems very nice," I say, "I just wish I could speak Spanish and talk to her more." I say while thinking that she wasn't all that charming, these are the kind of little hypocrisies we live with in order to smooth out our lives.

"Her parents hate me," continues Roland. "they talk really bad about me, but I just ignore them." He exhales luxuriously and drinks down his straight tequila, indicating he wants another to a passing waiter. His face has reddened more and his eyes appear slightly watery. I wonder what his wifes's parents say about him. Probably that he is a drunk I think and then try not to keep thinking those things.

Another lightning bolt strike nearby, out on the water and then the rain descends to act out its daily drama. The waiters run to close down the shutters, the lights dim. The sound of the surf pounding only a few meters away and the heavy rain create a cacophony of nature's symphony taking our total attention. The lights go out completely and we sit in the dimness, friends and strangers sharing an experience beyond anyones control.

Roland is smiling happily, enjoying the respite from normalcy. "This happens all the time,ª he explains, "the power will come back on tomorrow sometime, in the meantime we shall drink by candlelight, isn't this romantic?"

The waiters are busily placing candles inside of brandy snifters and distributing them among the tables. The candle light takes 15 years off of Vincent's face and I can't help but be amused by it all. He places his hand on my thigh and I place my hand over his to keep him from fondling me in this public place. He loves to do that. Breaking the rules.

At the bar they are lighting small kerosene lanterns. Just like when I was child on the farm I think. How charming this all is. More drinks arrive and we proceed with a certain controlled inebriation.

"Hey, look, its already nine o'clock," exclaims Vincent sitting up erectly in mock surprise at how fast the time has flown by. He continues to rub my thigh affectionately. "Hungry?"

"Yeah," I answer a bit slurrily.

Vincent raises his glass and drains the last drops of his margarita.

"*Las gotas de felicidad,*" says Roland, the drops of happiness, as Vincent signals for the bill. He pays and leaves a few coins on the table for the waiter.

The rain has stopped. We cross the street to the Malecon to walk above the waves. The air is clear and sweet, everything is bathed in a rosy glow from the sunset. It is beautiful.

The walkway of the Malecon is crowded with people, children, dogs and many vendors with cylinders of gas heating comales of different foods. We stop in front of an old Indian woman selling fresh corn steaming in a huge kettle. She smiles a semi-toothless grin and offers us a large corn cob steaming on a stick as though she reads my thoughts.

" I want one," I say.

"You could get sick ya know," cautions Roland.

"I don't care, I want to live recklessly for once, I haven't had corn on the cob in ages."

"Todo?" the woman asks, referring to the abundant condiments waiting to compliment the fresh corn. I imagine it comes from her own garden.

"Sí," I reply, pleased that I understand her.

First she squeezes lemon all over the corn, twisting and turning the gleaming yellow grains, followed by salt and chile pepper, then slathers sour cream and mayonnaise on it and finally rolls the whole concoction over and over in grated cheese. It no longer looks looks like corn on the cob but some kind of rare, cream colored, elongated, fuzzy edible object. With a pleased smile, she thrusts her creation toward me.

I accept it and Vincent pays. I crunch my teeth down through the layers of cheese, cream and mayonnaise to the sweet grains of corn. It is delicious.

"Want a bite?" I ask him as we continue walking, the surf tumbling the rocks below us for our pleasure. The waves quite high, no longer a gentle surf.

Vincent stares at the corn. I can almost hear him thinking about his dentures and if they are up to the job. He takes the stick of corn from me, then very deliberately and slowly bites down on it, I watch the teeth sink into the mass of cheese, cream and mayonnaise until they reach the grains lying beneath and then close over the corn. He does it and hands it back to me, smiling. "Good," he says, munching away. I am pleased for him and take a napkin to his mouth, whisking away fragments of cheese and cream.

Roland lays his arm across my shoulders, "Say," he says, "as soon as you finish that thing let's hit Las Margaritas, it's the only night spot in town. We can have a real dinner there. Rita, the owner, used to be a whore in Watsonville, in California. Oh, pardon me, a *lady of the night,* shall we say. A great lady, you will love her." He is weaving his way along the street, partially supported by his arm on my shoulders.

Within another block we can hear the music pouring from Las Margaritas. It is in a typical, old building now converted to a more commercial enterprise. Made of adobe bricks, there is the grand entrance with wrought iron gates, opening onto the center patio with rooms adjoining a corridor that surrounds the patio. Pots of palms and tropical flowering plants are everywhere. Lovely Doric columns support the cross beams that support the tile roof. A few puddles remain here and there from the late afternoon rain storm. The place is full of people, singing, dancing and drinking, even though it is a weekday.

A waiter with a flashlight guides us to a table in the back. As we walk through the crowd people stare at us. I must accustom myself to this, I think to myself as I straighten up, erect, trying not to look drunk.

The table is covered with a white cloth and adorned with a small vase of daisies in the center alongside a small lit, candle. The people at the next table lean forward and whisper to each other. The candle light reflecting off their faces make them look quite beautiful. I feel that one day I shall know these people, at least some of them.

Roland gestures toward the flowers. "Margaritas", he says, "that's what they call daisies in Mexico."

"And those great drinks!" adds Vincent just as a buxom woman with white blond hair flings herself around Roland's back and kisses him soundly on the neck.

"Rita, you old floozy you..you can do better than that!" exclaims Roland, standing up and embracing the woman, kissing her hard on the mouth. "You look great..here, I brought you some friends from *El Norte.*"

Rita stands back and with a slightly crooked smile appraises us. She looks long and hard at Vincent, barely glancing in my direction.

"Saay, don't I know you from somewhere, you sure look familiar," she says, "ya sure are a handsome s.o.b."

If it were any lighter in the restaurant we would see Vincent blushing as he rises to receive his kiss. "Licenciado Vincent Franklyn Cooper, at your service, Mam." he says as she reluctantly releases him. Except for the chaste look of her hand-embroidered Mexican peasant dress, she looks like a classic prostitute. Heavily made-up with false eyelashes, her bleached and lacquered hair piled high on her head and then falling down her back almost to her waist, her breasts large, and well exposed. She is incongruous, authentic and fascinating.

"And this is Joanna, she's from Frisco and is going to spend some time with us. She's an artist and plans to paint from life here," explains Roland, trying to make her like me. However, she looks at me with a cynical smile as she says, "How dee do Joanna, pleased ta meetcha." She does not like me. All I can muster is a nod in response.

That done, she turns her attention back to the men. "Let me buy you all a drink on the house, to welcome your visitors...I hope you will continue to frequent my establishment," she gushes with a wink at Vincent.

She is gone. Vincent and Roland sit down, smiling broadly.

"Quite a broad," states Roland, "she's got herself a Mexican lover, probably half her age who tends the bar here."

"Hmm," murmurs Vincent, contemplating the reverse gender age gap of this flambouyant woman ro his own situation.

The drinks arrive, they are of course Margaritas decorated with little sticks, tiny paper daisies on the tips. They are too cute. We drink to our health and happiness.

"Goddamn, if they ever put a road into this town, it will boom," says Vincent prophetically.

"Right now, tourism hardly counts, this place is more a center for agricultural trade in the area, fishing is big here, the ocean is so full of fish, we could probably feed fish to the whole world," explains Roland. "There are a few Americans and Canadians living here during the winter, they have created a colony called 'Gringo Gulch' up the river. They have built some really nice homes."

How nice Las Peñas is like this, a real place not a Mexican Disneyland, I think to myself. Not *developed*. Men take beautiful places like this and for money make them ugly, dangerous and ultimately redundant. *I guess I want money too, but on my terms,* I think my boozy thoughts.

Vincent and I dance to the Mariachi music, mingling with an International society of people that I find intriguing. We drink more until Roland decides it is time to go. Vincent pays and while we wait for change from the waiter I notice a table on the far side of the patio of Mexican men, well dressed and attractive. I see that the man who helped us earlier in the hardware store is there, talking in a very animated way, he looks to be important. There are a few quite beautiful women with them.

Roland catches me staring at them. "Ya see those guys, bad news all of them…gang of Mexicans up to no good. You better stay away from them, see the fellow at the head of the table? He's the one who stole our restaurant away from Smiley and me. Sergio Montes Cruz is the guy and the fellow next to him is his cousin who runs the tourist bureau, Antonio del Valle." I look away from them, I feel they know we are talking about them.

As we walk out of the restaurant I sense that now the Mexican men are watching us and *talking about us*. Back on the street, Roland hales a cab. We pile in as he directs the driver to 'Romanoff's on the Rocks'.

"Where the hell are you taking us now?" quips Vincent as he grips my hand. He leans over and kisses me wetly on the back of my neck.

"Just wait, you will love it, especially if you're hungry. It's like nothing else you have ever seen, trust me," counsels Roland.

The cab stops at the bridge and we continue on foot, following Roland. We are on a foot path that goes under the bridge and there camped alongside the rushing river on the rocks is the most outrageous outdoor restaurant I have ever seen. There are wooden tables and comales over simple wood fires, and tables with pitchers of fruit drinks and all of it tended to by robust women and their children. Some are making rich, yellow corn tortillas by hand and others are stirring great pots of soup suspended over the wood fires, There are beans, rice, tacos of all kinds, red sauces, green sauces and brown sauces of varying degrees of hot spicy. Chicken, pork, beef, brains, and kidneys, many kinds of fish to concoct with. Stacks of sliced cucumber, onions, chilies, tomatoes, avocado and lemons to name just a few of the choices. The women's faces are shiny by the light of the fires, they laugh and sing as they combine the foods together in their great creative endeavor. Feeding the public and earning money for their households. The area is full of people eating and drinking. The air is filled with the scents of food cooking, wood smoke and salt spray off the nearby Pacific Ocean. The rushing of the river over the rocks adds to the cacophony of the women's voices with the pleasant background of the mariachis playing under the bridge. It is all surreal.

"Pull up a seat," instructs Roland. We dutifully slide onto the rough, wooden benches, leaning forward in wonder.

A laughing Indian woman comes forth, she sizes us up. "*Que quieren Ustedes?*" What do we want? At that moment, we want food, we are very, very hungry.

"*Pozole para todos*," orders Roland, "*tacos de carne y pescado, guacamole y raicilla con agua fresca.*"

"Pozole is made with hominy corn, chicken and pork with various seasoning, like garlic and oregano," Roland explains to us.

The woman brings us the little clay shot glasses into which she pours the glistening alcoholic drink called 'raicilla', followed by bowls of hot pig skins along with a spicy red sauce and lemons. Roland passes us plates to fill with the oncoming meal. The woman brings large clay mugs for the sweetened rice water to soften the fire of the raicilla.

"Save room for the Pozole," he cautions as we emerse ourselves in eating the soft, rubbery pig skins doused in their sauces, lemon and supported by a toasted tortilla called a tostado. All washed down with the raicilla and rice water. The pig skins are called *brevas*, pure protein.

"Umm," sighs Vincent, chewing ostentaciously, "this is almost as good as sex," he laughs, "but not quite."

The woman returns, her strong muscular arm carrying a pot of the corn soup, Pozole, which she dishes out to us. A child arrives with a tray of the condiments needed to consume the soup; shredded cabbage, finely chopped onions seasoned with oregano, thinly sliced radishes, a hot sauce, a little clay pot of rock salt and lemons heaped onto a plate.

"With this ya don't have a hangover in the morning, I guarantee ya," says Roland between mouthfuls.

"What about *Montezuma's Revenge*?" asks Vincent.

"What's that?" I query, pouring more rice water into my mug.

"You know, the runs, trots, diarrhea in other words, they say it comes from unsanitary food."

"Oh." I keep eating. "Do you think this will make us sick Roland?"

"Well, maybe a little, but it's good for your immune system, if you get sick once, you won't get sick again, *comprende*?"

There are many people eating in this humble place, a class mixture of rich and poor, working men, fishermen, well dressed, important looking Mexicans, American couples who look as if they live here, laughing and talking among themselves. I feel a twinge of envy, *they must be rich to be able to live here I think. Maybe someday, I could live here and be happy like they are.*

We sleep late the next day. I awake to the sounds of children, laughing and screaming, dogs barking, adults calling out to one another on the beach below my apartment. Vincent is snoring next to me in the other bed.

I feel hot and sweaty, slightly nauseated as I make my way to the bathroom. There is a big cockroach on the floor. My instinct is to step on it but I am barefooted. The creature escapes into a crack in the floor. The initial onslaught of Montezuma's Revenge is rumbling in my lower intestines. I relieve myself of his curse on the toilet seat-less toilet which adds to my misery. I never did anything against Montezuma I think as I turn on the shower. In fact, I probably would have been on his side. The water is cold and refreshing but midway through my bathing, it turns to a trickle and then stops! I frantically rinse myself in the lessening drops of water.

I wrap myself up in a towel and awaken Vincent to see if he can do anything about the shower.

"No water you say?" he mumbles sleepily. He sits up and looks around him as though uncertain of just exactly where he is. He smiles at me. "See if the electricity came back on."

I press the light switch but nothing happens.

"No power, no water..can't run the pumps to bring the water up to the tank but don't worry, it will all come on eventually. Come here and let me make love to you, I need something good before I phone San Francisco and find out how my partner is screwing everything up at the office."

I slide into the bed next to him, not really feeling like sex at the moment, wishing the overhead fan could work to cool us off.

"Montezuma has taken revenge upon me for the sins of the Spaniards."

"Huh?"

"I have the trots and I feel like I am going to vomit."

"Don't even talk about it, drink water so you don't get dehydrated. I have a hangover I think and that's all I need…" He begins to fondle me. "Look what I have for you, that's how much I love you, not even a hangover can keep me from wanting you."

"Uh huh," I murmur as he slides into me. I think back as to when I inserted my diaphragm, yesterday I think, then as he continues I calculate how many days since my last period.

"Honey, what are you thinking about?" he murmurs through his sexual haze.

"How much I love you." I whisper into his ear.

I let him use me, for some unknown reason I feel distracted, perhaps the strangeness of everything has unsettled me. The failure of the water, the electricity, my queasy stomach or those unknown people last night.

Afterward, I make coffee and cut up some papaya to serve with cheese for a simple breakfast, the first in my new apartment. The food helps. The power returns and the refrigerator starts its noisy self. Somewhere in the distance I hear the rumble of the pump raising water to the tank on the top of the building.

After our cold water showers we dress, then walk to town to the public phone station located in the town pharmacy. It is starting to heat up for the day, the humidity is high and we are sweating profusely when we get to the pharmacy. I wait on a wooden bench as Vincent makes his phone call through a young woman operator.

I watch him through the filmy, rustic glass of the phone niche. His voice rises, then he shakes his head. Other people have lined up to use the phone. After ten minutes talking to his partner, Ralph Walters, he hangs up, drenched in perspiration still shaking his head.

"We're lying in a pool of blood," he exclaims morosely wiping his brow with a handkerchief. "Honey, I'm going to have to fly out of here at dawn tomorrow and try to make it back to San Francisco in one day. Ralph Walters cannot do pretrial negotiations worth a damn so I have to get my ass there and rattle a few swords. We are behind on the bond payments and the creditors are on our backs. It's a mess! Let's take a cab to the La Ramada on the beach and relax for a while, this is my last day with you sweetheart…I really don't want to leave you but my whole law practice of the last 25 years is on very shaky ground and we will need that in the future."

I experience a shiver of panic or something, is it fear of being here on my own in this strange place or is it the anticipation of freedom?

We spend the day at the beach at the La Ramada, swimming a little in the warm water, drinking, socializing with Roland, Smiley Jones and others. No one seems to work here.

A group of Americans saunter in, they are quite noisy; laughing raucously, waving to others as they sit down for lunch.

"That's the crowd from Gringo Gulch," Roland informs us.

"Oh yeah, say there's Sally Dimond, she still around?" Vincent waves across the table to an older woman in the group, very thin, her face still showing vestiges of former beauty through the ravages of age and excessive drink. Her hair is a bright gold blond, her lips painted a startling red.

She waves back, squints her eyes in an effort to identify the acquaintance, then screams "Vincent, you old son-of-a-bitch, when didja get here?"

She gets up and walks toward us, weaving slightly, grabbing hold of the backs of chairs as she makes her way forward, a mangy, brown dog follows her.

Vincent rises to greet her, she throws her arms around him and kisses him solidly on the mouth.

She stands back and studies him, smiling profusely, "Ya look great, handsome as ever, it's been quite a while since your last visit…we have missed you." She turns to Roland. "How the hell are yáll, how bout buying me a drink you old cheapskate." She pulls up a chair and sits next to Vincent.

"Oh, and this is my friend from San Francisco, Joanna, she's an artist," says Vincent, "she's going to stay down here for a while and paint."

Sally Dimond squints her eyes and looks at me and through me, like the way Rita grudgingly acknowledged my presence.

"Nice ta meetcha," she says accepting a cigarette from Vincent. He lights it for her, "They all say that don't they, artists, ha!" she snorts as she exhales.

This is going to be more difficult than I thought, the women don't like me right from the first, not the Mexicans or the Americans.

Drinks are ordered while Roland and Sally share the latest gossip.

I get up and excuse myself to go down to the beach to swim for a while, the water is calming. "Be careful honey, make sure there are no sharks around," counsels Vincent with a smile.

"I'll check," I mutter as I race down to the lapping surf and dive in under a wave. The waves are higher today than when I first swam here so I paddle out to beyond the breakers. Swimming on my back I watch the albatrosses flying overhead, then diving for their daily fish. They settle down close by me, seemingly unafraid of humans. *Not wise I think.*

I can see my apartment and the dock that extends from the street out into the sea. Children are gathered there fishing after school has ended. Fishing boats pull up to the dock to deliver their catch to restaurants, stores and homes. Las Peñas must be a town just like any other, families with children, the routine of meals, school, business, domestic life. The people I have met through Vincent, Roland and yes, of course, Doctor Kelly seem removed from what I have always experienced as normal life, more accelerated, more festive and less routine. *Is it because of their money I ask myself? Or the alcohol consumption? But my parents drank and they are well off.* Except for Hermalinda who appears to work in grim opposition to the rampant hedonism flourishing here. For her children I think. But can she ever overcome the influence of what is at this moment only the initial sprouting of what will become an overwhelming plague, extending it's tentacles of drug related vice into almost every household, taking its youth like a viscious, insatiable Pied Piper.

Feeling water logged after some time paddling about I return to the table where there are more drinks. I am getting tired of the drinking. I dry off and spread my towel on the equipale chair and return to the group, trying to figure out what the current topic of conversation is. It seems I have not been missed.

"Yeah," shouts Sally Dimond, to those of us sitting at the table, her voice hoarse and raspy, "then this ungrateful dog here, yeah, you Fido," she shakes her finger at the mongrel curled up at her feet who is seriously intent on licking a wound on his paw, "he just takes off for days after all I have done for him. Then I see him in town with a bunch of other curs and I tell you I just walked right past him as if I didn't know him, and after all I have done for him. He was practically dead when I took him in and fed him, doctored him and then he leaves, just like that!" She snaps her fingers. "And what do you think happens next? He shows up at Casa Cielo, my place on the hill wanting food and what not, well I tell you…get me another drink there wouldja?"

Sally speaks with a slight Texas drawl. She is from around Houston, divorced and well off. She wears a colorful, billowy long dress called a Mu-mu, and a wide brimmed straw hat, adorned with artificial flowers and a green satiny ribbon that trails down her back. Draped around her neck are several strands of gold necklaces, her fingers laden with various rings, obviously quite valuable, and a beautiful bracelet of Indian design of silver and turquoise around her wrist. She is getting quite drunk. I can't tell her age… but I view her with trepidation, the spectre of female self destruction hovers about her. *How can a woman who obviously had many of life's good fortunes at her disposal treat herself so badly, I ask myself.*

"Vincent," she says, waving a cigarette holder in front of her face as she talks, "whyncha all come up to my place tonight, I'm throwing a little party, bring your little artist friend along, how about it? We don't want anyone to get bored in Las Peñas ya know."

"Sure Sally, we'd love to come, I'm taking off early tomorrow for San Francisco so we can't stay too late."

"Off to Frisco, what a damned shame, the polo games start next Sunday, ya all are gonna miss a hell of a lot of fun." She douses her cigarette out on the floor. The dog is sleeping.

"Oh, well Joanna will be here for that," interjects Roland, "the polo games are between the Mexicans and the Americans, but instead of playing on horses, they play on burros. Great fun."

How am I ever going to fit into all of this I think.

Vincent looks at his watch. Mentally he is already leaving for San Francisco, facing the problems he is having there. He looks at me, smiles and takes my hand in his. "Let's get back to your place honey and take a little rest."

We say adios to everyone, even the dog wakes up, and return to my apartment, only a few steps away.

Vincent immediately crawls under the mosquito netting and into the bed, falling into a deep sleep within minutes.

To settle my own nerves I continue to accommodate my things in the apartment. I take the box with a few of my books in it. There is "Women in Love" by D.H.Lawrence, "The Sun Also Rises" by Hemingway and "Heart of Darkness" by Joseph Conrad. I look for grains of truth and inspiration in my literature and frequently find them in the books. However, my life seems so strange these days, I feel I am in uncharted territory and these books of men's lives hardly relate to what I am facing. I arrange them nicely on the bureau, a miniature library.

I wander across the open patio over to the kitchen to contemplate my easel with a canvas tacked to a board. Once I start painting, mixing the colors and applying them to the canvas I will feel more at ease here. I switch on the lights, the bulbs glow with a passive intensity. Getting down to business means preparing the canvases with rabbit skin glue and gesso. Then to the subject matter. Children of course, they are all over Las Peñas, no problem there. I can't paint adults, they are intimidating, too assertive and totally involved with themselves…either trying to make money or struggling to hang on to what they have. Money appears to be the answer to all of life's quandaries, even here, the people seem to suffer from loneliness and alienation, *but that is everywhere* inner voice asserts.

I check my camera. It is a very simple affair that slides out of its case on little rails and has a bellow type of photo imaging. It was my Mother's camera that she took to Mexico. Carefully I insert black and white film. It is a positive gesture which means I really intend to do some worthwhile work while I am here in Puerto de Las Peñas.

Returning to the bedroom, I see my love is fast asleep..better to leave him rest for the ordeal of the return flight tomorrow. The afternoon is slipping into evening, the sky darkening for the daily downpour. I walk onto the terrace and look out at the lush, dark green mountains, clouds are building up into shades of threatening gray and almost black descending over the tops of the mountains, the waves of the sea are a grayish color, crashing in a formidable manner onto the shore. They are higher and more menacing than they were this afternoon. I am entranced by the beauty and happy that I don't have to leave here as Vincent must tomorrow.

The boats bob around in the water. Some fishermen are leaving the dock carrying their catch over their shoulders. Big, strange looking fish, silvery in the diminished light preceding the storm. There is a boat struggling to come ashore amid the high surf, other men are waiting on the beach to help, to receive him. The men on the boat watch the rhythm of the waves, bobbing along just slightly beyond the breakers. Finally, judging the right moment, they begin rowing furiously toward the shore, a huge wave following them. The men on the beach wade out into the water to quickly haul the boat in just as the huge wave comes crashing down behind them.

The men wear only shorts, their backs are wiry and strong, a shiny dark brown. Their hair is very black. I like the way they look. They pull the wooden canoe, or panga higher onto the sandy beach and tie it down. In a few more minutes the deluge starts. I watch mesmerized, thinking that what is going to save me here is my art.

We never make it to Sally's party.

Roland takes us to the airport the next day. Vincent has only one suitcase. We wait patiently while he goes through the ritual of filling out his flight plan then walk out to where the Cessna is tied down. He goes through the flight check and turns to me for our parting.

He puts his arms around me, tightly and I feel close to tears. "You take care honey, be a good girl, paint like hell and when I come back to see you in a few weeks, I can take some paintings back with me for Aldrich. You stay close to Roland and Hermalinda, they can help you out if you need it. Remember, I love you."

"I love you too Vincent, I hope everything works out for you at your office."

"Don't worry about that, you take care of yourself."

Vincent and Roland embrace. "I'll look out after her Vince, she will be alright," says Roland earnestly.

Vincent pulls himself up into the left seat of the aircraft. Roland gives the propeller a few turns, then we both stand back as Vincent starts the engine. We watch as he taxis to the beginning of the runway, revving up the motor as he goes through his checklist. The plane begins its flight, speeding down the airstrip. In seconds it is airborne, the early morning sun flashing off its wings. We watch in silence as he dips his wings, the traditional aviator's farewell. Soon he becomes just a speck in the distance, then is gone.

I feel depressed, abandoned somehow as Roland drives us back to town in his rickety pick-up. He leaves me at my apartment with a kiss and an invitation for a drink. I think not. I throw myself on the bed, dripping with perspiration, wondering what to do next.

Well, says my inner voice, *you came here to paint, so you better get started.*

I walk through the patio-terrace to the kitchen and switch on the lights. *How sweet of Vincent to install lights for me,* I think, missing him terribly.

Disconsolately, I peel a banana and eat it as I peruse my paints, my brushes and the roll of linen that I will have to prepare in order to paint. I make an egg taco with some hot sauce for my lunch and then begin to apply myself to my work. I heat up the rabbit skin glue, cut off several pìeces of the linen of appropriate sizes and with a brush, slather them with the glue. I tack the canvases to the table, to a board and to the door in order to dry. That done, I return to my bedroom and lay down on the bed. The heat is intense, even with the fan blowing. I read a little, striving to ward off the loneliness I am feeling, then fall asleep.

When I awake it is already late in the afternoon. Feeling refreshed from the rest, I take my camera in hand and insert a roll of film, preparing for my first foray into this paradise, *on my own.* I take some pains with my hair, rolling it up into a floppy bun on top of my head, I push a stick through the bun to secure it, then a little makeup. I wear my bathing suit with a cotton lace robe thrown over it. I am barefoot. There is no full length mirror of course so I must have faith that I look just fine.

I'll go down to the beach and look for subjects to paint, maybe someone will invite me for a drink and conversation at the La Ramada.

Carefully locking my apartment with the big, iron key, I trudge down to the beach, wading through the gentle surf. The waves lapping at my bare feet feels wonderful, warm and soothing. The afternoon is bright and sunny except for the clouds growing over the Pacific, heralding the coming storm.

There are some children carrying roasted fish on sticks to sell, others are cooking the fish over hot coals on the sand. Some carry firewood. *Ahh, perfect subjects*, reminiscent of my photographic studies of children in San Francisco's Chinatown. There are about a dozen or so, ranging in age from around 5 years old to 12. They are very dirty from the work they are doing. The girls are in flowered dresses with lace and ribbon trimming, some quite ragged and the boys in shorts, all are barefooted, like me. They are brown skinned, with very black eyes and hair…their teeth sparkle when they smile; the commercial food corporations with their sugary, tooth decaying drinks and sickly junk food snacks have not arrived yet to this part of the country.

I try to sneak up on them so they will appear natural, so they don't become self-conscious and change their expression. I want to express them in all their simplicity. But they spy me. They of course consider me a tourist and run up to me presenting their fish to sell. They are poor children and I must appear wealthy to them, little do they know I barely have enough money to survive. I will have to sell some paintings to get by. That means I must take from them their beauty and innocence and transfer that to my canvases. I am a kind of thief but no matter, I must do it.

They clamor around me, I cannot be invisible. "Laydee, laydee," they call out, tugging at my beach robe. "*Pescado bueno, compra!*"

"No!" I shout, "No pescado," remembering the Spanish word for fish from High School classes.

I back away, take a picture, focusing on their laughing brown faces, the black, gnarled fishes on the sticks waving above them in the air, snap the shutter again then back off and continue walking along in the sand. Then I go to where a young boy is cooking the fish. He glances up, then turns back to his work, ignoring me. Perfect. I catch him absorbed in his work, beautifully posed.

Further along I see two little girls playing in the sand. I creep up to them and crouch down to their level. At the moment they turn to look at me I snap the shutter. I circle them steathily, they follow my movements curiously, wondering what this crazy gringa is doing. I take several more shots. A woman comes up to me suddenly, probably the mother of the girls, and begins talking rapidly in Spanish. Turning away I retreat rapidly looking for escape from the ranting woman.

The children have followed me and continue to shout at me to buy their fish. "No, no!" I say as forcefully as I can.

"Si, si," they chant, surrounding me, enveloping me in their messy midst. I begin to laugh and start to pull away but they follow. I make it to the La Ramada where they are halted by a waiter as I clamor up the stair to the restaurant. I see Smiley Jones and make for his table. Others seated there are watching my distress with amusement.

"Can I sit with you a moment Smiley. I'm a poor starving artist from San Francisco but those kids don't seem to understand that." Hanging on to my camera with one hand and the back of an equipale with the other.

"Sure, of course..you got mobbed by the kids, huh." He stands as if to help me seat myself but I handle it, uttering a sigh of relief, my camera at rest on the table.

"Thanks," I say softly, "I am going to have to rethink how I photograph them for my paintings."

Smiley is almost non-descript. Probably close to 60 years old, a round face with faded blue eyes, his gray hair thinning. He does smile a lot but I get the feeling he is basically depressed. The young Mexican girl is not with him.

"I just took some photos of some of the children, possibly to paint them and then this woman runs up to me talking a mile a minute in Spanish. I have no idea what she was saying."

He puts his head back and laughs, "She wanted money, sure, that you should pay for the photos of her children. These people have very little to sell here so if they see a chance, they grab it. There is a big gap between rich and poor, no middle class to speak of. Hell, I was just a poor working stiff in Happy Camp and here they think I am Mr. Got Rocks."

"Where is Happy Camp?"

"Oh, that's way up in Northern California, lumbering country, I did that all my life ya know. Then my wife left me and I decided to chuck it all, live the easy life down here. Ya know I own half of this place with Roland, we're partners in the business. After Montes-Cruz screwed Roland out of his half of the place across the street, Las Olas, Roland rents this part of the beach from Hermalinda's family, it was communal property. And then I came in with some money from Happy Camp and bought into it as a partner with Roland and we made La Ramada. Got it?"

"Yes, kind of."

"Oh say, how'd ya like a beer? Great in the afternoon to watch the rain and drink beer." I nod affirmatively.

He whistles to the waiter. "Well, well…did Vincent get off alright?"

"Oh yes, he would have liked to stay here longer but he had to get back to his legal practice in San Francisco. I am going to have to learn my way around here on my own I guess."

"Ha, ha, he's not like the rest of us beach bums around Las Peñas," he says as he pours the rest of his beer into his glass.

"I can see how easy it is to get lulled into the tropical atmosphere and just do nothing but enjoy being alive."

The waiter arrives with my beer and another for Smiley. He offers me a cigarette which I accept.

"Thanks Smiley," I say as we clink glasses.

I lean back in my equipale and look out at the beauty around me. The sky is a bright cerulean bluc with clouds gathering over the distant mountain peaks and out over the horizon. The jungle starts at the end of the beach in a tangle of rocks, boulders, palm trees and vines with stems as thick as ropes. Thunder rumbles in the distance.

"Tlaloque," says Smiley as he flicks his cigarette, "the Mayan god of rain."

"Really, you mean the thunder isn't the result of excessive moisture and negative electrical charges meeting positive charges? There is a god up there making all that noise?" I say, smirking slightly.

"That's what the Indians claim, and who are we to question them, maybe they are right and the scientists are wrong."

"It's more romantic for sure Smiley, I shall always attribute the thunder to Tlaloque from now on." I sip my beer.

The children have gone back to hawking their fish on a stick, chasing prospective customers. Fishermen returning from their work at sea are cleaning their catch, repairing their nets and selling off some of the fish. There are colorful beach umbrellas lining the shore shading a sprinkling of tourists having their lunch on the beach.

My eyes wander to the restaurant across the road. *Las Olas*, the waves, the forbidden place. They seem to have more people than there are here. There is a sign above the thatched roof that says 'Las Olas'. Music from the Mariachis playing is rythmic and pleasant, adding to the whole atmosphere of sensual malaise. There are no musicians at the La Ramada at this time.

Smiley catches me looking intently at the activity in the other restaurant. I think of the villain in all of this, Sergio Montes Cruz, and what a charming, handsome man his cousin Antonio was when we met him the other day in the hardware store. So helpful. Sadly, I will never be able to know him since I am under the care of these people of the La Ramada, as Vincent has ordained. I have become a part of a real, honest to goodness feud.

"Don't even think of going over there, they are really bad people and I have strict orders to keep you away from them," he counsels.

The shy young Mexican girl hovers behind Smiley. She appears to be about 15 years old. He turns, as if sensing her presence and gestures to her to sit down. She sits down on the edge of an equipale at an empty table next to us. She is waiting for him.

The aqua-drama is beginning. First the rumbling thunder, then the few drops of water announcing the big show and then the deluge. Water pours down in glistening sheets, drops make it through the roof thatching and pepper the table, the beer and us. I can no longer see across the road to the forbidden restaurant for the wind and the rain. It is marvelous. The waiters scurry about serving more drinks and food since the patrons are now captives for the duration of the storm.

After about twenty minutes it is over, the sun comes out in force, steam rising from the cobblestones, the air thick, hot and humid.

Smiley is smiling, "I just love the rain here, and you will too once you get used to it."

He stands and stretches his plump, stocky body a bit. "Gotta go," he says, "see you around on the beach." He pushes in his equipale, nods to the girl and walks out, the girl following along behind him.

I feel conspicuous sitting there alone, so gathering up my camera and my bag, I walk through the wet sand back to my apartment.

During the next several days I stay close to my new home. Leaving only to buy food, take photos in the streets, take film to be developed or to swim in the warm waters of the Pacific Ocean. I work on preparing canvases for painting. It is a struggle for me to familiarize myself with this strange land, and not to be a stranger. The men call out to me in the street and make what I imagine are suggestive remarks which fortunately or not I do not understand. I feel like I did after the divorce, facing a new life in an entirely new world. Only now I have experience.

Feeling the need of social contact, one day I visit Hermalinda in her home.

She is busy cooking in her simple kitchen. A big pot of beans is steaming on the stove while a servant is making tortillas. The children clamber about; the two little boys are climbing the avocadoe tree outside the doorway and the girl, Tammy, is sitting on the table nibbling on a tortilla. I see the box with the boat motor that Vincent had brought, still in its box, unopened in the corner.

"Hola Hermalinda, como esta?" I manage in Spanish.

"Bien, y tu?" she responds politely, wiping her hands in a towel, a faint smile of greeting flickers across her face.

Oh heavens, I think, *she is not going to switch to English.*

"Sientate!" she orders gruffly as she returns to her chopping.

Accordingly, I drop down into one of the wooden kitchen chairs.

I watch the maid making the tortillas with fascination: flattening the little balls of ground corn dough between the palms of her hands, then placing them on a wooden press to achieve their proper thinness and shape, then onto the firey hot comal, coals burning red underneath. She flips the tortilla over for a moment or two and then to a growing pile, going on to the next one.

Hermalinda pushes a plate of sliced avocados with salt and lemon toward me on the table. She indicates I should make a taco with the hot fresh tortilla. The little girl stares at me, dropping her tortilla momentarily, overcome by curiosity. The silence is broken only by the slap of the corn dough between the hands of the maid, the sizzling of the pressure cooker with the beans and the shrieks of laughter from the two little boys playing outside the kitchen.

"I've gotten started on my painting," I say conversationally, hoping for a positive response in English.

"Oh, esta bien," she says over her shoulder, continuing her work.

The silence extends. I suddenly feel profoundly unwelcome and this is the woman who is supposed to help look out for me. *There is no common ground for friendship* I think as I stare at her long black hair falling to her fat rear end.

"I really miss Vincent," I say, making one last stab at it.

She whirls around and looks at me angrily. Her face is shockingly out of Gauguin, I think of painting her.

"How ees possible you miss that mens," she cries out, "he like Rolando, chase any womans he can, run after them like dogs down the beach, no goot, no goot these mens, like Rolando." Her face contorts in fury.

I am shocked by the hatred she has for the two men.

"Before, I love Rolando mas then any mens," she continues, throwing down the towel with one hand and gripping the chopping knife with the other. "He like some white god to me, but all he do ees drink vino and chase after womens. He never pay mi papa for the land for the La Ramada…he jus care of hees self…no mi..no hees cheeldren…nada…solamente Rolando.

"Don you mees your mens Vicente, he jus same as Rolando, he cum here mucho and he jus the same, after las muchachas. I know zem now…I know…"

I breathe deeply, she has shaken my carefully constructed existence with her venom, however true it may be. I struggle on…"But they can change,.. with love and patience, maybe a psychiatrist…"

Hermalinda waves her knife, a bit too close for comfort as she screams, "estos gringos no vale madre."

I don't understand her words but somehow the meaning comes through. These guys aren't worth shit or something like that. I imagine that Mexican men have similar problems from what I have been told but don't bother to mention that. I feel the hopelessness of trying to defend my fellow countrymen to her. *No use in waiting around hoping to be invited for lunch* I think, *better to leave and search elsewhere for friendship.*

"I am so sorry Hermalinda," she may be crying, I can't tell if is from chopping onions or from betrayal. I kiss the little girl on the top of her head, she looks at me blandly.

"I'll have to be going now Hermalinda, have a nice day." I

say to her back, watching her arm move up and down over the chopping block.

"Adios." I wave to the little boys in the avocado tree. They wave back.

She says nothing as I leave. *I wonder why she is angry with me. It's not my fault men are so unfaithful, so intent on fucking every woman they take a fancy to. Maybe nature made them that way to insure the survival of the species, I surely am not to blame.*

I continue to concentrate on my painting. Socially, I make a passing acquaintance with a young Canadian woman who is living with a beach boy. Her name is Beverly, she has a child with the fellow and according to Smiley, her Canadian family has disinherited her. Another victim of social disapproval. I have passing conversations with various patrons of the La Ramada but still have not raised the courage to wander over to Las Olas, though the life there seems more glamourous somehow. I have noted a certain pall that hangs over Roland's establishment.

A young American drifter strikes up a friendship with me. He is penniless. We end up talking of Art and Philosophy on the beach sitting in the sand. His name is Mike. He thinks of himself as a poet. I confess to him that I have trouble relating to most contemporary poetry which seems to amuse him. We swim. Occasionally an American tourist eager for company will invite us for drinks. I have to make it clear early on in the relationship that I cannot have sex with him That I have serious relationship at this time.

My frankness amazes me. He is not deterred.

One Friday afternoon after I have been in Las Peñas more than three weeks, an American resident name Henry Swanson comes over to the table where I am sitting in the La Ramada with Mike and a few of the beach crowd. He carries a drink in one hand and a cigarette in the other. He introduces himself and takes a seat at the table, making some small talk with the others there. He is a medium sized man, not short, not tall, probably in his forties, close to fifty. A slender plain looking man with thinning light brown hair, his brown eyes twinkle impishly and there is something roguish about him.

He zeros in on me.

"I have a friend who wants to meet you and become *your* friend," he says, a slightly leering look hovering about his bloodshot eyes. He smokes as he speaks. To me he is unlikable.

"My very interesting friend is Cesar Cibrian Ramirez, the governor of Sinaloa!" Henry Swanson sits back in his chair, a smile playing on his thin lips, waiting for his words to sink in to those gathered at the table.

"Oh, well of course I would like to meet such an important man, why does he want to meet me?" I reply.

"He has heard about you, that you are an artist, here to paint scenes of Mexico and that your work is good. And of course that you are a very beautiful young woman. Come on now, be smart, this man may be able to help you with your work.." Swanson stands abruptly and looks down on me as if this is an order.

Overcome by curiousity, I excuse myself from the table of ex-patriots and follow Henry to the back of the restaurant where a large table is occupied by very serious looking Mexican men; talking, drinking, smoking, eating. All eyes turn in my direction as Henry and I approach. I feel I am on exhibition.

Henry takes over. In Spanish he introduces me, Joanna Botticelli, famous artist and then presents me to the Governor. "His honor Cesar Cibrian Ramirez, the Governor of the fine state of Sinaloa!"

A short, dark and rather swarthy man stands and comes before me, grinning widely. He has a heavy, Pancho Villa mustache, and thick, blue-black hair combed straight back across his head. His eyes are black and sparkling, his teeth large, white and gleaming in the late afternoon sun. Cesar exudes power, like a sleek cobra slowly hypnotizing his prey. A pistol dangles from a leather belt slung around his hips. He gently takes my hand and kisses my fingers. "I am soo huppy to meet wiz yu Madam. Forgeev mi pobre Engleesh pero pleeze seet down wiz us and geev us ze honor of you beeutifol presencia."

"Thank you," I manage to get out, and despite my inner voice screaming caution, caution and more caution, I sit down in the designated equipale chair that is being held for my occupancy.

The table is filled with bottles of different kinds of liquor; whiskey, brandy, beer and tequila and a forest of soft drink bottles, some empty and some half empty. There are dishes of cucumbers, peanuts and quacamole (avocado dip) seasoned with lemon, chile and salt.

"And what wud yu like to dreenk mi pritty arteesta?" he asks me as he slides into the chair next to me, leaning over almost to be touching me. I can smell the cigarettes on his breath. I back away slightly, not wanting to offend him and try to think of what to drink. He waits patiently for my answer. The other men seem to be hanging on my choice, their eyes fixed on me.

"Uhh, maybe a little Tequila with some water and ice, and oh, a bit of lemon."

"Hecho!" he pronounces and one of his men expertly prepares my drink.

They all sit back and smile in relief, their conversations resume. Henry Swanson has retreated.

"Yu have a very beuteeful face Senorita, but why yu here in Mexico? Yu like Mexico?" He places a plate of peanuts in front of me while the attention of his cohorts reverts to me and my answer.

I am nervous but plunge on, thinking my best defense is in the truth.

"Si, I like Mexico very much." I speak slowly and clearly so he can understand my English. This seems to please him.

"I am here to paint the beautiful life of the people of this country, the children expecially are wonderful to paint, their eyes, their expressions...everything here is beautiful."

Cesar throws his head back and exhales a long sigh of pleasure, then proceeds to translate what I have said to his retinue of secretaries, bodyguards, pilot and navigator.

The Mexican government plane at the airport was his.

I see Henry Swanson hovering in the background with a mirthful smile on his face. Like an immensely pleased Cheshire cat.

"There ees no place in zee whole world lak Mexico. We luv when yu people cum here weeth luv for our countrys, eet ees a mos wonnerful theeng for us, and from where do yu cum, pretty lady?"

"San Francisco, it is also very beautiful, have you ever been there?"

"Oh, si', si'," Cesar gestures excitedly to the others at the table, explaining to them that I am from San Francisco.

I cautiously sip my drink and pop a single peanut into my mouth. I feel hungry since I am living mostly on fruit, hard boiled eggs and cheese to save what money I have for the inevitable rainy day.

"Yu lak fly in my airplane? I hev a beeg aeroplane wiz two motos...I can take yu to fly in eet to see the beautiful Sierra Madre mountains of Jalisco state...very, very beeautiful for the Arteesta."

He is leaning over toward me, his arm around the back of my equipale, I feel his breath on my cheek.

"I am a pilot also, I fly a plane in San Francisco, I like very much to fly airplanes." I shift slightly in my seat in anticipation of his reaction to *that*.

He raises both arms into the air and pronounces, "Ay, Dios Mio, NO, it cannot be, a womans flying zee airplane, I don beeleeve zees."

Some of the men look alarmed, wondering what I said that evinced such a dramatic response from their boss.

I take a sip of my drink, smiling for everyone. *Maybe I should not have told him that,* I think to myself as he translates my remarks. The men begin to laugh and shake their heads, talking rapidly among themselves in Spanish. I have no idea what they are saying but have no doubt it is about me.

Henry Swanson moves in and affirms what I had just told Cesar, they all look at me as though I were an alien from outer space.

"I vant you to cum out weez us tonite…we go to Las Margaritas, hev a leetle fun. We eat feesh, drink more…we dance, yu lak cum weez us Madam Arteesta?"

"But Señor Cesar," I say as kindly as possible, "I am not free, I have a man friend that I am going to marry with." My Spanish attempts are corrupting my English grammar.

"No, no, no, for mi yu are free, don tell me about yur mens, I wan to know you bedder. Mañana I leeve in my airplane but I cum bak in two days and I luk for yu." He drops my hands and resumes his drink. I do the same, wondering how to get out of this.

Henry nudges me, mumbles in my ear, "Tell him yes, he's real important around here, he can help you a lot, come on… I'll go along to help translate and maybe look out for you."

I have been staying close to my home on the beach, working on my paintings since Vincent left. The idea of a night on the town with a Mexican politician seems like an interesting break in the monotony of my penniless existence.

"Yes, I mean si', Señor Cesar, I would like to go out with you tonight."

"Muy bien, bien, bien…now we dreenk a leetle more and zen we go to our home to rest and to dress very beautifool. I lak you very, very mucho Senorita Arteesta, yu es una mujer muy raro, and I lak zat very mucho. Salud!" he exclaims and again all the glasses go up in unison, this time I get it right and raise my glass on command.

One of his bodyguards stands up and points to his watch. Cesar nods and they all rise and gather their cigarettes and lighters. One of them signs the check. I notice that they all carry arms. Cesar leans toward me and kisses me on the cheek.

"Hasta luego mi amiga." Then they are gone.

Henry Swanson walks me back to my apartment. He acts as though we are old friends who have known one another for ages.

"This could really help you a lot, Cesar has a lot of power and influence. He is a top politico in Mexico, one of the big honchos."

"Like how could he help me?" I ask, as we walk barefoot though the sand, the soft surf lapping at our feet. The sky is assembling its clouds for the daily afternoon downpour, thunder rumbles in the distance. These things are reassuring.

"Oh, just about anything, he could give you a big show of your paintings in Mexico City if you play your cards right," says Henry, bending over to pick up a shell from the sand.

"How did you know I could fly an airplane? I could have been making that up you know. After all, I have just met you."

"It's my business to know about everyone who lives here." He says as we approach the entrance door to my apartment. I fumble for the big iron key, manage to turn it, forcing it to open the door. We go up the stairs and enter my humble living quarters. I wonder what kind of business he has.

Henry relaxes in the only chair in my bedroom and lights a cigarette, he offers me one which I accept. It was one of those spicy Mexican cigarettes, Faros. He takes a packet of matches from his shirt pocket and lights our cigarettes, then drops the burnt out match on the floor. I sit on the bed smoking.

"Yeah, Cesar is really taken with you," he says, laying his head back against the wall, exhaling pleasurably. The sky is darkening outside my terrace and the thunder is closer. "He's been keeping his eye on you all week long."

"Really, I never noticed."

"Got anything to drink?"

"Nothing."

"Hmm," he murmurs, not pleased. "Let me see some of your work if you don't mind."

We go across the open patio to my kitchen/studio. He stands in front of my easel where there is a half finished oil painting of a boy with fish on a stick looking out at the world in an intense, soul searching way. The work is on canvas tacked to a board since there are no stretched canvases available.

"Nice work," he says, grudgingly. "I used to paint myself but got out of the habit. Hardly anyone who paints does it down here, too much social life to work."

"I have been noticing that."

"Since you don't have any booze, I'll be on my way. Be ready at 8:00, we'll come by to pick you up."

I don't want to wear anything that could be construed as *sexy*. I put on some white cotton long pants with a Mexican peasant blouse and the traditional woven leather sandals. A bit of makeup and my hair piled high on the back of my head, held in place by a chop stick. Satisfied that I look chaste and plain I await their arrival.

Exactly at 8:00 I hear the pounding at the door. I rush down the steps and there is Henry, his hair all slicked back, wearing fresh, clean tropical garb and his leering smile. He takes my arm and walks me to the waiting Jeep where the governor is seated in the back, also with a leering smile. "You could have worn something more, well, more dressy," whispers Henry in my ear as he helps me into the place next to Governor Ramirez. It is starting to rain, the small leather tarp covering the top of the Jeep offers little resistance to what is building up to a torrential downpour.

"We are going to be wet, mi Chiquita," say Governor Ramirez as he puts his arm around me. Henry disappears into the vehicle behind us and the entourage is off for a festive evening.

The rain is pouring off the tarp in sheets while Cesar, seemingly immune to any discomfort, contiuously nuzzles the back of my neck. I shift uncomfortably under his attentions but he continues murmuring sweet nothings in Spanish of which I have no idea what he is saying.

We pull up in front of Las Margaritas. One of his pistoleros is waiting with a huge umbrella to escort us into the night club. We are all pretty wet by now, Lightening is crashing around us as though we were being announced.

We sit in the back of the club, the men with their backs to the wall which I understand later on is a safety precaution against any unforeseen assassination attempt. At least they will be able to see who it is that is trying to kill them. I am seated at the head of the table, my back fully exposed but oblivious to any danger. Many heads are turning in our direction. I see Roland with a group of people including Sally Dimond, at one of the tables, he seems to be ignoring me but that may just be my imagination.

The music is lively, flowers and candles adorn the tables, the atmosphere is truly festive. I want to dance, but Cesar says no, Too undignified. Drinks are ordered along with the ubiquitous snacks of tostadas with cheese, cucumbers with lemon, salt and chile, guacamole and little pieces of corn on the cob, slathered with butter and salt.

"*Comete, Chiquita*," orders Cesar, and I duly eat, hungry as usual. "Eef yu wan to dance mi amigo Alfredo will dance wis yu, okay?"

Alfredo leads me out to the dance floor and we begin something like a waltz. As we swing by Roland's table I wave at him in a friendly manner, but he is frowning at me. I am not supposed to be out partying with Mexican politicians. I smile at him as we swing by and then see at another table the man from the hardware store, Antonio del Valle and his cousin Sergio Montes Cruz. I sense wide spread disapproval with me and my company.

Back at our table Cesar is in serious conversation with Henry Swanson. Cesar bares his teeth in a big smile and puts his arm around me as I slide into my seat. He continues his conversation with Henry while occasionally nuzzling me on the neck.. I wonder what is going on, something is.

The night drags on. Dinner arrives which is wonderful; steaming chicken enchiladas with cole slaw. rice and beans. I devour it.

I excuse myself to go to the bathroom.

Sally Dimond is there with her daughter and some friends. They all stare at me. "Do you know what you are doing?" exclaims Sally.

"What?"

"Do you know who you are with?"

"Yes, the Governor of Sinaloa, Cesar Cibrian Ramirez."

She hands me a towel to dry my hands, "Darlin, you are naïve to say the least. What would Vincent say if he saw you out with a Mexican politician."

"This is just a friendly outing, I do need a break and Vincent isn't coming down here for another two weeks…I was just curious about Cesar."

"Just remember, curiousity killed the cat!" With that she turns and leaves, friends and daughter in tow, whispering and giggling.

I could use some friendly counsel just now, but there is none, so I just return to my fate. Cesar stands and holds my chair for me as I sit down, there are more drinks and even with the food I am beginning to feel the effects. I would like to go my little apartment and sleep but that does not seem possible in the near future but I will attempt it.

I lean over and whisper to Henry, "I would like to go home how."

He looks at me in alarm, "What! Home! The night is just beginning my dear, you better perk up."

No way to perk up, I think. I have to get out of this somehow. There seems to be something sinister about Cesar Ramirez and maybe if I weren't tired and a little bored I would try to find out what it is. I have to get out.

The mariachis are playing "Guadalajara" and people are singing along.

Cesar wants a song about Sinaloa and leaves to talk to the musicians.

"Henry, I am going to the bathroom, please excuse me."

"You better come right back you hear?"

"Sure, sure," I gather up my purse and quickly slide out of the equipale. I walk along the side of the restaurant,striving to be invisible, toward the door and out. Free! I have walked these streets everyday now for the last several weeks, this is no problem. I breathe deeply of the clean sea air. I walk briskly through the teeming cobblestone streets, fiercely alive with people, even children at one in the morning. Happy that I am wearing sandles for walking and not some high heels. Crossing the bridge over the fast moving river I see Romanov's on the Rocks below and remember when I was there with Vincent.

It seems like an eternity since that happy evening. Five more blocks and I am at Los Muertos and my apartment which seems like a palace to me at that moment. Wedging the huge key into the keyhole, making it turn, then locking it behind me, I rush up the stairs and fling myself down on the bed.

Taking a quick shower I put on some light cotton pajamas, turn on a little reading lamp above the bed and absorb a few pages of Hemingway's "For Whom the Bell Tolls" and fall into a deep sleep.

But not for long. I hear below me the music of the Mariachis playing below my window. Cesar. I will not go out on the terrace, I am not dressed to receive a serenade, I do not *want* a serenade. I want to be left alone, can't he understand that. I was as polite to him as possible but that is it.

The music drags on, song after song, of unrequited love, of desire, of a little lost boy..the whole repertoire but I remain glued to my bed, I am hoping he will think I am no longer there..that I have left for some unknown destination. Anything. Finally they stop, I hear them assembling their instruments and drive off. I drift back into a fretful sleep.

The next morning, Henry is at my door. He has a bag with tacos for breakfast.

"How can you be so rude to Cesar?" he says as he sits down on the edge of the bed. "Wanna cigarette?" He takes a package of matches from his shirt pocket and lights his cigarette. I refuse the offer.

"Look, I don't want to get involved with the man, period."

"You could have acknowledged the music he brought for you last night, he was crushed that you didn't come to the window."

"Sorry, but I had on an old pair of pajamas and curlers in my hair and I didn't want a serenade at all. And I left the restaurant last night because I was tired and not feeling well and that's it. Now why are you so interested in my relationship with the man?"

"Now that's a good question." He opens the paper bag of tacos and hands me one. It is filled with a mixture of meat, potatoes and onions. It is quite good.

"I'll make us some coffee."

We sit in the kitchen/studio, drinking coffee. It is starting to get very warm. The sound of the waves below my apartment is calming. I study this man's face, it is not an honest face, it tells of a man with limited resources, striving for gain in any way he can.

"Cesar took off this morning, but he will be back and soon." Henry sips the hot coffee and is soon perspiring. "He is not a man to be deterred."

He wipes the beads of sweat from his face with a crinkled handkerchief, stuffing it into his pants pocket.

I am still in my pajamas with a flimsey robe tied around my waist.

"What is going on here?" I ask, putting two plates down on the table for the tacos.

"Big stuff." he says, munching into his second taco. "A big film director from Hollywood is coming here to make a movie, the place is going to boom and everyone wants some of the action. Including me."

"Really, how interesting, when is this going to happen?"

"Sometime soon from what I hear, real estate is going to go through the roof once the rest of the world finds out about Puerto de las Penas. Oh, wouldja pass me the sugar please?"

"How sad." I say as he spoons several teaspoonfulls of sugar into his coffee.

"Sad? Are you crazy, that's great news, we'll all be rich, even you if you play your cards right which I don't think you will from what I know of you in the short time I have had to deal with you."

"I just think it's beautiful the way it is, once these people come in with their hotels, restaurants, discos, condos and all the rest, it will never be the same, The rivers will fill with garbage, the sea will be contaminated and all the turtles, mantas, whales, all of them will die off. The people will be contaminated with industrial food and drugs, families will lose their children to drug addiction and venereal diseases, crime will come and no one will leave their doors unlocked like they can now…it is going to be awful."

"Well, that's progress now isn't it..the maids and gardeners will have cars, they can drink good liquor, there will be highways in and out so you don't have to ride your burro to get anywhere, and we'll have money in our pockets, lots of it for the smart ones." He leans back in his chair as he challenges me to refute his rosy picture of this currently pristine tropical oasis about to be defiled by hoards of developers.

I shake my head sadly, thinking of how my ex-husband would see the foothills of the Sierra Nevada in Northern Califronia, covered with little houses…houses where the inhabitants spend most of their time and money on mortgages and on gas for their cars to get to their faraway jobs or to the super market to feed themselves. Houses too small to have kitchen gardens or family fruit orchards or to keep chickens or a cow so the family could eat even if the jobs failed. My ex is becoming rich but he has a rocky life in spite of his wealth.

"What can I say, everyone wants money of course but to lose the natural beauty and a healthy way of life for this amorphous idea of 'progress' doesn't make sense to me. Usually it is the banks and the government that profits most when these upheavals occur, and of course the big developers. Okay, I've said my piece, now what about Cesar…what is he up to?"

"He's just poking around, seeing who is in charge of things, meeting with the banks, that sort of thing. Apparently the director of the proposed film was here a while back and fell in love with Las Peñas, easy to do and wants it for the setting of his movie."

"That is a problem, first the artists discover a place, then the developers come and the place is ruined forever." I stand up abruptly, hoping he will leave.

"My goodness gracious, you are a gloomy one, I suppose you want me to leave."

"Yes."

"Well don't get mad at me, it's not my fault, it's just the way things are."

"I know, who am I to challenge the forces that be, but I do in my small way. Sorry Henry, I have to get dressed and do some shopping, then work on my paintings so I don't fall into the pit of irrelevance."

"Sure, you do that, I'll be around when Cesar comes back and maybe we can try Las Margaritas again, okay?"

He smiles sarcastically, takes a last sip of his sickeningly sweet coffee and leaves.

I sell two of my paintings. One to a long time American resident of Las Peñas and another to a German tourist. These sales have eased my economic situation considerably and renewed my enthusiasm for my work.

During the following week a little boy comes to my door to give me a telegram. It is from Vincent telling me he will be arriving here in Las Peñas within two days. I feel my heart flutter at the thought of seeing him again.

The day arrives. I can hardly work so I go to the La Ramada and wait for the inevitable fly over he has become famous for.

I sit at a table with Roland, Smiley Jones and Beverly, the young Canadian woman who lives with the beach boy. She carries a baby girl on her lap. An incredibly beautiful child with creamy beige skin and blue eyes, her hair a mass of golden curls. Beverly has a black eye and multiple bruises on her arms, cruel badges of domestic abuse. She sits quietly, rocking the child gently. I try not to look at her bruises, I don't want to disturb my mood of thrilling anticipation for the arrival of my love.

"Roland, how would you like to go to the airport with me to pick up Vincent?" He sets his glass of tequila down slowly, he looks at me inquiringly. I expect his next comment.

"What about the Governor from Sinaloa?"

I signal the waiter for a beer as I answer with a smile, "What about him?"

"Are you going to tell Vincent you had a hot date with Cesar Cibrian Ramirez, the infamous governor of Sinaloa?"

"There is nothing to tell, it was just a simple evening outing, he was very friendly and interested in my Art, that was all there was to it. And why is Cesar 'infamous'?

I take a swig of my beer, it is very cold and soothing.

"He has a bad reputation that's all, you don't know anything about him, the fellow is dangerous. He is mafia, drugs, who knows what else, you are being foolish to go out with him."

Roland's face is quite red, he has been drinking all day at the beach restaurant. I don't feel like justifying myself but go on to insist the man was perfectly nice with me.

Roland is unconvinced.

I hear the faint sound of an aircraft in the distance.

"Vincent is coming, can you hear the plane?" My stomach is doing double turns as the sound of the motor gets closer and closer. I run onto the beach along with the children, fishermen and tourists to welcome whoever it is that comes by air. Eyes all turn upward toward the North as the plane comes into view. It is a biplane, slowly descending toward the beach. It is the International red and white Staggerwing. I imagine all the things he is doing to bring the plane into position to buzz the tops of the restaurants, the shore, the waves of the sea. Pull back throttle, forward on the ailerons, maybe a bit of flaps and the flying machine is right overhead, So close you could almost touch it, everyone scatters as it roars above us and out to sea, to circle and return with all its force. I see him hanging out the side window, laughing and waving. The children jump up and down in excitement, the drunken tourists fall over in the sand. I wave wildly to him. Then he is gone. Gone to land at the airport North of town.

I run to Roland who is ready to go and we are off in his old pick-up to meet my love, the love of my life.

At the small airport of Puerto de las Peñas, Vincent's Staggerwing has already landed and he is taxiing to the airport building. I run to greet him as he gets out of the plane. He looks marvelous, heroic and handsome. Dressed in Khaki, like a model out of Banana Republic. He is thinner, his face ruddy, his blond/gray hair charmingly messed up. He smells of motor oil, cigarettes and sweat, a musky masculine smell that I love. He enfolds me in his arms in a kiss of pure passion. He does love me.

"You flew down here all alone?" I ask after he closes his flight plan and we sip beer at the airport bar with Roland.

"Yep, everyone was too busy, I'm a big boy now. I left San Francisco at dawn, made one stop in Guaymas with customs and here I am Honey, all yours for three days." He nuzzles the back of my neck, nibbling on my skin, if I were a cat I would be purring.

"What did you bring me Vincent, Las Peñás is heavenly but there is almost nothing to buy here."

"Oh, so you are going through consumer withdrawal?" he chuckles as he reaches into his travel bag and takes out a package wrapped in brown paper.

I carefully unwrap it. There are boxes of oil paint, alizarin crimson, cobalt blue, zinc white, raw umber, cerulean blue, Prussian green and more. I am delighted that he intuitively knew my needs.

"Oh, this is wonderful, I am running low on colors, you are so sweet, Vincent…I do adore you. What else do you have for me?"

"Champagne?

"Wonderful Vincent, have you missed me?"

"More than I feel like telling you, you may use it against me." he says, sounding like the lawyer he is.

"I have *really* missed you, more than I imagined I would..I almost would like to go back with you but not yet. I have sold some paintings and am a little better economically I am happy to tell you."

"Good, that makes it all worth it, now we only have to think of what we are going to do for the next few days. Of course you know what I want to do." He says as he rubs his hand along my inner thigh. "What's new and exciting in Puerto de las Peñas?"

Roland clears his throat ostentaciously. "Lots, actually Vince."

"Hollywood is coming to Las Peñas, what do you think of that?"

Vincent lights two cigaretts, the unfiltered Camels, and passes me one as he contemplates Roland. "What does that mean?"

"A famous movie director is going to make a film here, down the coast on the beach of Los Quelites. Raymond Morrison is the director, apparently he was down here a couple of years ago and loved the place, says it is perfect for the film..'My Beloved Iguana'."

"Strange name for a movie, what's it about?

"I'm not sure, it's based on a book by Alabama Witherspoon, he's a pretty famous writer I guess, but you know me, I'm not much for reading." His words are becoming a bit slurry as he raises his glass of Tequila to his lips.

"A lot of speculators are coming to town Vincent, it is changing the atmosphere of the place…some people like it but others don't. Money is in the air." I add.

Vincent laughs, his arm around my back, "Ah yes, I can imagine you hate the developers and the 'money in the air' knowing you, you would like everything to stay the same, natural, dirt roads, thatched huts, people eating from the land, climbing trees for coconuts, fishing with a line and a worm from a wooden panga, right?"

"Right, but I am fascinated by film making, it is an important art form you know. I can't wait till they come down here and get going on the movie."

Vincent frowns, I feel his disapproval. "Then when will you be coming back to San Francisco?"

"I'm not sure, is there a hurry?"

"No, I guess not, I would like you to be closer to me…things at the office are still in a state of flux with this problem of the missing funds but I hope by the end of the year it will be over with." He puts out his cigarette in a big oyster shell that is an ash tray. "Well, let's say we get going to town. I think I need a nap."

The afternoon rain has begun. We run to the truck, soaking wet in the process.. Vincent is going to drive since Roland is too sotted at this point.

We make our way through the down-pour, dodging the pot holes in the black top road. "How is Thom doing these days? I ask as we bump along .

"Good I guess, I don't see him too much, he has his secretary, Nancy living in your apartment and of course that bureaucrat is in my old flat, big change."

"So Nancy has my place, I guess that means I am out of there..but all my things are there still. What is going on?"

"I think dear girl that he is pissed at you and probably at me because you are with me. Simple. You didn't think you could keep on sleeping with both of us now did you" He turns his head away from the road and grins his evil grin at me.

I shift a bit uncomfortably and return his smile, "Maybe I did, I don't know what I thought, only that I was in love with you and that you are married."

"Not for long, I have discussed divorce with Phyllis and I think she will go along with it. I will be free for you… we will be so happy together, flying all over the continent, fishing trips, you can do water colors while I feed us from the land. We will survive on coconuts, berries and fish. How does that sound?"

"It sounds divine. I am thinking about this trip tomorrow. We should take a panga to Playa Dos Santos up the coast. It is really rustic, you will love it. No electricity, just little thatched huts for people to stay, the river is crystal clean and sand like a beige face powder, fish leap out of the water of the small bay there. The restaurant will cook up the fish that you catch for your lunch, or dinner or breakfast even. We can stay there for a day or two or forever." I lean over and kiss his cheek.

"Sounds wonderful honey, you take care of it

We stop at my apartment and take in Vincent's travel items, then he drives Roland to the restaurant, a block away and leaves him there to continue drinking.

Back in my apartment,Vincent falls asleep almost immediately laying down on one of the twin beds. I watch him as he begins to snore. His mouth slightly ajar. I wonder what the future may hold for us. I know he wants me to return to San Franciso but lately I am liking my freedom here, and more with the sales of my paintings. And then, there is the prospect of the film that is going to be made here, I find that exciting…all those creative people milling about in this small village where there is hardly any way to get in and out. Hmm.

When I go to make reservations for a two day stay in Playa Dos Santos, I find I have to go to the restaurant, Las Olas, the enemy territory of Rolando where I am forbidden to go..

As I wait at the desk in Las Olas I sense someone behind me and turn and there is Sergio Montes Cruz, the handsome head of Obras Publicas in Las Peñas. He smiles at me warmly and leans forward to kiss my cheek.

"Hola, Joanna, how nice to see you here, why you don come here to have a drink weeth us. I want very much to see your work and I think I would like to exhibit your paintings here in Las Olas."

"Oh, thank you Sergio, that is very nice…of course. Right now I have to hurry back, I have a guest from San Francisco." He is so good looking I find myself catching my breath.

"I jus want a few minutes of yur time, I want yu to meet some people, they have just arrived here in Las Peñas. pleeze, sit down with us a moment." And he takes my arm persuasivly and quides me to his table.

"But I need to make reservations at the hotel in Los Santos.." I protest.

"Don yu worry, we will make them from the table…just yu relax and seet weeth us a minute, what do you wan to drink?"

He acts like he owns the place and he actually does.

The people sitting at his table exhude positive energy, the cream of creative Hollywood and Mexican artistic endeavor. There is almost a collective halo shining around them. They are the *movie people.*

"And thees is Manuel Ortega, the famoso film photographer from Mexico City, Yolanda Fernandez who is doing the costumes, my cousin, the engineer Antonio del Valle who is in charge of designing and building the sets, Tony Pierce the artistic designer. Alabama Witherspoon the writer of the book that zee film is based on. And the artists/actors; Sheila Pendleton, Adele Ferber and Richard Peterson. That leetle fellow sitting there is my son Luis who ees too young to do anything yet." He laughs and the boy shifts in his seat under the scrutiny.

"My friends, thees is the very talented arteesta from San Francisco, Joanna Botticelli." The men stand up and offer their handshake to me while the women nod with polite smiles. It is rather overwhelming as I sit down in the equipale chair that Sergio holds for me, smiling furiously.

"And what would you like to dreenk my dear?" inquires Sergio as he sits himself next to me..

"Nothing really, I have a friend waiting for me in my apartment I really can't stay very long."

The man seated on the other side of me, Antonio del Valle, the man who had helped us in the hardware store, leans over toward me, he is more handsome than I remember. If that be possible. He has dark skin, thick black hair, a wide face with sparkling brown eyes…a mustache bristling over a wide grin exhibiting perfect white teeth. He is devastating. He speaks. "I want very much to see yur work Miss Joanna Botticelli, we are going to make art exhibits here in the restaurant, yu will be able to sell your work and make Las Peñas a more arteestic place here on the coast, more importante than Acapulco."

"That, that would be very nice Señor del Valle, I think next week I could show you my work, I have a friend here and…"

"No, no, yur friend can wait, yu must have a drink with us, eet is raining, just a little drink, not so much to make yur friend worry. Waiter," he calls," bring Miss Botticelli Ron Castillo on the rocks." No need for me to make a decision on what I drink, so familiar.

Those at the table are engaged in tense conversations among themselves concerning the coming film project. My drink sits in front of me, condensation running down the sides of the glass, the ice cubes rapidly dwindling in the tropical heat diluting the light brown rum. I take a sip, it is good, rather sweet and strong.

"Pleeze, call me Tonio," he asks and he lifts his glass to clink with mine. I lift my glass and then so does everyone else at the table and we all clink glasses. This is all very diverting but I do worry about Vincent back at the apartment.

"Antonio, can I come back another time to talk to you about this, I really have to go…I need to make reservations for tomorrow…"

"Si, si…there is the majordomo, he can make yur reservations."

I drink down my Castillo on the rocks, and rise. I want to just slip away, but Sergio and Tonio get up and escort me to the desk where I fill out the proper forms and put down a small deposit in pesos. La Ramada was never this exciting.

They both kiss me on the cheek and I take leave of this illustrious group of people for the time being to return to my sleeping hero.

Vincent is still sleeping. I lay down on the other bed and mentally peruse what has just happened. It seems an incredible thing that I should go to this very isolated place in the world and end up on the midst of the celebrity stars of the moment. The director, Raymond Morrison, famous for his rugged Western films, an imposing figure with white hair and a bristly white beard, a tall, lean man with a stentorian voice. Then there is Alabama Witherspoon, a writer of intense novels of disillusioned men and women coping with cruel and alienating environments. He looks unkempt, he drinks a lot and is gay. Manuel Ortega, the Mexican photographer is very dark, with long straight black hair, a very serious face, his eyes seem to glare out at the world, he is very much of Indigenous descent. Yolanda Fernandez, the costume designer seems to be a jolly sort, a plain woman, her hair pulled back in a bun, on the heavy side but very animated. Tony Pierce is from Los Angeles and has been the set designer on various films for Seven Arts, the film company producing the film, he is youthful and good looking with sandy hair and freckles.

The actors are another story, stunning with their familiar faces, the aura of their various film personages coloring their existence. The star is Sheila Pendleton, a striking beauty with alabaster skin, black hair flowing about her shoulders and perfect features. It is rumored that Adele Ferber, who is the lover of Richard Peterson the male star of the film, has arrived in Las Peñas to chaperone Richard. She is afraid that Sheila will take her lover Richard away from her. Adele Ferber is considered the most beautiful woman in the world, one would wonder at such insecurity on her part. She was a child star who matured into the beauty of adulthood to star in many films. She has jet black hair and white skin, her hair is short and fluffs out around her face, she is not very tall but with her lovely, violet colored eyes she commands those around her. Richard Petersen is ruggedly handsome, he has a broad face and intense blue eyes. He shows the beginning of the ravages of age, hurried along by too much alcohol. Sadly, it only seems to make him more attractive.

The rain is still coming down in sheets. Vincent stirs, the wind coming off the ocean is wet and chilly. I close the terrace doors and go to the kitchen to make coffee.

"Come here honey, I need you." He is awake. I slide in next to him and in a minute he is making love to me, hard and urgent. Everything is forgotten in the heat of our mutual union. After, spent, I lay in his arms, wet with perspiration, watching the rain pouring down almost next to us.

"Tomorrow we are going to the next best thing to the garden of Eden," I say as he lights cigarettes for us both.

"I can hardly wait," he says cupping my breast in his hand, then leaning over to kiss my nipple. Like a child of his will do one day.

The next day is bright and sunny, hot and humid, without a cloud in the sky. We wait on the rustic, wooden dock for our boat ride to Playa Dos Santos. We have a few clothes packed and a small ice chest with the champagne and snacks. I wear a bathing suit with with my home sewn, lacy robe over it, sandals and my hair in a pony tail, covered by a wide brimmed straw hat.. Vincent has on a khaki hat, shorts,and khaki shirt with huaraches on his tender city feet.

I love the boat trip, hugging the coast, the small speed boat bouncing over the gentle waves of the Bay. We are soon covered in salt spray. The deep emerald green high mountains are covered with thick, impenetrable jungle, tumbling down to the roiling blue sea take my breath away with their beauty. I love the farthest mountains, some over 12,000 feet, pale blue in the distance, I'm always wondering what lies behind them.

"Vincent, what do you think lies behind those high mountains off into the distance?" I ask loudly over the roar of the boat motor.

He turns to me smiling, "I know my dear, I have been there."

"Really? Tell me."

"There is a beautiful big mountain valley at around 4,000 feet. It is Shangri-la."

"You're kidding! Shangri-la, like the hidden valley in the Himalayas in the World War II movie, 'Lost Horizons', where the plane crashes and the surviving American pilots find a society where no one ever grows old?"

"Yeah, just like that except they call it 'El Valle Encantado', the enchanted valley. It's really beautiful, a few sprawling haciendas here and there, all pine trees and oaks, orchids hanging from the trees, and wonderful hospitable people like you have never met in your life. You would love it. We'll go on my next trip here, that is if you are still here."

"I will definitely stay for that."

We sit quietly, drinking beer for the rest of the trip thinking about the enchanted valley.

The boat eases up to beach at Playa Dos Santos, we jump out and wade the few meters of gentle surf to shore. Vincent pays the boat man, asking him to pick us up in two days. The boat is gone in a flurry of sea spray.

We sit down in some low slung beach chairs under a thatched palapa and have a delicious lunch of fresh water lobster and tacos of red snapper fish, all washed down with Bohemia beer. We doze after lunch in the beach chairs, the rising tide lapping at our feet, while our simple cabin of thatched palm leaves is arranged for us.

The cabin is more like a round hut, smelling of fresh cut palm fronds, two double beds with fresh, clean white sheets await our arrival. The floor is concrete, with a small bathroom and shower, a wash basin and toilet off to one side. The windows are simple square openings in the walls with wooden shutters to hold off the rain and cool winter nights.

"Which bed do you want?" Vincent asks as he takes off his clothes in order to take a quick shower.

"We'll sleep together of course, when we rumple the first bed we will change to the other bed and so on, okay?"

The rest of the day is passed in slow love making and sleeping, we are like two halves of a person, coming together like magnets to create one.

Night falls and the sounds of the jungle surround us, chirping, peeping, sometimes a screech in the distance as the animals prowl about their night business. The darkness is thick, impenetrable. Vincent and I sleep embracing each other, seeking comfort in this very primitive environment.

The day dawns bright with sunshine and the call of various jungle birds. Parrots of different sizes and colors. And then, as I step out of the door, there is an Iguana. A shiver of apprehension passes through my body. The Iguana is huge, like a prehistoric monster almost two meters long stretched out on the sand. All scales and wrinkled with dragon-like spikes flowing down his spine from his massive head to his tail, silver, gold and green colored with eyes like shining round crystals with dense, black mascara drawn around them. It sees me but does not move. I do not move.

"Vincent, come here quick, look!"

"Yeah, that's an Iguana alright, don't bother him, just walk around him." He takes my hand and we slowly creep around the creature on our way to breakfast in the restaurant.

"I hope he is there when we go back, I want to take his picture, I want to paint him, I have never seen such an exotic creature up close. Do you think he bites?" I ask after our breakfast of ranch style eggs.

"Probably, everything bites, including me…finish your coffee so we can go fishing, We are going to have to catch our lunch."

"The movie is going to be about an Iguana. How can people who have never seen one up close possibly imagine the thing realistically.?" I ask rhetorically.

"They'll figure it out, most people have never been in a gunfight at the O.K. Corral that doesn't stop them from enjoying it all vicariously in a film."

The man in charge of the pangas, pushes us off gently into the small bay of Dos Santos. The water is crystal clear. Myriads of fish from small to very large swirl beneath us. Vincent hands me a fishing pole with a shrimp-like morsel hooked on the end of the line for bait. Laughing at my ineptness, I drop my line and feel a tug immediately.

"Quick, pull it in!" he shouts.

I pull it in and there is nothing there, the hook, the bait and part of the line are gone!

"Where'd it go? How could the fish eat the hook. It must have been enormous."

Vincent fixes me another bait and we row out farther toward the sea. By now Vincent has caught several fish of various varieties and sizes. I finally catch one, and then more. It is so easy, there are *so many fish*.

We paddle around, absorbing the beauty of the shore line which is really a mountainside. There, several *real* huts are clustered on the slopes among the coconut palms and other tropical vegetation. Indigenous people live in them with their families, living off the land just as in my fantasy ruminations.

Back on shore, the cook takes our catch, selects what he knows to be the best tasting fish and goes about preparing it for us for lunch. The rest is divided among the workers at the hotel.

And so the days pass in Dos Santos in a lulling sensual bliss which neither of us have ever experienced before or since. The Iguana was gone from the entrance to our room when we returned from lunch, but there would be other Iguanas among the monsters I would experience before I leave Las Peñas.

Vincent leaves with a promise to return as soon as possible. I surprise my self by shedding a tear as he flies off. I hardly ever cry. I return to my apartment by the sea and my increasingly interesting life.

It is a bright, sunny and hot late morning in Las Peñas. I am wearing a tee shirt and shorts with woven Indian style sandals on my feet as I work on a painting in my kitchen/studio.

Cesar returns. The heavy twin engine Cessna over-flies Las Peñas, not actually buzzing the beach but enough to let everyone know he is back.

There is an ominous tightening in my chest and in a while I hear a knocking on my door, a loud insistant knocking. I look out from my terrace to the doorway below and there they are, the whole retinue of a Safari and two Jeeps with his bodyguatrds, pilot, navigator secretary, pistoleros is what they call them all since all are armed. Henry Swanson is doing the knocking and just behind him Cesar Cibrian Ramirez is standing. He is smiling his wide, menacing grin and waving to me. He is carrying a box under his arm. I slowly wave back

I open the door and Cesar immediately engulfs me in a tight embrace, his mouth on mine, the pistol on his hip pressing into my side "*Hola mi Preciosa, como estas?* Deed yu mees me mi amor?"

He takes my hand which is stained with oil paint and kisses it then with his own small, tough hand turns it over, examining the paint spots. "Oh, mi arteesta, yu are working, *vamos a ver.* Let's see what yu are doing."

Cesar, Henry and I go up to the studio where they examine my work.

My current painting is a study of two Indian women wearing colorful serapes in the market. Their hair is black, long and flowing. They cast purple shadows on the ground and in the background dimly depicted are piles of oranges, pineapples, bananas and other fruit.

"Beeutifull mi amor, I am so proud of yu...here mi chiquita, is a small present for yu, I luf yu." He hands me the package he is carrying.

Henry is smiling his Cheshire cat smile and smoking as they watch me unwrap my gift.

The flowered wrapping paper and garish ribbon bow fall to the floor as I slide out the blue fabric of a *dress*! It is a blue tafetta dress with a lace collar, and a tie that goes around the waist that makes a bow in back. It has short, puffed sleeves trimmed in lace and little buttons that go down the front. It is an appropriate dress for a twelve year old girl to wear to her graduation from elementary school.

"Oh Cesar, it is really pretty," I say, "but I cannot accept this gift from you."

His smile disappears and his mouth is set in a straight, stern line. "Yu must accept my gift to yu, it is with all my heart that I geev you thees dress…yu weel make me very, very sad, *triste*, eef yu do not take thees dress."

Henry waves to me, "I will wait outside," he says as he rushes down the steps leaving me alone with Cesar in my bedroom.

Cesar tosses the dress onto the chair and reaches for me. I retreat but he persists and grabs my arm propeling me to the bed. It is obvious what he wants. He takes off his shirt and his pistol belt and tosses them on the chair from which they slide to the floor. His skin is dark and smooth, his well muscled torso shiny from perspiration. A man who *gets* what he wants.

"Cesar, no, what are you doing?" I cry in alarm.

"I am going to make luf to you, I luf you, I luf you from zee time I first see yu on zee beach…yu cannot reseest me. I wan to geev yu pleasure mi Chiquita."

"No, I cannot, I have a *boyfriend*!" I scream as I wiggle away from him and fall on the floor between the twin beds. Now he has his pants down and off with a very large erection pointed in my direction. In an instant he is on top of me on the floor tugging at my underwear and my shirt while I struggle to push his hands away. I manage to get onto the other bed but he has my foot in his grip and then again he is on top of me, ripping at my blouse, tugging at my shorts.. "Stop" I scream, I am aware I am crying, he is too strong for me, I am naked. He slaps me in the face.

"*Lo siento*, I sorry, no yu scream, let me have yu, yu will like eet, stop fighting weeth me and let me make luf to yu…"

He has my arms pinned down and I can feel his cock moving against my inner thighs.

"Yu wan me to call mis amigos to help me control yu mi chiquita? Eff zey come up here zey will wan their turn weeth yu, yu wan that?"

"No."

"Mis amigos wud not hurt you, they would kiss yur cunt wiz zer tongues and make you cum and cum. Now calmate, let me go into you, don fight me no more…okay?"

He spreads my legs with one hand and fingers the soft folds there. "Yu are wet!"

How can I be wet, this man is attacking me, I am being raped I think..how can this be?

Cesar slides his penis into my body and fills me, I stop fighting him and accept the inevitable, his ferocious thrusting then the final ejaculation. He moans in ecstasy, then collapses on top of me. The eternal human life force satiated.

There is silence now, only our breathing and the sound of the waves below my terrace. He strokes my breasts absently,

After a while he sits up. He looks happy. "I do not like to force yu, but yu make me no choice what to do. *Me encanta tus pechos, blancos y rosas, como flores.* Now I wash myself in yur badroom."

My clothes are torn and in disarray. I pull the bed sheet up over me, waiting for him to leave to deal with this. He is trying to bathe in my pitiful shower, just a trickle of cold water.

As he dresses he is smiling. "I wan to buy yur painting Chiquita, the one yu are painting now…okay? How much you wan for dat painting?"

"Nothing, I don't want to see you again, ever."

He laughs, "I know yu need zee pesos, yu feenish the painting and geev eet to me, okay? I am sourry eef I hurt yu, I don wan hurt yu, I luf yu."

He leaves a wad of pesos on my dresser, turns and is gone down the stairs. I hear them talking and laughing below on the street, then the sound of the Safari and the two Jeeps starting up and leaving.

I can't work. My face is red where he slapped me. After a quick cold shower I put on my bathing suit and go down to swim in the purifying waters of the Pacific Ocean. As I paddle around on my back, beyond the waves breaking, I run through my mind what has just transpired. It was shocking, that never happened to me before. I am fortunate that I just had ended my menstrual period so I won't get pregnant. The rythmn routine is well known to me since my husband and I used it to get pregnant which never happened. I have a diaphragm which I can insert to prevent a pregnancy but it lies in my drawer along with the spermacide, only used when I am anticipating intercourse. But this was not anticipated, maybe I should have expected it but the reality is I did not. I consider myself invincible, *until now.*

I lie in the warm, salty water until I am exhausted. I shun any social involvement despite the invitations called out to me from the restaurants as I trudge through the sand on my way back to the solace of my apartment.

Insomnia shadows my nights as I relive the scene of my violation. I have failed Vincent. Guilt haunts me. He will probably never know what happened unless I tell him. I resolve not to tell him. Was there pleasure involved on my part as I succumbed to Cesar? Maybe there was some I think and then dismiss the thought. There can be no pleasure in rape. Or can there be? I can only overcome my mental agony when Vincent returns.

CHAPTER V

Interlude

During the following days the Hollywood film company delivers an old bus onto the beach below my apartment. It is a stormy day, there is a hurricane swirling off the coast. The clouds and the rain reach down to the sandy beaches obscuring the mountains and the town. High waves smash down and over the bus as men holding ropes tied to the raft carrying the bus struggle to bring it to shore. I lean out from my terrace, fascinated by the spectacle. The raft with the bus heaves and rolls, almost tipping into the raging surf. There must be 12 young men engaged in the effort, straining against the waves to safely beach the vehicle. There is no other way to bring the bus into Las Peñas. The bus is critical to the story of the movie they are going to make here.

Finally, with one final great effort between the men in the water pushing on the raft and those on shore tugging the ropes, they bring it all in to safety. There the bus sits incongruously on the beach of the dead, Los Muertos, as the men lay back in the sand to catch their breath.

Later on in the day I wander down to the restaurants, debating which one I should enter. I decide on Las Olas, the tie between me and Vincent's circle of friends has loosened and I don't often go into the La Ramada. Beverley is sitting with her small child at one of the tables and I sit down with her. She seems calm. Her bruises are healed.

She is a pretty woman of medium height, about 20 years old, with pale skin, freckles and blue eyes. Her blond hair falls loosely around her shoulders, she appears frail. The bulge under her smock suggests she is going to have another child.

"I am not with Jose anymore, but my little girl misses him." She reaches down and picks up the child who has a fistful of sand. She feeds the little girl a bit of avocado.

"That is too bad Beverley, what will you do? You are pregnant now."

"I am staying with friends of Sally Dimond in Gringo Gulch, they are helping me until I can figure out what to do." She is twisting a paper napkin in one hand, her predicament is palpable.

A waiter comes by for an order. I ask for lemonade for us both.

"Why don't you go back to Canada with your family?"

"I cannot, they have totally disowned me, I have no family." She begins to cry. I hadn't realized she was in such a bad place.

The day is still stormy, unusual for the rainy season when the sun shines in the morning and early afternoon and then the rain arrives later. The hurricane still rages off the coast. The sky continues to exhibit various shades of gray, almost blue black in places where it intends to rain down again. We sit quietly sipping the lemonade and watch the child play in the sand at our feet.

"I will probably go back to Jose," she says in a whisper, "at least with him I feel I belong, even though he is so brutal, I have no choice. He wants me back."

I have no experience with such profound problems, so enveloped in my own quandaries, but this situation seems unsolvable.

Suddenly she brightens. "Did you see the bus they brought in for the film?"

"Yes, they dragged it in through the surf right below my apartment. Whatever is it for, what is the story about?"

Then, suddenly a man comes by, stops and stands looking at us. He is the darkly handsome cousin of Sergio Cruz, Antonio del Valle, the engineer who I am told is in charge of the construction of the set of the film, "My Beloved Iguana."

"Hola Ladies, how very nice to see yu here, how do yu like our leetle hurricane? May I seet down weeth yu charming wimmens?"

"Of course Tonio, do you know Joanna?" says Beverley.

"Si, si.. we have met each other," he says as he sits down next to me, smiling. He takes out a package of cigarettes from his shirt pocket and offers us a smoke. Beverley refuses but I take one, cigarettes are hard to come by at times here in the tropics.

Tonio is very attractive, the men are driving me crazy lately. Except for Cesar it is a nice crazy. There is an awkward silence as we smoke.

"What is the movie about?" I ask, coughing a bit from the strong tobacco.

"Ees very, very eenteresting movie. Yu mus forgeeve my Eengleesh, Eet ees verey bad, But I weel try to tell yu thee story."

"Ees a grupo of turistas from the states, zay are very neurotic peoples. The Doctor who ees their psychiatrist, she is in charge of these peoples. She believes that zee people weel become normal when zey spend time weeth Nature. So zey go around the Mexico mountains in the old bus and finally they come to "Los Quelites" to a hotel on zee beach. We are making zee hotel now on Los Quelites beach. But in zee movie eet has a deeferent name. Okay, zen zee owner of zee hotel ees a drunken man who keeps a beeg Iguana in zis hotel, he lufs zee Iguana. He ees played by Richard Peterson. But zen, one of the wimmens, I think eet ees the Psychiatreest who ees played by Sheila Pendleton, she falls in luf wiz zis man…well, lots of theengs happens and at zee end, Sheila kills the Iquana, and then everything is a mess.

I theenk it is sumzing like dat. Eet is filmed in black and white. Alabama Witherspoon, yu know, the famous writer, he can tell yu better, eet ees his story, he is a character I tell yu."

Tonio signals the waiter. "Yu wan sumzing to dreenk? Some rum Castillo?"

"No, gracias, thank you, I have my lemonade. So what happens at the end?"

"Zee end ees very bad, I theenk the Psychiatreest drives off the cliff in the bus and keels herself…maybe she has zee Iguana weeth her when she go off zee cliff, I don know exactly the story. The Arteest, Tony Pierce, he makes the drawings and we make the building. That's what I know. "

He drinks his Rum Castillo over the rocks very quickly.

"Wow, how interesting." I say, slightly in awe…the making of an actual movie, practically before my eyes.

"Si, eet is interesting, but I theenk yu are interesting. I wud like yu to come to dinner weeth me tonight, Okay?"

I would like to have time to think about this invitation but there is no time so I just say, "Okay, I will go to dinner with you tonight."

"*Muy bien.* I will pick yu up at eight in front of yur apartment."

"You know where my apartment is?"

"Si, my dear Joanna, I know where yu leef. Now, *por favor, con permiso*, I must to go to an appointment weeth the Arteest. Beverley, yu take care of yur self and the niña, Joanna, I see yu tonight."

He gets up and kisses us both on the cheek and then is gone. He is like the hurricane, a rush of tremendous energy that sweeps over everything and then is gone.

The rain has subsided. I ask the waiter for the check but he tells me that Tonio has already paid.

I think the evening will be interesting. I am sure Vincent will understand that I can't spend every night here alone. I am sure.

I can't find anything suitable to wear. I leave to go to one of the many dress shops close to the hotel. I find an interesting black lace cotton dress in one of them and buy it. It is slightly sexy, or maybe more than slightly. It is low cut, with a lacy bodice, sleeveless, it fits tightly around my narrow waist, then descends into a flared flounce of tiers of black lace. The designer owns the shop and the clothes are quite unique. Rarely am I interested in clothes but there are times when I am.

Dressed and waiting, I smoke a cigarette and look out across the Bay. It is not raining and the air is fresh and clear. I see the blue Jeep of Antonio, pulling up in front of the apartment, turning around and stopping. He jumps out. I call down to him and in a moment I am down the steps, excited for a night out with this very compelling man.

"Where do yu wan to go?" he asks me.

"I don't know," I reply, the wind blowing my hair as we bounce along on the cobblestone streets.

"Las Margaritas?"

"Uhm, maybe not." I reply, thinking of Vincent's friends who are there almost nightly.

"Then I am going to take you to Las Conchas, ees up along the coast in the jungle on the beach, yu weel like eet. My friend, he owns eet, Dick Norwood, we call heem Ricardo, ees married with a womans from Columbia, yu will like him. He is American and very funny man. Always joking,"

Soon we are out of town driving North along a dirt road through thick jungle. It is almost dark and I wonder what would happen if we had a break down but I really don't expect it. I hear the calls of the night birds. The Ocean is on our left, the waves thrashing, thundering. Nature envelopes us making us sane perhaps, like the movie says.

"Yu like thees ride? Eet ees a leetle crazy no? But yu weel like the restaurant, eet is a Motel for tourists, fishermen from zee states."

We pull off the road into a clearing, there is a sign that says, "Las Conchas, Motel and Restaurant" The buildings are low and sprawling adobe, with thatched roofs, very rustic, right on the beach. We enter the simple reception room, a generator throbs off to the side. The air smells of wood smoke, sea urchins, cigarettes, cooking fish and chile.

A boy dressed all in white linen comes to us from what looks like the kitchen. He is smiling broadly, his brown skin and black hair make him a kind of jungle spirit.

He greets Antonio warmly.

"Thees is Toto, Ricardo's helper. Toto, meet Mees Botticelli."

The boy extends his hand and we shake. His hand is warm and soft, he is delightful.

"Come," he says, "we go to see Ricardo Norwood now in hees office."

"He speaks such good English, how is that?" I ask Tonio.

"He was abandonado as a small child, Ricardo took heem to the states for a few years, he raised heem like one of hees sons, zey went to school there, I theenk in Texas. He works now for Ricardo. He has, oh, maybe 14 years old."

Dick Norwood, or Ricardo, gets up from his desk and the accounts he is working on to greet us. He is tall, blond and handsome in a Scandinavian fashion. He has a natural smile and sparkling blue eyes, exuding male confidence.

"Well, ya finally got out here Tonio, left all your fancy film buddies to hob-nob with us lowly peasants." The two men embrace Latin style, patting each other on the back and hugging, there is no other word for it.

"And who might this lovely young lady be?"

"Thees ees Joanna Botticelli, she ees a great, great Arteesta. You weel luf her…and now we wan to eat, we are very, very hungry, what ees good tonight for dinner?"

"You are in luck, we have turtle steak tonight, fresh caught today. Just sit at the bar for a while, have some drinks and I will join you in a half hour, I need to finish some work here, I want to expand the motel into more of a hotel and need to present my plans to get some money for it."

As we turn to go Dick Norwood pats me on the back, gratefully, not on my bottom, and we retire to the bar.

The barroom is out of Hemingway, with a rustic Mahogony bar, thatched roof and huge shutters that open out to the sea. The light is all from kereosene lanterns and candles. It is excruciatingly romantic. A native man plays classical guitar in one corner. There are a few other couples and a group of men, fishermen I assume, seated at the tables with the leather equipales, drinking. Tonio and I slide onto the bar stools and relax, he smiles at me, his face crinkles and he strokes his mustache. He reaches for my hand and holds it a few moments.

"How yu like eet here?" he asks, as he takes out a package of cigarettes from his shirt pocket and offers me one. I slide the white missile from the package and pop it into my mouth. He lights mine and his on one match. I like that.

"It is incredible, nothing like this in San Francisco. You are old friends with Dick?"

"Not so old, he was here five years ago weeth his wife and a son…then he leaves for a while to Texas weeth the family and now he ees back. Everyone wants zee action here now. The newspapers in zee states are full of news of the movie and the actors and Puerto de Las Peñas..we are, how you say eet, booming!"

"Ooh, I had no idea, I thought this would be a quiet little village and it is more exciting and active than San Francisco, you never know."

"What you like to dreenk? Oh, perdon mi Engleesh, eet ees not too good but I try."

Toto appears behind the bar to serve us. He has a white apron on with a small turtle embroidered on the front. He has a little stool to stand on in order for him to work the bar. I think of child labor laws but then dismiss the thought as his wide smile and white teeth exhibit his pleasure at doing something worthwhile to help his patron. His job to is to get us drunk and happy.

"*Dos Castillos sobre las Rocas*" Antonio says, exhaling smoke luxuriously as I sit beside him contented to have him direct the events of the evening. He is exotic to say the very least and I am fascinated by him.

"And so, *Gringa Bonita*, what brings yu to Puerto de las Peñas."

"Hum," I clear my throat, set my cigarette down in a shell shaped ashtray and attempt to answer as well as I can this very common question I have been receiving.

"Well, I have always loved Mexico, from the time my parents came here when I was a child and brought me back a beautiful little Mexican Indian doll. Then, I grew up of course." (Here I give a self conscious little laugh) "When I was going through a difficult divorce, I came to Mexico City for summer Art classes at the University of Mexico. I studied with Raul Anguiano, who was very famous then. I loved every minute of it, the City had very few cars and no pollution, you could see the two Volcanoes every day and the people were wonderful. And best of all, I learned how to draw, Anguiano insisted we draw what we see, we even had nude, male models which would never happen back in Illinois."

"And there ees no other raison for yu to come here all alone to Mexico, no problemas with zee mens?"

Toto has our glasses before us and drops ice cubes from his fingers into the glasses. He glances up and smiles as he takes the bottle of Castillo rum and pours the glasses full over the ice cubes. Then takes a napkin and places it under each glass and presents his work to us with great pride.

"Salud!" says Tonio, "Salud!" I say and we clink our glasses which are so full that some of the drink spills out onto the Mahogony bar. We drink and the liquor hits us both, radiating from our stomachs to our brains, beginning the euphoria of inebriation.

"Now, pleeze tell me, why are yu here?" continues Antonio, determined to know my truth.

"Oh, you don't want to hear, it's a long story and really, I just needed a change and I wanted to dedicate some serious time to my painting and Mexico is such an inspiration."

At that fortuitous moment, Dick Norwood comes up behind us and puts his arms around us both.

"Ahh, compadre, I am so happy to see you and your pretty date. I wanted to talk to you about the film and also about some property I am selling on the point. I can't decide if I should sell the raw land or maybe build on it…when can we get together?"

"Aiee, Ricardo, I am so busy now, we are just feenishing the building of zee hotel for zee set and I need to be there everyday, Zees peoples are so exigente, how you say *exigente* en Engleesh?"

"I think it is *demanding*, that they want everything they want right at the moment they want it."

"Si, Si..eet is *muy dificile* My poor seeister Gloria is going crazy trying to manage everytheeng. Yu must wait until they feenish the film, they say three weeks of shooting and they are feenish, who knows. They are making me so tired."

He looks at me with a little smile, as though he didn't want to tell me all his problems on our first date.

"Okay buddy, I'll wait, in the meantime, your table is ready. Toto will take your drinks to the table. Say, we just got a generator, that's why we have ice,. It works for the refrigerator and freezer but not much else, oh the blender. No one wants me to put in electric lights, they say it'll ruin the atmosphere. Enjoy your dinner."

The breeze off the ocean has become a wind. A storm is coming up, the tail end of the hurricane perhaps. Suddenly there is salt spray from the high waves wafting into the dining room through the big wooden shutters. Then the waves come in, wetting the bar, knocking down glassware and bottles, and dousing those people close to it. They dash laughing to the back of the restaurant. Dick rushes to shut them down before the sea invades the restaurant. I love it.

"*Es muy rustico, no*?" exclaims Tonio between bites of turtle steak teriyaki. "Ricardo want to be close to the sea, but now he is *too* close," he chuckles as he serves me some fresh water lobster from a communal serving plate.. "Ricardo comes from Norte Dakota, verry cold and verry far from zee ocean, now he ees happy."

Our candle flutters in the breeze. The food is delicious and we suspend serious conversation for the duration of the meal.

"And you Antonio, why are you here?

His dark brow knits, and he leans back in his equipale and looks at me quizzically, his mouth set in a half smile. "Yu really wan to know about me?"

"Yes, of course, you know about me..are you married? Divorced? Engaged?"

He brings his hands together in front of him, they are good hands, with long artistic fingers. I like his hands

"Well my dear, I am deevorced..I married weeth an American woman, she was beeautiful and rich and ten years older than me and eet deed not work out. I was her pet and I got tired of being on her leash."

"Really, you were like a gigolo?"

"No exactamente, but maybe yu could say a leetle. I deed not like it and so we split up. No cheeldren which ees the good theeng. And I am an *ingeniero civil*, engineer yu say, but I can draw like yu can and I can design houses like an architecto. But I am neurotic, like the people on the bus in the film and I am trying to get better here in the tropics. I am from Mexico City where my family leeve. Sergio Cruz who ees in charge of construction of zee set for zee film ees my cousin. Here in Mexico, eef we get a good job and need more people to work we always employ our familee, eet ees zee custom."

Hmm, I think, nepotism is the rule here, keeping the family employed. I think it is a good idea. But no children, probably like my ex, can't have kids, probably just as well. "Do you see a Psychiatrist?"

"Not here, in Mexico City. But in Las Peñas, so many peoples have mental problemas that I don feel so crazy. Here ees normal to be crazy. I don need my Psychiatreest." He laughs richly at his observation.

It is true that many people who would be considered quite mad in the United States are doing just fine in the tolerant atmosphere of this country. I think of Roland and Beverley and Henry Swanson and Sally Dimond who are just a few of the people I have come to know here. Here you can be anything or anyone.

Toto appears to clear our table and asks if we want dessert. Yes, yes, I do. Dessert is a traditional Flan, a kind of baked egg custard with a brown sugar sauce, delicious.

"*La cuenta por favor.*" says Antonio to Toto who just laughs and says there is no bill to be paid.

"Ayee, Ricardo, he ees so generoso, we go to say good-by to heem, okay?" He tucks a tip of pesos into the boy's shirt pocket.

Dick Norwood is at the door as we leave. "Say, Joanna, you know you had dinner with one of the best Engineers in all of Mexico."

Antonio has my arm but I can feel him blushing. "And yu Ricardo, yu make thee best Turtle Steak Teriyaki een all of Jalisco."

"And not in all of Mexico?" he laughs. "I just want to say you two look great together, be careful driving back, lucky it stopped raining. See you soon Tonio about that property…"

We pull up in front of my apartment. Everything is glistening from the rain. Antonio has a flashlight since street lighting is quite sparse. He shines it on the keyhole as I insert the large iron key, turn it with some effort and open the door to my apartment.

Antonio is smiling, he reaches for me. I let him kiss me on the cheek. "It was a nice evening, Tonio..*Buenos Noches.*" I say as I make for my stairs. He holds me back gently, "*Buenos Noches, Reina*, I am happy yu enjoy the dinner and to meet my friend Ricardo."

"Yes, that was very nice but I am tired now and must go, *hasta luego.*" He lets me go, I turn to lock my door and rush up the steps to my little sanctuary on Los Muertos beach. I am attracted to the man but do not want any involvement…there is Vincent to think of and he will arrive one of these days, soon.

A few days later I am downtown buying a few groceries. As I walk by the Oceano Hotel I look into the barroom and see Antonio with a young woman. They are seated near the window, drinking and engaged in converstion. He is *holding her hand*! I rush past the window hoping he has not seen me and then reaching the next open window I peek in and he is kissing her! I feel the rare (for me) pangs of jealousy somewhere in my chest area and stop. I walk across the cobblestone street to sit on a bench on the malecon to get myself together again. I am shocked, thinking I was the only star in his sky but no, I face the fact I may be just one of many stars. *Humph, and he is supposed to be so busy.* Oh well, I do not lack for masculine affection. Watching the waves dashing and tumbling the rocks below me, the clouds gathering out to sea over the horizon, my inner voice comes to counsel me.

You have your work to do, Vincent is the love of your life so try to be faithful to him, go home and paint, and paint and paint. That is your life. Forget this man, he is a playboy obviously. You are better than that. You barely know him. Forget him. It is his decision and it is his loss.

Obediently, I trudge back to my apartment, my hemp bag full of fruit, fresh fish and vegetables. Inner voice is right I think as I prepare a substantial lunch of fresh red snapper, with tortillas, leftover beans, avocado, salsa Mexicana, a salad, and a big, sweet fresh yellow-red mango for dessert. I am feeling better, After a rest, I return to my studio/kitchen and paint.

The Las Olas restaurant wants to enhibit some of my work along with the work of some other local artists. Obligingly I tuck two pieces under my arm and walk over to the restaurant. Sally Dimond is there drinking with friends. She waves me over and I sit down with her while Sergio Montes Cruz and a waiter hang my work.

"Say kiddo, you're pretty good with that paint. I love that one with Indian boy and all the sticks..I guess the sticks are firewood."

"Thanks Sally, it's what I do, how are you?"

"Oh, Ah been kinda depressed lately…Ah'd like ya ta paint my dawg but Ah'm not speakin to him. He just leaves and doesn't come back, no gratitude.."

The dog is curled up at her feet, an incredibly ugly, mangy street dog who smells awful.

"Oh, Ah know he's no champion, and Ah'd like the maid to bathe him so he doesn't smell so bad but he tries to bite her so she won't go near the fella."

She takes out a little pill box, removes two small white ones and washes them down with her vodka tonic. "For my depression." She says, smiling a crooked smile.

Her face is pale and cruelly lined with wrinkles even though the scars of a surgical face lift are visible on the edges. Her lipstick is a startling bright red, rouge dots her cheeks like stoplights. The blue eye shadow makes her more cadaverous, she is frightfully thin under a brightly colored Mu-mu dress.

"How is Beverley these days?" I ask, almost not wanting to know.

"Oh, that's a sad one that, she's back with her boy friend and she's about to give birth any day. I sure hope he don't beat her up so she loses her baby. He's quite capable of that you know."

"That's terrible," I say rhetorically, not really knowing how to respond to such an intolerable situation.

Sally douses one cigarette and reaches into her bag for another. She offers me one but for some reason I abstain. She lights the cigarette, inhales with obvious pleasure then takes a swig of her vodka tonic. "Not much anybody ken do about it. She claims to love the guy, no one can do a thing. Ah tried to keep her at the house but she got bored Ah guess, says she misses him and went back to their hut on the hill. It's her life and of course the child's life also. Cute little thing ain't she."

I order a lemonade and sit back to absorb the social atmosphere of the restaurant. My paintings are hung among other works by local artists. Mostly fantasy paintings in bright colors, of flying children, colorful flowers and roiling sea with fanciful birds and fish The style is called Primitive, they are charming and sell well. They contribute to the generally unreal atmosphere of escapist utopia.

A small plane flies over head, low but not low the way Vincent flies.

Many rush to look at it. I go to the edge of the restaurant and stare into the sky at the plane. It is a Supercub. Hmm, I wonder, Vincent isn't due here for another week or so.

I return to the table. Sergio Cruz is sitting with Sally, He smiles at me and stands to help me sit down. They are talking about the film.

"Why you dreenk lemonade, I order you a real dreenk now, what yu want?" he says, his brown eyes twinkling, he runs his hand through his thick straight black hair. His face is broad, he is a big man and exudes charm and power at the same time.

"Okay, I'll have a tequila with mineral water and lemon over ice, how does that sound…rather like a lemonade, no.?" I smile back at him, I like him as do most people here.

He snaps his fingers at the waiter and I soon have my drink in front of me. The trials and tribulations of film making in the tropics are being laid out for us, it is very entertaining.

"Yu know, thees ees Mexico, (he promounces it May-hee-ko) and we are not so fast as yu gringos, for us, what we cannot feenish today we feenish mañana. That ees the law of the land. So now the Seven Arts company is screaming that we have not feenished the set, you know the hotel in Los Quelites where the movie takes place. Beleeve me, eet is almost feenished but they want it feenish yesterday, no ees posible. Alabama, he don care but Richard Peterson, he cares, the wimmen care and they are all unhappy with us. The sister of Antonio who was in charge of things like the gas and the water there, she quit and goes back to D. F. Mexico City. She no can stand it any more so I stay and fight weeth them. I theenk eet will be done in one week more…they must have to wait. They practice their lines, they swim in the bay and they eat and dreenk at night."

He looks at his watch. "I have to go now, the boat comes in five minutes to take me to Los Quelites to see how it all is going. Thank yu for yur beautiful paintings Joanna, Sally yu take care of yourself…I see yu all later." He leaves for the dock and shortly a speed boat pulls up, Two women step off, they are Sheila Pendelton and her maid. Sergio and two assistants board the speed boat and are gone to another fantasy land.

Sally stands up and calls out to the star. Everyone is fascinated as the beautiful woman strolls up to the restaurant with her maid behind her.

"Come sit with us!" Sally cries out.

Sheila is barefoot. Her pink painted toes are dusted with sand like sea shells. She wears a full dark, red skirt and a lacy peasant style blouse which droops off one silky shoulder. Her earrings are large gold hoops, her fingers sport many bright rings. Her thick black hair is piled on top of her head. Now, she has a displeased look on her face which is almost free of makeup but her lips are full and naturally red, her eyes large and dark blue with long lashes, slightly slanted and thick arched eyebrows. She is not too tall, but she is beautiful.

"Oh Gawd, what a goddammed trip this has been, Hi Sally, I think I will sit down a bit, I am going to meet some friends here for a late lunch."

"No, of course, we'all are happy as clams that you join us, this is Joanna Botticelli, she is an artist here. We all want to hear about the movie."

"That is a story in itself," she says as she puts her large hemp bag down on one of the empty chairs, "Maria," she says to the Mexican maid, "you watch this stuff while I go to the little girls room, be right back,"

When I was a child, I loved movies but it seemed to me that those marvelous creatures on the screen never went to the bathroom like the rest of us. That they belonged to a superior species that neither shat nor pissed. I feel vindicated that they are human after all, just like the rest of us.

Sheila returns, seats herself regally and requests a cigarette from her maid who produces a cigarette in a long holder. Then with a silvery looking lighter, lights the cigarette for Sheila.

All eyes are upon her. "Well, I tell you that is no picnic out there on that god-forsaken beach. Alabama and Morrison are in a big fight what to do about the death of that creature, what do you call it?"

"Iguana" says Sally, "it's an Iguana."

"Yeah, what an incredible creature, they let the thing roam around the hotel like he lives there and he is huge. I've seen some little ones around but no, they have to have this big thing like a pet dog but he is like a dragon or something prehistoric. He has a handler but still you never know if he is going to get into bed with you at night or not. They say he or she is not dangerous but I am not convinced. They say they eat insects but that is like eating meat isn't it, I mean we are like meat." She waves to the waiter to order a drink. He brings her a straight tequila with a beer as a chaser, some lemons.

"What are they fighting about?" I ask.

She sets down her tequila glass and studies me for a moment then answers.

"Well, you know Alabama Witherspoon, famous writer, he wrote the book that they are using for the film. In the book, the heroine, the psychiatrist, kills herself and the Iguana at the end by driving the bus off the cliff. Raymond Morrison, famous director in his own right doesn't like that ending and wants to leave the Iguana alive and just have me, who plays the psychiatrist, commit suicide in the bus. I like the idea of killing off the Iguana but not on the bus, if he's on the bus that means I have to spend time on the bus with that creature while they shoot the suicide scene and I dread that. Oh, I don't want to bore you nice people with these silly problems. Oh look, there's my friends, Maria, grab the drinks and we will join them. Nice to see you Sally and nice meeting you, whatever your name is, I like your work. Ciao."

It seems she leaves with swoosh and then a vacuum of air which slowly returns. Sally and I sit, a bit stunned by the woman. "Ain't she something now," says Sally, draining the last of her drink and ordering another.

I glance over to the entrance of the restaurant. There is a very disheveled Dr. Thom Kelly and another man I do not know standing there forlornly. I can hardly believe my eyes. That must have been him in the Supercub that over-flew the beach. I rush to meet him.

"Thom, what a surprise! I can hardly believe it's you."

He grabs me in an embrace, kissing me on the mouth as though we were long lost lovers. "I just got to missing you and thought I'd fly down here to see how you are doing, you look great doll, beautiful as ever…damn, I need a drink, let's sit down. Oh, this is George Foster, the new tenant in Vincent's old apartment. He's head of Transit in San Francisco. We are both dog tired but a drink and some food should perk us up."

Both men are dripping in perspiration, Thom's face is pale and haggard, he looks much older than I remember him. His clothes are stained and damp.

We sit down with Sally, I make the introductions, they order drinks and then I turn to Thom. "Why didn't you let me know you were coming?"

"Well, it's difficult, no phones and I don't know much about sending telegrams, so I just thought we would surprise you. We had to stop in Guaymas, the old Cub goes too slow and then the weather now is iffy. My god it's hot as hell here, how do you stand it?"

"Oh, you get used to it."

Clouds were gathering for the afternoon rain.

The waiter brings the vodka tonics and some cucumbers to nibble on. The two are hungry and end up ordering a full lunch.

"You want something to eat Doll?"

"No, thanks."

Suddenly George begins to cough and grabs a napkin as though he were going to vomit. Holding it to his mouth he moans.

"What's wrong?" Thom jumps up and goes over to the man.

"It's hot, something is hot on the cucumbers, my mouth, I am burning up!" He grabs his drink and downs the whole glass at once.

Thom sits down with a demonic grin on his face. "It's chile, he got some chile on the cucumbers."

"This is Mexico Thom, you know they put chile on everything, it is said it keeps the stomach bugs away."

"I prefer my medication in pill form." He says as he opens his pill box and takes out the little white round objects and pops four of them into his mouth.

George's face is quite red and his eyes are tearing, he looks very unhappy but says nothing. He is the typical bureaucrat from San Francisco. Normally very pale, his face small with a receding hairline of thin black hair, not very tall with a pot belly. He does not deserve Vincent's sexy, romantic flat on Upper Terrace.

"George didn't like the flight down here, long and boring, he says he prefers a big airplane, right George?"

George smiles weakly, obviously very uncomfortable in these surroundings.

Thom sits back after lunch looking over the scene. He takes out his Chesterfield cigarettes and offers me one, I cough a bit after inhaling this unaccustomed smoke. He laughs.

"So, when are you coming back to San Francisco, Or should I ask you *if* you are coming back,"

"Oh, I'll be back eventually, but I am enjoying it here, I suppose you know about the film they are making? And I am beginning to sell a few paintings here and there, look over there at that wall, we just hung those today."

"I don't imagine this salt air is going to do your canvases any good. You should think about that…this place is really brutal."

As he utters these words a shocking bolt of lightening strikes the water close to shore, rattling everything with its force. Then the rain comes, in sheets, obliterating the view of the ocean in a drenching, silvery curtain.

George cowers in his seat. Rarely does lightening strike in San Francisco.

"How are things on Upper Terrace?" I shout above the tumult of the storm.

"Oh fine, a lot calmer than when you were there I must say. Nancy is happy in your apartment and is wondering if you are going to give it up or what. She is divorced now you know."

"I don't know Thom, let me see how things go here. All my stuff is there…I love that apartment."

"Humph," he grunts, "so what is happening with you and Vincent, you still screwing him.?"

"That's not a nice thing to say Thom, but really, it is none of your business whether I am screwing him or not."

He is obviously perturbed. I never used to talk back to him, he was always right and had the right to be rough with me verbally but not me with him.

"Vincent should be down here soon, he is taking me to Shangri-la." I say as I snuff out my Chesterfield cigarette in a large sea-shell ashtray.

Thom laughs sarcastically, "What kind of nonsense is that?"

"No, really, it's a valley up in those mountains where no one ever gets old, like in the film, 'Lost Horizon'," I wave my hand up toward the west where the Sierra Madre Mountains rise, tall and misty.

"He's crazy and you are a fool to listen to him."

"Let's not talk about him anymore. Where are you staying tonight?."

"Some dump I imagine, this place is the pits. Look at that rain out there, how can you stand it every afternoon?"

"I like it Thom. Now, I think you should stay at the Oceano hotel, it's close to everything and it is nice, right on the water."

"Whatever you say. I would like to see you tonight after we rest up a bit, have dinner with us, okay?" His tone is softer now, accepting my assertiveness finally, but there is now a larger void between us than before. I had almost forgotten about him and the times I had spent at his knees listening in rapt silence to his counsels. The relationship will deteriorate without my subservience to his dictums.

Sally takes all of this in with an amused half smile. She stands to take her leave of us. "Nice meeten ya'll, Ah'll be on my way, don't forget yer gonna paint my dawg Joanna, he is expecting it."

The rain has slowed down. Thom pays the bill and we go to the street to look for a cab.

"They call those rattletraps taxi cabs?" he comments as an old chevy sedan, in very poor condition, pulls up with a smiling chauffeur behind the wheel. "*Donde van*? he says, a cigarette dangling from the side of his mouth.

"*Al Oceano*," I instruct, my Spanish having improved somewhat due to necessity.

"I will come by the hotel about eight. I'll wait in the lounge for you. Okay?"

"Yeah."

And my disgruntled visitors continue on their wretched way.

In the evening I wait in the lounge of the Oceano for the two men. The people from the film are gathered at one of the low slung tables, boisterously enjoying their drinks. Henry Swanson comes by to greet me.

"You're looking quite lovely, how come you're all alone?" he says as he sits down next to me.

"I'm waiting for some friends from San Francisco, Henry."

"Cesar is coming here in a few days and wants to see you." He signals the waiter for a drink.

"No, I do not want to see him."

"He wants to know if you are wearing the dress he brought you."

I laugh, "Please don't bring him around me, the man was awful. Oh, here come my friends."

Thom looks much better now than this afternoon, his white hair combed carefully across his noble head, his features relaxed, A nap and a shower has done wonders for him. He is even smiling pleasantly. George is in tow.

"Hi there, waiting long?" he says as they take their seats at the table "No, Henry, I'd like you to meet Dr. Thom Kelly and his friend George…I'm sorry I forgot your last name."

"You never were good at remembering names," remarks Thom as he shakes hands with Henry. "What are you drinking doll?"

"Nothing, I was waiting for you. I will have a Margarita."

"What the hell is that?"

"You'll see." I say squirming as I notice Henry giving his order to the waiter, knowing he will probably not pay for what he is ordering.

Thom's attention is taken by the table of Raymond Morrison, the director of the film and across from him the writer, Alabama Witherspoon, along with the actors Richard Peterson, Sheila Pendleton, Adele Ferber and their various assistants. They seem to glitter as they babble away, drinking and laughing on a level most of us can not imagine. Thom bares a striking resemblance to the director, Raymond Morrison. I believe he is aware of it and amused. Tall and gaunt, abundant white hair combed with care and appreciation. Morrison has a beard, which Thom does not sport, but no matter.

"Lots of talent over there," comments Thom.

"They are the aristocracy, like you told me, right? The aristocracy of the creative is what you said." I say as the drinks are being served along with the peanuts, the cucumbers and all the rest of the customary snacks.

"Did I say that?" says Thom.

"Yes, you said that, I learned so much from you, I hope it was all true."

He laughs, "So do I."

We clink our glasses and say 'salud' in hopes of a pleasant evening ahead.

The atmosphere is convivial, musicians play soothing Mexican melodies, the waves tumble the rocks on the beach next to us with an agreeable rhythm, the people are all attractive and well dressed, the moment has the feeling of well being and my guests seem to be enjoying themselves, finally.

We end up at Las Margaritas, Henry still tagging along. There is a twenty minute wait which is unheard of.

I wave to people as we enter and find a convenient table. The place is crowded tonight, the news of the film has brought the multitudes to Puerto de las Peñas.

After dinner, Thom excuses himself to go to the bathroom

George leans over toward me and puts his arm on mine on the table.

"You are quite lovely tonight, Thom talks about you all the time and finally I have met the talented and beautiful Joanna." He leans back, his face in a tight little smile.

"Well, thank you for the compliment George, I am pleased to meet you also, how do you like living on top of San Francisco…on Mount Olympus no less?"

"Oh, I like it very much, it is close to my work and it is quiet. Thom says you used to have parties there all the time but now there are few parties. He misses you very much, he still loves you and wants you to come back to him. He is prepared to forgive you for everything. Is that possible dear?"

This takes me by surprise. Thom behaves as though he despises me. I take a moment to consider my response.

"No, I am afraid it is not. I care very much about Thom, he helped me through a difficult time in my life and I believe I helped him also. We spent a lot of time together but for me he is now a very good friend, I respect him very much and wish all the best for him but we are not really compatible, we are not what you might call soul mates if you know what I mean."

The smile vanishes from George's face replaced by a deep frown. He sits back in his chair and looks at me almost angrily. Henry, who has listened to this exchange is smiling his cynical smile. I take a deep breath and look for Thom to return soon and remove me from this interrogator.

Thom does return and he too is scowling. "Damn Mexican bathrooms, don't have paper, soap…nothing and they always need a good cleaning."

He sits down and looks around. "So why is everyone so quiet? What say we have a round of cognacs and head for the sack, I think we are leaving tomorrow."

"Why you just got here.." I say, reaching for a cigarette. Henry dashes forth with a lighter.

"I know, but it's not what I thought it was, oh, I don't know, I'm just ready to go, I've had enough of this place And besides, I have surgery at the end of the week."

"Oh, are you operating on Mrs. Van Rohr."

"Well no," he grumps, "she died."

"She *died*?"

"Yeah, she went under the anesthetic and we began the procedure on her back, the thorax, you remember, inserting the bone plugs to free up the nerves and then she just stopped breathing, like that. Cardiac arrest." He snaps his fingers. "We tried everything to get her going again but she never regained consciousness unfortunately." He takes a big gulp of the remains of his vodka tonic, his face twisted at the memory of the loss of his patroness.

"That's terrible," I say weakly. "But still, you could stay here a day or two longer. This place is beautiful, the people in general are sweet, kind and thoughtful. Why there are foreigners who have built expensive homes here just to be part of it all. What has happened to you? You always had an adventurous spirit, you loved the exotic and now?"

"Let's just say I've grown up at this late date." He chuckles at that.

The cognac arrives. I am already woozy from the drinks and the cigarette smoke around me and in me. The music has become loud and boisterous, people dancing, laughing shouting at one another. I too feel the need for quiet.

"Say there, Henry, is it? You want anything else? Thom sweeps his fingers through his glistening white hair.

"No, no, many thanks sir, this has been a wonderful evening for me."

"I didn't get to talk to you much, what do you do here in Las Peñas?"

"I am a..a consultant to new arrivals." He says with a sheepish grin, draining his glass of the last drops of cognac.

"You will obviously have many clients now with all the publicity about the place."

"Yes, I think so."

The waiter comes with the bill. Henry makes a feeble attempt to pay his part but Thom pays the whole thing.

The air off the sea is refreshing as we walk along the Malecon, teeming with people at one in the morning. The sky is clear and the stars bright, filling the sky to excess. Thom takes my hand as we walk. Reaching the Oceano we get a cab for me.

"How about breakfast tomorrow, then go to the airport to see us off, that will make me very happy."

"Sure Thom, what time?"

"Let's say early so we get a good start…seven too early for you?"

"No, I'll be here."

He kisses me goodnight. A bland kiss like a father to a wayward daughter. He is not happy with me. I know I have lost his support and my lovely little apartment, cheap, and with a view, all at the same time.

The next morning I walk to the Oceano for breakfast with Thom and George. Afterward, we clamber into the miserable taxi for the bumpy ride to the airport at the edge of town. I can see why Thom is so dismissive of this place where others consider it to be a paradise. Paradise is not *comfortable*. And is not necessarily luxurious. He is older and accustomed to his pleasures which include good streets, nice taxis, English spoken and familiar food. Here, it is all strange, rustic and sometimes not too clean.

The Supercub sits waiting for them. It has been gassed and checked out. He fills out his flight plan at the desk in the shack which is the airport office. We walk out to the plane.

The sea is not far away, almost like Half Moon Bay but tropic and sultry. Sea gulls scream in the breezes, albatrosses wing their way to wherever it is they go. The morning is warm, promising to be a hot day.

The two men look pale. They don't look adequate for the flight they are about to take. Thom nervously walks around the fragile looking little aircraft, tugging at the ailerons here, moving the rudder there. I think of Vincent's admonition concerning Thom's flying ability but hope for the best.

The airport attendant loads the plane with their luggage. George squeezes his ample self into the back seat, reaches his hand out to me as a gesture of farewell. His hand is cold and clammy in this heat. His face is twisted with fear.

"Here doll, hold my notebook while I get into this claptrap.. oh, I don't mean that. It is going to be a difficult trip I am afraid. If we can make it to Culiacan I think we'll stop and rest up there. Guaymas is too far for me, I'm kind of tired."

"Maybe you should stay another day and get some rest."

"No, I'm ready to leave and when I am ready to leave, I go!"

"Okay, well good luck, I'm sorry you didn't like it here. Be careful, it's actually better that you go to Culiacan..maybe take three days to get back..you have to consider the rains that come in the afternoon."

"I know, I know..,we'll be alright, don't worry about me. Worry about yourself."

I think I see tears in his eyes. This is too much for me. I reach for him, I hug him and give him a nice farewell kiss. He struggles to get into the front pilots seat and I hand him his notebook. With one last look into my eyes, he slams the door to the cabin and I hear the lock click into place. The man is heartsick and angry at the same time. Not good.

The attendant gives a few turns to the propeller, stands back while Thom shouts "clear"! The motor starts, the prop begins its spin and the tiny plane slowly turns toward the runway. Just a mass of canvas, aluminum struts and a motor to take those two men all the way to San Francisco. I watch as Thom waits at the start of the simple runway and goes through his checklist. Then the plane begins its roll forward, gathering speed and in a few moments it is airborne. Soon it becomes only a speck in the distance and then disappears.

I feel very sad as the taxi bounces along the pitted black top highway back into Las Peñas . Why can't life be more simple I ask myself. Why can't Thom and I remain friends even though I am not in love with him? Why? My inner voice is silent.

A week later a telegram arrives from Vincent. He will be arriving in a few days and plans to go to Shangri-La! Or, El Valle Encantada as it is called. I become terribly excited about this and can hardly focus on my painting.

Vincent lands the Staggerwing directly at the airport without the familiar buzzing of the village. I walk out with Roland and the attendant to receive my lover. "Please don't mention about Cesar, I think Vincent can be jealous but I am not sure." I whisper to Roland.

He looks at me with a wicked grin. "Of course he is, no, I won't say anything about Cesar but you better be careful," he warns.

"You look wonderful," Vincent says as he embraces me, his arms passing on a wonderful feeling of security and love. I have missed him. He is sweating profusely, perspiration dripping from his face onto his shirt. His daughter Alice is with him, a teenager 16 years old, blond, blue eyed, dressed in a silky blouse and blue jeans. She is laughing nervously, greeting me in a friendly fashion with a kiss on the cheek. I had met her briefly before at the house on Upper Terrace and noted that she was very possessive of her father but she seems to have forgiven me, possibly because she has become accustomed to her father's female liasons.

"My god, what a trip!" she gushes breathlessly, "I thought we would never get here." She grabs her suitcase while the attendant carries the rest into the office. Roland and Vincent tie down this monstrous bird so it won't fly away on it own. Vincent gives maintenance instructions to the attendant concerning fuel and oil. We move on to the office to close the flight plan.

"Have you missed me?" Vincent asks, rubbing his hand up and down my back as we stand at the desk.

"Terribly." I answer truthfully, Antonio del Valle, Cesar and Doctor Kelley don't count, mere distractions for better or for worse.

Blanca, the airport wife is there at the bar smiling her broad, ingratiating smile. "Cerveza?" she asks.

"Si, si," we respond, almost in chorus.

Vincent continues, "You are going to love where we are going, up over those mountains." He says, sweeping his arm toward the hazy Sierra Madre lying await in the Eastern distance. They are beautiful mountains, beckoning, beckoning.

"When can we leave?"

"Tomorrow, Alice and I are going to stay with Roland, we'll pick you up in the morning, be ready and have a fishing rod."

"I don't have one."

"I have one for you and one for Alice, also a rifle to shoot ducks."

"Shoot ducks? Poor ducks, why do you want to shoot ducks?"

"Cuz that's what guys do, we are hunters, you know that. That's what you love about me, don't you?" He says lightly as we sit down at the bar for the traditional beer at the end of a flight.

"I'm not sure, I don't like the idea of killing wild life." I mumble, knowing how hunting is such an important part of his recreational life.

"There are hundreds of thousands of wild ducks migrating and many of them land to rest, feed and mate on a lake up there where we are going. I won't shoot a lot, just a few for lunch, I don't like to kill them either but it's something I have done since I was a boy. It's a part of me.."

He takes his cigarettes out of his shirt pocket, the package is crumpled and damp but he extracts two unfiltered Camels, lights them both and passes me one. I have missed this. The cigarette is quite strong and I cough slightly. He laughs. "Out of practice, huh?"

"Pass me one. Dad." says Alice as she sips her seven-up.

"Oh no, you're too young to smoke, stunt your growth you know.."

He turns to Roland, "So how are things going in Puerto de las Peñas? Lots of action because of that movie they are shooting over in Los Quelites I hear."

"It's a godamned circus in town now. Tourists from all over coming in planes, boats and burros to see the rich and famous. It's turned Las Peñas into a carnival," says Roland as he orders another beer from Blanca.

"Tourism is money, is it not?" exclaims Vincent exhaling smoke and blowing a few smoke rings into the air. Alice pokes her finger through them like a child, giggling.

"Yeah, I guess. Everything is crowded now, Las Margaritas is full every night, people are renting out their homes to tourists and the beaches are so crowded that the fishermen hardly have room to work."

"That's not good, we are going to have to find another undiscovered place to go to enjoy the peace and quiet." Vincent lifts his finger as a signal for another beer. "Would you like another cerveza" he asks me.

"Oh, I like your Spanish, okay, *quiero uno*." I reply. He is rubbing his hand up and down on my thigh. The beginning of foreplay. The beer relaxes all of us.

"How is Hermalinda and the kids?" inquires Vincent, dousing out his cigarette under his heel on the dirt floor.

"The same, fatter than ever and madder than ever. She wants to put me on a leash and tie me to the house if you know what I mean." He laughs acidly. "The kids are great, growing like weeds, little Tammy is cute as a bugs ear, wait till you see her."

"Well, here's to my co-pilot and Navigator, my lovely daughter Alice." He lifts his glass to her. "She did great on the trip, I'll make a pilot out of her yet, like I made one out of Joanna, right Joanna?"

I smile at this, since I have not flown since my solo at Half Moon Bay almost 6 months ago. There has been no opportunity.

"I hope I haven't forgotten how to fly," I answer, wistfully.

"Nah, never, it's like riding a bike, you never forget, we just have to get you up there in the sky again." He chuckles while caressing the back of my neck with his strong fingers, I feel like purring.

CHAPTER VI

Shangri-la

"How are we set for a trip up to the mountains?"

"Good, I sent a message to Don Pancho Ocho to expect us tomorrow or the next day, what do you think?" asks Roland, fumbling for a cigarette in his pants pocket. Vincent obliges him by striking a match to light the Faro cigarette and then blows out the flame.

"I am at your disposal in this Roland, the sooner the better, I have promised my girl here to show her Shangri-la so let's go ahead with it tomorrow. I'm stealing time away from the office, many problems there that I don't think can ever be fixed but for the moment, let's enjoy it here, that is what it is meant for, right? Life is short." He leans over and pecks me on the cheek and pats my knee, I am part of *his* escape.

The morning dawns bright, clear and hot. We are in late summer. The mountains shimmer in the distance, a faintly purple tone. I study them as we pack our things into the Staggerwing, sensual and inviting, hiding what mysteries there. I look forward to knowing their secrets. What is behind them?

Alice is laughing gaily, attired in shorts and a frilly blouse with her blond hair pulled back in a pony tail, she is youth personified. I am feeling almost maternal, older and wiser? I am not sure about the wiser part but I too am thrilled to be going on this trip.

"Vincent, you've got everything here except the kitchen sink! What is this thing?" asks Roland, holding up a shiny metal contraption.

"Oh that, that's for making biscuits in the mountains, it's a solar oven, it works great. I brought along some foam pads to put on the ground under our sleeping bags, so we will be more comfortable and a tent. It could rain up there. That other box has my little alcohol cook stove, tin plates and cups, a coffee maker to make coffee over a fire, spoons and forks, some towels, lots of things."

"Why didn't Hermalinda come along?" I ask Roland as my overnight bag gets tossed into the back of the plane.

"No, she's not interested in the outdoors or going up to the mountains, to her it is something to get away from. I did ask her. If my two boys were older we could take them, they would love it, but their mother loves town life. Period." He smiles a bit wanly then helps Alice and me up into the back seat.

We are surrounded by a retinue of Mexicans, watching our activities with thinly veiled amusement. *"Es un avion muy grande, no?" Muy muy grande, me da miedo."*

Vincent pulls himself up into the pilot's seat with Roland on the right side as navigator. "What are those guys saying"? he asks Roland as he begins checking the instruments preparing for take off.

"Oh them, they think we are crazy gringos going to our doom, they would be terrified to get into this plane. They are very superstitious, they think that if men were meant to fly we would be born with wings."

"Hah, they are probably right, but I have been flying on canvas wings since I was fourteen years old," replies Vincent, "and I am still here."

The attendant gives the propeller a few turns then stands back as Vincent yells "Clear!" The signal to start the engine.

"Isn't this fun?" giggles Alice as we taxi toward the landing strip. She grabs my hand and squeezes it. "I'm glad you are along, I kinda do get scared sometimes, my father is so reckless."

"We got a little bit of a cross wind, hang on back there," shouts Vincent over the roar of the engine.

He dips the left wings slightly into the cross wind, we gather speed rushing, bouncing down the runway and then comes that miraculous moment when we are airborne, on wings of canvas, just like the canvas I use for my art. Once in the air, Vincent throttles back and we begin the climb into those mysterious mountains of purple and blue, with silvery rivers of water wandering along their skirts. He makes some lazy turns to gain altitude and then we head east with a compass heading of about 90 degrees.

The sun shines into our faces as we go higher and higher to 6000 feet which he will hold until we reach the landing site which is at 4000 feet. We pass between high peaks soaring above us on either side. The mountains are lush with tall pine trees and oak shrubs. Here and there are waterfalls tumbling down over the jagged rocks. A very dramatic entrance to the land of eternal life, Shangri-la.

In about ten minutes we break out of the mountains and there beneath us is the valley, the beautiful El Valle Encantada. We see great squares and rectangles of cultivated earth supporting a massive amount of corn, interrupted by the sprawling, tiled roofs of the haciendas. A river snakes down the center of the valley, meandering from one side to the other.

"We'll buzz the town, like before, there's the Ochoa place, there at the edge of the village, are they expecting us?" shouts Vincent.

"Yeah, of course, I sent them a telegram to expect the gringos from San Francisco," says Roland, his face pressed against the window of airplane door, as if he wanted to actually lean out of the plane to get a better view.

We hit turbulence, the plane bounces up and down. back and forth erratically, tending to make us all a bit nauseous. "Dad, stop the bouncing, I'm gonna get sick," says Alice weakly, her face quite pale, she grips my hand tightly, her fingernails dig into me but I accept the pain since she is the beautiful daughter of Vincent, my love.

"This won't last long, it's because we are coming down into the air currents caused by the mountains," explains Vincent as he banks low over the large, sprawling house of the Ochoas, making two vertiginous circles above the home. I look out at the people of all ages gathering on the cobblestone street in front of the house, children jumping up and down in excitement, grown men waving their sombreros at this god-like, creature in the bulky form of the Staggerwing roaring over them.

The house is in line with the approach to the airfield. Vincent adjusts the flaps and airspeed for landing.

Fortunately we touch down before any of us throw up. The plane lurches along the potted field and stops. Vincent throws his head back and expresses a great sigh of relief, he is a bit greenish white also.

We slowly and carefully get down from the plane, stretching in the refreshing cool breeze, a welcome relief from the heat of the coast. The men go to the other side of the plane to urinate, for them it is easy.

"Now what Dad?" asks Alice, in an irritated tone of voice, her childish patience exhausted.

"Calm down honey, they will be here before you know it to take us to their humble home with all the animals living right there with the family," says Vincent, yawning as he leans against the plane. "This is old Mexico, ya gotta be patient here, they'll be along soon."

"You mean the animals, like the cows and horses and chickens live in the same house as the people?" says Alice, aghast at the thought of joining this menagerie.

"Well, not exactly but almost," says Vincent, amused by his daughter.

I sit on a convenient rock, my stomach accomodating itself to this more serene environment. After the prolonged roar of the engine of the Staggerwing, the silence is divine. But it is not truly silent. There are so many birds singing, insects humming, and what looks like vultures, hawks and swallows dipping and diving after those insects which abound. The sky is a deep cerulean blue, clear. I glance over toward the town which is dominated by a church spire rising above the many tiled roofs of the homes. Behind and all around are the mountains. Between the moutains are seas of green, young corn fields spreading from north to south, east and west, until they abrupt with the mountains that define the enchanted valley.

Vincent rummages in his shirt pocket for his cigarettes, takes out two and lights them for us. "Feel better honey?" he asks as he shakes out the match. "Sorry about all the bumping but sometimes that's how it is when you fly, it's not for the faint heart or the faint gut, but admit it, wasn't that fun, I mean, wasn't that a beautiful flight through those incredible mountains? If we didn't fly over here you would never see it all. This is the Sierra Madre Volcanico, Transversal; part of the ring of fire surrounding the Pacific Ocean, all these mountains were once volcanoes, just look at the shape of them. Why they might blow again someday the way they must have millions of years ago."

I study the mountains, and yes, they do look like extinct volcanoes with deep cavities at the center and some with long flowing sides, like a bride's veil that I know to be a lava flow from ancient times, now long hardened and weathered to support forests and crops.

Roland continues to educate us. "Volcanic soil is very fertile which is why you see cultivation all over the valley. The fertility is the result of those violent explosions."

We are silent as this sinks in, the image of the roiling volcanoes in our minds eye spewing forth huge quantities of smoke and fire all over this valley. Eventually closing all the exits so the water and all the minerals, stone and rocks from the inside of the earth settle down and form the valley.

Vincent and Roland begin the ritual of unloading the plane. They search for the tie-down amidst the weeds and finding the obscure loops secure the plane to the ground. Then comes the rumble of a truck, or possibly two trucks.

The Ochoas et al turn onto the airfield, stop and many children hop off the back of the trucks like so many rabbits.

The men stride forth to greet us, They are dressed in big straw somberos, white shirts and dark trousers with high boots. Some wear fringed leather vests. They all have Pancho Villa mustaches and are smiling huge grins, showing off their big white healthy teeth in contrast to their dark weathered faces. They all have big bellies, a sign of their prosperity.

The women are laughing, also quite fat, wearing lacy blouses and big colorful skirts to which are clinging small children and some not so small.

Roland and Don Pancho embrace, Latin style, their arms around each other, patting their backs. "*Como estas Don Pancho!*"

"*Muy, muy bien compadre y Don Vicente, que bueno que tu lo trajiste el y la familia. Bien venidos!*"

Roland translates Don Pancho's greeting and welcome. Then presents his wife and older sons and daughters. I am overwhelmed; there are so many of them and they are so effusive. Alice and I are accustomed to the reticence of our anglo culture and here, the kissing and embracing cancels it all out. We must learn to be outwardly affectionate and demonstrative. I begin by smiling as does Alice. They are telling us that their house is our house! How can that be I think? If we took their house for our own, where would they live? They think I am Vincent's wife and Alice my daughter. Roland explains that I am a friend and they accept that.

Our suitcases, bags, gifts and boxes of camping equipment are loaded onto the trucks and Alice and I are squeezed into the front seat. Vincent and Roland ride in the back with all the children. My sense is that we have landed in another world, much like the land of Oz. The only way to handle it is to relax and enjoy it with all senses alerted.

Our chauffeur, Gustavo, the eldest son of Don Pancho is driving and Alice is right up against him, uncomfortably so. He is smiling and laughing, asking us in Spanish what we think of their valley. He smells of the earth and fermented sweat. Not an unpleasant smell but quite distinctive. His boots on the pedals are encrusted with mud, manure and pieces of hay. I am sitting next to the truck door and turn my head now and then to watch the minor drama as we drive the short distance to the family home. Gustavo's hand is moving on Alice's thigh, just below her shorts in a suggestive manner. She tries to squeeze up against me but I am already squashed against the truck door. I look out the non-existant car door window at the passing scene, pretending that nothing is happening. She pushes his hand away.

"Quiero estudiar ingles," mutters Gustavo meaninglessly as he leaves off Alice's thigh and down shifts. We pull up in front of the Ochoa residence. Gustavo has to come around to open the passenger door as there is no door handle on my side.

"Oh my god," mumbles Alice quietly as we gather our belongings and enter the home of our Mexican hosts.

The men are jovial, joking and slapping each other on the back. The court yard of the house is cool and airy, filled with pots of palm trees and flowering plants. A corridor surrounds the court with rooms branching off to the sides. We are told that electricity has come to the Valle just recently. We are happy to hear that. We are taken by a maid up the stairs to the bedrooms on the second floor. The court yard is open to the first floor with the bedrooms and a bathroom off the surrounding corridor.

Alice and I have a room together while Roland and Vincent will be down the hall from us. Our room is painted an appropriate pink, some of the paint is chipped. There is a large, wooden wardrobe on one side, beautifully carved with floral images, to hold our clothes. Two twin beds will accommodate our sleep. There is a vase with plastic roses on a dresser and a pitcher of water with two glasses. We drink copiously of the water. A carved wooden cross of Jesus hangs over each bed, meant to protect the sleeper. A print of a painting of the Madonna and Child is framed and adorns one of the walls. There are some Indian patterned throw rugs on the floor, but no windows.

Alice throws herself down on one of the beds and exclaims, "I can't believe it, did you see what that guy was doing? He is outrageous, what should I do, should I tell my Dad about him?"

I suddenly feel a tinge of mature authority and decide on caution. "No, no, don't say anything, that's how the Mexican men are, they feel challenged to assert themselves sexually, I don't mean that he plans to rape you or anything, just forget about it, Vincent will be disturbed and it will overshadow the trip, ruin it."

"Whatever you say," she says, unconvinced and craving retaliation against this very forward Mexican boy.

We can hear the men laughing and talking loudly down the hall.

"Well, I am going to really stear clear of Gustavo, and he wants me to teach him English, can you imagine?"

"I think we have to find the bathroom, I need to wash up…I feel covered with dust." I say as I open my suitcase, rummaging for a towel I remembered to include.

The bathroom is on the other side of the hall way and it is *inside*.

We use the toilet, wash our hands and faces, comb out our hair, apply some light make-up and feel ready to face this new, rustic world.

Alice and I walk down the stairs to the court yard where a long table is set with plates and food of all sorts. Vincent, Roland and Don Pancho are already seated, enjoying the first of many tequilas.

"Ladies, ladies, you look beautiful, sit down with us and have a tequila," orders Roland. The men rise and help up to our places.

Alice looks around furtively to be sure Gustavo is no where near, then she relaxes and we both sit back on either side of Vincent to receive the adoring attention of the men…I feel happy.

We are hungry and the dishes of avocado guacamole, tostadas with bean mix, various types of sauces, some hot and some not so hot, piles of steaming hand-made corn tortillas, boiled potatoes cut into cubes, seasoned with onion and chile, beans, home made cheeses, cheese covered chips and large bowls with chunks of roasted pork meat, called *carnitas,* all quickly vanish and are just as quickly replenished. There are pitchers of sweet fruit water called *aqua fresca* placed along the table with sparkling clean glasses. The fruit water is made with guavas, blended with some sugar and water added. This beverage can be made with any fruit; pineapple, watermelon, mango, oranges. It is one reason why these people are so healthy with those glistening great teeth. Coca-cola and all the carbonated sugar drinks with their chemical additives have not yet arrived to the Valle Encantada. In fact everything on the table before us is from the garden, orchards, stables and fields of this valley. Organic, natural, by default.

We fill our plates and glasses, Vincent who is next to me pours me a tequila in a skinny, tall glass.

"That is cute," I remark as he lifts his tall skinny glass of tequila and clinks it with mine in the classic toast to our health. He leans over and kisses me on the side of my cheek.

"You happy?" he asks sweetly, smiling, obviously very happy himself with whom he calls his two favorite women in the world with him.

"Of course I am happy, I am in this beautiful place with you, my love."

"I do hope you mean that," he says, a shadow passing over his face.

"I do, Vincent, you know I love you."

I wonder to myself if Roland has mentioned any of my escapades to Vincent, Las Peñas is so small, it is hard for anything to be secret.

"Good news sweetie, Phyllis has agreed to give me a divorce, I don't know what happened but all of a sudden she relented; she told me that if I didn't love her enough to stay married to her she didn't want to stay with me anymore, that it was too painful. Then her lawyer contacted me and says she wants just about everything I have in order to alleviate the pain." He fumbles for a cigarette in his shirt pocket and takes out the familiar Camel cigarette pack of unfiltered nicotine deliverance. He lights two and hands me one. It is time to smoke, I am satiated with the meal.

He exhales profoundly, sits back in his equipale chair and makes a few smoke rings for Alice who sits on his other side.

I don't want to pry into what he has that he may lose so I say nothing in response. I don't know that he may be facing poverty in the future. He has already lost a house to a former marriage and now this on top of the fiscal problems of his law practice.

Alice is laughing and poking her finger through the smoke rings, I imagine it is a game they have had since she was a child.

Gustavo and his brother Arturo have seated themselves across the table from us, Gustavo with an impish grin on his face as he delves into the lunch. Their mother comes out from the kitchen with more food which she lavishes on the boys.

Their sister Letti helps her serve. Some other male relatives are also at the table and it seems strange to me all of a sudden that there are only men at the table except for Alice and I.

"Vincent, why don't the women sit down at the table with us, they seem to be eating in the kitchen."

"Here the women don't eat with the men, the women wait on the men…everyone seems okay with it. For you and Alice they have made an exception. Have another tequila and don't worry about it, just feel special, which you are."

Hmm, I think…curiouser and curiouser. But then it gets more interesting.

"See that little toddler running around?" says Vincent nodding toward a plump little cherub bouncing around in infantile joy among the flowers, chasing a puppy who is as delightful as he is.

"Well," he leans toward me in true gossip form and says, "that little child is Don Pancho's son from one of the young women around town here and he has brought him home for Doña Maria, his wife, to raise."

"You mean he brought to his home and to her home a child he had with another woman and Doña Maria doesn't object?"

"No, not at all, these women love children, *all* children. Would you take care of my baby from another woman?"

"I…I don't think so Vincent I am not that noble.
You should ask Phyllis if she would take care of a baby I had of yours and couldn't care for it for some reason."

"Wow, honey, I seriously doubt that, you want a child don't you? I'll be happy to give you one, a really beautiful baby, when the time is right, let me get through this divorce first, okay?"

"Okay."

I ask to see the kitchen. Leti takes me to where the wonderful food originates. It is a very large space with several stoves along the colorful, tiled walls. Huge pots and pans hang from the wooden beams of the ceiling and cutting boards are placed strategically next to the comales. Cupboards are stacked with colorful plates and glasses. Steaming pots are cooking on the stoves while women continue chopping and peeling to keep the bounty flowing. They are prepared to feed the multitudes.

I want to see where the animals live. Leti opens a large wooden door on the side of the kitchen and there we are in the stable. She explains in slow English that before the kitchen was open to the stable but they have since put up a wall. Flies are a problem even though ceiling fans turn slowly in the kitchen trying to alleviate the problem

The cows, with their large brown eyes look up from their meal expectantly. Their calves are nursing vigorously, tugging at the udders of the mother cows. In the stalls further back I see the horses stamping their feet and whinnying. Chickens flutter about. Leti picks up an egg from the hay strewn floor and slips it into the pocket of her apron. The air is pungent with animal smells. The walls are hung with saddles, reins, ropes. branding irons and various tools. To me it is surreal but this is the reality of a working ranch.. We walk along in front of the stalls, Leti stops in front of one of the horses and begins to caress the soft nose of the animal.

"Ella es mia," she states, her mare. A lovely creature, a palomino with creamy white mane and tail and golden fur coat, she is gorgeous. Leti's fingers lovingly stroke the mare's neck and side of her large head. The animal obviously adores the attention and whinnies softly.

How wonderful that would be I think, to have my own horse, but it is something I have never considered remotely possible.

After lunch we excuse ourselves for a much needed siesta. The change in altitude makes us all very tired along with the rich food and strong tequila. Thunder is growling close by and the afternoon rains will soon be upon us, the dark clouds crowding the cerulean sky.

As we go up the stairs to the bedrooms, Vincent puts his arm around me and whispers that he is dying to "get into my pants". Not very romantic but a true expression of how he is feeling. Following the rules is hard for both of us but we must respect the customs of the family which demand that we make an outward show of virtuous celibacy, no matter what the reality of our relationship may be. Even if Vincent is close to 50 years of age, which is quite mature in their eyes.

As I drift into sleep the thunder crashes around us and the rains arrive with a fury. The rain is a welcome guest here on the ranches, soaking the corn fields and filling the springs and rivers with water for the coming dry months.

The evening passes pleasantly enough. We move to the dining room where more food, coffe and tequila is served. A friend plays the guitar in the corner and we switch to candle light as the power went off during the afternoon storm. Leti brings me a bright red and black wool serape which is draped around me. The garment is very warm as the evening has turned surprisingly cool after the rain. The men discuss the impact of tourism on the way of life here in this isolated place and on the coast.

I sit next to Vincent and suffer for lack of Spanish.

I lean over to Roland and inquire, "Roland, please ask Don Pancho if people here in El Valle Encantada live forever."

"What are you talking about?" he says, looking at me strangely.

"You know, Shangri-la."

Vincent is laughing.

Roland then asks Don Pancho in Spanish if in fact the people here never get old and never die. Don Pancho throws his head back and laughs uproariously at this question, his large abdomen undulating from the effort "*Ojala!*" he ejaculates. This means something to the effect that *wouldn't that be wonderful.*

"No my dear, Vincent is just pulling your leg, although Don Pancho admits that many people here live into advanced old age, like a hundred or even a hundred and twelve in one case. But not forever, but who would want to live forever?" Roland asks rhetorically.

Vincent hands me a cigarette with a devilish grin, "Sorry honey, but really the population does live long and is very healthy, it's a great place. Tomorrow you will see the beautiful volcanic lake high up in the Sierra Madre."

"I didn't actually believe you Vincent but it is a nice thought and it almost seems as though it could be true, but only if the valley is left alone. That so called *progress* doesn't wreak its usual destructive force. Like in the film, the woman was young and beautiful only as long as they remained isolated up in their valley but as they advanced down the mountains toward civilization she became older and uglier."

"Honey, progress is inevitable, nothing can stop humans from wanting something better in their lives, not all the books, demonstrations, politicians with their ideologies and it does not matter what a mess they may make of the world." Vincent asks Roland to translate for him.

"Well, on that depressing note. I think I will go to bed, what about you Alice, tomorrow is a big day, right?"

Alice already looks half asleep as I rise. Vincent looks at me sadly, I know he is suffering for lack of sex but this chaste way of life has it's charms.

We kiss Vincent, Roland, Don Pancho, his wife and others there, goodnight. Alice avoids contact with Gustavo who is sitting with a stone face next to his mother.

Alice and I sleep profoundly in our not very soft beds with all the religious icons around us and the security of a strong family home.

We rise early the next morning, excited to be on our way up into those beautiful mountains. We dress appropriately in jeans, shirts with neck scarves and boots. Vincent brings us spurs to put over our boots so we are authentic and tops it all off with cowboy hats donated by Don Pancho. We are far away from bikini-land.

The sons of Don Pancho have brought horses from their ranch in Ocotillo, as well as including the beautiful Palomino mare of Leti and a burro, for all of us. They struggle to urge the reluctant beasts up onto the back of two big pick-up trucks. Another truck is for us and all of Vincent's gear for camping.

As we drive out of town I take careful note of this most different place from San Francisco. We pass the plaza, with towering date palms surrounding the square which is dominated by a lacy kiosk. Many varieties of flowers proliferate in the gardens around the kiosk, roses, daisies, jasmine, copa de oro and bouganvillia. There are many stone benches placed around the plaza with the names of the persons who have donated them and sometimes their ranches.

People of all ages are seated there; talking, laughing or just resting. The sun is bright and there is not a cloud in the sky. A gentle breeze from the mountains fans through the town, the flowers perfume the air. Birds dart among the trees, calling and singing to each other while butterflies ply the floral display. For a moment I forget myself and my problems and just enjoy that such a beautiful place can exist on earth. It seems that these people have not a care in the world, their valley providing for them all that is necessary for a good life. I sigh.

"You alright honey?" asks Vincent, "want a cigarette?"

"No, this air is so clean it seems a shame to contaminate it with our bad habit of smoking."

He looks at me askance. "Really now, you gonna quit?"

I laugh at the notion. "I am just as addicted as you are, I am afraid I can never quit unless for some extraordinary reason."

"Well, I guess we will just take a break from our vice and fill our lungs with nice clean air. Our lungs will never know what hit them after all these years of inhaling tobacco smoke."

Vincent leans back and strokes my hair as we begin rumbling up the mountains. We pass humble homes along with sprawling haciendas, their tile roofs extending over all the forms of life here. Homes for people, for dogs and cats. for the chickens, for the horses, for the cows, for the sheep for the workers and their families. There are family fruit orchards with lemons, oranges, avocados, gauvas and fruits I know not the names of. Then there are the great fields of corn which are truly impressive, the tassles forming a sea of waving gold going on forever it seems, only stopping when coming up against the steep, formidable mountains.

Halfway up the mountains we stop to put water in the steaming radiators of the old trucks and for some of the men to pee. Water circulating in the name of life going on.

Then we pile back into the trucks, the horses stamping their feet and complaining of their unpleasant situation, anxious to be out and roaming the verdant grasses covering the mountains.

"What do you think?" I ask Alice curiously, wondering how she is accepting this most unusual of outings.

"I like it, this place is so different, it's like..like going back in time, ya know what I mean? People going around on horses, no supermarkets or department stores, no telephones and they all seem happy."

"Yes, there is a kind of peace here. They say that during the last revolution there was fighting here in the town and the people had to hide the priests and the nuns from the rebels. The rebels were against the church."

"That seems strange, the church is supposed to do good for the people, right?" remarks Alice, looking very pretty, her blond hair flowing in the breeze.

"Uh huh, that does seem strange, but I don't know my history well enough to explain why they went after the church, maybe they felt the church had too much power."

The trip passes without a problem until we reach the stretch of very steep road. The final grade to the lake. The trucks stop and we all get out to see what happens next.

"We can't go up from here in the trucks, you are all going on to the camping site by the lake on foot or on the horses," declares Gustavo in Spanish.

Leti takes my hand and tells me in Spanish which is translated by Roland, "You can ride my mare, she is very gentle, her name is Adelita. That was the name of a woman warrior in the Mexican revolution. You will love her, don't hit her as she is naturally obedient."

The young men saddle up the horses and strap our camping gear and food to the burro. Then they all three get back into the trucks, turn them around and leave us to our fate.

"Well," says Vincent with authority. "It's time to mount our steeds and be off to the mountains. Here Joanna, you first, you get this beautiful Palomino. She is a powerful animal, well cared for and well fed…almost fat."

A little nervously I slip my foot into the stirrup and with a push from Vincent swing up onto the saddle. Adelita gives a little shudder and turns her large, beautiful noble head to look at me. I look back at her and smile. She also smiles and turns her head back to the road ahead. I take the reins, give her a little prod in the side with my spurs and we are off.

The pine trees tower on each side of the horse trail, which appears to be well used. The air is much cooler than down in the valley, enough to warrant a sweater. A few clouds float across the sky possibly foretelling a storm later in the afternoon. The trail ends on the shore of a beautiful,deep blue volcanic lake that stretches out and around for several kilometers. Wild ducks, geese and herons fly over head, this is their stopping off spot for the southern migration. It looks like a bird sanctuary which my love and his friend Roland are going to upset with their rifles. I brush the thought away as I don't want to ruin the trip with my environmental concerns.

Vincent quickly sets up the tent for Alice and I. The men will sleep outside. Then he makes the fire surrounded by stones and sets out all the cooking parafanalia. Alice and I stand by and watch, the women's job of preparing the meals has reverted to the men and it is pleasant. I take out the cigarettes from the back pack and light one for me and one for Vincent who takes time out from his work to smoke. He looks very handsome, his face is ruddy and lean from the exercise, I feel I love him very much. Roland is more or less useless in this endeavor and occupies himself by fixing drinks for everyone except Alice. She gets lemonade. Somehow, they managed to bring ice up here so we drink tequila over ice with lemon juice from real lemons. This is a special treat as the ice will obviously not last too long. Vincent has me slice up some cheese and cucumbers for a little snack before we are off to hunt the main course, wild duck.

Alice and I put on bathing suits, hiding behind the bushes for privacy while Vincent and Roland load their rifles, putting extra shells in their pockets. I take out my sketch book and some drawing pencils to record the day. We walk along a trail that follows the shore and the men begin shooting.

"Hey, I got one!" shouts Vincent, "look, it's dropping way off there, who is going to swim out to fetch it?"

"Me, I will," I yell, happy to be of service and an excuse to swim in this exotic lake.. I leave off my drawing of the lake and surrounding forest and dive into the cold water, swimming out to where the poor creature is floating, very dead. I take the bloody, bedraggled thing under my arm and side-stroke back to shore. The duck's dream of a wonderful warm place to spend the winter, maybe have ducklings, now shattered.

"Good for you honey, you are very good to have along on a hunting trip. I think we may need one more, maybe Alice can get that one." Vincent says as he takes aim and continues shooting. Roland is not too enthusiastic, I am thinking he does not like to hunt very much. He returns to camp and fixes himelf another drink and is happy with that. I return to my drawing.

Vincents ends up with three ducks for lunch. Back at the campsite, he cleans them and adjusts his cooking fire with the three ducks speared on wood sticks to roast. He heats up a pot of beans and some tortillas. Doña Maria has made us a tomato hot sauce with which we make duck tacos. He serves it all to us on dented, metal camping plates. The food is delicious.

"I bet you never had anything so good in your life," murmurs Vincent between mouthfuls. We are washing it all down with the tequila, lemon and water. The ice is almost gone.

"You really know how to make a camp old buddy," says Roland as he helps himself to more roast duck. "This is better food than the Fairmont hotel."

"You betcha," agrees Vincent, "now Joanna and I are going to take a walk in the forest and you and Alice have to clean up, The cook never cleans up."

Alice pouts a bit but begins by going down to the lake for a bucket of water to heat up.

There is thunder in the air as Vincent and I walk along the lake, hand in hand. It is late afternoon and suddenly it begins to drizzle.

"Let's get under a tree until this passes," says Vincent pulling me along into the forest. The trees are swaying in the cool wind as the rain comes down, the scent of the forest is sweet and musty. The forest floor is covered with pine needles, grasses, stones, pieces of dead wood and mushrooms. Lots and lots of mushrooms. He pulls me under a fallen log. A frog hops away, startled by this invasion of his space.

"I have been waiting for this for days my darling, this has been very difficult for me, you know, not being able to make love to you." He talks to me as he undresses me and then himself.

The rain is falling heavily now as he begins the lovemaking. We kiss and then his hands are all over me. I spread my legs to receive him.

"You are wet down there, I like that, you want me as much as I want you, I have missed you so much. I want you for my own, to have you whenever I want you and none of this chastity thing.."

I giggle a little at the "chastity thing" knowing how much he hates it.

"No more talking, just feel me inside of you. isn't this wonderful, that we can do this anywhere just with our bodies..I do love you Joanna."

The rain is coming down in sheets, hard around us but we are partially sheltered by the log as we wallow in our passion. Nothing else matters except the frenzy of our bodies matching the frenzy of the storm. Rivulets of water pass over my feet and under my back. I pull lightly on his wet hair, loving the incongruity of our place on the floor of the forest.. He comes with a low moaning sound while I am still hot.

"Don't stop," I moan until finally it happens for me. I cry out, he keeps going and I cry again. Gradually we slow down until exhausted. He flings himself off of me onto the wet earth and lets the rain wash over him.

We lie there naked, not speaking for an unknown time, utterly soaked. I sit up. There are crushed mushrooms under my back. I feel like part of the earth.

The rain slows down and stops.

The sun is getting low. "They will worry about us," I say, struggling to get into my wet jeans.

"Yes," he says with a sly grin, "We'll just say we were caught in the rain, but really we are caught in each other...I'd love a cigarette but they are all wet." He holds the soggy package of unfiltered camels in front of me, useless now.

We walk back quietly. I can hear Alice calling out for us. We are very bedraggled.

"Dad, I was so worried about you, you are all wet. We stayed in the tent, it's really quite water proof...but you guys, look at you."

We change clothes, hanging our wet garments from the trees, knowing they will probably not dry during the night. I am feeling chilly as the sun goes down.

Vincent manages to get a fire going from some wood he had protected in the tent. He fixes coffee for us as we prepare to sleep, really not able to do much else.

I sleep deeply until suddenly I wake up in the middle of the night, sweating and terrified. A nightmare. I try to think of what is frightening me and then it comes to me, *housewife!*

Vincent wants marriage, he needs marriage, he needs a wife and even though I love him very much the thought of becoming a wife is horrifying to me. Unpaid domestic labor, I think of my mother and how she suffers with her husband even through she has all the material advantages available. I have protected myself against pregnancy with a diaphragm so for the time being there is not that to worry about.

I can see the many stars through a window in the tent but the night is very dark, there is no moon. An owl is murmuring in the distance and a whippoorwill calls out. I hear a shuffling outside, like little creatures roaming around us. Alice sleeps quietly beside me, a sweet child, willing to accept her father's whims and deviations from what is considered normal middle class behavior. I have been faithful to Vincent, more or less, except maybe being attracted too much to Antonio del Valle but ultimately he did not seem interested in me. My thoughts range over my relationship with Vincent and how intense it has been until I came here to Mexico, and now? Eventually I sleep, a rather troubled sleep.

The next day is filled with early morning sunshine and not one cloud in the sky. The air is cool, a soft breeze ruffles the leaves of the oak trees. Birds flit around us, singing and calling to each other, nibbling at crumbs around the camp site.

"Hey, look, some animals got into our beans, we were not alone in the night." says Vincent, happy to be where we are. "Today we are going to catch fish, lots of fish for lunch," he announces,…."I am going to teach you all how to cast a line and catch fish."

After a breakfast of eggs, corn muffins baked with Vincent's solar oven and the beans that the squirrels left us we march down to the shore with all the fishing gear. I take along my sketch book determined to finish the drawing I started yesterday.

They do catch many fish for lunch and I finish my drawing despite the fact that Vincent is not pleased with me preferring to draw rather than catch fish.. Vincent cleans the fish and prepares them as fish tacos. It is all very, very good and then it is time to break camp.

"I would like to stay longer here," I say as I help him fold up the tent.

"I know honey, so would I but I have to get back to work. You start thinking about when you want to go back to San Francisco so we can make some serious plans."

I nod quietly, not wanting to make any plans.

We pack up the burro and saddle up the horses, stuffing our wet clothes into plastic bags, The beautiful Adelita, the Palomino mare is happy to be on our way. I stroke her soft nose, then with some help from Roland, swing up into the saddle. This is fun I think as we make our way down the mountain, and as for my quandary over my love life, I will put that aside and just enjoy these very precious moments in this very beautiful place.

Back in El Valle Encantada, we are welcomed back into the Hacienda quite exhausted.

"You all look so healthy, but such a short time to spend here," declares Don Pancho in Spanish as he helps us with all the suitcases and camping gear. His sons take the horses and the burro to the stable and we collapse in the dining room, wanting nothing more than to sleep.

The next day we prepare to leave. I feel sad to have to leave this valley which does seem like Shangri-la. Doña Maria kisses us all telling us that her house is our house (*mi casa es tu casa*) and that we must come back soon. Making a living has enslaved Vincent but that is how it is for most everyone I think. That's how it has to be for me too, then brush aside the unpleasant thought. What if we could just live here on practically nothing, wouldn't that be nice, maybe we would become immortal, maybe. Like Thoms' fantasies of the Grecian gods living on Mount Olympus.

We fly over the mountains in the Staggerwing then the great Pacific Ocean stretches out endlessly before us on the horizon. Puerto de las Peñas is a small speck on the arc of the Bay of Banderas. The jungle is thick, dark green and at this time, it is impenetrable. I see one small road leading into the village as we descend to land. I have never been to a place so isolated and so intriguing. I feel glad that I do not have to return to San Francisco and the infamous rat race.

The next day, we return to the small airport to say good-by to Vincent and Alice and wish them well on the their return trip to Half Moon Bay and life in the San Francisco Bay area.

Vincent holds me tight and smothers himself in my hair as we stand by the plane before they take off. He has tears in his eyes.

"I love you so much Joanna, I want you for myself," he whispers to me. I feel choked for words, I don't know what to say to him...I am having doubts and then what...?

After doing a final check of the plane, Vincent swings his still lithe body into the pilot's seat, then Roland helps Alice fit in next to him as co-pilot. She is smiling, pleased to be with her Dad for the long trip home. They both wear dark glasses to guard against the fierce sunlight. The plane door is shut fast and locked. The airport assistant gives the propeller a few turns then stands back

The plane turns majestically for the taxi to take-off. Stops while he runs it up to test the motor then begins the acceleration for the thrill of the take-off. The engine roars reassuringly and soon they are speeding across the runway and shortly, they are in the air. Flying. It still seems miraculous to me. Roland and I watch until they are just a speck on the horizon and then disappear.

"Well, I hope they make it okay." Says Roland as we walk back to the airport shack. "How bout a beer for the road?"

"Okay, why not, I feel a little sad that they are gone." I say truthfully.

"Only a *little* sad?" say Roland, "I should think you would be devastated that he has left you here alone, why didn't you go back with him?"

"I don't know exactly, I am not ready to go back yet, I have three more months on my visa and I want to stay and see how the film goes, I like it here Roland, I feel free and the people mostly have been good to me."

"You mean the *men* have been good to you," he says acidly as we sip our beers.

"It always comes down to that, my relationship or non-relatioship with men. Did you mention any of that to Vincent?"

"Not exactly, but you better be careful," he says ominously, "especially with Cesar Ramirez, he's not one to fool around with…mafia you know, drugs they say. He can be dangerous."

"I think he got what he wanted from me and will leave me alone from now on. Anyway I hope so, you are right, he is not a very nice man."

"Why, what happened with him?"

"I'd rather not talk about him, let's go back to town, I feel like I need a good nap."

"Can you pay for the beers, I'm a little short of cash right now," he mutters, symbolically digging his hands into his empty pants pocket, "Vincent gave you some money didn't he?"

"No, but I have some change…I'll pay."

We get into Roland's old pick-up and soon I am back in my little apartment on the beach. I throw myself on the bed and sleep.

Meanwhile. Vincent has taken the Staggerwing up to crusing altitude, which he will hold more less at the same, 8500 feet. Alice begins to doze, her blond head falls against his shoulder. The altitude and the drone of the engine are sleep inducing. He glances out at the ocean below him, they will be skirting the coast all the way back to San Francisco. The day is bright and shiny and he hopes it stays that way, He contacts Mazatlan just to let them know he is in the air. He talks in English to the control tower, it is the international language of aviation. He lets them know they will be landing in Guaymas in order to go through customs and enter the United States. If he makes the mistake of even one word in Spanish, all the information will come in unfathomable, at least to him, Spanish.

His mind wanders, rehashing the events of the past several days.

The trip was good but for some reason he feels that Joanna is different somehow, not so dependent on him…maybe because she is selling her paintings or could there be something else? Or *someone* else.

He may as well face it, he does not exactly trust her. She is too young and too pretty. The Artistic part makes her more interesting to men he thinks. Maybe he should wait before divorcing Phyllis. Thinking realistically about the situation he knows he *needs* a wife. Joanna is too involved with her Art, she doesn't seem like a woman who will be happy cleaning house, cooking, washing, ironing and all the other drudgery that goes along with marriage. Maybe he could get her a maid he thinks. But no, they are too expensive in San Francisco,, $20 dollars or more for the day and imagine every day how much that would cost. Especially now with the finances of his Law practice all up in the air. I will have to come down here more often he thinks, to make sure I don't lose her, maybe in another few weeks if I can get away from the office. I can't forget her just like that, I love her, she is a special woman, that is the problem.

He feels drowsy himself and nudges Alice to wake up and keep him alert.

"Hmm, Dad, let me sleep," she murmurs.

"Talk to me," he orders, "if I fall asleep we will crash."

That wakes her up. "What do you want to talk about Dad?"

"Oh, anything, well lets start with Joanna, what do you thing about her"

"She's okay, she's like your other girlfriends more or less, she's good looking and does something interesting. But really she is too young for you, you should fine someone closer to your own age, and you should get rid of Phyllis."

"Why don't you like Phyllis?"

"She's nice enough but she drinks too much, that's not good for you because you drink along with her."

"You don't like her because your mother hates her."

"Yeah, because she wrecked your marriage, of course she hates her."

"Hmm," Vincent frowns, he hates criticism, especially from a minor and especially from his daughter.

"Do you think you could fly this thing for a little while, I need to sleep a little, not a whole lot, just a little cat-nap would do."

"Are you serious? Me, fly this thing?"

"Don't you remember I showed you how to fly the Super Cub when you were six years old. You couldn't reach the rudder pedals but we went up and down and back and forth, remember?"

"Yeah, but we if get turbulence, then what?"

"You just ride it out, flying is really easy once you are in the air, the hard part is taking off and landing. Look, you just watch two things, your altitude and heading. These two instruments do all the work…here take the stick. Just remember its not like the steering wheel of a car, it controls the up and down motion of the plane..take it, it won't bite."

Alice places her well manicured, nail polished hands, (now a little soiled from the camping trip) on the control. She tentatively pushes forward a little and the plane dips.

"Ohh, did you feel that? Okay so this thing here tells me what our altitude is and this other thing, this circular thing tells me what direction we are headed, right?"

"Yeah, they are your instruments, so you have been watching and learning, you are a smart blond Alice, I like that. Now you just keep the heading at 310 degrees and the altitude at 8,500 feet and we will be fine. Keep an eye out for other aircraft just in case…and now I am going to recharge my batteries."

Vincent slides down a little in the leather pilot's seat and lays his head back. In a few minutes he is snoring.

Alice hums to herself, wishing they had a radio aboard, keeping the plane perfectly under control. The sweep of the earth beneath them is awe inspiring. They have left the tropics and now are over the desert with its jagged, rocky mountains stretching out as far as she could see. It all seems totally deserted of people. The enormous Pacific ocean laps at the shore, the wetness of it contrasting dramatically to the dryness of the desert.

After about a half hour, Vincent jolts himself awake. For a moment wondering where he is

"Boy oh boy, I needed that. How you doin darling, we're not in Timbuktu are we?"

"No Dad, we are just fine, how do you know where we are?"

"We'll give our co-ordinates to Mazatlan and they will tell us, and then of course we have a map we can consult. I am very proud of you, you are one smart little girl."

"I'm not a little girl Dad, I am going to be seventeen years old in a month and a half…and I have a boy friend at school, his name is Bob."

"It seems every fellow is named Bob, but aside from that, he is a lucky guy to have girlfriend like you, I hope he appreciates that."

"I think he does."

"Are you sleeping with him? You still a virgin little girl?"

"No, I mean yes, I am still a virgin and really it is not nice to ask a person a question like that."

Vincent slides his hand onto her bare thigh, below her shorts and begins to caress her. She wriggles a little and the plane bounces a bit, still under her control.

"I would like to make love to you Alice."

"How can you say such a thing, you are my father!" The plane drops 20 feet, sliding off course as Alice expresses her outrage at her father's suggestion.

"Here, let me take over, I'm just kidding, let go of the stick or we'll go into a spin.

Her face is crimson as she berates him. "What is wrong with you, you are like some kind of oversexed animal, no wonder Mother kicked you out."

"Sorry, I didn't mean to upset you, I just said it that's all, you are so pretty, so young…and me, I am facing old age, I would just like to possess your youth and beauty that's all, you can't blame an old man for that."

He has the Staggerwing back under control. Alice is crying silently.

"I am sorry Honey, I didn't mean to upset you, forget it okay, I can't stand to see you cry, here take my handkerchief. I just want the best for you and I hope Bob is good enough for you but there will probably be other Bobs in your life before you settle on one."

"Everything you say just makes it worse," she mumbles, wiping her eyes dry. "I would like a cigarette."

"Anything you want, they are in my pack behind the seat, light one for me too."

He slides the side window open slightly to eliminate the smoke. They sit in silence smoking, the engine humming as they fly through some cloud formations.

"I just can't believe what you said, it's just too much."

He blows some smoke rings for her to play with but she ignores them.

Their relationship has become fraught with emotions neither can understand. He knows he has a problem with sex, he seems to need it more than other men he knows, in fact he is rather famous in the male circles around San Francisco as a ladies man. Now he has managed to alienate his daughter whom he adores. *Maybe I need to take a pill so I don't get a hard on all the time, whenever I am around an attractive woman, he thinks Some guys need to take a pill to get it up but me? Never.*

He glances over at Alice, she seems to have calmed down and is looking out the window. *Maybe it will be alright, I hope so he thinks as they get closer to their destination, she is my beautiful, darling daughter and I can never part from her.*

Guaymas is looming in the distance, they are almost half way home.

I stay close to home in the coming days, focusing on my my painting and taking care of myself, eating well, swimming in the afternoon and sleeping deeply. After several days of this I feel a need to socialize. The opportunity is always there at my door step. The La Ramada or Las Olas, the beach front restuarants and bars are teeming with people at all hours of the day and night.

Las Olas beckons, the forbidden place the more exciting, interesting place…I go there.

"Hey, where ya bin?" says Henry Swanson, patting me on the back as I take a seat at one of the few empty tables at the restaurant. He sits down across from me, smiling profusely.

"What are you doing here, I thought you weren't supposed to come here from the La Ramada.?" I say.

"I go where I am needed," he answers, arrogantly, taking his cigarettes out from his shirt pocket and offering me one.

I take one of the Faros and he lights it for me. I inhale and look around me at the many different types of people drinking, talking, talking and drinking and some eating and drinking and talking, mostly talking it seems and drinking. I order a drink as does Henry.

"How's the painting coming along?"

"Very well, I just thought I would take a break and see what is happening in the world."

"Lots of things, the film is about to wrap up, lots of parties, haven't seen you at any of them..you're kind of a hermit these days."

"I just don't want to get into trouble."

"Speaking of trouble, Cesar was here last week looking for you but couldn't find you, no one was at your apartment."

I laugh a little, "I was in Shangri-la."

He looks at me crookedly, "And where may I ask is that?"

"Up there, over the mountains in a valley very beautiful where no one ever gets old, can you imagine? It's called 'El Valle Encantado' and it really is beautiful."

"Why would you want to go up there, it's just a bunch of ranches, cows and trees, nothing is happening, it's all happening here you know. So what are you going to do about Cesar? He says he is in love with you and wants to see you again."

"Not after what happened. I don't want to see him ever again."

"Well, if you think you are such hot stuff you can just toss off a man like that, you don't know what you are doing miss."

I see Antonio del Valle standing across the restaurant, talking to someone close to the desk. He looks my way and starts walking toward the table. My heart starts pounding and I wonder how I look. I unconsciously pat my hair in place and sit up a little straighter. Henry takes notice and turns to see what I am seeing. The drinks come, tequila with lemon and fizzy water as well as a plate of the ubiquitous cucumbers with lemon, salt and sprinkled with ground, red chile. The air has become charged.

"Hola," says Antonio with a very friendly smile, "*Como estas Señorita?* He stands with his hands on the back of an equipale. He looks quite handsome, with this small, thickly mustache adorning his upper lip, his hair thick, curly and black. His eyes dark and intense. He ignores Henry. I smile back at him. He sits down in the equipale across from me without asking. He takes out his cigarettes from his shirt pocket and offers me one, then signals a waiter for a drink. "I been very busy." He states in a conciliatory way. "Zees movie ees making me crazy." He continues, "One of zee producers fell off zee terrazo of the hotel set at Los Quelites and broke hees arm, almos he keel hesself. Zee directoro, Raymond Morris ees going to sue us in zee courts."

Henry bursts out in laughter. "That's because of bad Mexican construction, the railing of the terrace just gave way when he was leaning on it, but you all know no one gets sued in Mexico, especially an American suing a Mexican, it just doesn't work." He takes a long swig of drink, he is irritatingly smug.

Antonio's smile fades and he abruptly gets up and moves over to sit next to me, obviously angered by Henry's denunciation of the Mexican court system along with the integrity of the construction practices.

"I know eet was made too fast, the set I mean, zee construction was not always good. Mi cousin, Sergio feels real bad about eet but we are almost feenish wiz zee movie, and I am very glad about zat. I went to see yu at yur apartemento las week but they say yu were away…where yu go?"

"Up there, over the mountains to La Encantada, it is very beautiful, I made some drawings and spent time camping by the lake with some friends." I wave my arm airily toward the towering mountains to the East.

"De veras, Sergio has sum money for yu, they sell one of yur paintings from here in zee restaurant, yu are a very talented person Joanna, I wud like to help yu exhibit yur Art, weel yu let me help yu?" His arm slides around behind me, resting on the back of the equipale. Henry stands up suddenly, finishes his drink and leaves. His task of coupling me with Cesar Cibrian Ramirez now apparently further complicated.

"That Henry ees no good person, yu must not be friendly wis heem, he ees like a, how yu call eet in ingles, peemp? Sumzing like zat. He ees no good."

"But he seems to want to help me out here..how do you know what he truly wants from me. I do wonder."

"Yu are too, how yu say eet, naïve, too trusting."

"I am curious about people, I have been married most of my adult life, I really have never had to judge people on my own, my husband choose our friends and that was that." I eat one of the cucumbers and wait for his response. He is amused.

"I want to see yu more, I am so sorry I deed not see yu after we went to Las Conchas, I wanted, but I was selfeesh and went wiz another girl but I cannot forget yu. I wan to take you to dinner thees night, we go again down the coast to Las Conchas, we see Ricardo and eat Tortuga steak, yu like zat?

He reaches for my hand and slowly envelopes it into his hand, I feel he is enclosing all of me slowly and I flow with it. I look down at our hands, hidden under the table, his a dark brown and mine paler in contrast. Interwoven. I feel the energy running between us, like an electric current, potent and pulsating through my whole body. His hand is strong and warm.

"Uh, yes, that would be nice Antonio," I answer with a slight tremor to my voice. *Damn*, I think, *what is happening to me, what is this man doing to me?*

The afternoon rain begins with an explosion of thunder. Then almost immediately, the rain pours down. A few drips fall on us, the table and those around us. The roof thatching is not impermeable. No one cares, the air is very warm and the drops are refreshing.

"Yu like zee rain Joanna?" he asks while caressing my hand with his fingers, sliding sensuously over my fingers, the palm of my hand and my wrist. I feel that I am naked. He distracts me so I can hardly maintain a conversation…he smiles, knowingly.

Abruptly, I slip my hand away and reach for my drink. "Yes, Antonio, I love the rain, it cleans everything."

"Zee rain cleans our souls Joanna and blesses us, eet ees good to be here in zee rainy season. Now mi chicquita, yu cum weeth me tonight, *verdad*?"

"Yes," I answer helplessly, the huge threatening future hangs over me now, and this man is leading me into the wild unknown. I cannot resist him.

The sky has cleared in the late afternoon and dusk is about to fall as we enter the restaurant Las Conchas. Ricardo is there to greet us, wearing a white chef's apron over his clothes and with a great smile on his face.

"Hey there you two, you make a great couple, I can just feel how you are feeling…great turtle steak tonight and a new case of champagne, Moet Chandon, from France no less, to celebrate."

Antonio is laughing, "To celebrate what Ricardo?"

"To celebrate that the two of you are as happy as pigs in a blanket for god's sake, that is something to drink to, right?"

He takes us to a corner table and lights the candle in its little chimney. I am happy as a pig in a blanket,

"The place is yours old friend, here comes Toto to take your order, whatever you need, just let me know. I am at your service."

The champagne is very cold, beads of moisture form on the glasses as we carefully clink them together and wish for our mutual health.

"Salud!"

"Yu are a most beautiful woman, Joanna, why you not married?" he asks, his face ruddy, intense, in the candlelight, as leans toward me.

"I told you I was married, I did not like being married. Please don't ask me any more about that, talk to me about you about your work about the crazy people in the film and let's just enjoy this place and the turtle steaks and the champagne and the rain."

"And yu and me, Joanna, mostly yu and me."

They bring the dinner. Turtle steaks, medium rare with beans, potatoes, fresh dinner rolls, hot tortillas and a salad. It is delicious and revives my half starved body.

We are not aware yet but soon the turtle steak will be unavailable due to over fishing, it will become an endangered species Like so much other wild life on the earth, but it has not happened yet. All that concerns me now is romance. It never occurs to me that all this beauty is transient, for the moment it seems eternal

""Here mi querida, try thees sauce, eet is a specialidad of Ricardo."

"Hmm, it is good, really good, kind of like tartar sauce."

The champagne goes quickly and another bottle takes its place. I am feeling very good, full of good food and wine and thinking about what is going to follow.

After dinner he takes my hand and gently leads me out the door to one of the unoccupied cabañas. He stops in front of a room, number seven, he opens the door slightly. A sensual aura floats out, of candlelight, air perfumed by jasmine, of sex.

He looks at me, smiles and says "Yu want?"

"Si, Antonio, I want." I am helplessly out of control with desire for this man.

The room is simple, a concrete floor covered with throw rugs of animal fur, a thatched roof, a large king sized bed with a colorful bedspread and some simple paintings in a primitive style on the walls. Toto has already been here to light the oil lamps, one in the bedroom and the other in the bathroom off to the side. The whole room glows softly.

Antonio holds me in his arms, he is a little taller and of a more slender build than Vincent but my thoughts are far away from Vincent.

We can hardly let go of each other, rapidly he flings the cover of the bed down and we are on the sheets frantically removing our clothing until our naked bodies are merged in love's embrace.

"Aheii, yu smell so good mi amor, I have wanted to do thees theeng weez yu from zee first time I see yu," We have intercourse twice since we are so passionate, the first time we both climaxed almost immediately, He blames that on the turtle steak for overstimulating our senses but I blame it on extreme sexual attraction which has surpassed what I had felt for Vincent.

We lie together afterward, I stroke his lean, smooth body, the color of coffee with cream. I run my fingers through the stiff, curly black hair of his chest. I touch his mustache and ruffle it a bit. He likes that, time is standing still for the moment.

"Yu know Joanna, I believe that making luf like we jus deed ees like praying, eet is like communicating weeth zee gods, eet takes us to heaven."

His hand is fondling my small breast, he kisses the pink nipple and I think I will melt.

"And now, mi Chiquita, what are yu going to tell to yur boyfriend from San Francisco?"

"How do you know about that Antonio?" I ask, sitting up in surprise.

"I know everytheeng about yu," he says as he reaches down between my legs and fingers me there with all the juices of our love making. He mounts me again and we make love for the third time.

We lay back, he pulls the covers over us and we sleep until early morning.

The day dawns fresh and fragrant here in the jungle. Colorful, exotic birds call out to each other, filling the humid air with a cacophony of nature's music. There is the rushing sound of the sea, its waves slapping the sandy shore behind us. As we leave, Antonio plucks a golden flower from one of the shiny bushes and carefully arranges it behind behind my ear. He is smiling. For the moment there is not a care in the world for either of us but that will change as it must.

We are quiet on the way back to town in the jeep. This is the beginning of a torrid affair and we both are aware of how disruptive such a thing can be, but there is no escape. We are destined to see it through

He leaves me at my apartment with an embrace and a good-bye kiss. He orders me to be ready for him in the evening as I am now his official girl friend and will accompany him on his social rounds about town. The parties, the restaurant dinners, the drinks at the bars are all part of his job, It is something I can very easily do without but for the time being I am his.

A mad world of social activities begins for me, something I am not accustomed to. Every evening I go out with Antonio, he expects me to be beautiful and glamorous so he buys me clothes since my clothes are mostly home sewn by me, though attractive in their own way, they are not up to high fashion standards which seem to prevail now in Puerto de las Peñas. I take to staying at his place in town. It is a simple antique home of adobe, right up against other houses, one story, painted bright blue, right on the Malecon. It consists of one big room encompassing bedroom, kitchen and living room with a bathroom built into one side of the room. In the back is an unkept garden called a patio and a few straggly coconut palms. It is overgrown with weeds, The front wooden door opens out onto the street and then there is the sea wall and the sea in all its glory. Half the top of the door opens while you can keep the bottom half closed. I like to hang on the bottom half and watch the world go by. We spend a lot of time there in that blue house on the sea, nursing our hangovers and preparing for another foray into what has become jet set society in this isolated village.

"There are going away parties for zee stars of the film, " says Antonio as he combs his hair in front of the bureau next to the bed. ·"Yu be better to rest today, yu don look too good."

I turn over in the double bed that has become home to me lately. It is unbearably hot, the bed sheet is damp from the perspiration from the two of us. I don't know how he can be up and about after our late night carousing the night before. We went to bed around four in the morning. I don't think I can face another party.

He hands me a glass of water. "I don't feel very good Tonio, I think I am going to be sick."

He laughs, "I don give yu permission to be sick, yu rest and be ready for me at nine tonight. I have a meeting with zee Taylors from Canada, zay wan me to make zem a house on the cliffs over the ocean, zey wan me to build in the air, and I weel do eet, yu weel see mi pretty arteesta. I weel sell zem yur paintings to put in the house, zey luf yur paintings."

I drink the water and it helps, then fling myself back on the bed. Too hungover to even talk to him or notice when he leaves.. I just nod and smile wanly and then he is gone. I drift in and out of sleep. Then manage to get up and fix myself some coffee. I brush away the tiny ants munching on some sweet bread I find on the kitchen counter and eat it myself. The maid has come and gone while I slept.

It has been almost a week since I have last been to my apartment at the beach on Los Muertos. I must go there, I must reconnect with myself, the apartment is the key. I need to paint again. Tonio has completely absorbed me into his life, his friends are my friends, the clothes I wear he chooses, I even have my hair cut to please him…it seems like I have been here before. Like in my marriage. Am I doomed to repeat a life of servitude to a man I ask my inner voice?

Only if you let it happen my inner voice whispers. I am happy to hear even a whisper since I have not heard from the voice for a long time. *Go to your apartment and see how you feel.* Good idea I think, and dress myself for the street.

Inserting the huge key into the door of my apartment feels exciting, as though I were doing something very important. An act of rebellion. The studio looks as it should look, abandoned. A half finished work sits forlornly on my easle, a study of two women in close proximity in the market casting long purple shadows on the street, The back ground is just indicated, bins of lush tropical fruit. A brush lies on the table next to the palette. It is dried up. How could I do that, leave a wonderful sable brush uncleaned to dry up to uselessness. The bedroom is a mess, Antonio and I had made love there and then left it all in disarray. I force myself to start picking things up and cleaning in a perfunctory way. The residue of drinking all night, night after night is taking its toll. I have no energy.

Earlier that week I had received a telegram from Vincent saying that he was coming to see me but did not know exactly when he could get away. I felt convulsed with guilt and have no idea how to handle this. Of course, as soon as he arrived everyone would inform him of my infidelity, but when would he arrive? There was no way to prepare myself for him.

I go back to the kitchen/studio and open the refrigerator. I am hungry. It is still working, miraculously. There is some cheese and tortillas, a little sauce that might still be good and some eggs. After a breakfast of fried eggs and cheese tacos, instant coffee and some juice I begin to feel a little bit normal again. The bed beckons me and I sleep until late in the afternoon.

As I lie there listening to the waves ebbing and flowing, the thunder off in the distance heralding the daily storm, I realize that I do not want to go out tonight again to the party. All the main actors and actresses have already left for California and their lives there, the party is mainly for the Mexicans;

supporting characters and workers. Tonio is going to bring the photographer of the film here to see my work at some point this week. I should stay here and work on my Art…but I can't. I have to go with him, there is no choice. The photographer, Manuel Ortega, is famous in Mexico for his talented film work. Tonio says what they all say, *he can help you*. I think I am the only one who can help me and for some reason I am caught, like fly in a web, I can only struggle but it is hopeless. But maybe not, there is the Mexican government and the limitation on my visa. I have to leave in two months or else. Or else what? Jail? No, Antonio and his friends and relatives will not let me get away, they have incredible influence but still the option is there.

I work on cleaning the studio. The maid I had has not come around so I have to look for her if I want her to work here again. Late in the afternoon I walk back to Antonio's place. As I enter I see that he is there. I feel his disapproval.

"Where yu been?" he asks angrily.

"I just went to my apartment to clean it up, I need to start working again Tonio, you know that… you tell me that an artist has to work or they die, you say that and it is true.

"I don like to come here and yu are not here, it makes me feel bad, yu understand me, I need you, cum here, I want to kees yu."

He holds me close, his tongue probes my mouth, arousing me. There is no way to deny the passion I feel for him. I can feel his erection pressing against my lower belly. His arms circle me, he pulls me down to the floor, opening my blouse, kissing my breasts, his hands roam my whole body. He pulls my underpants to one side and directs his penis into me, we are both panting as he thrusts…" I wan to shoot yu," he cries as he nears his climax, my head is against the foot of a chair, my arms around him as he finally comes, crying out in total ecstasy. I have been "shot".

We are still half dressed, our clothes dripping from perspiration. We lie flung out on the concrete floor, recovering our senses.

"Yu deed not cum?" he asks as he sits up.

"No".

"I weel make you cum. Go on zee bed."

He gets up and brings a damp towel from the bathroom and carefully cleans my oozing cleft. Then burying his head between my legs he sucks and licks until I am crying out with sexual tension which suddenly releases into utter uncontrollable pleasure.

He laughs. "I like when yu cum, I like when yu scream out…eet is like eet is happening to me all over. I luf yu Joanna, yu stay weeth me, okay?"

I answer with a perfunctory "okay". Not knowing if I really mean that or not.

"Tonight I wan yu to be very very beeuteeful, Yu wear zee gold dress I bought you from Mexico City, yu look spectacular een zat dress."

I wear the gold dress that evening. The dress is floor length, with thin spaghetti straps supporting a criss-cross bodice. It is a light weight silky material and has a lacy gold stole to throw over my shoulders. The afternoon nap has helped me enormously to confront the evening. I wear my hair piled high on my head with fluffy bangs fringing my face. I know I look good.

"Yu are too beeuteeful for words, not Spaneesh not Engleesh," states Antonio as we walk arm in arm the two blocks to Las Margaritas where the fiesta is to be held. It is ten o-clock at night, the time the parties begin here. We walk into the raucous atmosphere, redolent with smoke, cooking odors, women's and men's perfume. A rock band is playing in the corner, we find our reserved places at a large table of

Antonio's relatives, friends and trusted workers. Everyone is happily inebriated which we soon will be also. The table is loaded with bottles of whiskey, brandy, tequila and various soft drinks. There are shiny glasses waiting to be filled; bowls of ice cubes with pinchers to handle the frosty objects, hors d'oeuvres which here in Mexico are called botanas, occupy any empty spaces on the tables.

We walk around the tables, greeting those there with a hug and a kiss or a handshake. There is Antonio's cousin, Sergio Cruz and his wife, Delila, Manuel Ortega, the film photographer, Tony Pierce, the artistic designer, Dick Norwood and his Chilean wife, Antonio's sister Estella, Roberto and Blanca who run the flight service at the airport, Sally Dimond and her friends from Gringo Gulch, young architects who work in Antonio's office along with the engineers who constructed the set for the film. The Mayor is there with his wife and his entourage…it is a sea of faces and we must connect with each one before taking our seats. It is the protocol of the parties here. It is all so different from the parties at Upper Terrace with Thom and his friends, there is not even any way I can compare them. There is a formality here that exists even when a person is falling down drunk. It is accepted that some are going to be falling down drunk and they are quickly and happily conducted to a safe place and the party goes on.

The music is so loud conversation is almost impossible, but no matter. Sally Dimond sits next to me. I want to ask her about Beverley and finally get a chance when the musicians break.

She is wearing diamond earrings and a diamond necklace. She is already on her way to oblivion. Her eyes are glassy and her lipstick is smudged.

"You look cute tonight now don't y'all," she slurrily comments.

"You look great, I love your necklace," I lie, as Antonio lights my cigarette.

"Thanks, my diamonds, just like me. From my second husband, he was great but died before his time…since then there are just my boys." She says, patting the brown hand of a grinning young beach boy sitting on the other side of her. This is truly another world for me. *How can she do this I wonder, my Midwestern prudery surfacing as it sometimes does. Don't make judgements, it could happen to you, you never know what lies ahead, says my inner voice, who seems to becoming more vocal lately. Never, I answer virtuously, I would never lower myself to sleeping with an inferior man, a worker!*

Ha! Answers inner voice in a very knowing manner, a voice I am lately not agreeing with.

"Who yu talking to?" asks Antonio, pouring glasses of rum for us from a bottle of Ron Castillo, the tawny liquid spilling over the ice cubes with the promise of relaxing euphoria.

"No one, really what makes you think I am talking to someone who is not here?"

"I feel yu are talking to someone who ees not here, because I know yu and yu are leetle beet crazy like me…here, yu dreenk weeth me, Salud mi amor!"

The sweet drink flows into our bodies, releasing us from the daily concerns, I can see why people become alcoholics, it is all so pleasant at this stage.

I turn again to Sally who is fondling the young man's knee. "How is Beverley doing?"

"Ohh my gawd, that poor thing, she just had another baby, a boy this time and she is back with her fella, just like Ah feared. She can't stay away from him no matter what he does to her, Ah don't know what is going to become of her, Ah really don't. And say, when are you going to paint my dawg? Fido is behaving himself lately, I feed him ground beef with his croquettas and he stays closer to home, I washed him so he doesn't smell so bad."

"Oh, I don't know about when I can paint him, I have to leave in a while, my visa is going to expire."

"Ahh, come on honey, you can find some time, I'll pay you." She says, snuffing out a cigarette and lighting another one with a silver lighter.

She turns her attention to a friend who comes up behind her, thankfully taking the matter of the "dawg" off the table.

I am disturbed by the news of Beverley. not knowing what to say about such a difficult situation, wondering how a beautiful young woman like Beverley could allow such a thing to happen. A beach boy. A boy who lives and works on the beach, in the Sea..not in an office cubicle in some high rise building with elevators and windows that don't open. What would happen if all women choose to love beach boys I ask myself, what would the world be like. But beach boys who did not beat them up of course. But the office men can be brutal also...my mind trails off and my attention returns to my lover, Antonio.

"I wan yu to talk to Manuel Ortega, he ees very, very famous in Mexico, He ees incredible, a first class arteesta weeth a camera."

"But I can hardly speak Spanish.and I don't think he speaks English, how can I talk to him?"

Antonio wants to bring me into the Mexican Art scene, it is something I should want also but the language is a barrier. Later on we sit with Manuel and he talks to me in broken English about the Artists working in Mexico City. Many of them are acolytes of the late Frida Kahlo and Diego Rivera. Manuel is very intense, a dark swarthy man, heavy set and not too tall, with thick bushy eyebrows and a big mustache. He intimidates me with his personal force.

"I weel go to yur studio mañana Señorita, eef yu invite me." Manuel says with that curious mixture of humility and arrogance so common in the Mexican man.

"I invite you Manuel, I would like you to see my work… tomorrow."

The party ends on a raucous note. Everyone begins throwing their drinking glasses over their shoulders to crash on the floor behind them. The tables are surrounded by a sea of glass and people laughing in a deranged manner, searching for more glasses to break. It is a traditional way to end a successful party.

Manuel Ortega, the famous film photographer from Mexico City stands silently in front of my paintings in my disheveled studio stroking his large, abundant mustache. He rocks back and forth, ever so slightly. Antonio and I wait for the verdict. He is merciless.

"Yur painting is good, yu have talento, but yu are a dilettante," he pronounces, with great authority.

My world crashes around me. "I am a dilettante? That is not good, that means I am superficial, an amateur, not to be taken seriously…but it is what I do."

He turns to me with a mean smile, "I am sourry Señorita, now I must leefe."

"I see yu tonight," whispers Antonio as the two men turn and rush down the steps to the world outside.

I am crushed, after my successes, how could this man say that? Maybe I am wasting my time painting, I could use a dose of Thom Kelly and his relentless ego support right now. And Antonio, he also was always supportive of my work, he has sold many of my paintings to his clients, why did he not defend me? So much for the Art scene in Mexico City.

That night at dinner I question Antonio. "Why did he say that Tonio, *dilletante*, that is not a good thing to be if one feels serious about ones work, you know what I mean. And you like my work, you have truly helped me survive here, "

"Si, si, I know…I should not have brought heem, he is old anyway and maybe he deed not like that a woman, young and preety like yu ees maybe a successful arteest, he is a successful arteest so maybe he does not theenk yu are any good. Yu are good, forget heem, I weel order yu lobster tonight so yu eat good food and forget about Manuel Ortega. Okay mi Chiquita? We drink tequila and just theenk about yu and me."

I am feeling agitated, something is wrong, I need to change. It is mid day and I am recovering as usual in Antonio's house. He has gone to work to his architectural design studio while I lay around like a kept woman…which is what I am becoming.

A plane flies low overhead, I rush to the door and look out. It's there, the Staggerwing buzzing the beach restaurants, soon to land and then what.

My heart starts pounding furiously, I lay down and press my hand against my heart, I wait. After a while I return to the door. A few cars are passing, the day is bright and sunny, it may not rain as we move into the fall and the dry season. The sea is calm, lazy waves stroking the rocks of the shore. And then they come.

A Jeep full of white men from "el norte", loud and clamorous looking forward to the freedom of a holiday in this relatively lawless place.

And there is Vincent, laughing and gesturing as the Jeep slowly makes its way to Los Muertos and the promise of food and drink after the long, ardous journey by air. He looks handsome and confident, seated on the back edge of the Jeep as it moves slowly in the traffic over the cobblestones. I can hardly breathe. I back away from the door so he doesn't see me. My world truly feels shattered, he is lost to me, possibly forever.

I can see him now, sitting down at the rustic tables in the La Ramada, the musicians playing in the back ground, the men ordering their first tequilas of the afternoon. Roland happy to see his countrymen and eager to impart the latest gossip, my gross infidelity, my brazen affair with a Mexican man.

"Yeah, I was afraid this would happen," says Vincent, lighting up an unfiltered camel cigarette, He is sweating profusely, taking a handkerchief and wiping his brow. His stalwart friends, Roland Adams, Jake Moretti, Ham Sado and Ted Burkhart are with him.

He leans back in his equipàle and stares wistfully up at the thatched roof of the restaurant, as though seeking help from above.

"What should I do, should I shoot the guy?" he asks rhetorically to the men around him. They laugh, uncomfortably, downing their tequilas rapidly, the waiter standing by to keep their glasses filled.

"Not a good idea, maybe shoot her, the Mexican police would be more lenient with ya," says Roland with a smirk.

"Hum, I guess it's all for the best, the babe was just too young for me and wants to play around, can't blame her.."

"Come on Vincent, she double crossed ya, and you stupidly fell in love with her...just forget about her. Ya got a wife back in San Francisco who loves ya, Phyllis might be kind of an alcoholic but she is true blue." Jake growls his words. He is angry at the situation, his good friend Vincent made a fool of. "Ya can't trust most wimmen, Vince, you know that..now just forget about Joanna and let's have a good time. Line up a boat for tomorrow and lets go deep sea fishing, no more mooning over wimmen, ya hear."

Roland signals one of the waiters to see about a fishing boat and orders another bottle of tequila. They proceed to get very drunk, forgetting about the pitfalls of love and anticipating a day at sea fishing for Marlin and Tuna,

I am too distraught to stay in Antonio's house. I make my way to my apartment and huddle on the bed, miserable. Too miserable to even cry about the situation. A situation that I have created, I wallow in it until nightfall. I can hear the music and loud voices from the restaurants down the beach. I suddenly want to get away. I feel fed up, like eating too many chocolates or too much ice cream, I *need* austerity, discipline. I need to be on my own whatever that is, I need to suffer for my art, for my fleeting youth, for my unborn children. I need to leave here.

Someone is pounding on my door on the street. I know who it is. I run down the steps to open the door. Antonio stands there looking at me sternly.

"Why ju leeve zee house, why? I no geev yu permeeshun to leeve."

"I just need some time to myself Tonio, you must understand…I am an artist after all, I need my own space."

He is not impressed and walks up the stairs with me behind him. We are NOT happy.

He sits on the bed, his face twisted in anger.

"What can I do weeth yu?" he asks the air around him.

I stand looking at him then walk to the terrace to look out at the ocean, not knowing what to say, how to get around this. My passion for him has dwindled and he has become my nemesis. I think about my apartment in San Francisco and realize I miss it. This affair is over but how to end it?

"Come here Joanna," he orders.

I turn to him. He pulls me onto his lap and nuzzles my neck.

"We weel go out tonight, yu weel go weeth me. Yu weel forget yur boyfriend from California, he does not luf yu like I luf yu…yu put on a nice dress and we weel go to Las Conchas… we weel not stay out late, we weel rest, yu are very tired."

He stands and takes me in his arms, gently and kindly. I begin to cry, I who never cry. He likes that, and dabs my tears with his handkerchief.

"Yu cry, eet is good for yu to cry, now come weeth me."

I go with him, my clothes and personal things are at his place, I feel torn apart but helpless for the moment. The easiest thing is to comply. He is not a violent man so there is no worry about that. But I no longer care for him and I know I am going to hurt him when I leave.

The days pass. It is almost November and my visa is about to expire.

I make plans to leave Puerto de las Peñas. Antonio objects. "Yu no have my permeeshun to leave here, Yu cannot leeve."

"I have to leave, I have to back to San Francisco, I need to take care of things, I have an apartment there, you have to understand Tonio. I must go back."

He pounds his fist on the table as he speaks.

I feel nauseous. I make it to the toilet in the bathroom just in time to vomit profusely. Gagging and spitting, I am utterly miserable.

He stands by helplessly, handing me a towel. I rinse my mouth in the water from the faucet and wipe my face. This is not sexy. He says he is sorry.

"It's not your fault," I stammer, "too much booze I think."

He looks unkept, we cannot stop the socializing for some reason and it is ruining both of us. I am feeling weak lately and craving solitude. Craving my little apartment on Upper Terrace. It is like a cave I can go to to lick my wounds. There are the problems but it has all evolved into something else. Vincent no longer lives there and I have heard that Thom is now with his secretary, Nancy. There is still my work, I can paint for Aldrich galleries, I can do medical drawing. My escape is ending

The day comes when I must go. With my boxes of paint material, my luggage and personal things packed, Antonio drives me to the airport where I wait for the plane to take me back to reality. This is much more complicated than when I came down with Vincent in his plane.

I feel sad, my sojourn is over.

"I weel cum to San Francisco, yu are mine Joanna, I weel not let yu get away from me…yu must understand that," he says as we drink a beer at the airport bar while waiting for the plane.

"I know Tonio, I love you (I lie) but I have to go back, I need time to think, I need to be alone for a while and figure out what to do with my life."

"Hah," he grunts, as though figuring out what to do with a life is a silly concept, a futile effort.

"Here, you finish my beer, I can't drink any more…look they are starting to board the plane."

We embrace on the field, he has tears in his eyes.

"Please Tonio, I will see you in San Francisco, please take care of yourself, I love you…"

"Yu don luf me, eef yu luf me, yu don go to San Francisco," he mumbles bitterly, ashamed of his tears he wipes the back of his hand across his eyes.

The steward motions me to hurry up the steps of the plane. They slam the door behind me. I sit down in a window seat with a sigh of relief. I am free, I am flying out of paradise, maybe never to return. The roar of the engines is exhilarating and the take off is ecstasy. The warm, blue Pacific Ocean churns beneath us as we gain altitude and slowly leave the tropics behind for the cool North. I imagine the pilot going through all the manuveurs of piloting, maybe I will fly again I think, but how? Vincent must hate me. My life is a mess but it is soon to become messier.

CHAPTER V11

San Francisco

I fumble in my purse for the key to my apartment. It is late at night and I have just taken a cab from the airport. The cold fog is swirling around Upper Terrace and the top of Mount Olympus. The Eucalyptus trees sway in the damp wind, dripping, dripping. I am shivering so hard I can hardly push the key into the familiar door but it does not turn. The lock has been changed. Frantically I run around to Thom Kelly's entrance and press on his doorbell. Nothing. I lay on it this time, knowing what an umpleasant sound this bell has. Finally he calls down.

"Who the hell is down there at this godawful hour." He growls as I ascend the stairs.

"O my god, look what the cat dragged in, why didn't you let us know you were coming?" He stands in his white silk pajamas in the doorway, I almost have to push my way in. I am freezing cold.

I sit in his golden living room, shivering. He brings me a cup of tea and I can finally talk.

"I forgot how cold it can get here, this morning I was in Las Peñas in 90 degree heat and now…." I sip the hot jasmine tea slowly.

"And now you are back, well, you have been gone almost 6 months. Nancy is living in your apartment until you come back. And now you are back." He lights a Chesterfield cigarette and hands it to me..

"No, no thanks, I haven't been feeling well lately and smoking seems to make me sick. Where can I sleep? I'm really tired Thom and all my luggage and boxes are still out in front of the apartment on the sidewalk. I need a key to the place, you changed the lock, why?"

"We lost the keys somehow, Nancy will give you a key tomorrow. Now, there are your things out there in the wind." He sits down next to me, obviously exasperated.

"You are a problem child Joanna, I will have to rouse Nancy, she can stay up here with me. She's divorced now you know."

"No, I didn't know but it was inevitable. Sorry to be such a nuisance Thom, my visa was about to expire so I had to come back. There are no telephones in Puerto de las Peñas as you know so I couldn't call you to say I was coming. I forgot how cold it gets here in wintertime..sorry."

"I'll put up the heat so you defrost a little, you don't look too good."

I hear him talking on the phone in the bedroom to Nancy. I seem to have stopped shivering somewhat. I feel like a refugee.

"She'll be right up." He says as he sits opposite me on the sofa. He looks very pale. His thinning white hair lying carelessly around his head. I see a slight tremor in his hand as he lifts the cigarette to his mouth. The match falls to the floor. "So what happened to you and Vincent?" he continues the interrogation.

" I would rather not talk about it Thom, it just all went bad somehow, my fault I guess but I need to be back here and get back to work...forget about men for a while, you know what I mean?"

He smirks. "Let me get myself some vodka to help me digest all of this. "

He looks almost angelic in his white silk pajamas,his floppy white hair, he seems to float out of the living room into the kitchen where his stash of liqour is stored.

I lay my head back on the sofa and close my eyes, feeling inadequate for this. He no longer loves me, or maybe he does a little, I will need him now. Nancy will have to step aside for the moment.

"Here doll, take a shot of this, it will make you feel better." He hands me a shotglass of vodka and plops down on the sofa beside me. He smells like soap and antiseptic. All I want to do is sleep.

"I heard you were playing the field down there in Las Peñas…what happened, it all got too much for you? You got out while the getting was good…what happened?"

"Can we talk about this tomorrow Thom, I am really exhausted…I need to sleep more than anything. That flight seemed to take forever."

Nancy arrives by the kitchen. She wears a blue bathrobe over her pajamas. She looks bleary eyed, her night's sleep rudely interrupted by me, the bad girl on the block.

"Oh, hi Nancy, sorry to wake you up, you don't mind if I sleep downstairs in my apartment, we can figure all this out in the morning…could you help me bring in my stuff, it's out on the sidewalk."

I know she is reluctant to help me but I also know she is a "good" person. She has a bit of the martyr in her DNA.

"Sure, I'll help you out, you did lend me your place after all."

I toss back the shot of vodka, sip the last of my tea and we go down the stairs to get me organized. Nancy is truly noble.

Thom is left with his burning curiousity of what happened between Vincent and I. The truth is almost banal. I was unfaithful to my lover Vincent and took another lover to whom I will probably be unfaithful to also. It is ancient history of men and women, the back and forth of love, the waning and waxing of emotional attachment, of sexual passion, desire. The tiring of it all. Nothing new and exciting to tell him about tomorrow.

The whole top of the little mountain at the center of San Francisco is shrouded in a cold, biting fog. It is as though we are alone in this misty, damp cold world, the fog trying to enter our bodies.

Nancy and I haul the boxes and my suitcases into the small apartment and she quickly departs up the back steps. I hardly recognize my apartment but no matter, I find my night gown in the suitcase and my toothbrush, take care of my necessities and slide into the bed. It is still slightly warm from her. Dreading tomorrow, I still fall asleep from total exhaustion.

In the morning Thom calls me upstairs for breakfast. He has the places set on the terrace table outside the kitchen. The view of the City is fantastic as ever. The fog has lifted and the sun is shining brightly. How can I be so miserable in the midst of such beauty I ask myself. I slip into one of his chairs and wait to be served, unable to do anything else.

He serves his usual overcooked scrambled eggs and almost burnt toast with a few dry pieces of bacon. I eat slowly while Thom and Nancy go over his appointments for the day.

"Okay, now you." He stares at me balefully. " You are going to have to go to the Doctor and get totally checked out, you never can tell what you might have picked up there in the Tropics, Amoebas, Hepatitus, you name it. I called Ted Burkhart, he is expecting you this afternoon for a one thirty appointment."

"Does my car work?"

My little Triumph was still parked out front by the so called garden wall.

"It's fine," says Nancy, stirring some sugar into her coffee. She is dressed in a Navy blue pant suit, her brown hair pulled to the back of her head in a bun, with a little make up and some low high heels, a plain looking woman, she is ready to go to work. "I have been using it, I hope you don't mind, but it would just deteriorate sitting there in this weather you know."

She is a good, decent person I think as I nod in her direction.

"Thanks Nancy, I just need a little time to rest and get myself organized here, this is a big change."

Thom grunts in disapproval. I feel his anger and hostility under control but I can only get on with my life. The next step is getting a health check from one of Vincent's best friends. As I leave, Thom hands me a little plastic cup for a urine specimen. I grimace as I accept it, my former glamourous image totally shattered by my desperation.

I make my way down the hallway of the medical building on Sutter street to Ted Burkart's office. The antiseptic smells assail my nose, nothing like the sweet smells of the flowers in Puerto de las Peñas, or the smell of the sea, or the wood fires cooking lunch on the beach. I hope he doesn't tweak my breasts the way Annette told me he liked to do when he examined the stewardesses. I open the door to his reception room, announce myself to his receptionist and plop down in a leather lounge chair to wait. There is a pile of aviation magazines lying on the table, I take one and thumb through it aimlessly. The beautiful planes in bright colors, overflying strikingly gorgeous landscapes are in another world. I have just come from a strikingly beautiful landscape and was crushed by it, I close my eyes and wait.

"Joanna, how the hell are ya?" calls out the Doctor, poking his head out from the office door. "Come on in and let's see what all we've got here."

Friend or enemy I think. He reminds me of a giant cat, his eyes glinting in a round face with his inscrutable, wicked smile.

I shyly hand him the paper bag with my urine sample and take a seat on the examination table. The nurse takes a blood sample from my arm while he checks out my heart with his stethoscope.

"How do you feel?" he asks, logically.

"Kind of tired, probably from the trip back from Mexico."

"Y'all had a pretty good time there in Las Peñas Ah hear." He chuckles cynically as he checks out the glands in my neck.

"Your periods are regular?"

"Yeah, mostly, I'm kind of late now."

"Oh. Well, we'll run the lab tests and get back to you tomorrow with the results."

"Thanks, I don't have too much money to pay for this... how much is the exam?"

"Don't worry your pretty head about it, Kelly is going to foot the bill for you, still cares about you."

"That's amazing, I thought he hated me."

"Who should hate you is Vincent after you shafted him with that Latin Lover in Las Peñas...how could you do a thing like that?"

I feel shrouded in guilt. I shrug my shoulders as I put my jacket on and prepare to leave this inquisition. "It just happened, that's all, and Vincent is married. How is Vincent?"

Burkhart sets his stethoscope down on a table of instruments and folds his arms over his chest. His blue, cat-like eyes bore into me.

"Do y'all really care now?" He leers at me.

"Yes, of course I care about him, we were quite close you know."

"Well, he's back with Phyllis, his wife and we're all going up North for a fly-in this week end. He's got the Staggerwing in good shape."

"That's nice, I'm glad to hear he is alright tell him I said hello."

"I don't think so. Y'all take care of yourself now."

He leans over and kisses me on the mouth. I rush out of the office more upset than ever, surrounded by hostile, disapproving people in this beautiful City.

I spend the rest of the day in the apartment, putting my things away, resting, reading. I have very little money, I am going to have to get my studio going again, maybe ask Thom for some work in Medical Illustration, anything to get back on my feet again. I need money for food, gas for my car, rent...it is overwhelming.

The next day, Thom calls me up to his apartment in the afternoon.

"So, how are you doing?" he asks, his eyes cold and forbidding. Nancy is seated on the Pouf in his living room, her legs crossed, one leg gently kicking back and forth, waiting in anticipation..

"I'm okay I guess, a little overwelmed by everything."

"What do you expect?" he says icily as he stands in front of me with my medical test results on a sheet of paper in his hand.

"Well, I have good news and bad news for you doll, you don't have amoebas, parasites, or hepatitis. However, you are going to be a Mother!"

"What?" I cry out, "What are you saying?"

"You are very pregnant my dear, you are going to have a baby."

"No, it can't be, I just can't imagine such a thing…I can't. I'm not ready for that, it's not the right time." I feel the tears of panic welling up, I fight them back, no crying now.

His face is twisted in a classic smirk of pleasure, the old Catholic is pleased at my punishment, no matter how much he has protested his rejection of religion, it's all still there. Original sin and all. I hate him, he is a bona fide hypocrite.

Nancy rushes to the kitchen to get me a glass of water.

"So now what are you going to do?" he asks as he throws the cigarette butt into the fireplace.

"I…I really don't know, I think I need time to think about this…You know I spent so many years trying to get pregnant when I was married and now, what? I didn't think I could get pregnant even though they said that my husband at the time was sterile."

"You will have to move out of here you know, I can't have you walking around my place with a big belly, pregnant by an affair with some Mexican peon."

"He wasn't a "peon" Thom, he was a handsome, well educated architectural engineer. I just don't love him, I have to have time to think about this." I am winning the struggle to regain my composure.

"You know you don't have too much time dear, if you are going to terminate the pregnancy, the sooner the better. This is your doctor talking."

Terminate the pregnancy. Abortion. I will have to have an abortion…what a nightmare this is. How stupid I was not to use the diaphragm more diligently. I vaguely thought that Tonio was sterile, he had been married before and never had children. Or maybe I was sterile. Dumb.

I rush out of the living room to my apartment down below, although it no longer feels like my apartment but it will have to do for the time being. My mind is in a turmoil, having the baby will tie me forever to Tonio and forever keep me from Vincent. Vincent, I keep thinking of him. Keep wanting to see him… this is a mess.

Staring out of kitchen window of the downstairs apartment, I see the tops of the towers of the Golden Gate bridge poking out from the early morning fog, as though they were floating. I wish for an answer. The fog stretches out towards the horizon, hovering over the intensly blue Pacific flowing into the City to isolate us all. I am isolated with this problem, No one can help me decide, I pace back and forth in the small studio space in my bedroom. The skeleton that Thom has loaned me for my medical illustration is still there, smiling broadly, its eternal, knowing smile, amused at us the living, with our mortal problems.

I mount the three steps to my bed which is unmade and lay down, wishing for escape. But I have already escaped. There is no escape. I sleep. Nancy comes and goes quietly, some of her belongings are in the closet here and some are upstairs in Thom's bedroom.

It is early afternoon when the phone rings. It is Antonio, I had given him my phone number before leaving him on the landing field in Puerto de las Peñas. Some sixth sense must have informed him of my plight.

"Hola, Tonio, how are you?"

"No muy bien mi querida, I miss yu muchisimo. How are yu? How was zee flight to San Franceesco?"

"It was alright, it took a long time and I am still tired from the flight."

"I want to come to see yu, I cannot leeve weethout yu …yu cannot know how sad and lonely I am here in La Peñas, for me the sun does not shine, the sea is gray, the sky is dark and the flowers do not bloom.---I need yu so much."

I can hear that he is crying. This is unbearable. Am I that great that he should be so miserable? According to Thom l am a disaster. I struggle with the decision of whether to tell him about the pregnancy or not…*not,* says my inner voice who has been seriously absent lately. The responsibility hangs heavy on me, weighing down every other concern I could have. I must decide and fast.

"Tonio, please, l am sorry..I don't want to hurt you, you have been a good friend, we had so many good times together, I miss you too but it is not the time for you to come here. I have to move from my apartment and get another apartment. I have very little money."

"I weel send yu money, how much you wan? Tell me, I send it to yu"

"No, that is sweet of you but I can borrow from my ex-husband, he owes me money…something to help me get started again here."

"I don wan yu to borrow money from heem!" he says emphatically.

"Tonio, can you call me back, later on, I have to go now, please…"

"No, I wan to talk to you, I wan yu to come back to Las Peñas..I wan…"

I slowly drop the phone into it's cradle, knowing that was not a nice thing to do but not wanting to talk to him another minute more.

In the evening, I meet with Thom and Nancy in his flat.

"So, what did you decide to do about your pregnancy?" Thom asks, leaning against the mantle of his fireplace, swirling the ice cubes in his vodka tonic.

"I think I need to have an abortion Thom, I don't want to but I need to work now. There is no way I could take care of a baby under these circumstances." I fumble with the hem of my sweater, my breath is labored, I feel I am choking but beg my body to carry on.

"Yes, that is what we were thinking, it's the best thing to do if you don't want to go back to Mexico and marry the son of a bitch." He gulps down the last of the drink, Nancy takes his glass to refill it in the kitchen.

I ignore his profanity, not having the energy to defend Tonio. "No, I do not want to marry him, I just feel very confused…this situation is too much for me. How does one deal with it?" I lean back on the Chesterfield and sigh, struggling to control myself.

"Take it easy doll, we are here to help you, why I don't know, you have been very reckless and inconsiderate…well, I guess I don't need to lecture you at this point. You will have to go to Tiajuana Mexico for the operation as it is illegal here in California.. Nancy will go with you and we will make the reservations right away so you get prepared."

"I have no money."

"I'll pay the godamned abortion and the flight for the two of you, why I don't know, but I still hate to see you ruin your life, no matter how intent you are on doing just that." He takes the fresh vodka tonic from Nancy and drinks. "You can pay me back with work once you get back on your feet."

"All I can say is thanks Thom, I really don't know what to do.'

"You'll be fine, just learn to keep your legs crossed in the future and stay away from Latin Lovers."

Yeah, right, I think, *that's all I have to do to have a nice wonderful life..well….*

The next morning, Nancy and I board a four engine Boeing airplane for the three and a half hour trip to Tiajauna Mexico. I feel like an empty vessel, without feelings, without energy, just to follow this woman and do what she tells me to do, No will of my own. I cannot think of the potential baby inside or me or I will crack, my shell will break. It takes all my strength to stay calm.

We disembark in Tiajuana. I am back again in Mexico, but this is different. It has the dreary neglect of a border town starting with the airport. We take a cab to the address that Thom has given us. It is an old house on the edge of town. The street is unpaved, the wind blows the dirt, bits of garbage, torn and dirty plastic bags bounce around in the sandy road. We go up the rickety stairs and ring a bell. An elderly woman lets us into the house. It is cold and bleak. She does not speak.

"This is pretty awful," I whisper to Nancy.

"Shh, what we are doing is illegal in the states and maybe here too but it serves a need for women in your situation."

The doctor's office is almost barren, concrete walls and folding chairs in the waiting room. The walls are painted a sickly green, there are no plants, no pictures on the walls, the atmosphere is cold and unhospitable. What I would imagine a prison to be like. Another woman sits quietly facing us as we takes our seats. She also appears to be an American.

A Mexican woman in a white nurses uniform emerges from the operating room and beckons me to follow her. She is dark with long black hair braided down her back. She smiles at me in a friendly fashion as she gestures to a screen behind which I can change clothing..

"Hola, como estas?" she asks as I remove my clothes and put on a hospital gown.

"Bien," I answer, my Las Peñas Spanish coming back to me. "Muy nerviouso." *I am very nervous.*

"Yo entiendo," she says, she understands.

She instructs me to lay down on the operating table and shortly the Doctor comes in to check me. He is smiling in a reassuring way as he greets me in my humiliating situation, my bare ass exposed to the world. He has that Mexican charm which is an asset in my situation.

"Relajate." He commands as he groups around my lower innards.

I grunt and groan as he pokes and manipulates those mysterious objects in my lower abdomen.

"Todo esta bien," he says as the woman prepares me for the surgery, She passes me a mask with a whiff of gas and I fall into a trance, vaguely aware of the activity going on in my body but utterly passive as they perform the abortion.

I wake up as they are packing me with a diaper like bandage to contain the bleeding and I realize *it is over, my body is mine again.*

"Eet is feenish my dear" says the nurse in English. "Eet is okay, yu no bleed much, yu healthy lady."

"Can I have more children?" I ask fearfully as I emerge shakily from the gas, an aspect of this that I had not considered, that I may never be able to bear a child after this.

"Just as many as yu can afford to have," the doctor answers with a smile as he washes up in the sink.

The nurse helps me dress, I am shaky, then takes me out to my caretaker, Nancy. I sit down to fight off a need to faint.

"Yu need to rest, here, yu lay down for a while…yu have to recover."

I lay down on an old sofa in the corner. Nancy hovers over me.

"How do you feel?" she asks needlessly since it is obvious I feel shitty.

"Not too good, but I think I can make it back."

We have a return flight scheduled for the late afternoon.

After a half hour, several glasses of water and a cookie of some kind, I begin to feel stronger. Nancy pays them…they call a cab and we retrace our steps of the morning.

I sleep on the flight back. Thom is there to meet us in San Francisco and whisk us to Upper Terrace. The nightmare is over, more or less.

CHAPTER VIII

Vincent yawns ostentatiously. Fatigue is plaguing him. He is alone in his big white Buick pulling into the driveway of his suburban home in Redwood City. He grabs a bag of groceries he bought at Petrini's in San Francisco on the way out of the city.

"Phyllis, I'm home," he shouts as he enters the sprawling ranch style home and makes his way to the kitchen. He drops the bag of groceries on the counter rather roughly. There is no response so he mixes himself a drink of Tangueray gin on the rocks, lights a Camel unfiltered cigarette and turns on the TV in the adjoining family room, comfortably ensconced in his favorite brown leather lounge chair.

He has a terrible headache. He takes two aspirins from a bottle in the kitchen and gulps them down with his gin. He needs to rest after the grueling drive down 101 with all the rush hour traffic to contend with. The Television is crammed with news of the assassination of John Kennedy which took place the week before. It depresses him even further to watch as Lyndon Johnson takes over the power of the Presidency and the futile efforts of the investigative branches of the government to find the culprit. The main suspect, Harvey Oswald had been shot while in custody further degrading the proficiency of government officials.

He thinks about what to make for dinner, he bought some sweet breads which he loves but Phyllis hates and would like to prepare them as brochettes on skewers over a charcoal cooker he has on the patio. He debates with himself if he has the energy to do this.

The situation at his offices has deteriorated and their entire law practice has been forced to leave their ideal location on Post street, right off Union square in downtown San Francisco. Walters, his partner has found office space close by on the Peninsula in Burlingame at a much lower rent. Legal costs and interest payments have skyrocketed let alone what they owe on the principal of missing Trust funds. Most of his time now is spent arguing for more time to make good on their debt. The new offices are not as glamourous or well situated as they were in San Francisco but they have no choice. He had to let go of most of the staff and only retain one secretary in the new space. The rent and office expenses in San Francisco were too much money under their reduced circumstances.

He thinks of Joanna and the bad ending to what he is forcing himself to think was just a pleasant affair. She was just too young he has decided and switches off the TV. He hates the constant interruption of the commercial breaks. Apparently she is back in the City according to Kelly. *Maybe I'll see her again.* He finishes his drink and goes to the kitchen to fix another.

He runs his hand through his thinning gray hair and lights another cigarette before going upstairs to see if he can rouse Phyllis who lately has been passed out by the time he comes home from the office.

Poor girl, he thinks, *nothing much too look forward to these days.*

He pushes aside the bedroom door and there she is snoring away, the empty gin bottle on the floor. He goes over and shakes her gently.

Her red hair falls over her face as she struggles to sit up in the bed. A lacey nightgown, badly stained sags to one side of her shoulder…her breasts are visible through the thin fabric. They are still high and firm as she has never nursed a baby.

That's what I need he thinks, *a good roll in the hay, a good fuck to keep me going….*

He pulls back the covers exposing her body. She is thin. She doesn't eat enough but it is sexy for him as he undresses and flings his clothes all over the floor.

"Hi" she says."I didn't hear you come in, I didn't make anything for dinner.".

"You are my dinner, spread those long legs of your and let me in…" He thrusts his hard penis into her, she gasps as there was little preparation for sex. His head is aching more as he continues the ritual and feels closer and closer to ejaculation when suddenly everything begins to grow dark, Phyllis seems to fade from his sight, moving father and farther away, the room turns gray and then it all goes black. He falls to one side of her on the bed, breathing laboriously, semi-conscious.

"Vincent," she screams, "Vinceent.." are you alright, what happened?" He does not answer. "Speak to me damn it what's wrong with you?" She feels trapped under his body, now heavy and leaden. She wiggles away from him, breaking their sexual connection, pushing on him and finally slides out from under his weight then tries to get a response. But there is nothing, he is very pale and slips into unconsciousness without speaking.

"O my god, are you dying?" she exclaims. He has had a stroke. She stands up next to the bed and stares down at his crumpled body, *I can't deal with this,* she thinks. She rushes to the phone and calls their doctor to get an ambulance over right away.

She is sobbing profusely as they wheel his motionless body onto the ambulance to take him to the hospital in Redwood City. She throws a long coat over her nightgown, unable to do much more and goes with the doctor in his car to the hospital.

Ted Burkhart meets Phyllis in the waiting room outside the operating room at the hospital. "The doctors say they must operate immediately as he has had a ruptured aneurysm and the parts of his brain that are denied blood will atrophy," he explains.

She falls into Burkhart's arms. She smells strongly of booze. He is reluctantly sympathetic to her.

"I can't bear this," she wails, "why is this happening?"

"Calm yourself down Phyllis, he'll be alright, y'all know Vincent is tough and those are the best neurologists in the whole damn country workin on him."

She sits down, he sits next to her, she dabs her face with Kleenex, she looks wretched, her face blotchy and pale, her breath is atrocious. Other people seated in the waiting room watch them curiously, also probably in the thros of extreme anxiety.

"What are they doing to him?" she asks fitfully, "I know a little about surgery…I worked in a hospital for a while.."

"Well, ah talked to the head surgeon, he came here from Palo Alto to work on Vincent…it ain't pretty Phyllis. They'all are gonna open his skull and expose the artery that has ballooned and ruptured."

"Ya mean they are gonna saw his head open?"

"Yeah, that's about it honey, they are going to do what is called a lobotomy on your husband, it's to save his life. They'll remove a piece of bone from his forehead, tie off the artery, remove the necrotic brain tissue and put the bone piece back, like a puzzle. He ain't gonna be the same man ah'm afraid to say. He may not make it through the surgery, y'all have to be strong now."

"I can't imagine this is happening, he is always so…so healthy, how could he collapse like this, I can't believe it."

"He doesn't really take care of himself ya know, he smokes a lot and drinks and he's under a lotta pressure in his office, with all the problems of the missing trust fund money…it just got to him, that's all. When a guy is over 50 it's not the same, he just hasn't the same resistance as a younger fellow. Vincent just didn't want to accept that, ah mean that's what ah think."

"Maybe it's my fault, I don't really take care of him, I drink too much I know but I can't help it, I'm such an alcoholic." She says as she cries into the Kleenex which by now is thoroughly soaked. "He's never really loved me," she sobs, "there's always another woman, for a while there was that lawyer he had working in his office and now this, this artist person with that funny Italian name who lives there on Upper Terrace, always another one..she must be about 15 years old…I think I love him but maybe I hate him."

"Time will tell," says Doctor Ted Burkart in his most philosophical manner. He has never really accustomed himself to the fragility of human life, something he faces all the time in his profession. A profession that has rewarded him well, a ranch in New Mexico, a private plane of his own, an apartment on Nob hill and lots of disposable income.

CHAPTER IX

Joanna

I am shocked when Thom Kelly tells me what has happened to Vincent. I am incredulous, he had seemed almost immortal to me when I was enraptured with him. And foolishly I was planning, without even being aware of it, of going back with him, telling him how sorry I was to treat him so badly, that I truly loved him…that he is the love of my life. *And now this!* He may die and I will never see him again, can never tell him how much I love him. No more flying lessons, or making love on the beach or in other unusual places, never to cook dinners together, never to have babies together, nothing! I know in my bones I will never love another man, that no one could ever compare to Vincent.

My heart feels as though it is breaking as I drive my little sports car to Baker's Beach, my favorite place to commiserate with my personal tragedies. The beach lies almost at the entrance to the Golden Gate bridge, facing the open water of the Pacific Ocean. The waves are treacherous, dramatic in their power and yet somehow consoling to a turbulent soul.

I take off my Mexican sandals, roll up my jeans and walk through the cold surf, nothing like the warm waters that lap your feet in the surf of Las Peñas. I climb the rocky cliffs at the end of the beach, practically in the shadow of the bridge. There I find a smooth rock to sit down on, then fixate on the waves crashing against the rocks below me. People look at me curiously, probably thinking I am suicidal but that I am not, but miserable, yes, that I am, profoundly miserable.

The sun is warm on me and there is solace in the sea. I think and think and try to know what I must do. No matter what becomes of Vincent, I must immediately find another place to live, to get out from under Thom and Nancy and to seek work…I will have to pay rent on a regular basis, not like with Thom where he would forgive me for non-payment. I can no longer escape adulthood, much as I enjoyed my interlude in life, I will have to be strong…anything else will be a disaster and life is precious. I watch the fog out on the horizon, beginning its journey to land, the mountains stretching out in all directions, the beautiful sea. I love being alive and will have to go on from there.

I lapse into reverie, dreaming of a distant future, to escape the horrendous reality of the present. There we are, Vincent, and I and our new baby in our beautiful ranch home on the slopes of Mount Tamalpais. Somewhere in Marin county. Not in Sausalito as that is too steep for our ranch home. He has recovered from the aneurysm and the surgery, a truly miraculous recovery which has become the subject of various articles in medical journals. His law practice has resumed and the problems of the missing trust money have been resolved. We live in domestic bliss. I sit in one of our designer living room sofas breast feeding little Vincent junior. An adorable bundle of love at one month of age, already smiling and looking around him with his big blue eyes, wondering at the world he has just entered.

Vincent, looking handsome and distinguished in a slightly rumpled gray suit, has just returned from his office in downtown San Francisco, early, to escape the bridge traffic and has brought bags of groceries from the City.

"Honey, I bought some sweet breads and chicken livers, I will make us brochettes for dinner, you think the little fellow will like that?" he grins at us as he carries it all into the kitchen where he deposits it on the island in the center of the well appointed kitchen.

"I'm sure he will enjoy the brochettes tonight for his evening meal after I have digested all that great food. You are so wonderful darling. And how is the dental work coming along?"

He sits down across from me and opens his mouth to show his new teeth. "Just a few more implants to go darling and I will have perfect teeth of my own, right there embedded in my mouth, how do you like that?"

"That is wonderful my dear love of my life, no more bother with false teeth or eating corn on the cob…and how are the payments on our lovely new home coming along?"

"Well, light of my life, I just made the final payment from the income on a case I just finished for Lloyd's on that BOA crash in the South Pacific three years ago. BOA finally settled rather than have me trying the case before a jury since I always win and we now own this lovely house with the beautiful view of the coastal mountains and the forests."

"When can we start the pool?"

"Next week sweetheart and by the time little Vincent is a year old he can be swimming in his own pool."

I sigh happily, he has been a wonderful husband and the future with him and our child stretches out into infinity, wealth, health and happiness will be ours and our children's.

"By the way," he says as he lights one of his camel unfiltered cigarettes, "I love the way you look in that silk dressing gown I just bought you at Magnin's," (a green and lavender floral print,) "with our baby nursing happily on your teat, look how his little fist beats on your breast. He is growing so fast, I almost wish I were the artist and could paint you both exactly the way you are in this moment with the setting sun lighting up your heads, like a halo."

I giggle self -consciously. "You do flatter me dear love," I remove the baby from my breast. The child tries not to relinquish my nipple, gripping it with his tiny gums, stretching it out as though it were rubber, it finally gives. I cradle him over my shoulder and pat his tiny back so that he burps up any air he may have taken in with my milk. This would cause gas for the little creature. The infant regurgitates a bit of milk onto the shoulder of my silk dressing gown but no matter. He is a strong baby and already is holding his head up.

"Oh honey, please don't smoke in here, it is bad for the baby you know."

Vincent quickly crushes the partially smoked cigarette in an ash tray and smiles at me. "You are such a good mother..by the way, did the new maid come by today?"

"O yes, I forgot to tell you..she is wonderful, Spanish speaking so that I can keep up with my Spanish. She cleaned and cooked and did the laundry while I organized my studio to start painting again. Maria is her name and she even had time to hold the baby when he was crying for no reason that I could tell."

"Oh, dear love, I am so happy that you are able to get back to your painting again, I know how important it is to you to work. I could not stand it if you left your art work to do housework, that would be criminal."

"That makes me so happy, dear heart, that you understand how important it is to me to continue my work as an artist."

"Did Maria mention her cousin who wants to take care of the vegetable garden…we are so fortunate to have that extra acre along side of the house to make a kitchen garden."

"Yes, she did, we need to make a list of seeds that we want to plant and he, I think his name is Juan, will take care of it."

"Great, we won't be running into town for every little herb or thing and the vegetables will be clean and fresh when we need them…I like that. Come into the kitchen with me and talk to me while I fix the brochettes and have a little drink of Tangueray gin on the rocks.. I will have to wash the mushrooms

I think…..I think….." Slowly it all fades away and I am back on the rocks mesmerized by the ocean waves, waiting for an answer to this tragedy.

If your lover survives, you must go back to him, have a child with him, he is the best man you have come across in this lottery called life. Maybe he will be alright.

My inner voice is back and not a moment too soon. But what it suggests is outrageous, my child might be a bastard if Vincent does not divorce, my parents will be furious that I didn't marry a stockbroker or a corporation man…someone designated by the society we live in. But I have to admit to myself, inner voice has spoken the words I have been mulling over now since I returned to San Francisco. But still, I am not sure I can do such a thing on my own.

You must do this, your child will have some of what you had before with Vincent. If you do not do this thing you will regret it the rest of your sterile life.

What if he dies, what if he lives but cannot impregnate me, then what?

You will have to wait and see what is left of the man when the doctors finish with him. If he does not survive, well, you will just have to go on with your life…just hope for the best.

I shift uncomfortably on the rocks, my butt beginning to hurt but I stay put until the end. The tide is rising and I will have to walk through the surf to get back to my Triumph. I have lost track of the hours I have been here.

Just think about it, bastards can be very interesting people, some of them have become famous in the past. They are usually love children and the world can certainly use more love children, no?

Hmm, the future is being laid out for me and it is one that will certainly be very interesting but also difficult…but what the hell, I have nothing to lose by becoming a single mother and perhaps, much to gain. I will support me and my child with my Art, by painting beautiful paintings that people will buy. I will think of something, I will not only survive, but like my little sports car, I will *Triumph!*

My mind is made up as I make my way carefully down the cliff, avoiding the sharp rocks, reaching the icy cold surf now swirling up to my knees. The cold, gray fog has rolled in and the beach is deserted. Straggles of yellow brown sea kelp litter the beach, washed up with the tide. The magnificent bridge is now obliterated by the roiling gray mass. The hill and small forest at the other end of the beach is no longer visible, Buoys are moaning their warning calls, like sick seals, to the ships passing through. The waves slap against me, trying to take me down. My hair has escaped the pony tail and is now hanging in salt water clumps around my head. I struggle through the surf which now has a strong under-tow. I am totally drenched and freezing cold. I manage to reach the dry sand, exhausted by the effort to escape the sea. Then make my way to my little sports car sitting alone in the parking area, I pray to my guardian angel that it starts.

And on to Mount Olympus and the rest of my life.

To be continued …